24 X 7/08 ✓ 3/09

Springer's Gambit

ALSO BY W. L. RIPLEY

Dreamsicle

Storme Front

Electric Country Roulette

W. L. RIPLEY

Springer's Gambit

THOMAS DUNNE BOOKS
ST. MARTIN'S MINOTAUR ⚹ NEW YORK

THOMAS DUNNE BOOKS.
An imprint of St. Martin's Press.

SPRINGER'S GAMBIT. Copyright © 2001
by W. L. Ripley. All rights reserved. Printed in
the United States of America. No part of this
book may be used or reproduced in any manner whatsoever without written permission
except in the case of brief quotations embod-
ied in critical articles or reviews. For information, address St. Martin's Press, 175 Fifth
Avenue, New York, N.Y. 10010.

www.minotaurbooks.com

Design by Lorelle Graffeo

ISBN 0-312-27456-4

First Edition: June 2001

10 9 8 7 6 5 4 3 2 1

FOR BOB FARRINGTON:

Coach, mentor, friend.

ACKNOWLEDGMENTS

Thanks go to Steve Ketchum for his hospitality in Aspen.
Also to Dr. Paula Baker for proofreading.

And special thanks go to Ace Atkins, who fed my own
pep talk back to me.

CHAPTER

One

WHEN MAX GOT BACK THE RESULTS OF THE BIOPSY HE knew he wasn't going to pay any more tribute to Nicky Tortino. No more laundering the guy's hooker money, no more vig right off the top. Fuck Nicky T. Way Max figured, a guy who only had six weeks to live could thumb his nose at people like that. Besides, if Nicky clipped him or hired it done it'd be better than lying in bed with an IV in your arm, waiting for it to happen.

So Max had chased off Nicky's torpedo, Gerry Knucks, last time Knucks came by. Gerry got the name Knucks because way back he carried these brass knuckles that had a pewter handle with the word, Knucks, engraved on it. Yeah, this is the kind of people Max Shapiro had gotten himself involved with. Guys with little kid nicknames they engraved in brass knuckles. Could you believe it?

Max had made himself a ton of money as a real estate developer but had to admit that back in the seventies with the interest rates hovering around 22 percent and nobody building shit, except disco owners who always defaulted, Nicky Tortino had been a windfall. Max set up some dummy development corporations, then took out phony loans which Nicky wrote off on his taxes. Then Reagan and the eighties came along and it was boom again so Max had made enough money that he didn't need Nicky's laundering business anymore. By the mid-eighties Max had a beach house in Malibu next to a movie star, two Jaguars in his garage, and a line of credit like the defense department. But he still had to piece off all his action and they sent Gerry Knucks around every month to collect and inform him of any deals that Nicky T had cooking. Max was sick of it.

But you don't get to quit the wiseguys. They had no retirement plan.

So Max had to keep working.

It was funny how he had taken the news about the cancer. Like something was happening that was just part of the next thing he had to do. Like watching it on television or something. He didn't really feel sick or anything. He'd had these pains in his stomach, sure, but they weren't unbearable like his Uncle Ray who had just withered away to nothing, a bowling ball head on top of a neck that was all corded muscle and skinny, the bones in his face and shoulders pushing against the skin as the cancer ate him up. Wasn't like that. It was more like he had indigestion or something.

Max was fifty-seven years old and was still in pretty good shape even though he had the beginnings of some love handles and his hair was receding. He got out and golfed every week. Played racquetball down at the club about five times a month. And he could still water ski, which he loved. So, he decided that he was going to spend his last days in Aspen, maybe learn to ski and hit the spots where he could watch the swells drinking Dom Perignon and pretending they didn't have shit where their brains were supposed to be.

Besides, he hadn't seen much snow in his life and that would be different. Snow was clean. Aspen was clean and the mountains were nice. Might as well get shot in a picturesque place as not.

So, when Gerry Knucks came around, Max was waiting for him. He'd gone out and bought himself this Beretta nine, like the one Mel Gibson used in the *Lethal Weapon* movies and when Gerry Knucks came by Max had whipped out the gun kinda off-hand, like he did it all the time, and Knucks said, "Come on, Max, cut the fucking horsing around, I ain't got no time for it," which Max had to admit was kind of cool on Knucks's part.

"I'm not paying you guys nothing anymore," he'd said.

Then Knucks had frowned, a little furrow of skin forming between his eyebrows like he'd just been given an algebra problem he hadn't seen before. Even though he had a dumb nickname Gerry

Knucks was sharp. "Come on, Max. What the fuck is this about? You been paying for twenty years. You know Nicky's not going to like this. And, then I've got to give him the bad news and he'll act all pissed off and then I'll have to come back. You know how it works."

Max thought about it a moment, shrugged his shoulders and said, "Well, I'm not doing it anymore."

"Why not?"

"I got cancer."

"I guess that makes sense. But you don't need the money. Just pay this time and let me get going."

"I'm not paying."

Gerry Knucks looked around the room as if he'd landed on Mars or something and said, "Dammit, Max, just give me the fucking money and go die in peace. Take a vacation, go somewhere, spend some money, have a good time. Get drunk. You gotta pay. That's the way it is. You know what's going to happen if you don't and I won't like that. Hell, we been friends."

"Nothing personal, Gerry. Just don't want to pay anymore. It's the principle of the thing."

Knucks nodded his head. "Well, I can sorta understand that. But, you know what Nicky's reaction's gonna be."

"Well, fuck him."

"Yeah. Fuck him, fuck me, fuck you. Fuck us all. That's what you're doing. You're just creating extra work."

"Tough all over," said Max.

Gerry Knucks rubbed the side of his face. "Well, I'll go then. Unless you're gonna shoot me or something." Real cool. Gerry was a tough guy, no doubt about that. "You gonna shoot me, Max?"

Max shrugged. "I don't think so."

"I appreciate it. Always were a decent guy, Max. I may have to shoot you, though."

"I understand."

Knucks sighed. Puffed out his cheeks and exhaled. "I won't enjoy it though. And I'll make it quick. You won't feel a thing, I promise."

"I'd expect nothing less."

"Aw, you know. Old friends and everything. You care if I have a cigar before I go?"

Max nodded at the humidor on his desk. It was walnut and had three drawers and gold handles like a piece of bedroom furniture. "Help yourself. Take one of the Cubans. Third drawer. Got a couple of Montecristo number two's in there."

Knucks opened the drawer and pulled out the torpedo-shaped cigar. "Thanks, Max."

"It's a good smoke."

"Well, gotta go. Be seeing you, Max."

Max nodded. As Knucks reached the door, Max said, "Hey, Gerry."

Gerry Knucks paused at the door and turned around. "Yeah, Max?"

"Knucks is an asshole name."

Gerry looked down at the floor, nodded his head, then looked up and smiled at Max. "Yeah, guess you're right. Thanks for making it easier for me, Max. Gonna miss you."

And he left.

So Max packed some stuff and caught the next flight to Colorado.

And then after he'd moved to the Aspen lodge he'd bought a couple of years ago on spec, Max got the call from the doctor telling him he wasn't going to die, after all.

"Well, that's just fucked up, Doc," Max had said. "What kind of thing is that to tell a guy? I'm going to live now. That it? Where'd you get your medical degree? Correspondence school?"

"I thought you'd be happy to hear this." Max's doctor was some goy asshole from a bigshot California family whose father-in-law had been a candidate for governor back in the eighties. See what happens when you back a loser, thought Max.

"I'm supposed to be happy because I'm going to live? What's the matter with you? How's a guy supposed to plan anything if you can't make up your mind? You want to tell me about that?"

"Well . . . a . . . I'm sorry about this, Max. I'm sure it's a shock to you and all, but after it sinks in I'm sure you'll realize that you've got a long life ahead of you."

"You'd think that, wouldn't you?"

"We still on for golf next week?" asked the doctor.

Max said, "No, I'm afraid you wouldn't give me the right score. By the way, what's wrong with me if I don't have cancer?"

"Looks like you have an acute case of indigestion."

Max hung up the phone.

Could you believe it?

CHAPTER

Two

"SO WHAT ARE YOU GOING TO DO, NOW?" SUZI CHANCELLOR asked him. Suzi was Max's girlfriend. She used to be a cigarette girl in Vegas. Her name used to be Suzi Craig but she changed it to Chancellor when she became a dancer. Great legs, nice smile. Ears were a little big, but she kept them covered with this cascade of red hair, same color as Ann-Margret's. Suzi was no dummy. She wasn't no genius either but had a lot of sense. She'd attended UNLV for a couple of years before she decided to see if she could make it as a showgirl. Max had met her while he was playing the tables at MGM Grand, Suzi bringing him cigars and him tipping her big.

Suzi liked him because he hadn't come on to her like the other guys did who came to Vegas. He didn't tell her how great her legs were, which were spectacular, but seemed more interested in her background and seemed genuinely interested. Max thought it was charming and fascinating that she was a Mormon girl from Salt Lake City who'd came out to Vegas. He wanted to know if things really did float on the Great Salt Lake. She'd told him how when she was in high school she and her friends used to get some beer and drive out there and float on their backs. "But, you had to make sure you toweled off real well or the salt would eat up the upholstery on the car."

He'd ask how her parents felt about a Mormon girl working in Vegas and she told him that her dad had died in a plane crash years ago. "He was coming back from a business meeting in Provo. It was a charter. Somehow, one of the turbines fouled and they went down in the mountains." He told her he was sorry about that and she said it was okay because her dad had cancer anyway and didn't have much longer to live. Go figure that one, would you? thought Max. Then, she'd told him she had a business in Vegas, a dress shop for large-figured women and she did the cigarette gig because it got her out among interesting people and she made some business contacts that way. "They have to buy somewhere," she said. "And they don't want to be embarrassed by trying on something next to the chorus girls that buy clothes around here."

Max said that made sense and he knew this girl was pretty sharp and he asked her to have a drink with him and she accepted even though he was twenty years older than she was and it had gone from there. They'd been going together about a year now and even though Max had offered to pay to expand her dress shop, Suzi didn't want that. "I'm your girlfriend, not your business partner."

So when he told her that the doctor had said he wasn't going to die, she asked him what he was going to do now.

"I thought about calling Nicky T and telling him I'd pay." He pursed his lips and confessed, "Well, anyway, I thought about it."

"And now you don't want to." Her hands on her hips, looking at him. "That it?"

The snow was coming down through the big window behind her. Max liked the snow. He'd been raised in L.A. and hadn't seen any snow except in the mountains when his parents took him to Denver once. He'd loved the way it looked, like a big ice cream sundae and had loved the mountains ever since then. He liked the way she looked with the snow coming down behind her.

Max shrugged. "Not sure. Maybe. I'm tired of working for Nicky. I didn't mind Gerry Knucks so much except sometimes he made my secretary uneasy because he's a thug, even though he's pretty polite for a guy from the Bronx. He doesn't look like a thug so much as he has this . . . I don't know, some sort of menacing thing going. And, he's not a dumb guy, either. Smart. Smarter than the guys he works for who're a bunch of wop dimwits. But . . . aw, you know."

"You know what?"

"After I decided not to pay him it felt pretty good. Like I was a free man or something."

"Not if they kill you."

"Some things are worse than that. Paying some festuring ass-hole like Nicky T part of your business and washing his sleazy whore money as if he were some desert rajah makes me feel like a putz."

"Desert sheik," said Suzi.

"What?"

"You mean desert sheik. Not rajah. That's Indian."

"Like Indian from India?"

"Like that."

He nodded. "So, anyway, it started to feel good, not paying. I like it. I got money and I've been busting my hump for ten years longer than I wanted to and I don't need Nicky in my life. Besides, I don't think it'd make any difference if I called and said it was all a joke and I'd start paying again. Nicky's thought processes went stagnant in about the fourth grade and all he's thinking about is respect and how this affects his reputation with the wiseguys down-town. He wants to be a made man, which I never understood."

Besides, and this is the part he hadn't told her, he was kind of looking forward to living large and dangerous. Max liked to visu-alize things. Dying from cancer and Nicky sending guns after him didn't scare him so much because he imagined doing all the things he wanted to do before it happened. It was like a kind of freedom. At first, it had been like that old TV series with Ben Gazarra where they tell him he has only one year to live and so he goes around having adventures. Then, after the doctor had told him he was going to live, the irony of the show's name came to him. *Run for Your Life.*

"You given any thought to what you're going to do?" Suzi asked. "You know he's going to send Gerry or some other thug to come after you. You better put something together."

Max liked the way she approached it. She didn't panic or get emotional. She thought things through. She had good business sense. She just wanted to make sure he had a plan.

"I can shoot pretty good. I was in the service, you know? Went to Vietnam in 'sixty-five. But I didn't see any action. Supply. What the guys get shot at call a REMF."

"REMF?"

"Rear echelon motherfucker. Only shot my gun on the range once in a while but I was a pretty good shot anyway. I thought about that, you know, walking into Nicky T's and blasting him like the Wild West or something where we shoot it out."

"That's not using your head, Shapiro," Suzi said. "That's letting your testosterone do the thinking and that won't work."

He nodded. "I'll give you that." But he didn't tell her how he secretly fantasized about busting a cap on Nicky Tortino. Just walking up to him and pulling the Beretta and shooting him in the nose job he'd got himself. Mess up all that cutting and plastic surgery. At first, when he thought he was going to die and he had nothing to lose, it had made sense. Different now. Boy, was it different now. "But, I don't know what else to do."

She put a finger to the corner of her mouth like she did when she was looking at a new fashion line at the dress shop. Considering it, looking at it from different angles. She was a thinker, that's for sure. "Didn't you say you knew a guy here in Aspen? Some guy who used to be a secret service agent or something that played piano in some lounge here in Aspen?"

"Yeah," said Max. "Guy's name's Springer. Cole Springer. He plays the piano and tosses off smart remarks at the ski morons who tip him, not knowing he's making fun of them. Used to work on the president's detail until he quit. I heard he got canned because he made some funny remark about the president to a newspaper guy or something."

She cocked her head and smiled. "A man with a sense of humor."

"Maybe what I need is a man with no compunction about shooting a greaseball degenerate like Nicky T who would think no more of whacking me than what shoes to wear to the mall."

"This guy's got experience protecting people. Who else are you going to be able to get on such short notice?"

He thought about that. "Nobody, I guess."

"That answers your question then."

"Yeah, well, he'd be good but I sold him a plot of land once that was in a red zone."

"A red zone?"

"Yeah, a fly-over. Where they re-route jets from SAC head-quarters in Colorado Springs while they were making some changes. He was going to put up a piano bar in Colorado Springs but the noise from the jets screwed it up so he had to sell at a loss and blames me. Took the money and moved here. That was about five years ago."

"Why'd you do that?"

He shrugged, his palms up and level with his shoulders. "I didn't know they were going to fly the damn things over. I'd never even seen the land. I sold it for Nicky T. That's who he should be mad at."

"You need him now."

"He doesn't like me much."

She leaned over and stroked his chin with her thinking finger. "Then, charm him, Max."

It was eleven o'clock on a snow-covered October night when the football players tried to throw the little guy out of the Whiskey Basin Tavern. Normally Cole Springer was neutral about such events but it was the tattoo on the man's forearm that caused him to intervene. Also, you couldn't have that kind of stuff going on in this business as it made the crowd nervous—especially in Aspen—and they would soon move on to someplace where people didn't get picked up and hurled bodily from the place where they came to relax.

The Whiskey Basin Tavern was a nicely appointed lounge, at the base of Ajax Mountain, which catered to both the ski-resort crowd of semi-celebrities and wannabes as well as the land rapist developers and millionaires and movie stars who came in now and then. There used to be racks of antlers on the roofed deck as you entered the establishment and inside artwork by Frederick Remington and, paradoxically, prints by Renoir and Monet. Very eclectic. But then the antlers had to go as it made some of the vegetarians uneasy. Springer kind of missed the horns.

Some of the regulars were there. There was Ski-Bob sitting at one table. Ski-Bob was a pretty good guy who wore a cowboy hat with a feather in it and always came to the place with an illegal smile on his face. Ski-Bob drank Crown Royal whiskey and Molson's Golden Ale in a cycle of whiskey, beer, whiskey, beer. Sitting with Ski-Bob was his newest snow bunny, a nice-looking blonde who was a little wide in the seat but looked serviceable enough. At the bar were Coyote Creek Jack and his buddy Chance McCoy, a couple of guys who were old enough to remember Aspen when it was just a backwoods ski resort. They could still remember when Hunter S. Thompson, the outlaw journalist, ran for sheriff of Aspen. Thompson himself had once been in the place, a fifth of Chivas Regal in his fist and demanding Red Stripe, which they didn't have, so he left, screaming gibberish.

Then there was the odd sprinkling of Aspen chic. A successful middle-aged divorce lawyer named Caldwell was sitting two tables over from Ski-Bob. Caldwell had this silver hair contrasted by a strawberry-blond mustache and he always wore some kind of leather—cowboy boots, leather-fringed jacket, or even leather pants on a couple of occasions. He also had a split-leather cowboy hat with a conch medallion band. Caldwell had a couple of ladies who were on the cusp of their forties—both good-looking and both probably married. Caldwell was kind of a jerk but he ordered Dom Perignon about twice a week and he tipped good. Also, the leather cowboy act was amusing to Springer.

It was Wednesday night. Talent night. Anyone who could play was welcome to step up to the piano and play something. At ten o'clock, Springer was sitting at the baby grand playing a section of Chopin's Concerto no. 2 in F Minor, a square glass of Glennfiddich Scotch sitting on a short table beside the piano bench. He had learned the piece in totality from an arrangement that provided segues to account for the loss of orchestral accompaniment. Though it made the piece a bit erratic, Springer was more concerned with romantic expression than with musical cohesion. As he played, a few people in ski clothing looked up at the man with the lumberjack build sitting at the piano. The tavern regulars paid little attention.

When he reached the somber Larghetto in the Concerto, Springer begin to think of her. He became immersed in the piece as the music both freed him spiritually while sending him to the blue world of melancholy.

He missed her.

As he neared the end of the interlude his despondency turned to resentment and he attacked the Allegro Vivace, aggressively fingering the cascading finale.

There was a smattering of applause as Springer finished. Ski-Bob nodded at him and Caldwell raised his champagne glass to him in salute. Usually, Springer saved the emotional performances for home, resorting to the piano at the Whiskey Basin as an outlet for frivolous, even whimsical displays. He acknowledged the applause and then started fingering the opening of Beethoven's *Moonlight Sonata*. As he moved into the melody line, he abruptly struck the keys hard with both hands and queued up the computer soundboard beside him which launched him into "Unchain My Heart." As usual, the sudden tempo and music change got everybody's attention and Springer had fun with the piece. He didn't have a great voice, but it was gravelly enough for "Unchain My Heart."

When he finished he noticed the football players, guys who played for the Colorado Golden Buffalos, hassling an older guy who was very out-of-place for an Aspen night spot—a wiry little guy who drank Budweiser straight from the red-and-white can. Springer noticed the bouncers edging closer to where the little guy was more or less arguing with the beefy college guys. Way out of his league.

Then, he saw a couple of the football players stand up and grab the little guy by the arms. When they did, Springer noticed the airborne tattoo on the guy's forearm. The bouncers moved in and were telling the tattoo guy that he would have to go when Springer intervened.

"What's the deal here, Bruce?" Springer asked one of the bouncers who also served as a bartender, Bruce Caspar, a big, beefy redhead with freckles like the Milky Way. Bruce read his horoscope daily and lifted weights religiously.

"Nothing, Cole," said Bruce. "This guy—" indicating the guy with the tattoo, "has had a little too much to drink and it's time for him to go."

"What's your name?" Springer asked tattoo.

"Wilson. Jake Wilson."

"You a 'Nam vet?"

"Yeah," said Wilson.

"Hundred and first?"

He nodded. "Balls-out rocket riders and no-mercy commie killers. How'd you know?"

"Tattoo. My brother had one like it."

"Yeah? What's he doing now?"

"He didn't make it back."

Wilson's face softened. "Sorry."

"It's okay. Been a long time ago and I was in grade school at the time. But thanks anyway." Springer smiled and looked at the bouncer. "Let him hang around, Bruce."

"What the hell you got to do with it, piano boy?" asked one of the football players. He had a crew cut and sideburns cut off square. Big guy with a big jaw. Looked like a linebacker or a tight end. The other guys with him looked like skills players—running backs or defensive backs. This was the biggest guy who was talking to him now.

Springer smiled at the guy. "I don't have anything to do with it. This guy fought in 'Nam and I've got some respect for that. I'm sorry for the trouble he caused you. I'll move him to a table away from you guys. No reason for anyone to get worked up, huh? So, let's just everybody relax and I'll buy a round and—"

"Naw," said the linebacker, waving a hand. He pointed a beefy finger at Wilson. "This guy's got mouth problems and he's gotta go. You understand that, piano? I'm a customer and you're just the hired help—"

"Cole doesn't work here," said Bruce.

"What's he doing up there then?"

Bruce started to say something but Springer held up a hand to stop him. "I just like to play," said Springer.

"These guys were making cracks about Vietnam," said Wilson. "I'm just minding my business, drinking my beer and they made a crack about 'Nam vets."

"What did you say?" Springer asked linebacker.

"You ain't no 'Nam vet. The fuck's it to you?"

"Maybe nothing. Maybe you don't have the mettle to say it twice."

Linebacker's eyes narrowed and his jaw clenched.

"Better watch yourself, piano. Before I toss you out in the snow."

"Well, you look big enough. And we know you can talk big but I haven't seen anything else."

"What's that mean?"

"It means I'll bet you I can take you and another guy of your choice."

"You wanna fight us?" said linebacker, amused. "Piano here wants to rumble with us."

"No," said Springer. "Arm wrestling. Two of you at once. You pick somebody and I'll take down one of you right-handed and one of you left-handed. At the same time."

"That's crazy. We'll break your arms."

"I lose I'll pay your tab and Wilson goes outside. I win, Wilson stays, you go and you pay Wilson's tab."

The big kid looked at his buddies, and smiled with the confidence that had increased over the years with his neck size. "You're on, piano."

Springer loved being called "piano." It was right up there with "hey you."

Over Bruce's protests, Springer pulled up two tables and three chairs. He placed one chair between the two tables and a chair on the opposite sides. Springer seated himself in the middle chair and indicated to the linebacker and another football player—a black guy with big shoulders and a thirty-inch waist—to sit in the other two chairs. Linebacker took Springer's right hand and the narrow-hipped guy took Springer's left hand.

"Now, I'm a little older than you guys so be nice." While he was talking, Springer hooked his feet around the legs on his chair. "Say go, Bruce."

"Aw, come on, Springs, this isn't right. My horoscope said to stay away from—"

Springer said, "Say go, Sergeant Wilson."

"Go!"

They were young and strong. Springer knew that. But they were also cocky and drunk. Too drunk to see that he had hooked his legs around his chair or notice that he could put all his weight forward and go in the same direction with his arms which increased his leverage. He pushed hard against the combined strength of the two men and they pushed back. It was a dead heat for a brief moment. Then, abruptly, Springer slammed both football players hands down on the table. Hard. The running back yelped in surprise and linebacker cursed. Then Springer stood and bounced linebacker's knuckles against the wood one more time.

Linebacker jumped out of his chair and rubbed his hand. "You sonuvabitch."

"Figure up their tab, Bruce. Pay up," said Springer to linebacker. "And go."

"I'm not giving you shit," said linebacker.

Springer shrugged. "Figured you for a welcher."

Springer saw it in his eyes way before it happened. He was going to take a swing at Springer. Well, what could you do about it? As the ham-sized fist came at him, Springer moved aside, slapped the back of the football player's forearm and then slammed the side of his hand against the big man's nose, breaking it. He knew he shouldn't do this as soon as it started.

The linebacker's nose exploded in a spray of red and Springer side-kicked him in the knee. The guy went down like a gut-shot buffalo. One of the other football players stepped up like he was going to come at Springer, but Springer was in his stance now—legs wide and balanced, hands relaxed, eyes focused and hard—and the football player put up his hands and shook his head. Linebacker was laying on the floor clutching his knee and rocking back and forth in pain.

"You sonuvabitch," said linebacker. "You fucked up my knee."

Springer relaxed.

Bruce and the other bouncer helped linebacker up and escorted the Colorado Golden Buffalos to the door. Bruce came back and said, "We might get in trouble over that."

"Yeah. About time for me to call it a night, anyway."

Max couldn't believe what he just saw. Surprised him so much he didn't go over and talk to the guy, even though that had been his intention. Not that Springer wasn't a big guy. He was. But he had put both of the college guys' hands down on the table like he was slamming down a five-spot on a horse. Sure he'd suckered the guys, but Max couldn't see anyone short of Arnold Schwarzenegger in those *Terminator* movies doing that. Then, he'd dodged the hay-maker and put the big guy on the floor.

Strong, quick, and smart. That's what Max needed. Guy had a soft spot, too. Max saw it with the little guy and heard it in the guy's music. Guy was a walking, talking contradiction. A tough guy that played the piano and could strong-arm people.

Perfect.

"That's the guy?" asked Suzi.

"Yeah, what do you think?" said Max.

"You didn't say he was cute."

"I'm not going to date him for chrissakes."

"He'll do," she said. "But—"

"But what?"

"Something about him. He's got a look about him. I dunno."

"Whatta ya mean, a look about him?"

"He might be hard to handle."

"You're the one wanted me to come here," said Max, not be-lieving how changeable Suzi was.

"Let's talk to him," she said, like she'd decided something.

"Might not be a good time. Maybe his blood's still up."

"Then don't arm wrestle him," she said, smarting off like she did once in a while.

"In the morning, maybe," said Max.

"Good idea," she said, giving him this wise-assed look. "Put-ting it off."

What do you do with a woman like that?

CHAPTER

Three

"SO WHERE'S THE FUCKING JEW?" NICKY TORTINO ASKED
Gerry Knucks.

"Aspen, Colorado," said Gerry. They were sitting in Grotto #9
on Fisherman's Wharf, eating lunch. It was Saturday. Gerry liked
this place. The food was fresh and good and he liked looking at the
fishing boats coming in and out. He envied the people in the boats
leaving the dock at times. Just get out on the open water without
anyone around. No phone, no interruptions, no imbeciles talking
out the side of their mouths.

"Send Auteen."

"You're not seriously going to send Auteen, are you?" Gerry
Knucks said as Tortino spooned another oyster.

"What's wrong with Auteen?" Nicky asked him, slurping the
oyster. Gerry looked at the big black guy sitting next to Nicky. The
man's bodyguard. Auteen Phelps.

"First, he weighs three hundred pounds. Second, he's black.
And third, it's fucking Aspen."

"So?" said Nicky, in that tone that suggested that you were the
one that was stupid, not him. Nicky didn't know shit about geography but let on like he knew. Once Gerry was talking about fishing
in Ontario and when Gerry asked him where he thought Ontario
was, Nicky got all defensive and said, "Hey, I ain't fucking stupid,
you shithead. I know where it is, I just can't remember what state
it's in."

"Look, Nicky," said Gerry, wanting to avoid a geography

argument. "It snows in Aspen. All the time. All the people there are rich people. Celebrities and shit like that. People who ski. Auteen don't look like he skis much, y'know? Max is gonna make him if you send him up there. Max ain't stupid."

"Sure he is," said Nicky, talking with his mouth full of chomped-up oyster, which looked like shit to Gerry who tried to look at something else. Guy had no class. Nicky thought you bought style at J.C. Penney's. "He's stupid for thinking he can just quit doing business with me without permission."

"He thought he had cancer."

"He shoulda died of it then. That would've been the smart thing."

"Well, you can't send Auteen. I'll go."

"No, I need you here. Fucking chinks are crowding me downtown. Kim Li's all pissed off and I want you to go to Chinatown and see what his fucking problem is."

"Auteen's gonna stick out like a turd in a bowl of whipped cream in Aspen."

Auteen looked up from his steak, considered Gerry. "You saying something, Gerry?"

"Just eat, Auteen," said Gerry. God, what he had to put up with.

"I'll send Ray Dean with him," said Nicky.

"Ray Dean's dumber than shit," said Gerry. And Ray Dean was a fuck-up. A walking disaster and functional illiterate whose idea of class was the silver-capped cowboy boots he wore.

"Yeah, but he's white."

"I didn't say you shouldn't send Auteen because he's black, Nicky. I said you shouldn't send 'im because Max will make him."

"So, now you're the fucking brains of the organization? That it?"

Sometimes Nicky got on Gerry's nerves. But, what were you going to do? Doing independent work was bullshit. You sit around doing nothing and got sent places and maybe they hooked you up with somebody dumber than Ray Dean, who was a greasy cracker shitheel, and Auteen, the bull elephant. Hard to imagine but sometimes they could find somebody that dumb and it happened. Nicky paid him good and paid him regular. Let him run things to a point, but like some of the other dago dipshits he'd known, he was all bent out of shape over the respect thing.

When he was in New York the guys had been sharper. Knew how to dress. How to act. That's the way Gerry had learned the business, from guys who knew about style and keeping a low profile, not slurring their words and using mutants for bodyguards. But things had got hot in New York. Feds shutting everybody down. Gerry jumped to the West Coast where he'd hooked up with Nicky on a reference from Benny Lovitz, a smooth operator who got sent up for a dime jolt when he wouldn't rat out some of his business associates but helped Gerry out before they turned the key on him. Stand-up guy with honor. Some integrity. Did things the old way.

Nicky T wore disco necklaces and talked like he thought he was Robert De Niro. It was fucking tiresome. It was like you had to tell the man everything three different ways until you got it delivered in a way the guy would accept. Or understand. Gerry didn't know which.

"Okay," said Gerry. "I'll go to Chinatown and see this guy. Auteen and Ray Dean can go to Aspen. Maybe we'd better contact somebody local, who knows the territory, to show them around."

Nicky nodded his head like he was considering it, putting on an act for Auteen like maybe if he didn't think it was a good idea he wouldn't do it. Nicky knew Gerry was right and Gerry knew Nicky knew it, but you had to play the game with the man.

The shit he had to put up with for money.

Springer didn't like Max Shapiro and the other sharks who were paving over Colorado so when Max came over to his table in the Wienerstube, a little bakery/restaurant on East Hyman and asked him if he remembered who he was, Springer said, "You're a guy never saw a meadow didn't look like a parking lot."

Shapiro had looked at his girlfriend like, "See what I mean?" She gave him a look like, "So what, do what you came to do." Then he'd told him how he wanted to hire him as a bodyguard.

"I don't do that anymore," said Springer, spearing a piece of French toast with his fork.

"Yeah, I know. You play the piano. And play games with college boys." Shapiro getting testy now, more from exasperation than anger, Springer thought. Springer had learned to watch and gauge people's moods from his days in the service. Max was an older guy who looked pretty good for his age which Springer guessed at late fifties. Medium build but not sloppy. Not muscular either. Built about like Paul Newman.

"What do you need protection from?" Springer said. "I think you have a captivating personal manner."

Shapiro looked at his girlfriend, making a face. She said, "Well, Max, he's right. You've got to do better than that. Can't make fun of what he does."

"He made a crack about what I do," said Shapiro, in self-defense. She smiled, shook her head, then looked at Springer. Shrugged her shoulders.

"He really needs your help, he just doesn't like to ask," she said. She had nice green eyes and a good voice to go with it. The kind of voice that got things done. Got people to go along with her. "He's really quite a lovely person when he's not acting out."

He indicated a chair, inviting her to sit down. Max sat down also, though nobody asked him to.

"What does he need protection from?" Springer asked her.

"Some nasty guys in San Francisco don't like him anymore."

"Why don't they like him? I know why I don't like him."

"Let's just say he is no longer fulfilling their wishes."

"He's involved with criminals. That it?"

"Like that."

"What the hell?" said Max. "Am I invisible? Don't talk about me like you were watching me on television or something."

"Sorry, Max," she said, patronizing him a little. Teasing him with it. "Tell the man what you want."

Max gave her a look, then said to Springer, "I want you to watch my back. Like I was a politician or something."

"You'd be a step up from that."

"I'll pay you whatever you want."

"That suggests you have some hard people after you. What did you do that pissed them off?"

"Why does it matter?"

Springer shrugged. "Want to know what I'm up against."

"I'm not gonna tell you about myself."

"Max Shapiro, man of mystery," said Springer, smiling.

"You just need to take the money and do the job."

"I'm not going to do it blind." He took a sip of his coffee. "Besides, maybe you have it coming."

That stopped Max for a moment. "What is it with you? You got some sort of moral dilemma about taking money? You're hard to talk to, you know that? Probably why you have to work for other people instead of running your own show."

Springer smiled at him. Amused now. Guy could piss you off without trying, thought Max.

"What's it pay?"

"Pay you a grand a week and if you have to take anybody out I'll pay a bonus. Twenty-five thousand. You get beat up, I pay the doctor bills. You get clipped, I'll spring for the funeral. I might even get you a wreath. Hire some mourners."

"What could be better than that?"

Max looked at the woman. Nodded his head. Then back at Springer. "You go way out of your way to be smart-assed, y'know?"

"Really not that much trouble. What about the Whiskey Basin?" Springer asked.

"They'll get another piano player."

"Maybe not one who can arm wrestle football players," Suzi said.

"I own the place," Springer said.

Shapiro turned his head and looked out the corner of his eyes at him. "You own it." Not a question.

"My place."

"Shitty location."

"Least it's not in the SAC flight pattern."

"You want the job, or not?"

"Probably not."

"Not enough money? What?"

"Wouldn't pay my bills. Three grand a week's what I have to have."

"Three grand? A week? Are you fucking kidding?"

"Everything's higher in Aspen. Besides, I'm giving you my land-raper rates."

Max made a face, shaking his head, teeth clenched. "This fuck-ing guy," he said, under his breath.

"Pay what he asks," Suzi said, prodding Max. He frowned.

"What are you, his agent?" said Shapiro.

"What are you saving it for?"

"Just because I got guys after me doesn't mean I start throwing money away."

"Just do it," she said.

"I'll pay two five a week," he said.

Springer shook his head.

Max appealed to her, "Will you look at this guy?"

"How much is your life worth to you?"

"Nothing I go broke saving it."

Springer smiled. Sipped his coffee.

"I'll add another five hundred myself," said the girl.

"You got five hundred a week to add?" asked Shapiro. Springer saw the change in the guy.

"Yeah, I've got that much. Besides, I never liked Nicky all that much. Don't want to lose you to him."

Springer looked at the girl and she gave him a look that asked him to do it. Not a pleading look. It was a look that *demanded* that he do it. She definitely had something going in the insight depart-ment. Forceful without being intrusive. He needed to watch her. He wondered if Max had figured out what he had in her.

"I'll give it some thought," said Springer. "While I'm thinking about it I might know someone you could call and he could help you out while I consider it. Retired cop."

"Well don't go out of your way to do me any favors."

Springer smiled. "Last thing on my mind."

Suzi chuckled at that.

Sitting here with two wise-asses, thought Max. Who needed that?

CHAPTER

Four

TOBI RYDER KNEW SHE SHOULD'VE BROUGHT IN HER HAND-
bag and kept the gun in it while she was in the restaurant but she
was stubborn. She didn't like the way it felt under her left arm
when she was sitting. The .40 Sig was always uncomfortable but
she didn't like the way the smaller autos shot. The male cops would
tell her to get a "lady's gun" or ask her if she was going to take
down a buffalo and she would look at them, smile through her
perfectly straight teeth, and tell them to "eat shit." The Sig wouldn't
fit in most of her purses and she couldn't wear it on her belt and
keep it out of sight so the only alternative was the shoulder holster.
Sometimes, though, the holster strap chafed against her bra strap.

But she could hit what she pointed at. First time, every time.

Still, she never learned to adjust to sitting in trendy night clubs
and restaurants around Aspen among the Donna Karan costumes,
armed with the clip loaded with ten 190-grain bullets and one in
the pipe.

"So, what do you think?" Summers asked her.

"Can't figure it," she said, looking at the guy with the large
shoulders and delicate hands sitting with Max Shapiro and an attractive woman who seemed to be with Max. The trio looked somewhat out of place among the beautiful people. Max and the woman
dressed expensively while the guy in question dressed well but
looked like he shopped the racks at J.C. Penney's. Actually, the guy
looked like he belonged in a beer commercial with trees and mountains and streams bubbling in the background.

"Maybe the guy's dirty."

She shrugged. "Could be. Doesn't show in his jacket."

"They kicked him out of the secret service."

"I thought he quit."

"He made some crack about the president. Newspaper guy asks him if the president was a pussy-hound and the guy says something like, 'if my gun had perfume on it he'd be on top of it in two seconds.'"

"That's not the way I heard it," she said. "What happened was the president summoned some showgirl to his room and the news guy got wind of it and followed her up to his room. Springer, and this is the part I'm not sure about, stops the reporter, telling him he had to leave and the reporter asks him what the president was doing with a beautiful woman in the room and he says, 'You're the reporter. What do you think he's doing?'"

"That wasn't smart."

"On whose part?" she said, reaching under her arm and adjusting the holster.

"How you figure a shithead like Shapiro gets a babe like the redhead?"

"Women go out with you. Figure that one."

"I could remind you why."

"And I could shoot you through the heart," she said, not kidding. Glasses clinked and voices chattered away, tailing off to nothing.

"Come on, Tobi," he said, smiling. Actually, it was more of a leer. Jack Summers was a pain in the ass. He had always been a pain in the ass. It was his life's work. He was a handsome guy with a good line but she'd played that hand and folded. A smooth user of women who could convince you he was telling you the truth while hiding the silent lie. "How long are you going to stay mad at me?"

"What makes you equate disgust with anger?"

He had been trying to hit on her since the FBI sent him to Aspen. He was an expert on Max Shapiro and the San Francisco rackets and Tobi Ryder of the Colorado Bureau of Investigation knew the area, so when Shapiro cleared out of the Bay area and headed for the mountains they became a duo. They had been an item briefly two years ago when she was on the rebound from her ex-husband—David, the asshole—another federal hotshot who thought "dodging bullets and fighting crime" was an aphrodisiac to helpless women all over the Rockies. Her mother adored David because he was handsome and what her mother called, "focused with good business sense." Her father had been less kind.

"He's a piece of shit with legs," he'd told her. "You shouldn't marry cops. They're unreliable." Then he'd smiled at her, enjoying his irony. Her dad was a cop, too. Her mother was a powerful, tough woman, a former assistant district attorney in San Francisco, while her dad had been a carefree risk-taker who'd died five years ago in a motorcycle accident. At the funeral her mother had been a rock. Not a tear. Took care of all the arrangements. The press slobbered all over her toughness. Her stoicism. Tobi had tried to be tough like her, but had started crying like a little girl, missing her daddy, when the SFPD color guard handed her a flag and his badge.

He had been her hero—her ideal—and now he was gone. So, she'd taken this job and moved away from the foggy, misty curtain of San Francisco to the Rockies where the air was so crisp and clear that it was like looking at the mountains in a mirror's reflection.

Jack Summers said, "Maybe I like tough women."

"Unrequited love's the worst," she said, sipping her coffee. She looked at the Springer guy, talking to Max Shapiro and the redhead. Springer was a good-looking guy with broad shoulders. Dark hair. Dark sad eyes. Hell of a piano player. A guy who could play Chopin and take out a two-hundred-fifty-pound athlete in a matter of seconds. They'd followed Shapiro to the Whiskey Basin and she noticed Springer right off. When Springer came to Aspen she had run background on him because of his security clearance. Cole Springer, age 35, white male, 6-1, 200 pounds. Desert Storm veteran. Special forces. Widower. Considered a loose cannon by White House aides. A practical joker who was a dead shot with a pistol—held the secret service record on the pistol range. A dangerous man who could make you cry the way he played a piano—like he was lost in it.

The Bureau had been trying to make a case on Max Shapiro

for ten years, Summers told her. Money laundering. Underworld contacts. But Max was smooth. He kept himself out of trouble. The Bureau wasn't really that interested in Max as he was just a conduit. They wanted Nicky Tortino. Summers wanted Nicky bad as he had been close a couple of times. But Tobi knew Summers would take Max as a bonus—or squeeze him to get what he wanted. But things had gotten weird in San Francisco.

"There's been some kind of change in mood between Shapiro and Nicky," said Summers. "Something doesn't add up. Don't know what it is yet."

"Shapiro doesn't look like a criminal," she said.

Summers looked at her. "So, tell me, what does one look like?"

"Not like him."

"So now you're clairvoyant."

"It was an observation of his physical characteristics. Clairvoyance would require me to intuit his disposition."

"Well, he's a dog-ass and I'm going to turn the key on him." Always talking tough, that was Summers. Like they were in the movies or something. Jack Summers, G-Man.

She watched the three of them—Shapiro, Springer, and the woman—their body language suggested that the discussion was business. But what business? Shapiro's girlfriend looked sharp and poised; not the kind of woman that hung around with mobsters and crooked real estate speculators, though she had the flavor of bright lights about her. Something was wrong with Summers' picture of Max Shapiro and Tobi thought she knew what it was. The fact that Shapiro was in Aspen talking to an ex-Secret Service agent was a hint.

"You said things had changed between Shapiro and Tortino, right?" she said. "So, maybe Tortino is mad at Shapiro and wants to have him killed. So, he visits a former Secret Service man. The only one in town. A guy who has been a high-speed bodyguard."

Summers looked at them, turning his head sideways, as if he were considering something deep and deliberative. "That's a stretch. Maybe the Springer guy is dirty and Shapiro is cutting him in on a deal."

"Now Springer's dirty too?" That's another thing about Summers. He was so cynical it made your teeth hurt. "Everybody's a criminal to hear you tell it. There is a term for people who are not criminals, Jack. They're called citizens. You remember them, the ones we're sworn to protect?"

Summers leaned his head back and looked down his nose at her, which he did when he thought he was imparting wisdom or telling one of his fabulous lies about "how special" she was to him. Back before he quit smoking, he used to hold the cigarette alongside his face when he'd do that. She almost wished he hadn't quit smoking because he had a couple of mannerisms with the cigarette that tipped her off when he was lying.

Summers said, "The rumor is Springer got the money for his place by raiding crack houses in Denver."

She looked at him like she didn't believe him.

"Way it went," he said, "he dressed up like DEA and went in hard and confiscated their money, leaving the bad guys cuffed to each other."

"Went in by himself?" She thought about it and had to smile. "Plays the piano and takes down crack dealers."

"He took a guy with him. Some outlaw guy around here works at a ski resort. Don't get yourself all lathered up. He's not Robin Hood. But he's capable of doing a deal with Shapiro."

For a half-second she could see herself stabbing Jack in the throat with her fork. "Why would Shapiro need to do that?" she said. "You said yourself that Shapiro dealt in large money with big companies. Why would he need a piano player in Aspen?"

"You can't figure the way these recidivist reprobates think." He did a double take with his eyes. "Hey, they're leaving."

"You take Shapiro," she said. "I've got the piano player."

Springer was up and moving around by six o'clock. He'd always been an early riser. He ground some coffee and got the coffeemaker started, then sat down and looked out at the snow which gleamed with moonlight, waiting for the sun to peak over the mountains and break the day into different colors. Thought about Max Shapiro's offer. Springer could use the money. Paying for and operating the club was costing him big-time and if it wasn't for the deal on his living quarters he wouldn't be making it. Aspen was high-rent.

Max's girlfriend, Suzi, was an interesting person. Good-looking woman about Springer's age, maybe older. Street smart with good sense. Not the type who had a huge vocabulary but was expressive and thought before she said things. Kind of kept Max on task is what it seemed like. She had this reddish-gold hair like his wife Kristen had had.

He could still see Kristen if he closed his eyes. Her smiling when he said something she thought funny. Frowning at him when she disagreed with him or thought he was over the top. Then the cancer got hold of her and didn't let go. It had been hard to watch. She went a piece at a time. And each piece chipped away at him— like being skinned with a plastic spoon. She told him she was worried about him after she was gone because women functioned better without a husband, than men did without a wife.

"Promise me you'll find someone," she'd said.

"I'm not going to make this mistake again," he said, trying to lighten things up. She didn't like it when he cried. It made her feel bad, like it was her fault she got cancer. She'd smiled and told him how she didn't want him to sit around feeling sorry for himself and playing melancholy pieces on the piano like he did when he was thinking about something he regretted.

"I can always tell what's going on with you by listening to you play," she'd told him right before the end. That's what he liked about her. She was tough-minded. She didn't whine or complain about her disease. And, she was perceptive and knew how he worked inside his head. She didn't press him on things, just knew how to react to him. It was like their relationship was symbiotic so when she died it diminished him more than if he'd been cut in half. More like two-thirds gone.

Long time gone.

He got a cup of coffee and looked out the frosty bay window of his apartment. He lived in the second story of a turn-of-the-century house that belonged to an actor friend of his. Nice place. Halfway up Red Mountain. Worth about 3.5 million. The actor, twice nominated for an Oscar, would come in on weekends and holidays and stay in the main floor, bringing in politicians, celebrities, and family. Springer watched the place for the guy when he wasn't there and paid minimal rent. Minimal rent for Aspen, that is. He could barely cover the rent and the interest on his business. In fact, he couldn't cover both. Thirty-six years old, a widower with no children, and living in somebody else's place.

You're really going places, kid, he thought.

Looking down he noticed the dark brown Explorer. Smoke coming out of the exhaust. Where were those binoculars he'd bought when he went elk hunting last year?

Tobi Ryder had gotten up early and provisioned herself for watching Springer. Coffee, doughnuts, a couple of sandwiches. Newspaper and a novel to read. Nice place he had. Beautiful house with a wrap-around porch and a large upper deck. Surveillance work was boring work, not like television and the movies where the cop or detective is sitting there about two minutes and then something revelatory happened. Once, in her first year with CBI, she'd sat outside this alleged paper-hanger's house for four days waiting for him to emerge so she could follow him and find his connection only to learn she had the wrong address.

Now she had sat in front of this house for an hour in the dark, drinking hot tea from the thermos and munching the French pastry she knew she shouldn't be eating since everything went right to her hips, trying to keep the crumbs off the upholstery of her new Explorer.

She'd followed him home last evening, waiting for the lights to go out before heading home for a few hours of sleep, then back here to wait and see where he went, what he did. Maybe he was involved with Max, maybe not. It was more an excuse to get away from Summers for a while. She was starting to harbor thoughts of macing the guy.

Couldn't believe she had ever dated Jack Summers, FBI lounge lizard. But, he'd been slick. A predator male whose dating persona was vastly different from the real Jack Summers, who was only interested in her as a trophy fuck. Too many of those guys around.

They ought to start a special department downtown and put her in charge—round up all the phoneys and incarcerate them. Unfortunately, that would only leave married men and widowers. Stop it, Ryder, she chided herself, you're becoming way too cynical.

She started the vehicle because she was getting cold. The radio guy said the temperature was in the thirties, felt like the teens. Lived here five years now and had never gotten used to the cold mornings even though when the sun was up she barely noticed the cold. She'd grown up in California. Carmel. It got cool there sometimes, with the Pacific Ocean breezes and all, but nothing like this. She shivered as the heater began to warm the cab. She picked up the binoculars and rolled down the frosty window so she could scope the grounds and the windows of the house.

There were no lights on in the lower part of the house but there was a glow in the second story. She glassed the bay window and jumped back from the lenses when she picked him up in the window.

He was waving at her. Looking back at her through his own pair of binoculars.

What a smart-ass.

Springer smiled as he watched her double take. It was like that Eastwood movie where Clint and Lee Van Cleef are looking at each other from their hotel rooms and Van Cleef puts his telescope down then raises it back up to look at Clint and gets that cryptic Clint smile in return. That man-with-no-name smile that was like a blink of an eye.

He'd noticed her and her partner in the restaurant. Watched them come in the place and studiously avoid looking at him, as if they weren't aware of him, which is one of the things they taught you to look for in the service. From force of habit, Springer had memorized every face in the room and picked up on their mannerisms. The pair had tried to affect nonchalance like a couple out on the town, but their mannerisms and body language wasn't companionable. It suggested two people thrown together by circumstances and purpose. Especially her. By watching her out of the corner of his eye he could see that she was only with him out of necessity.

There were other clues. She wasn't carrying a purse and the way she avoided sitting with her left side against either the table or the chair back, her body turned ever so slightly to avoid contact with that side of her body. She was carrying a weapon. And a big one. Nice-looking lady with a big heater that didn't like to carry a purse. Tall girl with chestnut-colored hair and an expressive mouth that curled up on one side when an amusing thought came into her mind.

Cops. Had to be. No mistaking them. The guy with her was a federal cop. You could smell it. See it. Taste it. Brooks Brothers suit, hair cut razor perfect. Following Max? Yes. And now following him. Why?

So, he waved to her and she surprised him by smiling back— a brief Clint smile—before putting the vehicle in gear and driving away. He'd see her again. Maybe he'd bring her a cup of coffee or something next time. You never know.

He smiled to himself and sat down at his piano and played the intro to Leon Russell's, "Roll Away the Stone."

Smiled some more.

CHAPTER

Five

RAY DEAN CARR COULDN'T BELIEVE HOW MUCH FOOD Auteen Phelps could eat. Look at this fucking monstrosity, shoveling that shit down his neck like he needed a ramrod or something to get it all in. Guy orders four Big Macs, three orders of fries—large orders of fries—two cherry pies and a large Coke and ate it, breathing through his mouth at the same time, if you could believe it. He'd ordered two large Cokes, but Ray Dean had pointed out that all he had to have done was order the value meals. Then the drinks were free for crissakes.

Look at him, shit coming out the side of his mouth while he was eating, leaving mayonnaise skid-marks on the corners of his mouth which looked like pus. "Wipe your mouth," Ray Dean told him, holding a hand up, disgusted. "Shit."

Auteen dabbed at his mouth with a napkin. "There, that make you happy, man?"

Make me happy? Make me sick, maybe. This is what it was like, eating lunch with this guy. This Aspen was a weird place. Everything expensive-looking and the people talking about weird shit like "powder" and vintage wine and all of them dressed up in fancy shit or weird shit. Even the little kids had ritzy looking coats and boots. Ray Dean felt out of place and had the feeling people were looking at them. This McDonalds looked and felt different from the ones back in Frisco. Wasn't some drive-in place. It was a store-front type that you wouldn't even know was a Mickey D's unless you were looking for it. It even had an upstairs room where you could look out across the west part of town.

A tall big-boned woman dressed in ski clothes walked by and they both watched her.

"You ever watch that show?" said Ray Dean. *"Third Rock from the Sun*? You think that tall alien bitch, the one that Newman got the sweats for, looks like her?" He indicated the tall woman in ski clothes with a nod of his head.

Auteen looked at her. "Man, the bitch on the show is a dude."

"What does that mean?"

"I mean that's a man playing the part."

"Where do you get this shit?" said Ray Dean, his arms out, eyes squinted like he was trying to see something more clearly. "She ain't no guy."

"Man, I'm telling you she's a dude. Got an Adam's apple and a dick."

"You need to quit reading *The National Enquirer*, man. It's fucking your head up."

"There's some good shit in there."

"No, it's all made up. Like wrestling. Y'know?"

"What do you mean, like wrestling? You think Goldberg hits you upside your head that ain't gonna hurt?"

Man, you couldn't talk to this guy sometimes.

Ray Dean had never seen much snow growing up in Houston. It was only October and the stuff was everywhere. Aspen. Weird place. It was limp dick central. Guy could go platinum here if he cornered the Viagra market. And the names of stuff around here? Straight out of some mind fart. He took out the "Guide to Aspen" he'd picked up when they came into town.

"Whacha doin'?" asked Auteen. "You think they got a map here, tells us where the man is, with a star on it showing where his crib is?"

Ray Dean winced. He raised a hand. "Man, don't talk when you're eating. Okay? Let's agree you're not going to do that shit anymore. That's gross. And I'm getting a feel for the place, see? Getting familiar with it. So I'll know where everything is."

"Seems like all we got to know is where Max is."

Ray Dean kept his head down, his knee moving up and down, looking at his map, rolling his eyes so Auteen couldn't see it. Auteen didn't look or act smart, but he wasn't stupid either. He was just so big that he didn't figure anybody was crazy enough to be messing with him. Like Gerry Knucks messed with him. All the time. Gerry was always fucking with the both of them like they were something stuck on the bottom of his shoes. Ray Dean would've given up his entire Randy Travis collection to cap Gerry. Let the guy have it right in the throat, then ask him, "What the fuck did you say? I can't hear you." Then pop him again.

But you didn't mess with that man. Gerry Knucks was stone-cold hard. A nasty guy with eyes that cut you. Had a way of looking at you that froze you up inside. Supposed to have killed five guys. No convictions. Hell, not even ever detained. When Gerry Knucks did you, that was it. You were DRT. Dead Right There. And nobody knew nothing about it. And the guy didn't talk about it, either.

"After we find Max," said Ray Dean, "and after we do him, then we gotta get outta here you know. Gotta know the way out. What do you think we're going to do? Ski out like fucking 007? You gotta plan these things. Do it right or we have to listen to Nicky T give us shit about what a couple of fuck-ups we are while Gerry sits there staring at us."

"Yeah, man, I hate the way the man look at me sometimes. Pisses Auteen off."

There was another thing the guy did, called himself by his name, like he was some fucking celebrity instead of a mountain of shit. "Yeah. So we do this right, maybe he don't need Gerry no more. Show the man we are all the muscle he needs."

"Knucks say to not take Max light. Say the guy foxy smart."

"Max ain't shit. We're gonna blow holes in him and laugh."

"You ever cap anybody?"

"What're you talking about? Of course I have."

Auteen turned his head sideways and looked at him. "Naw, man. You ain't killed nobody before. You a cherry. You my little bitch."

"You think this is my first time?" said Ray Dean, his arms out and looking to each side of him like he was appealing to someone. "That it?"

Auteen chuckled. "Who'd you kill? Somebody's pet cat? Some junior high kid sometime."

"I shot that guy last year downtown. Remember that?"

"You mean that faggot boy tried to hit on you? Shit. That don't count, baby. I'm talking about icing somebody for real. Somebody know what the count is and know it's coming."

"I got a dime jolt for shooting a guy back home. Only had to do a deuce."

"They probably let you out 'cause you such a badass they 'fraid to keep you."

"Hey, that's funny, Auteen. I don't hear Letterman calling though. They let me out because they got no room for cons that kill perps. Guy had a sheet and a warrant on him. He was crowding my play one night down at the pool hall. Killed his ass when he pulled a knife on me. And who are you to talk? What've you done?"

"You're asking me that? Guy from South Central L.A.? Shit. I broke a nigger's neck once."

"Why? What did he do?"

"Told me not to talk while I was eating."

Oh yeah, this guy was a comic.

"So, he was looking back at you," said Jack Summers, sitting in one of the guest chairs in her office, "while you were looking at him?"

Tobi shrugged, annoyed having to explain it. "Yeah, it was like that."

"Then what did you do?"

"I smiled at him and I drove off."

"You smiled at him? Like you thought it was funny?"

"It *was* funny, Jack."

"What was funny about it?"

"The situation. I'm staking him out, glassing his place, so he gets out his binoculars and looks at me and he waves."

"Why's he waving?" Summers asked, getting bugged by it now.

She exhaled. Closed her eyes. God, Jack was thick. "To let me know that he knows what's going on. You don't see the irony?"

"I see that you screwed up the surveillance and thought it was romantic like you were starring in a Hitchcock movie or something."

"I think it would be more like Sergio Leone myself."

"What?" Summers leaned forward in his chair, his forearms shoving her dad's framed photograph. She reached up and pushed his arm off her desk and rearranged the photo.

"Never mind," she said. She looked away from him. Maybe he would disappear if she didn't look at him. What was it with guys like Summers? She'd had three brothers. The only girl. Mom favored them but she had been her dad's pet. And they had picked at her. Sometimes in fun and sometimes just to get at her. Jack was nothing compared to her brothers. They could really get you going but she loved them anyway. And if somebody bothered her they would be all over the guy. She hadn't wanted them to do that as she could take care of herself so sometimes she had to do things and not tell them about it.

Then, Summers said, "You've got it in your head that this guy has some kind of special condition that makes him not a puke. Maybe we need to discuss that. What gives you the impression this guy's so stylish?"

"I'm just relating what happened."

"I think you're hot for the guy."

"And I think you need to give some consideration as to why you harbor those thoughts."

He sat back and stared at her. "I'm jealous? That's what you think?"

"There. Don't you feel better? Confession's good for your personal wellness."

"Well, from now on if he needs surveillance, I'll do it."

"I don't remember anybody putting you in charge," she said, warming a little.

"I'm federal and I've been doing this longer than you."

What a conceited asshole. "And, this is my territory. So, maybe we'll play it my way."

"There's more than seniority on my side."

"Meaning," she said, then making her eyes mock droopy to piss him off, "that you're the big strong G-man and you won't be blinded to your duty by wanting to hop in bed with the guy?"

"This isn't personal, Ryder. This is business."

"That's right," she said. "And, I know what I'm doing. It was

a situation that I thought was humorous and I thought I'd share it
with a colleague. Instead I get this reaction like we were still dating
or something. Which, if you don't mind my saying it, was a enormous mistake on my part. If I were a man I wouldn't have to put
up with this crap. You'd have laughed and we'd have gone had a
beer over it."

"Don't give that feminist shuck."

"Get over yourself, Jack. It wasn't that great."

He leaned back, offended. God, now with the injured male thing.
"Don't tell me that our time together wasn't memorable for you."

"It's not like I have it circled with little stars on my calendar.
And you lied about not seeing anyone else, too." Not that she gave
a rat shit, now. But, at the time his lying really annoyed her—she
had been vulnerable and on the rebound from her divorce and this
guy swooped in like the vulture he was, telling his silent lies and
feigning affection when all he wanted was to get in her pants. Never
again.

"Oh," he said. "I guess the next thing you'll be telling me is
that you were faking the orgasms."

She was shaking her head now, her teeth set in an even line.
"You're such a shit, Jack."

"Just trying to get things straight."

"Kiss my ass, Summers."

"Okay. All right." He was backing off now. He wasn't always
stupid. Just most of the time he was stupid. And, all the time he
was a smooth snake but she'd unmasked him for all time in that
part of her mind where she kept such information. "Let's move on.
So, what do you want to do?"

She shrugged. "I'm going to drive back over and follow him
around. See what he does with it."

"What do you think that will accomplish?"

She smiled at him. Coy now. "I don't know. Maybe I'll get lucky
and he'll ask me out."

Max couldn't believe it when he saw them. But there was Auteen,
three times the size of God, sitting in McDonald's. And Ray Dean

Carr with him. He figured, hoped actually, that Nicky would send Gerry instead of these two imbeciles. Not because he wanted Gerry to come or because they were scarier than Gerry. Gerry was a sure thing. If Gerry came after him it would be quick and painless. With these two guys it could get messy.

But, at least, with this pair Max had a chance.

So Max had left McDonald's and checked in at the Ritz-Carlton lodge. Once in his room he called Suzi and told her to bring his stuff.

"We're going to hide out in a hotel?" she asked.

"For a while."

"That's kind of romantic."

"I saw Auteen and Ray Dean in town."

"Auteen and Ray Dean. Sounds like a comedy act."

"They are. But, you don't need a Ph.D. to kill somebody. I'll be just as dead as if they were smart if they catch me."

"Okay," she said. "So, you'll need some clothes. I'll bring you those new hiking boots I bought and a pair of regular shoes, some jeans, a couple pairs of slacks, some sweaters . . ."

"Bring my cigars, would you?"

"Anything else?"

"Yeah. Bring the Beretta."

"Okay," she said, and hung up. Not whining about it. Just okay. Making it an adventure they were sharing. She'd bring the gun. Suzi knew the score. She was something special. Sometimes he took her too much for granted.

He tried to call the Springer guy. Talk him into coming over and talking about the bodyguard thing again. The guy's phone rang four times and a recording came on. "Leave a message," said the recording. That was all. No amenities. Just "Leave a message." Like he was annoyed anyone would call. This Springer guy could irritate you even when you weren't talking to him.

Max hung up and ordered a bottle of Scotch and some ice from room service. He tipped the room service waiter and made himself a drink. He sat at the window and looked out at the snow and the mountains.

There was a lot of snow here. He'd never seen so much snow.

She was back now. She had a different vehicle this time. A big dark blue Mercury. Springer had spotted her in town, tailing him, trying to lay back so he wouldn't pick her up and yet not appearing to care if he saw her or not since Aspen wasn't a big place like people thought and there weren't too many places to go. He'd driven up to the Whiskey Basin and spent a couple of hours going over the books. Still not good. Just enough to cover the rent. There wasn't going to be any money left over at the end of the month. Like every other month.

Then he'd gotten a call from his banker. He was behind on the payments. The guy was nice enough but told him he could only extend him until Wednesday. He had to come up with his payment. Four thousand dollars. He had maybe seven hundred dollars in the bank.

He'd been thinking about buying a bottle of Glenfiddich and getting plastered, but thought better of it. Couldn't afford the Glenfiddich and the thought of getting drunk on Crawford's wasn't appealing. He couldn't decide if there was some sort of ironic symmetry involved in getting drunk on expensive Scotch while defaulting on a loan or if it was only perverse.

He gave some thought to Max Shapiro's offer. Three grand a week would pay a lot of bills. It would hold the bank off for a while. But he'd have to hang around Max. That'd seem like he was working again. No more shaking down crack dealers. Last time it had gone bad. There had been shooting and though he didn't like guys who sold rock, he didn't want to have to kill one of them. So he'd shot one of them in the shoulder and the others ran. But there were only about five bills in the house. These were dysfunctional crack dealers. They were eating their own product and spending the money on cars and stereo equipment.

He'd headed back home to change clothes for the evening and had seen her in his rearview. She followed him almost to his place before turning off. He sat in his car for a few minutes, waiting to see if she drove by but she didn't so he went inside.

Back in his apartment, he put on some Bob Seger, took a

shower, and shaved while he waited for a frozen pizza to bake. Even the insolvent must eat, he thought. Things sure weren't going the way he'd hoped when he'd left the service. If this kept up he'd be experiencing a midlife crisis ten years before his time.

He opened a Heineken and took a look out the window.

He saw her sitting out there on the street in the blue Merc. Thought about the way she'd smiled when he'd waved at her. No anger, no irritation. Just a quick smile then she was gone. Then, he had a thought. Wonder if she'd like a beer. He remembered all the times he'd been standing outside a hotel room or the Oval Office wishing somebody would bring him a beer. What the hell, huh?

He grabbed another Heineken and a bottle opener and went out the back way. At the bottom of the stairs he could hear his phone ringing.

CHAPTER

Six

TOBI LOOKED UP AND SAW THE PIANO PLAYER WALKING right toward her. She looked at him, trying to give him a hard look then gave up on it. She put both her hands on the steering wheel, closed her eyes, let out a big breath. Smiled to herself.

Jack was going to love this.

He tapped on her window with a green beer bottle and she considered starting up the car and just driving away. She looked at him—he shrugged, palms out—and she rolled down the window.

"Nice day, huh?" he said.

"Yeah, it's wonderful," she said. "I may go to the beach later. You want to cut the crap and tell me what you're doing?"

He leaned back from the car and looked down the street. Smiled. Smug bastard. Look at him standing there knowing he's made her again but not knowing she wasn't trying to hide from him. He was *so* hard to anticipate.

He held up the beer. "You know, I looked down here and saw you sitting in your car and I thought about the times I was standing outside some room or in a hall or at some meeting, just standing there with nothing to do except look steadfast and I used to wish somebody would bring me a beer and maybe shoot the breeze with me."

"Steadfast?"

"As opposed to bored out of my skull."

"Why do you think I'm here?" she said.

He smiled at her. "Figure you're a groupie."

Her eyes flashed hot. There. What a look. She looked good when she did that, he thought. Like lightning in the Rockies.

"That's not why I'm here."

"You're a cop."

"And you're a sarcastic prick."

"I'm at least sarcastic. The other?" He shrugged and left it hanging.

"Pretty sure of yourself, aren't you?"

"The guy with you the other night? He FBI?"

She wasn't going to be drawn into becoming the person answering questions. "What are you doing hanging around with Max Shapiro?"

"He's a piano music fan and he had some requests for pieces. You see, he really likes Van Cliburn but I think most of Van Cliburn's good stuff was when he was younger. On the other hand—"

"Did you quit the service or did they force you out?"

There. Right at him. Trying to knock him off his mark. He said, "You want a beer or not?"

She popped the auto locks button on the door. "Step into my office," she said.

It hadn't gone well in Chinatown.

When Gerry Knucks walked into the back office of the Red Dragon Restaurant, Kim Li had another Chinese guy and two of his torpedoes standing around looking tough at him. All the chinks thought they were Bruce Lee. Also, Kim was giving him the hard act for the benefit of the other Chinese guy. That damned Nicky, what had he got him into this time? Always cleaning up the guy's messes. There was an overlap on collections and a guy owed Nicky and Kim at the same time. How smart was that? Getting your ass in the sling with two of the nastiest guys in town at the same time?

So, anyway, the guy was making the pay-off to one of Kim's lieutenant's when Nicky had run onto the pay-off scenario by accident and so he had Auteen shake him down for what the guy owed Nicky. Told the lieutenant to eat shit when he complained which is easier to do when Auteen Phelps is standing beside you.

A million to one coincidence. Of course, Kim Li, being a guy who didn't like coincidences, was pissed off about it and called Nicky so Nicky told the guy to go fuck his ancestors, which isn't the way to talk to people who thought their ancestors were their link to heaven. Nicky had a right to the money, but things would go easier if Nicky'd just learn a little about culture. Then he'd know better than to insult a Chinese guy's heritage.

Kim's response was to have a couple of his goons intercept one of Nicky's runners, bounce the guy around, and relieve him of about three G's. Chump change, but the respect thing was an issue now so Gerry had to go over and tell Kim to knock the shit off and let's leave each other alone, okay? It's a big town and there's room to operate for both of them. But Kim got all animated and started talking Chinese at him, which Gerry didn't particularly like as he suspected he was being cussed at and insulted. But he stayed cool and checked out the two Kung Fu warriors standing around with their arms crossed, one of them with those Tong tattoos on his forearms.

So Gerry said, "Look, I'll come back later when you're in a better mood. Maybe I'll have some of the pepper beef out front. Is it good here?" Nobody was talking to him so he left the place. But apparently that wasn't good enough for Kim so he had the bad asses follow him out. Gerry made them about two blocks from the restaurant. They were driving a blood red Mercedes, for crissakes. Inscrutable, huh? Gerry always drove a white Taurus—of which there were about a million—when he was on a job so nobody would notice.

Also—and it was a funny thing, because the chinks have this idea that white guys thought all Orientals looked alike—Gerry recognized the guys in the Mercedes because Chinese *didn't* all look alike to Gerry. He made it his business to remember faces, and clothing, and mannerisms. You had to if you wanted to stay alive.

Gerry maneuvered them to follow him to a loading dock down on the wharf he knew about, a union dock, which was closed down for improvements and if there were any guys there they weren't going to say anything. He had a key to the supervisor's office.

Gerry pulled leisurely around the corner of the dock warehouse, parked the Taurus behind some loading crates, and got out of the car. It was a noisy place with seagulls squawking, water breaking against the pylons, and the sounds of ships horns and construction machinery clanging and banging all over the place. Fish smells in the air. He climbed the stairs to the main office where he could see everything, got out his Colt Gold Cup .45 auto. He liked the big Colt. He liked one shot and the thing was over. Everybody used nines nowadays but he'd seen guys take a couple of hits from the nines and keep coming. One shot from the Colt was like being hit with a wrecking ball no matter where you hit them. Hit them in the ear lob and they rolled. He lit a cigarette and waited.

You know, Max Shapiro was right. Gerry Knucks was an ass-hole name. He'd been thinking about that some lately. It was lim-iting. How far could a guy go in life with a name like Gerry Knucks? Was he going to be a leg-breaker all his life working for a festering asshole like Nicky T? There was no leg-breaker's pension fund. He had put away some money but it wouldn't last him forever, what with his expensive taste in clothing and booze and food. He was getting older. A lot smarter but his legs weren't doing him any good anymore. His knees hurt all the time. He could still shoot and po-sition himself and could still hit as hard as ever but getting out of the way was getting to be more of a problem. Besides, the work was getting boring, even depressing. You found some poor shit and you threatened him and while he was pissing himself and shaking and begging you to give him another chance you had to stand there and listen to it. It was getting old.

Fifteen minutes passed and the chinks showed up, rolling slowly through the docks in the crimson sedan. Stupid. They should have parked somewhere else and walked in or just waited for him to come out. Maybe they were late for a ping-pong match or a Godzilla festival. But Godzilla was Japanese, not Chinese, right? Maybe he was as bad as Nicky about the culture thing sometimes. Gerry watched them park and get out of the car. Gerry eased down the steps and walked up right behind them. All that Kung Fu, feel-the-earth shit was garbage. Walked up right behind them, didn't even hear him.

"You looking for me?" he said, and they turned around, one

of them reaching inside his jacket. Guy had the gun halfway out when Gerry shot him in the face. The guy fell dead on the ground. The other guy, the one with the tattoos, reached inside his coat. Gerry shook his head at the guy. The guy froze, looking at Gerry. Gerry gave him the stare, the one that said, "You're mine. Nothing you do matters."

"He didn't leave me any choice," said Gerry, trying to calm the guy. "That's what you need to take away from here. I don't want no shit over this. He was going for his gun and I had to take him out. You see it that way, don't you?"

The chink's face twisted into hatred. "We will find you and we will kill you, you shitbag."

Gerry turned his head sideways and looked at the guy. "What did you say?"

"I said fuck you, asshole."

Gerry squeezed the trigger on the Colt and shot the guy in the throat. The guy flopped around and made fish noises for a few seconds. Gerry put the gun away, nodding his head.

"Yeah, that's what I thought you said."

"So, now you're telling me you had a beer with him?" said Jack Summers, sitting in her Explorer. Didn't ask, just climbed in on the passenger side before she could hit the door lock.

"He brought it to me," Tobi Ryder said. Jack never gave up. Like he was her big brother or a shiek and she was part of his harem.

"Just like that, huh? Why didn't you drive off?"

"I wasn't trying to hide from him. He already knows we're cops."

"Now he does, anyway."

"No," she said, shaking her head. "He made us the first time he saw us. In the restaurant while he was talking to Shapiro and his girlfriend."

"How do you know that?"

"He told me. He told me if I was going to carry the big weapons that I was going to have to learn to sit so I wouldn't give it away. Also said that you had out-of-town cop written all over you. Said your clothes were all wrong for an Aspen native and tourists don't wear Brooks Brothers suits in ski resort towns. Said you were 'ob-trusive.'"

"So now he's giving Dick Tracy crimestopper tips, that it?"

"That's not really a crimestopper tip when you think about it." His left eye twitched. She was enjoying pissing him off. "He just notices things like that. He's a pro."

"So, if he's so damn good why isn't he still doing it?"

"He explained that, too."

Sitting in her Explorer, both of them sipping beer, Springer had told her, "It was kind of a mutual thing. I didn't want to work for them and they wished I would die in a flaming car wreck. Chief of staff was this repugnant asshole that thought the moon couldn't change phases unless he gave it permission. 'Everything goes through me,' he was always saying."

"The story about the perfume on the gun crack. Was that true?"

He'd shrugged, said, "You hear a lot of things. I had a smart mouth sometimes, but mostly it was because I was bored and they insulted your intelligence telling you things that were unmitigated bullshit and you were supposed to swallow it like a good Nazi. I said the perfume thing once, but not to a reporter. I said it to a friend who repeated it to a reporter but that's not what got me in trouble."

She asked about the other incident, the one where the reporter asked what the president was doing in there and he said, "You're the reporter, what do you think?" But, he said, that wasn't it either. He had said that but the reporter didn't tell anybody about it until after Springer left town.

"So, what was it?" she asked.

"He raised his voice to me."

"You mean he yelled at you?"

Nodded.

"The president?"

"No, I think he kind of liked me. It was the chief of staff who got bent out of shape."

"And that's why you quit?"

"That's not all of it." God, getting anything out of this guy was like mining sand at the beach with a pair of tweezers.

"What was it then?"

"I think I may have told him that I'd break his nose or something like that."

She leaned against the seat back and looked at him. "You threatened the chief of staff?"

"More or less. I said something like he should learn to modulate his voice when he talked to me or he'd be blowing his nose next to his ear for the rest of his life."

"So they fired you?"

"I'd already given them notice. It was my last day anyway. It was kind of fun to blow a fast one under his chin. May have been the defining moment of my government career."

"Before that you won a medal in the Gulf War."

Then he did something odd. It knocked him back some. He'd looked like he didn't want to talk about that and asked about her to change the subject. Gave her a funny look like she had stepped over the line, but that wasn't it either. More like a little boy with a secret he didn't want to tell. He asked her how long had she been a cop? What made her decide to do that? She'd told him about her dad and how much she'd idolized him. And then he asked about the little half-moon scar on the side of her chin.

She said, "This dirtbag Russian mafia guy, one of those imported thugs who think they've found heaven in the American rackets, hit me with a big diamond ring. Broke my jaw. My badge of courage."

"So, what happened to him?"

"He came at me with a fireplace poker and I shot him but I got in trouble for shooting him. Got suspended for a while."

"Why's that?"

"I shot him twice."

"Why'd that get you in trouble?"

"One of the shots was post-mortem."

Springer shrugged. "So, sometimes you need two shots. You can't always tell if the first one did it."

"The second shot castrated him."

"Oh." He looked out the windshield of the Explorer, then back at her, giving her a little smile. "Be a good thing not to piss you off then, huh?"

And, then he'd said, "What does your mother, the district attorney, think about all that?"

She looked at him. Yeah, he was trying to see if he could get a reaction from her.

"How do you know about that?"

"Wild guess."

"My guess is you don't make wild guesses." He'd shrugged at her. She didn't know whether he was trying to be enigmatic or if he *was* enigmatic.

She said, "So Max Shapiro visits with you. What's that about?"

"You're the cop," he said, mimicking the reporter story. "What do you think it's about?"

"He wants a bodyguard. He's got somebody after him, doesn't he?"

He smiled. "That's a pretty good guess."

"It is, isn't it?" she said, realizing he wasn't confirming it, but not denying it, either. "It's Nicky Tortino, isn't it?"

He looked at her. Smiled. Didn't say a thing. She felt a measure of satisfaction because she knew that he knew she was on it.

And now she was telling Summers, sitting in the same seat as Springer had, about the whole conversation and he didn't like it but he had to admit she had added a significant piece to the puzzle.

"Nicky T's out to get Shapiro," said Summers. "That's interesting. There may be some way to use that to my advantage." She didn't miss the use of the personal pronoun. *My* advantage, he said, like she was decorative. "Did he say whether he was going to take the job guarding Shapiro?"

"Said he hadn't decided yet. Said he could use the money and he liked Shapiro's girlfriend so that was working in Max's favor."

Summers looked away from her, then down at the dish of honey-roasted peanuts the waitress had set on their table. He picked a couple of them up, then threw them back in the dish. "Well, you and Mr. Springer are big sweethearts now, that it?"

"We're going to be married and have six children, none of which will be named Jack," she said, looking right back at him. "Why don't you just get off it? I found out some things we need to know and it didn't cost us anything and it didn't take very long."

"What if he tips off Max?"

"He might. So? He may've told him before now. I told you already. He knows we're cops. It's not Max we want anyway, is it?"

"Not really." Thinking about it now. Hopefully, thinking like a cop instead of a potential boyfriend; the captain of the football team jealous of the guy who rode a motorcycle to school, which would be a good thing. "You know, if Springer could do something besides try to get in your pants he could help us put Max and Nicky T and the whole operation away." But, there it was again, he just couldn't get it out of his head.

"See?" she said, not going to let him get to her about the crack about Springer wanting to get in her pants. "If I'd have been some macho boy cop we wouldn't be this far along would we?"

"I meant we could possibly enlist Springer to help us get inside information on Max and Nicky."

"That would be a nice thing."

He nodded at her. She could see that he hated to give her anything. "Well, just don't get carried away with the flirtatious aspect of the thing. Springer's a variable. I looked at his file and he's unpredictable. There's no telling what he likes and doesn't like and which way he'll jump. I'm sure you're smarter than to indulge some fantasy about an aimless shithead you perceive as some kind of romantic rogue who plays the piano for a living."

She stared at him for moment, not believing anybody could be so self-absorbed. "Maybe I like romantic rogues who take chances and work for people because they like their girlfriends or like to play the piano and ride motorcycles. But don't get yourself all worked up, dwelling on it. There's nothing happening there."

"Good," he said, not looking like he understood a damned word she'd just said. "That's better. I'll stop bringing it up and we'll proceed along professional lines. I'll find out exactly what's going on with Shapiro and you talk to some locals. So, what's your next move?"

She smiled, couldn't resist one more dig. "I think I'll take piano boy up on his offer of dinner tomorrow." Summers responded by giving her the look she wanted. A pissed-off look. "He's a local, you know."

Sometimes, she was *just* like her dad.

CHAPTER

Seven

MAX WAS GETTING APPREHENSIVE. WHERE WAS SUZI? AT first, he'd gotten antsy because he wanted his cigars, then it had turned into impatience at having to wait. He started watching a movie, one of those deals where you punched the numbers up on the remote and they billed the room, automatically. Then, he got to thinking about it. What if they found her at his place? Auteen and Ray Dean wouldn't have any hesitation about squeezing her. He wished he had told her to just get over to the motel. Now he was worried about her. He shouldn't have involved her. Now, she could be in danger. What had he been thinking about? He tried calling but there was no answer. Maybe she was on her way.

He tried calling the smart-assed piano player again, have him go check on her. No answer there either.

Where the hell was she?

Springer thought about his encounter with Tobi Ryder. She was sharp. Not just attractive but straight-out intelligent. Tough, too. Shot the guy after he broke her jaw, and then still ticked off so she shoots him in the privates. He whistled lowly when he thought about that. She could get mad.

He was also thinking about Max's offer. Maybe he'd go over and talk to him about it. He'd given him the address and Springer knew the place he was talking about—a modified A-frame over on

Cemetery Lane that looked like a Swiss chalet—so after Tobi Ryder left he got in his car and drove over to Max's place. What else was there to do? Think about how broke he was?

He found the place easy enough. He drove by once without stopping, a habit from his days in the service, to recon the layout. As he turned around to go back he had the feeling that something about the place wasn't right. What was it? When he drove by the second time he knew what it was. It was the rental plates on the Cadillac. He remembered Max saying he had two Jaguars in his garage that weren't worth anything in all this snow and that he was talking to a guy about a Land Rover.

Maybe it was just somebody visiting. Nothing to worry about.

But his internal alarm was humming with the kind of low buzz it made just before it started clanging. Max had bad guys after him. Max wasn't from around here. Doubtful he had people who just dropped by to see him. So, Springer drove down the street and parked and got out and walked back to Max's place.

Before he walked back, though, he got the Beretta Tomcat .32 out of the glovebox and dropped it into his coat pocket.

Suzi was looking for that sweater, the one that looked so good on Max when the men walked into the house. Surprised her. They walked right in like they were part of the family. Two of them—a gigantic black guy with chin whiskers and a silver earring and a weird-looking guy wearing a bolo tie and black silver-tipped cowboy boots and this enormous mane of hair which he wore long and sprayed up like a seventies country-western star. The hair was like a helmet, or a lion's mane: unmoving, covering his ears and neck and curling up at his collar.

"What the hell do you want?" she'd said when she saw them.

"Where's Max?" said the guy with the hair.

"He's not here."

"I don't believe you."

"Suit yourself," she said.

"Take a look around, will ya?" Lion's mane said to the big man.

"This a nice crib," said the big man.

"Yeah, I'm crazy about it. I may move here," said lion's mane, looking annoyed. "Now, see if you can find Max."

"Look around all you want, but he's not here," she said.

"Where is he then?"

She gave him a pained look. "Like I'd tell you, right? Who does your hair, anyway?"

"What's that mean?"

"You look like the bride of Frankenstein."

He looked at her like he was trying to figure out what he was seeing. "Look, lady, I don't want to spend a lot of time fucking around, see? So, you need to close your hole and answer my questions or some serious shit's gonna start happening. That connect in that stupid head of yours?"

"If I close my mouth how am I supposed to answer your questions?"

That's when he slapped her.

Auteen was enjoying himself, looking around the place. Man, Max knew how to live, that's for sure. Saw the bar. The man had about every kind of shit there was. Jack Daniel's, Stoli, Beefeaters, Chivas, the whole thing. He picked up a bottle of tequila because he'd never tried any and took a swig of the stuff. Kinda sweet with a wang in the aftertaste. Wouldn't want to drink that stuff all the time. He set the bottle back on the bar without putting the lid back on.

Auteen was getting a little tired of Ray Dean's mouth. Like he was the boss or something. And him with hair like a Martian. And those fucking clothes which made him look like Joe Pesci in the "Cousin Vinny" movie, the one where the guy played the city lawyer in the deep cracker South.

Nicky and Ray Dean was both prejudiced which got on Auteen's nerves, though he knew they were dumb about the race thing. Knucks wasn't prejudiced and even though he gave Auteen a bunch of shit, at least Knucks was a bad-ass motherfucker who you could respect. But Ray Dean was a cracker-ass redneck who didn't have good sense. Someday, Auteen might have to squash his dumb ass a little. Don't know why he was involved with these guys anyway except Nicky T paid good. The man liked having a big black guy standing next to him when he was talking shit to someone. Sometimes he treated Auteen like he was some kind of trained zoo animal. But he paid good. It always came back to that. Someday soon Auteen needed to be finding himself a new gig. That's for damn sure.

He was walking through the rec room where there was this big-screen television when he spotted the chrome-finish refrigerator. The biggest refrigerator he'd ever seen. Like the kind you saw in restaurant kitchens. He opened up one side of it. There was just about any kind of beer you could think of in there. He took out a bottle of Michelob and opened it up and drained it in one swallow. Felt it slap against the back of his throat all cold and foamy. Got out another and opened it. Take his time with this one. There was some kind of fancy meat tray like they made up in grocery stores in the fridge, except fancier. Huge slices of turkey and beef and ham and different types of cheese on it. He peeled back the plastic wrap, grabbed a handful of turkey and cheese.

And that's when the guy put the gun against his neck and said: "You oughta try the corned beef."

Could you believe this bitch? thought Ray Dean. You smack her upside her head and she starts talking shit, telling him what's going to happen to him. Snarling at him. Like she wasn't the one looking up from the floor.

"You bastard," she'd said. "You touch me again and I'll cut your balls off."

There, see? What's wrong with a woman like that? "You better get a machete, then," he said. "And back out of the way because they're the size of coconuts. They fall on you, they'll break your back. You ain't hurt anyway. But you don't shut up I'm gonna make it hurt."

"I don't know where he is," she said.

"You're packing his shit up and I'm supposed to believe you're taking it to the Salvation Army or something? Come on lady, I'm getting tired of this. There's no reason for you to get messed up.

Just tell me where the guy is and we leave. Nothing happens to you. You get this place and live happily ever after."

He helped her off the floor and sat her down on the side of the bed. He lifted up her face by pinching her cheeks between his fingers like a parent scolding a child so he could have her full attention. She had nice skin. Maybe there was something she could do for him besides provide information.

"Now," he said, "you only get one shot at this and then it starts happening. Where is Max?"

"Fug you," she said, the words garbled because of the pressure on her jaw.

"Say what?"

"Fuck yourself with a can opener, prick."

He let out a breath and shook his head. "You shouldna said that." Then he knocked her off the bed. She hit the floor in a heap and he moved in on her.

"Had to be a tough bitch, didn't ya? What good is that, huh? You don't get nothing for it. Now I'm going to fuck up your world, lady," he said. He grabbed her by the arm and jerked her to her feet.

"You do," said a voice behind him, "and it'll be the last thing you ever do."

Ray Dean turned around and saw this big guy standing behind Auteen. Guy with a gun.

"What's this?" Ray Dean asked him. "Who the hell are you?"

"I'm from the abused women's crisis center."

"And you carry a gun?"

"We've gone militant."

A wise guy. Just what he needed with everything else. Ray Dean looked at the situation. The guy had a gun on Auteen. Look at Auteen, docile as a puppy. Three hundred pounds of worthless.

"What the fuck are you doing?" Ray Dean asked Auteen. "How'd you let this happen?"

"You talking to me?" said Auteen.

"No, I'm talking to the seventeen other stupid fucks in the room that let some off-the-street peckerwood walk up on him with a gun."

"Man, you better get off me, Ray Dean."

Ray Dean rolled his eyes. They had a situation here and Auteen takes an attitude at him. Someday he was going to have to shoot this nigger. Not now, though. Besides, he had the immediate problem to deal with.

"You okay?" the guy asked the girl.

"I'm okay."

"I didn't hurt her," said Ray Dean. "Just trying to get her attention."

"That's all you were doing, huh?"

"Yeah," said Ray Dean, shrugging. "That's all."

"Well, I guess I can understand that," the guy said, cool, like it was no big deal.

"Sure, we can get along."

"Lay on the floor," the guy said, nudging Auteen. Auteen lay down on the carpet. "On your face. Fingers laced behind your neck. Do it now." Voice was hard-assed, like he was used to giving orders. Who was this guy? Auteen complied.

"Now, roll over, Auteen," said Ray Dean. "Sit up. Speak."

"I'm warning you, man," said Auteen, talking into the carpet.

"Look, buddy," said Ray Dean, talking to Springer now. "This ain't no big deal. We're together on that, aren't we? We'll just go. This isn't something we can't work out."

"Now you," said Springer, gesturing with the gun. "Move away from the girl and get on the floor, like your friend."

"Aw come on, there's no use in that."

"Need to do what I say. Let go of her."

"Or what? You gonna shoot me? That it? Shoot holes in Max's place?" This freaking vanilla cookie wasn't going to shoot nobody. Talk to the guy. Keep him thinking. See if he could maneuver the girl between him and the guy while he got out his nine. Look at the way he was dressed. Dockers and one of those jackets like you'd see in a Sears catalog. Little bitty ladies gun. He wasn't no hard-on.

"You right-handed or left-handed?" Springer asked.

"What's that mean?"

"I'm through talking to you now. Let go of her and get on the floor."

"I think I'll hold on to her just a little while longer while we—"

Springer shot Ray Dean in the foot. Took off part of the little toe on the right foot. Ray Dean screamed and hopped around on his left leg. He made it to the bed before he fell onto it.

Damn, it hurt.

Who was this guy?

CHAPTER

Eight

"YOU KNOW HOW TO USE THIS?" SPRINGER SAID, HANDING
the Beretta to Suzi.

"Yeah." Suzi took the gun and pointed it at Ray Dean. Springer could see her jaw muscles working and her eyes were blazing. Enough so that Springer became concerned. Ray Dean too.

"Don't give that crazy woman a gun," said Ray Dean. "What're you thinking about?"

"Ah . . . Suzi," said Springer. "I don't think we need to murder this guy. At least not right at this moment. He isn't going to be making any sudden movements, anyway. But, if the black guy moves, shoot him in the head. He's a big guy, so if you start shooting, don't stop."

"Tell the bitch be careful," said Auteen, "Auteen ain't movin'."

Springer put his knee in the small of Ray Dean's back and relieved him of his pistol. Then, grabbing a handful of hair he jerked Ray Dean off the bed and onto the floor.

"You shot me," wailed Ray Dean. "You fucking shot me, you . . . What are you thinking about when you do something like that?"

"Just trying to get your attention," he said, mimicking Ray Dean. "That's all."

"Shoulda laid on the floor like the man told you," said Auteen.

"Shut up. Shit, I'm bleeding all over the place."

"Keep your foot elevated and it'll slow down," said Springer. "And, quit crying. It's unbecoming."

"Should I call the police?" Suzi asked.

Springer thought about it. Shook his head. "I don't think so. These guys work for somebody else. Somebody with money and connections. The police will lock them up and some lawyer from the coast will be here within twenty-four hours to cut them loose."

"You bet your ass," said Ray Dean.

"Nobody asked you. I want anything out of you, I'll beat it out of you."

"Why you gotta be such a hard-ass all the time?"

"I had an unhappy childhood," said Springer. Then to Suzi, he said, "They'll just send somebody else, anyway. Maybe somebody not as ear-to-ear dumb as these guys. We know who these guys are. These guys are Abbot and Costello."

Max was on his third Scotch—had a nice buzz going—when Suzi finally showed up. Well, about bleeping time. She had the piano guy with her. Max had quit watching the in-room movie, some bullshit love story with Sandra Bullock in it. He'd only wanted to see it because he liked the way she looked. The story was sappy. You could never believe the shit Hollywood put out anymore. Everything was on the surface, like the writer had to slap you in the head so you wouldn't let your attention wander. Bullock was cute and good with the lines they gave her, but there was no fire. Now Rita Hayworth. There was a woman could make you pay attention.

So, he'd changed over to another channel and watched a college football game. Colorado State versus Air Force. It was in the third quarter and Air Force had the ball third-and-long on State's forty-five when Suzi knocked on the door.

He opened the door and let them in.

"Where the hell've you been?" Max asked.

"Good to see you too, Max," Suzi said, like she was pissed off.

"What?" he said, opening his arms. What had he done now?

"Max," said Springer. "Don't open the door until you're sure who's on the other side."

"Why I got to listen to you?"

"Just do what he says, Max," said Suzi, tired of his attitude. "He's your bodyguard, now."

"He took the job?"

"After you pay me three grand up front," said Springer, as he looked out the window.

"That wasn't the deal."

"It is now."

"Why three grand?"

"I'm running a blue-light special," said Springer, smiling.

"Just pay him, Max," Suzi said, running a hand through her hair. "I've been through a lot in the last hour. Those two guys you were telling me about? Ray Dean and Auteen? They broke into your house looking for you. Ray Dean slapped me around and Cole saved me."

"How'd you do that?" he asked Springer.

Springer shrugged. "I have a way with people."

What a wise guy. "Just talked them out of it, that it?"

"He shot Ray Dean in his foot," said Suzi.

"I'd like to have seen that," said Max, thinking about it. Then he thought of something else. "Where'd this shooting take place?"

"Your bedroom," said Suzi.

"You shot a gun off in my house?"

Springer chuckled to himself and sat down in an overstuffed chair, his hands dangling off the sides of the chair's arms.

"That's funny?" asked Max.

Suzi said, "Max, Ray Dean was beating me up."

"Is there a bullet hole in my house?"

"Right through the carpet," said Springer. "He bled some too. I clean it up I have to charge you more."

"You already want three grand."

"That's for the rescue and shooting my gun. Fifteen hundred for each. Ammunition's expensive."

"Especially yours."

"God, Max," said Suzi, pouring herself a drink. "You're incredible."

Max frowned and took another sip on his Scotch. "You had to shoot him, huh?"

"I gave some thought to hypnotizing him," he said and shrugged. "But the gun was in my hand and all."

There it was again. Guy was always smarting off about something. Like Max was working for him instead of the other way around. Like Max was the straight man in some Vegas comedy act.

"So, now what?" asked Max.

"Pay him," she said.

"That'd be a nice beginning," said Springer.

Tobi Ryder got a break. She was talking to a Pitkin County sheriff's deputy—a friend of hers named Belinda Talbot—who told her she had been called to the ER to investigate a gunshot wound. All gunshot wounds had to be reported by hospital personnel to the authorities.

"This guy, a real puke-looking guy with a do like Conway Twitty on a bad hair day, says he shot himself accidentally in the foot," said Belinda. "So, I ran him through NCIC and he's a bad actor. Did some time for shooting a guy in Texas. Turns out he muscles for this creep in San Francisco—"

"A guy named Nicky Tortino," said Tobi.

"Yeah, that's right. How'd you know that?"

"So, where's the guy now?"

"I questioned him and the hospital turned him loose so he could report to the Aspen Police. It looks like he *did* accidentally shoot himself. It just took off part of the little toe. He kept whining about how it hurt and giving the nurses shit. Huge black guy with him that you could tell thought the whole thing was funny. Wonder what a turd like that is doing here in Aspen?"

"I think I know," said Tobi. "Where's this guy staying?"

"That place right across from the Ritz. The Mountain Chalet."

So that's why Tobi was back in her Explorer on her way across town. Thinking about the situation. Thinking about the guy, Springer.

Max Shapiro was in town. Shapiro laundered money for Nicky Tortino, a San Francisco hood who operated with the permission of the mob. Tortino wasn't a made guy, just some punk who'd made more money than he deserved and paid out tribute to the wiseguys. That's what Summers had told her.

"Tortino is a real case of diarrhea," said Summers. "He's built himself up a business in numbers, loan-sharking, some drugs—only coke because he's leery of crackheads—and has managed to insinuate himself into some legitimate businesses like construction, trucking, and he owns a restaurant downtown. He's a major player in the Bay area rackets but he's a caricature of a wiseguy. Makes Gotti look demure. Dresses flashy-trashy. Talks loud. Another one of those guys who thinks he's Tony Montana."

"Who?"

"Tony Montana. You know. Al Pacino in *Scarface*. You haven't seen that one?"

"So, if he's such a moron, how's it he's managed to elude a high-speed crimebuster like yourself?" Smiling when she said it, enjoying watching his forehead wrinkle. Knowing she had irritated him again. It was like a game. Except he was too easy sometimes. Her brothers would have come back at her with something, trying to knock her off her feet. But not this guy in his Bostonian tassled wing tips and his rep tie. Not super-cop, God's gift to middle-aged cheerleaders everywhere.

"Nicky's got the connections, that's all," said Summers, controlling himself. "He lucked onto a shylock with style and brains. A leg-breaker named Gerry Nugent. They call him Gerry Knucks."

"Gerry Knucks?"

"He makes things work for Tortino. Without Nugent, Tortino is a small-timer. Nugent is one of the sharpest operators in the Bay area. Never spent a minute inside. In fact, he's never even been arrested."

"Maybe he hasn't done anything."

"How do you manage to ever arrest anyone? You don't think there are any criminals?" She let it pass. Let him have one. "We suspect him of four killings, maybe five. You can never connect him up, but people that screw around with Tortino get a visit from Nugent. Doesn't threaten or act tough, but everybody in town's afraid of the guy. And, by association, everybody's afraid of Tortino."

"What about Ray Dean Carr?"

"He's dumber than toilet paper. But a total sociopath. Dangerous. A mean little bastard who once barb-wired a guy's nuts because he made fun of Carr's hair."

And now someone had shot him, she thought, as she maneuvered the Explorer through the light traffic on Main Street. She put a Celine Dion disc in the CD player and thought about Springer. He was a paradox. This guy who played the piano and, according to Summers, hit crack houses when funds got low.

"You always wear slacks?" Springer had asked her, sitting in her car.

"What kind of question is that?" she said.

"You look like you have nice legs," he said, shrugging, like he was talking about the weather. "I've been wondering what they look like."

"Where have you been during the past decade?" she asked. "You don't think that's a bit sexist?" Not minding it at all but trying to see if she could get him to register something approximating remorse.

But he brushed it aside. "You want to see my legs?" he said, "that it?"

She smothered the smile. "I've seen enough and I'm not that impressed."

"You're not dazzled yet? Wondered why you hadn't tried to frisk me. You're not a lesbian or anything, are you? Usually only lesbians can resist me."

"It's not that tough, believe me."

"You ever wear a skirt?"

"Sometimes," she said. "On a date maybe. If I really like the guy."

"Yeah?" he said. Then, looking out her windshield like he was settling something in his mind, talking to himself, he said, "Huh? If I really like the guy. Okay."

Just like that and then he was out of the car and headed back into his place.

So, that was what she was thinking about when she pulled into the parking lot of the Aspen police station, shut off the Explorer, and walked inside to talk to someone who might know the desk people at the Best Western.

———————

When Springer pulled up in front of the Whiskey Basin they were waiting for him. Two uniforms in an Aspen police unit. It was early evening and he needed to make some arrangements with the staff for the next few days. Tell them what to do while he was protecting Max. Then he was going back to his place to pick up some clothes and another gun and his shaving kit before heading back to the Ritz.

"Mr. Springer?" said one of them, a weight-lifter type with a square jaw shaved close.

He admitted that's who he was.

"I have a warrant for your arrest, sir," said the policeman.

"For what?"

"Assault?"

"Who did I assault?"

"A man named Garrison Pierce signed a complaint against you, sir."

"I don't know the guy."

"He plays linebacker for Colorado University."

He pursed his lips and nodded. "Oh, that Garrison Pierce."

Tobi liked visiting the Aspen police station. They treated her like a celebrity there. The guys flirted with her, nothing vicious, and the female cops were friendly. Aspen PD was not like a city precinct station. Things were new and clean and the perps were mostly DUI's or traffic violators processing through. No crackheads or pimps or cheap hoods with jailhouse tattoos. They shared the jail, a new facility, with the Pitkin County sheriff's department.

She was able to get the information she wanted. In fact, the cop, a young guy named Proctor, who looked like a male model in a freshly-pressed uniform and laser-precise sideburns called over for her and got the room number after pouring her a cup of coffee.

"Room Two-twenty-five," he told her, after hanging up the phone.

"Thanks," she said. She sipped her coffee and made a face. She held the coffee cup up and pointed at it.

Proctor smiled. "Yeah. It's like battery acid except not as tasty.

Happens every time Sergeant Gordon makes it. Good cop, bad cook. You're the second person who's complained about it." He laughed thinking about it. "Guy we just processed opened his eyes wide when he drank it and asked if we could just slap him around with our nightsticks next time instead of making him drink our coffee."

"What was he in for?"

"Assault. Brought him in last evening. He broke some football player's nose the other night. Sprained the guy's knee too." This was beginning to sound familiar to her. Proctor said, "You know what he said when we were bringing him in? He asked if we saw the guy he was supposed to have assaulted. I said yeah and he said, 'Would you assault a guy looks like that?'"

Springer.

"Where is he?"

"He's in the detention room, trying to make bail."

"May I use your phone?" she asked.

"Sure."

"I'm going to order some real coffee," she said. "You want some?"

Springer called the Ritz-Carlton from the police station and asked for room 307. He'd tried the night before but didn't get an answer which meant Max and Suzi had gone out even though he told Max to stay in the room until he got back. He tried calling the club but no one answered there, either. Which didn't make sense. When he got the front desk he didn't ask for Max Shapiro because that would be stupid on a number of levels. Also, Max had registered under the pseudonym, Micah Sharone. He was hoping that Suzi would answer the phone but Max answered.

"Max," said Springer. "I told you not to answer the phone."

"What? I had to answer. Suzi's taking a shower. Besides, I knew it was you. Nobody else knows where I am."

"Where were you last night?"

"We went out to eat. That okay with you?"

"I told you to stay inside."

"I gotta eat. Besides, where the hell are you?"

Springer wasn't going to argue with him right now. "Look Max, I need you to send Suzi downtown with a hundred dollars and bail me out."

"A hundred bucks? What'd you do? Litter?"

"Assault. Just send her."

"You don't have a C-note on you?" asked Max, perplexed by it. Max always carried between two and five thousand dollars himself so he couldn't understand how someone could function with less than a hundred dollars in his pocket. "You're getting expensive. First, it's three thousand up front and now it's a hundred dollars for bail. You're not going to want to get your teeth capped are you?"

"Fine, Max," said Springer. "I'll sit down here then. It's not a bad place except for the coffee. Just stay away from the windows and don't answer the door or the phone until I can figure out a way to get out of here."

"I'll send Suzi down," said Max, resigned to it.

Springer hung up the jail phone and sat down on the bench. He'd spent the night sleeping in the detention room, the dispatchers watching him through the big glass window. He picked up a month-old copy of *Time* magazine and leafed through it. Magazines. A padded bench. Covered in *Naugahyde*. Hard to respect a lock-up that had lounge furniture in the holding cell.

He was reading a book review about an historical romance entitled "Crimson Lace" when she came into the room. She had a tray with two cups of coffee and some pastry on it. He looked up at her and saw she was smiling like she had told herself a private joke.

"You know," she said, segueing into it, "I was just thinking of all the times when I was on stake-out trying to be alert and stalwart and wishing someone would bring me a cup of coffee and a doughnut."

"Stalwart?" he said.

"As opposed to bored to tears and freezing my cute little ass off," she said.

Springer smiled. This was a pretty sharp lady. *Special Agent* Ryder. And he had to admit it.

She did have a cute little ass.

CHAPTER

Nine

RAY DEAN'S EARS WERE BURNING. IT WAS BECAUSE WHEN he called Nicky he got Gerry Knucks. After Ray Dean told him about the mess-up at Shapiro's house Gerry jumped all over his ass.

Ray Dean had his foot wrapped and elevated and had taken a couple of the pain pills the hospital had given him. Washed them down with Jim Beam. His head was humming seven different ways so he didn't get what Gerry was talking about. Gerry always had something to say though.

Knucks said, "You go to Aspen and you let some resident shoot you? That's what you're telling me?"

"It's Auteen's fault. He was downstairs fucking around and the guy snuck up on him."

"You want to explain this to Nicky?"

Not really, he thought, but what was he gonna do? So Nicky got on the hook and tore him a new hole.

"You got shot, huh?" asked Nicky.

"He shot me in the little toe."

"The *little* toe? What was he aiming for? Your big toe? I hope you die of the gangrene you fist-fucking imbecile," said Nicky. Sometimes Nicky thought he was comical instead of a guy who talked while he was eating, like Auteen. "How'd you and the other halfwit manage to get shot and let the guy get away? The guy's a local, for crissakes. You wanta tell me about that shit? I'll walk you through the procedure. Tell you how it works. Are you listening? First, you make the guy. I mean you know for sure where he is physically, then you walk up to him and you shoot him. Am I going too fast for you? You don't just wander into his fucking house like it was a fact-finding survey, you understand what I'm saying, you dumb Texas shit? And, you don't let accountants or whatever this guy is, front you and take your manhood."

Fucking Nicky, thought Ray Dean. "Guy came out of nowhere. I don't know why he showed up. Who could figure something like that? We'll take care of this, Nicky. Not a problem."

"I'm gonna send Gerry out there."

Not fucking Gerry. "You don't need to do that. We got this covered."

"That's why you're shot in the foot, right? Cause you got it covered?"

"We'll get the guy, Nicky. Don't worry."

"Worry's all I do when I put you on something. You got two days, then I send Gerry. Y'understand? Oh yeah, you and the chocolate buffalo don't let any vicious insurance salesmen roll you or nothing before then. Some of them carry letter-openers and fountain pens and I wouldn't want you should get hurt. Okay?"

Ray Dean hung up the phone. Asshole. Last thing he needed was Gerry coming around and giving him daily shit sandwiches. Besides, he wanted to show Nicky that they didn't need Gerry. Fucking Gerry, with his frostbite eyes and his wise mouth, making remarks. Who needed that? Speaking of nasty eyes he could still see the way the local guy's face changed just before he shot Ray in his foot, saying, "I'm through talking to you now." Meaning it. He needed to find out who this guy was and what he was doing in Aspen.

"What he say?" asked Auteen. Look at him, eating Kentucky Fried Chicken out of the bucket and watching *Wheel of Fortune*.

"He said you fucked up the job."

"Naw," said Auteen. "Ate your ass, didn't he?"

"No, he told me to go buy you a big watermelon you did such a good job."

Auteen chuckled to himself in that deep-throated way he had. "Ate your ass out."

"We got two days to whack out Max."

"You still saying things like 'whack out'? You a priceless white boy. I keep you around for something to laugh at."

"That right? Well, let me tell you something. Are you listening? As a bonus, I'm gonna burn the smart-ass that shot my foot."

"How you gonna do that?" said Auteen. "We 'bout run out of bitches for you to slap around."

Now, even Auteen was giving him shit. "We'll find him. And Max, too. And the girl with the mouth problems. Before Gerry Knucks gets here and hogs the credit."

"I'm with that," said Auteen, dropping a leg bone in the trash can. "And knock off the racist shit, you redneck, no-toe-having, Texas peckerwood. I don't even like watermelon."

"But fried chicken's on the list, right?"

Gerry watched Nicky hang up the phone.

"Two days, huh?" he asked Nicky.

Nicky shook his head for several seconds, then said, "No. Go out now. They're gonna fuck it up if I leave 'em there. Catch the next plane out."

Gerry nodded.

Nicky said, "You want to say it, don'tcha?"

"Want to say what?" said Gerry, putting on his jacket. But he knew what Nicky was talking about.

"You want to say 'I told you so.' "

Gerry shrugged.

"So, go ahead. Say it."

"I'll call you when the job's done," said Gerry.

Suzi got lost driving over to the Aspen police station even though it was right along the main drive, so she had to stop and get directions. Also, Max was pissed at her because she forgot to bring his cigars from the house after the incident with the weird hair guy.

"Sorry, Max. What was I thinking about?" Sarcastic, now. "Only thinking of myself when I'm attacked by two hoods when I should have been thinking, what will Max do without his cigars?"

Max put his hands out and gave her that expression like he didn't know why she was on his case.

She was getting tired of Max's narcissism. She hadn't noticed it before. Ever since they'd been in Aspen he'd been acting like a child. At first all he could talk about was how pretty the snow was in Aspen and now he was even bitching about that.

"You ever seen so much snow?" he'd asked, for no apparent reason. "I'm gonna go ape-shit if I don't see some grass pretty soon."

"Grass?" she'd said. She shook her head in disbelief. "Now you want grass? You don't have any grass at your office in San Francisco. For the last ten years you lived in a building with no grass around it. So I don't know what you're talking about with the grass thing."

"Yeah, well, grass is at least a possibility in Frisco," he said, making no sense but always wanting the last word. Which was another thing she hadn't noticed before. Max always wanted the last word like he was keeping score or something. That's why Springer annoyed him so much. It was because Springer could always say something Max wasn't expecting. Max, the millionaire land developer. Max, the human punch card for hoodlums whose vocabulary couldn't break the three-syllable barrier. Max, who always wanted the last word.

But she *would* like to go and check on her dress shop. A couple of days in Vegas might put Max in a better mood. But only a couple of days for her. Since she'd been in Aspen she'd taken a look at her life in Vegas and was starting to re-examine herself. She liked the mountains and the snow and the quaint shops and the clean air and the lack of neon. Vegas was neon signs blinking twenty-four hours a day. A place for pretenders to hide out in a sham universe. Hadn't noticed she didn't like it until she wasn't around it. Aspen might be a good place for a queen-size dress shop. Full-figured women wouldn't have to shop next to a snow bunny with a twenty-three-inch waist.

So she called the airline and got the tickets for Vegas. Three of them. One for Springer, though she didn't think he was going to like the idea.

When she finally got to the police station she found Springer with a woman cop named Ryder. Ryder had a flavor that Suzi couldn't quite put her finger on at first. Then, when they were leaving, Suzi figured it out. Ryder had the same type of confidence that Springer had, like she could handle anything that came her way. Then there was the cop flavor that went with the confidence thing.

Also, and you could see it right off, there was something in the air between Springer and the woman cop. Electric stuff. She wondered if either of them were aware of the vibes they put off. Which was too bad since Suzi was starting to have feelings for him. Not intimate feelings like she wanted to marry him or be his girl. It was sexual. She could see herself going to bed with this guy. Sleeping with a guy who didn't complain about everything like a spoiled child. A guy who knew what to do instead of bitching about not having grass to look at.

She was tired of Max.

But now was not a time to duck out on him. No, that wouldn't work. Suzi thought too much of herself to look like she was running out when things got tough. She'd get over this.

Still, it'd be nice to run into a guy who was in charge.

Springer asked Suzi if she'd drive him home to get some money and then by his club before heading back to the motel and she said fine, she was in no hurry to go back to the boring hotel. He told her he was sorry but they had seen her now and it'd be better if she didn't go out for a while.

"So, how long are we going to hide out while these two guys are running around?" she asked him.

"Until I think of something."

"Max and I need to go to Vegas." She said it tentatively, like she was looking for his approval which made him smile.

"Why not?" he said, surprising her. "Might be a good idea to get away from Ray Dean and Auteen for a couple of days. Throw them a curveball and see what they do."

"Still don't see why we didn't have them arrested."

"Wouldn't help. They'd just send someone else. No, I like it this way. I know who they are. I can see them coming. Subtle's not their style. Otherwise, we're going at this blind."

"How's Max ever going to get out of this?"

"There are ways. Either we make a deal or we make them think Max is out of reach or dead or—" He tailed off.

"Or what?"

"Or, I have to figure out some way to take Nicky out of the picture."

"You mean like kill him?"

He shrugged.

"You'd do that?"

"If it gets down to him or Max. And, if it's Max, that means me too."

"You'd die protecting Max?" What kind of man *was* this Cole Springer? "Why?"

"That's part of it when you take the money."

"What's it like?" she asked. "Being in the Secret Service?"

"I don't know. Boring mostly."

"Why'd you join then?"

"Thought it'd be interesting. You know, going places, protecting hotshots. Wearing a communicator and a gun, looking tough."

"You ever in love?"

"Was married."

"Divorced?"

"She died."

Uncomfortable now, she said, "I'm sorry."

"It's okay."

"What have you been doing since?"

"Mostly feeling sorry for myself."

She didn't expect that.

Gerry Nugent was looking through the magazines at the airport newsstand. Get something to look at while he flew out to Aspen. His flight included a stop-over in Vegas because Nicky wanted him to see a guy in Vegas for him. A bookmaker named Sudden Sal. Gerry picked up a copy of *Sports Illustrated* and a *GQ* magazine. There was an article on former pro athletes that caught his eye.

What'd those professional sports guys do when they got too old to play the game? They'd still be young. In their thirties, most of them. Had led active lives. Exciting lives. Couldn't just check into the retirement village and suck their teeth. They'd want to do something. Some of them didn't know what to do. Or, what they wanted to do. Sometimes Gerry felt like that.

The *GQ* he bought to look at men's clothing styles. Maybe try something different. Not some college-kid thing with the slouchy jackets and T-shirt. But something different. He ran his fingers along the lapel of his jacket. Nice jacket. Four hundred bucks. Nice material. Looked nice. But it made him look like the other guys in the life—a little more subdued—but he still dressed like what he was.

What was he?

A leg-breaker? Probably. A shylock? Sometimes. A shooter? Well, he'd done that. Mostly though, he was a guy that somebody else told where to go, what to do. Which was okay. Paid good. Wasn't very fulfilling though. But, now he was thinking like some mid-level executive who'd punched a clock for twenty years. *Fulfilling?* But why try to hide it?

He felt funny without his Colt. Couldn't get on a plane with one. Get one when he got to Aspen. Wasn't worth the trouble or the risk to smuggle one on a plane. That's how he had stayed clean all these years, he didn't force things. Didn't take unnecessary chances. Didn't talk about what he did. Not even to Nicky who he didn't even tell about the two Chinese guys he'd had to do. Nicky didn't know, Nicky couldn't tell nobody. If Nicky knew he'd blow it all over Frisco. Bragging about it like Gerry was a prize dog or something. Put a bull's-eye on Gerry's back for the chinks and the cops. Nicky was high maintenance. What with the jewelry and the partying around and the ridiculous clothes Nicky thought were chic instead of shit.

Nicky didn't understand you couldn't buy class. Couldn't even make a down payment on it. Class was hard, but style was attainable if you knew how to carry yourself.

As he boarded the plane the stewardess smiled at him which she was paid to do. Nice to have a girl smile at him that wasn't wearing too much makeup or flying on some pharmaceutical like the girls that hung around Nicky and his crowd. How long since he'd talked to a nice girl? The stewardess's eyes lingered on the G-shaped scar alongside his left eye where he'd gotten careless once. Hadn't been ready when the guy went at him with the broken bottle, twisting it. Gerry had dodged away at the last second, avoided losing his eyes and nose and maybe his life. Hammered the guy alongside his jaw then got his gun out and shot the punk. Nobody knew about that one, either. Wasn't a contract or work related. Just a couple of juiceheads working a beg-and-bag scam on him. One of them bugging him for pocket change while the other guy came at him with the bottle. Got the bottle guy. The other guy ran.

He had stitched up the wound himself, looking into two mirrors—positioned so he didn't have to look at himself in reverse. Waiting a couple of days holed up in his room until it healed enough to remove the stitches. Had one of the guys he worked with score him some Percodan and some morphine to get through it. Put ice on his face and waited. Wasn't medical-school quality but he'd closed it up pretty good. He'd learned how to do it when he was in the marines. His best friend in the marines had been this medic that bought it in Vietnam. Pretty good guy who didn't deserve to die that far from home.

The pretty good guy didn't make it home to his wife and kid. Gerry Knucks, the mob enforcer, did. Didn't seem right to Gerry.

Now he was going to have to go out and clean up the mess Ray Dean and Auteen, the traveling squirrel act, had made for him. He was interested in this guy that had drawn down on them. Ray Dean always underestimated people. Thought his tough guy act made him immune. It's what made him unreliable. This guy had snuck into the house and put a gun to Auteen's head. What had he said to Auteen? Oh yeah, "You oughta try the corned beef." Not, "Freeze." Or, "Move and I'll splatter your brains all over the refrigerator." Instead, something funny, like the guy was amusing himself. Then shoots Ray Dean when Carr didn't do what he told him.

A professional.

That's what Ray Dean didn't see. The guy was a pro. Knew what he was doing and was willing to shoot to get his way. Didn't call the cops because he knew it wouldn't do him any good—probably because he knew who they were and could keep an eye on them instead of someone taking their place—which is what Gerry had warned Nicky about but had been ignored. This wasn't some local like Nicky or Ray Dean thought. This guy would have to be taken into consideration.

That's the way it was. Don't take any chances. Don't force things. Before he did anything else he would have to see this guy and size him up. No use getting taken out by some guy he didn't know. It could happen.

He didn't have no red "S" on his chest.

When they pulled the car into the parking lot of the Whiskey Basin, Springer saw Bruce Caspar standing beside his car. He also saw the chain and lock box on the doors of the Whiskey.

Springer got out of the car and said, "What's going on, Bruce?"

"Cole," Bruce began. "I've been trying to get hold of you. We're locked out. The bank they . . . a . . . they called in your note because you were in jail."

Springer looked at the club, then back at Bruce.

"They moved pretty fast."

"Bank president is a CU grad and a big Golden Buffalo booster. They called him and I guess he took a personal interest."

"Looks like it."

"So what do we do?"

He reached in his wallet and took out fifteen one-hundred-dollar bills. Part of the money Max had given him. Handed the money to Bruce.

Bruce asked, "What's this for? You just paid everybody."

"Pay everybody for the rest of the week. Keep them on staff. Anybody wants to leave or get another job, I'll understand. I'll give good references to everybody."

"So what are you going to do?"

He looked at the building and the vacant parking lot.

"I'm still thinking about it."

Mostly he was thinking, what else could happen to him?

CHAPTER

Ten

AUTEEN COULDN'T BELIEVE IT WHEN HE SAW HER.

It was Max's girl. She was walking out of the fancy hotel right across from the place they were staying. Knew it was her. Watched her get into the Jag and pull out into the street.

"Her and Max must be staying in the Ritz," he told Ray Dean— who was taking a bath—his bad foot outside the water to keep the stitches dry. This white boy had flabby arms and round sissy shoulders and his skin was pale like a fish. A little guy who thought he was a bad ass, his pasty white foot bandaged and propped up on the side of the tub. Had himself some ugly toenails—all yellow and unhealthy looking. A dirty white boy. Had a glass of whiskey on the closed stool lid and smoking a cigarette. Probably didn't have inside toilets where the man grew up.

"How do you know that?" Ray Dean asked Auteen like Auteen was making it up. Always talking to Auteen like he was the help. He told him he saw the girlfriend, Suzi, get in the car and drive away.

"Why'nt you follow her?" Ray Dean asked in that way he had like Auteen was stupid or something.

"Cause you got the car keys, fool."

"You coulda gone across the street and grabbed her. Made her tell you where Max is."

"Good plan, Ray Dean. Grab her in broad daylight. A black man grabbing a white woman in the parking lot of the whitest town I ever saw." Auteen shook his head. What's wrong with this guy?

"Shit, you been eating too many them pills. Messing up your thinking which wasn't nothing special in the first place."

"What if she don't come back?"

"You think she be applying for a housekeeping job? Man, shut up. She be back."

"Well get over there and wait for her."

Auteen leaned his head back and looked at this little white boy, skin all puckered up from the water. "Man, who put you in charge? We're back to me being black still which you can't seem to keep in your head. I can't go over there and hang around. They'll have the Aspen po-lice over there faster'n you can say Rodney King. You haul your wrinkly white ass out of the tub and limp over there your ownself."

"Might as well. I do everything else."

"Yeah, I be lucky to have you around so you can get shot in the foot and such."

"Yeah, well fuck you."

"I been *thinking* about fucking you, honey. You kinda cute, all naked there in the water with your foot sticking out."

Then Auteen laughed because he could see he was pissing Ray Dean off. Ray Dean was funny to have around. Didn't mean to be, but he was.

"Slow down," Springer told Suzi as she approached the Ritz.

"I'm not going that fast."

"That woman walking in the door," he pointed in the direction of the front door of the hotel. "That's the CBI agent you just met back at the police station."

"Did she follow us?" Suzi asked.

"No. She was ahead of us. No way she could know you're staying here." He'd kept an eye out for a tail anyway and didn't see anybody.

"What do you want me to do?"

"Pull to the back of the hotel and let me out and then drive somewhere and I'll call you on the mobile phone when it's safe to come back."

"Is it going to be all right?"

"I don't know. Sure a lot going on, though."

Tobi Ryder pulled the Explorer to the side of the street and couldn't believe it when she saw the guy limping across the street in the direction of the Ritz. Her cop instincts were buzzing. She *knew* that it had to be Ray Dean Carr. Summers had told her about a short guy with really weird hair that worked for Nicky Tortino. One of the guys she was looking for.

What was he doing?

She drove on down the street, turned around and pulled into the carport of the Ritz, badged the valet, and followed the limping man with the bad hair into the lobby.

Before she got out of the car she checked the Sig-Sauer. Racked the slide and thumbed on the safety.

Ray Dean had his story all ready when he walked into the lobby. He'd found this fifty dollar bill in the parking lot and the woman had driven away before he could give it to her. He just couldn't keep it, you know. He wouldn't feel right if he didn't give it back. No, he didn't know the woman but she was driving a red Jag and he'd gotten the license plate number as she was driving away. The desk clerk, some Joe College-looking guy with a ski tan, said he'd be sure they got the money, but Ray Dean had told him how he'd feel better if he gave it to her himself and would he just call the room?

Sounded good to college boy so he picked up the phone and dialed the room. Ray Dean watched him punch in the numbers 3-0-7. College boy waited awhile and then said, "I'm sorry, sir, they're not answering."

"That's okay," said Ray Dean. It'd been about an hour since that dumb shit Auteen said he saw the woman leave in Max's car. Car wasn't in the lot. She was gone. Max was alone. "I'll check back later. By the way, where's the nearest men's room?" College boy pointed around the corner and told him they were next to the elevator.

Ray Dean thanked him and headed for the elevator. He punched the up button and the doors slid open. Inside the car he pressed number three.

He smiled to himself as the doors closed. Pulled the silencer out of his coat pocket and fixed it into the end of the Ruger .22 automatic pistol. It made a solid click sound when it seated. He heard the electronic whoosh as the car lifted him to the third floor.

Here I come, Max.

Max was starting to go ape-shit. Sitting around in the motel room watching daytime television and drinking Scotch was making him crazier than a two-dollar crack whore. No cigars and Suzi mad at him because he asked her why she didn't bring them from the house. Got all pissy about it. They were getting on each other's nerves penned up inside this place. He was looking forward to flying out to Vegas for a couple of days and seeing the neon signs.

He missed the signs. Weird what you missed.

Aspen was this place that was all wood and mountains and snow and people in Eddie Bauer clothes, sipping wine and not smoking. Couldn't smoke anyplace around here. Wasn't supposed to smoke in this place either. That's what the guy at the desk told him when he called down to see if they had any cigars.

"The Ritz-Carlton is a smoke-free establishment," the tight-assed guy who answered the phone had told him, like that was his ticket to heaven or something—the fact that they didn't allow smoking. Soon as he got his hands on a cigar, Max was going to smoke the shit out of it, smell the room up and then smoke it in the lobby when he checked out.

Watch their faces as he perpetrated the transgression. Blow smoke in the guy's face. Maybe ask where a guy could get some money down on a dog fight around the place. Ask it real loud.

Like Bill Murray would do it.

The room phone rang and Max started to pick it up then re-membered that the piano guy told him not to answer the phone. He almost answered it anyway, but if it was Springer then he'd just give him some more shit about it. Or ask for more money. It rang again. It'd be like that smart ass to call just to test him.

It stopped ringing.

That's probably who it was. Take that, jerk-off.

Max was playing with the Beretta now. Loading it and unloading it. Pointing it at people on the TV screen. Racking the slide. Made a nice sound. Visualizing himself as Alan Ladd now in *This Gun for Hire*. Imagining himself shooting Nicky. *Seeing it*. He could do it.

"Yeah, Nicky," he said. "You total dirtball scumbag. It's me, Mad Max Shapiro. And I got a bullet with your name on it." Pointing the gun at the TV. "What's that? You don't think I'll do it, huh?" Laughing to himself, now. "Well, put your head between your knees and kiss your ass good-bye."

He pulled the trigger, forgetting it was loaded and the television set exploded into a cascade of glass and sparks. The sound was deafening.

"Well, shit, Max," he said to himself, his ears ringing. "Look what you've done now."

Then he heard somebody yelling in the hall. Then, a man screaming in pain.

Tobi Ryder badged the desk clerk and asked what Ray Dean Carr had been talking to him about.

The desk clerk told her that Ray Dean had told him he'd found a fifty dollar bill and wanted to return it to the owner.

"Who did he say it belonged to?"

"Said he didn't know the people but he had the plate number of the car and I checked it against our records."

"You didn't give him the room number, did you?"

"No, of course not," said the young guy, assured. "That's against policy. Didn't give him the name either. I called the room and no one answered."

"Where was Mr. Carr while you were calling?" she asked, getting worried now.

"He was standing right where you are."

She pointed at the house phone on the wall behind him. "Did you call on that phone?"

He nodded. Shit. Ray Dean had the room number. "What's the room number you called."

"I'm sorry . . . we're not allowed—"

"Cut the company-line crap and give me the number," she said. "He watched you dial the room. He's a criminal. Give me the room number. Now."

"Three-oh-seven."

"Where's the elevator?"

"Around the corner," he said. "You want me to call the police?"

"You weren't paying attention," she said. "I am the police."

Ray Dean got off the elevator and looked for something to jam between the doors. There was a potted plant right across the hall. He grabbed it and ran back before the doors closed and stuck the plant between the doors so no one could use the elevator. That done, he checked the layout of the third floor. He found a house-keeping closet with a laundry chute. That's how he'd do it. Knock on Max's door, tell him it was room service. Pop Max, then down the hall, wipe the gun, and drop it down the laundry chute and walk out.

He couldn't wait to see Gerry when he showed up. Gerry, good to see you. What're you doing here? Everything's done. Max's taken care of. How about a drink? I'll buy.

Yeah, it could be like that. For once maybe Gerry wouldn't have nothing to say.

He made his way down the hall, checking the rooms closest to Max's and listening to them. No sounds of people or television sets going. People in Aspen didn't watch daytime television. Too busy going to wine tastings and save-the-snail-darter rallies. Quiet everywhere.

Perfect.

He found 307 and waited outside. Could hear the television. Max was in there. He heard Max's voice.

". . . You don't think I'll do it, huh?"

What was this crazy-ass shit? Who was he talking to? Then he heard Max say, "Well, put your head between your knees and kiss your ass good-bye."

He liked to shit his pants when he heard the gun go off.

He'd jammed the elevator, Tobi decided, after she'd waited much longer than it should have taken. She looked for the service elevator but when she found it it was full of housekeeping staff and carts. She ran back to the lobby, found the stairs and ran up them two at a time. She was on the second floor when she heard the gun go off.

Ray Dean didn't wait around to find out what happened. He limped down the hall to the housekeeping room and dumped the pistol and silencer down the laundry chute. Hated to do it, but had no choice. He was on his way to the elevator when this tall, good-looking bitch stuck a gun in his face and said:

"Police officer. Get on the floor. Now!"

"What's the problem, lady?" he asked her, trying to get her to calm down. Shit, women anymore. Now they're carrying guns. Next thing he knows she kicks his legs out from under him and he was on the floor, face down, her knee in his back, which mashed his bad toe against the floor. He screamed and she told him to shut up.

Fucking bitch.

"Where's Max?" she asked.

"Max who?"

She gave him more pressure with the knee. It hurt. She frisked him.

"You might check under my zipper," he said.

"Shut up or you won't need a zipper anymore. What did you do with the gun?"

"I don't know what you're talking about. I'm walking down the hall and you give me this Xena routine. I'm a fucking citizen minding my own business."

"A citizen, huh? You're a dirtbag who doesn't belong here. I heard the shot."

"I did too. Scared the hell out of me. What's going on here, people shooting off guns and shit? Getting so a decent person can't walk around in broad daylight."

That's when she cuffed him.

"Ouch," he said. "You don't have to get 'em so tight. You're cutting off the circulation."

"Tough," she said. "Bite your lip."

He gave her a mock laugh. "I'll give you something to bite."

Then he felt a sharp poke when she stuck the gun up his ass. Felt like he was getting a prostate exam.

She said, "You say anything else and you're going to get a nine millimeter suppository. That connect for you?"

Everybody was a comedian, anymore. Like that guy that shot him in the foot and now this girl cop.

What was it with women anymore?

CHAPTER

Eleven

SUMMERS WAS STARTING TO GET A BAD FEELING ABOUT the way things were going with Tobi Ryder. It had been like that when he was seeing her. Always playing word games with him. Thought she was being clever telling him she was having dinner with Springer after he warned her against getting too close to the guy. Then when she told him she didn't really have a date with the guy, acting like she thought he was dense, not getting the joke. Thing is, he wasn't sure whether she was kidding or not when she told him things.

This was an FBI operation not a high school dance. Besides, he preferred working solo.

He'd done some background and found out that there was definite animus on the part of Nicky Tortino against one Max Shapiro. Shapiro had been incorrectly diagnosed as a terminal cancer victim and had told Tortino he was out of the life on a permanent basis. Lots of irony here. Shapiro's clean bill of health was his death warrant. Also, a couple of Tortino's employees—a couple of low-echelon hoods named Auteen Phelps and Raymond Carr, aka Ray Dean Carr, aka R. D. Carson—were either in transit or had already arrived in Aspen.

Two years ago he'd had to watch Nicky T walk on a case Summers had built for two years when the key witness suddenly disappeared. They had the witness under protection, an Albanian guy who stole cars and delivered them to a chop shop. He'd had the Albanian guy over a barrel—looking at a five-year fall for transporting stolen property across state lines. Guy went out to get a pack of cigarettes and never came back. Never found the body or the guy. Never knew what happened. A Gerry Knucks kind of operation. Had to be.

He could still see Tortino smiling at him when the judge dismissed the case, telling him, "Tough luck, Columbo. You got dick for your trouble."

Summers wanted Nicky T. Wanted to put him inside. Turn the key. *Personally*.

And now he had this ski-bunny for a partner who thought the whole thing was some kind of romance novel where she falls for the bad guy. As for the piano player, Summers made a couple of calls and learned that Springer was *persona non grata* with his former superiors. "The kind of guy who was always pushing the envelope," said one of the district supervisors in D.C. "See if he could get you going. Never should have let him in the Service in the first place. Once, after one of our guys got a little rough with a protester, all a big misunderstanding, Springer got into a shoving match with the officer. Two Secret Service guys scuffling over some dipshit with a protest sign. Springer, while he's getting his ass chewed, tells me he didn't know he signed up to be a Brown-shirt. A real piece of work, that guy."

So, *why* did they let him in the Service?

The supervisor said, "Oh, well, the guy had tremendous instincts and natural ability. War hero. Desert Storm. Then, he maxed his PT."

And now Springer was here in Aspen, cluttering up an investigation with his dark anti-hero act going, impressing Agent Ryder. That's why you couldn't have females involved. They were too emotional. Got themselves involved with the principals.

He punched up the number of the Colorado Bureau of Investigation. Time to let somebody know what was going on.

Springer hung back in the lobby watching her talk to the geek at the reception desk. Tobi Ryder in action. Sharp. Intense. He could see her get the guy's attention, now. Getting her way. She looked good in her jeans and jacket, nice pair of boots with short stacked heels. Looked good and was in charge. Saw her running off to the elevators then up the stairs. He went up behind her, careful not to let her see him.

Then he heard the shot.

He pulled out the little Tomcat and headed for Max's room. Bet that hardhead answered the door himself. Didn't listen and got himself shot. Too bad, he was counting on this gig to bail him out on his club. Oh well, what did he expect from a guy who'd sell you real estate in a flight zone?

When he got to the landing he heard Tobi yelling for somebody to get on the floor, then the sound of a man's voice followed by something dropped to the floor, some screaming and then her telling the guy he was going to get a "nine-millimeter suppository." Not a bad line.

He came around the corner, gun up and saw her with her knee in the guy's back. Ray Dean, the woman-hitter.

"What's up?" he said.

She looked up at him, her eyes bright with adrenaline and pointed this big Sig at him. She said, "Put the gun on the floor and step away from it."

"She'll shoot you, that's no shit," said Ray Dean. "She's got something loose in her head."

"How's the foot?" said Springer, letting the gun relax down to his side. "You keeping it elevated like I told you?"

"How'm I supposed to get it up with this broad standing on it?" Ray Dean's face was screwed up in pain. Springer was enjoying himself now.

"Better watch him, Agent Ryder," said Springer. "He beats up on women, don't you, Ray Dean?"

"I mean it," she said. "Put the gun down or I'll shoot."

He smiled at her. "You do that and you'll never discover the secret inner me. Come on, you know you want to. I'm going to go down the hall and check on Max. You want me to call nine-one-one?"

He turned his back on them and walked down to Max's room.

Tobi watched him walk away. Just turned his back on her, little smile before he turned around. Daring her. That pissed her off.

She wanted to pull the trigger, put one into the wall right by his head. Scare him a little, but that would get her in big trouble at the office. Pissed her off knowing he knew she wouldn't shoot. Couldn't. She pulled the hairball to his feet, him whining the whole time.

"I wanta talk to my lawyer," he said.

"Shut up," she said, watching Springer walk down the hall, ignoring her.

She thought about what he'd said. "You do that and you'll never know the secret inner me." Not a bad line, but still too sure of himself.

Smug bastard.

Springer knocked on the door and said, "It's me, Max. Springer. Open up."

"Yeah? How do I know that?"

Springer exhaled. This guy. Answers the phone when he's not supposed to but won't answer the door when he knows it's you standing outside. "I don't have any secret codes or anything. Just open the door. There's a police officer out here with Ray Dean on the floor and Suzi's waiting for us to call."

The door opened and he walked inside. Max all jumpy and wired, his eyes bright with alcohol.

"Ray Dean's out in the hall?" he asked, eyes nervous. "What's he doing out there? You say the cops got him. How'd he find this place?"

Springer saw the busted television, the glass on the floor, the bullet channel in the wall behind it. He looked up from the TV to Max, and said, "So, what is it, Max? The TV try to get the drop on you?"

"It was an accident."

"Well, Max, the way I see it, it was either you or the appliances. Anybody would've done the same."

Max gave him a look and said, "I've got a situation here and you think you're Henny Youngman. Just what I need. I'll bet Ray Dean followed you here. Some bodyguard. You're leading the fucking bad guys here."

"Your thought processes amaze me. I don't know how he got here, but the female cop saved you. How much cash you have on you?" Springer asked, looking at the shot-up room.

"This another touch? I already gave you three grand."

"You're going to need to bribe the hotel people before the cops get here. If you want to go to Vegas you'd better do it quick."

"Yeah, yeah. You're right," said Max. "First time."

"Then call Suzi and tell her to pull the car around front. We're checking out."

"How come you're all the time telling me what to do? You're working for me, right? I mean, that was the deal, right?"

Springer said, "You've got a state cop and a hit man out in the hall who knows where you're hiding and you want to argue. I just don't understand that. I'm trying to but I don't think I can."

"I'll do what I have to."

"Commendable," said Springer, picking up a shard of glass. "Call them and tell them you didn't like the way the in-room movie turned out."

Max started to say something, but instead he shook his head and picked up the room phone. Max did what he needed to do. Springer was impressed the way he handled the hotel people.

"I'm very sorry," Max told the hotel manager on the phone. "I'm just so scared anymore when I travel. That's why I carry a gun with me. I'm extremely embarrassed by the whole episode . . . Yes . . . Please, let me know what the damages are and I'll pay them plus the room rate for every day you don't have the room available. And a fifteen percent gratuity for yourself and your staff . . . No, I *want to* . . . Yes, I realize how irregular this whole situation is and let me repeat how disgusted I am with myself . . . No, no police . . . Yes, I know there's a policewoman came here. But, she's got the whole thing under control."

Now Max was making a face like he was disgusted with the manager rather than with himself.

"Are you a Bronco's fan? You are? Hey, that's great. John Elmore is a great quarterback, isn't he? My favorite. I can get you Broncos tickets to any game you want. Sure, and the rest of it too . . . No problem. Thank you so much, you bloodsucking bastard." The last part he said after he hung up.

"Well, that's taken care of," said Max to Springer.

"It's Elway," said Springer.

"What is?"

"Your favorite quarterback's name is Elway, not Elmore. And he's retired."

"Elway, Elmore, what's the difference? Just another jock who has too much money. Bet you were a jock too, weren't you? Yeah, you got the build. What was it? Football? The important thing is that the snotty manager went for it. Why do you have to be critical all the time? Just keep me from getting shot, that's all."

Man, he was going to earn every penny, working for this guy.

The uniforms arrived within five minutes of Max calling the manager. Ray Dean Carr walked when they found out Max was the one who'd shot off a gun. Nothing else to hold Ray Dean on. The cops were suspicious and asked questions of Max but the hotel manager showed up and took care of things. Just an accident and no, the hotel was not pressing charges. Mr. Shapiro had already arranged to pay for the damages and the hotel was satisfied with Mr. Shapiro's explanation.

Agent Ryder was less satisfied.

"I want to know what the hell is going on?" she asked Max, but looked hard at Springer after she said it. "I had to cut loose a low life with a sheet like Charles Manson and I've got an ex-Secret Service agent show up, gun in hand, who I think is protecting a guy who shot up a television set. So, I'm going to learn what's going on. And I don't want any bullshit out of anybody, either."

Springer shrugged and tried out a smile on her, but she wasn't buying it. Didn't always work. Liking the way she looked when she was mad, but not playing games with him, either.

But, she didn't shoot him.

"I accidentally discharged my gun while I was cleaning it," said Max. "That's all."

"That's not what I'm referring to. What is Ray Dean Carr doing in the hallway?"

"I don't have any idea," said Max, selling it with a wide-eyed expression, his palms showing. Max had possibilities. Had to be some reason he'd made so much money. But you could see Ryder wasn't going for the innocent act.

Suzi had shown up right after Tobi Ryder. "Anybody want something from room service?" she asked, breaking into the conversation. You could see Ryder was getting warm behind her eyes. "Some coffee? A cocktail? I haven't had a thing to eat all day and I'm starved. What about you, Officer . . . Ryder, isn't it?"

"Yes, that's correct."

"Would you like something?" asked Suzi, sincere. Smart girl. Max would crash in five seconds if she wasn't around.

"Coffee would be nice," said Tobi. "Thank you."

"What about you, Cole?" she asked him.

"Get me a bottle of Scotch," said Max before Springer could answer. "Johnnie Walker Black."

Suzi smiled at him. Patient. "I was talking to Cole, dear. And, you've had enough to drink already," she said, nodding at the empty Scotch bottle on the bureau.

"Coffee's fine, thanks," said Springer. Suzi picked up the phone to call room service, ignoring Max who was glaring at her like a little kid.

"Look, Mr. Shapiro," said Tobi. "Ray Dean Carr works for Nicky Tortino. Do you know Mr. Tortino?"

"Tortino?" said Max, into his act now. "Seems I heard that name before. Isn't he from Frisco?"

Ryder waited. Giving him a few moments in the hopes of getting him to say something else, thought Springer. Now, all Max had to do was shut-up, not offer any information and she would have to ask a follow-up question. But Max couldn't do that. Max hated dead air.

After about seven seconds of silence, Max made a face like he was thinking about it, then said, "Yeah, wait, I know the guy. Nick

Tortino. Owns a restaurant over by Golden Gate Park. I been in there a couple of times. They say the guy's a gangster or something. Is that true?" Redeeming himself with Springer a little by asking her a question.

But she was too smart to take the side road he offered. "Why is Ray Dean Carr here, Mr. Shapiro?"

"I tell you I don't know."

"Did you take a shot at him?"

"A shot at him? Hell no. Why would I do that? My gun went off while I was cleaning it. Ray Dean didn't even come in here." A mistake to call Carr by his first name, thought Springer, instead of saying "the guy" or something. He was sure Ryder didn't miss it. "Hell, I didn't even know he was out there. He say I shot at him?"

The coffee came and Max signed the ticket and tipped the guy with a ten, still mindful of his situation with the motel management.

"You are worth a lot of money, aren't you, Mr. Shapiro?" said Ryder.

"I make out all right."

"Better than all right."

"Okay. Better than all right. So, what's wrong with that?"

"You ever do business with Nicky Tortino?"

"What's Max done?" said Springer, trying to break up the interrogation trance Detective Ryder was trying to create.

"Excuse me," said Ryder, holding up a hand. "I'm talking to Mr. Shapiro."

"And I'm talking to you," Springer said, watching the storm build behind those great eyes. "Are you investigating Max?"

"Shut up, Springer," she said.

He did so, seeing she wasn't kidding. A tough girl in a tough job, pissed off now and not playing games anymore.

But, she hadn't shot him yet.

That was something to think about.

CHAPTER

Twelve

TOBI RYDER SLAMMED THE DOOR TO THE EXPLORER WHEN she got out. Still mad. Knowing she couldn't do anything except hassle Shapiro and the Aspen police weren't any help, accepting the manager's story, not wanting to make any waves. The last thing the tourist industry in Aspen wanted were reports of guns and low-life thugs apprehended in the Ritz-Carlton. Then there was that smug bastard—who knew all this—standing around with that contented smirk on his face the whole time. His idea of flirting, she guessed.

And, what was Ray Dean Carr doing in the building unless he was there to shoot Max? But the guy had no gun. He must've ditched it. Maybe she could get a warrant and check the place out, but that would be difficult, if not impossible, with no probable cause and the manager already on record as dismissing the whole affair as an accident. Springer was right there with a gun out. Expecting trouble. He was working for Shapiro but she could see there was tension between the two of them. Something had thrown Shapiro and Springer together. But what?

She was anticipating an ass-chewing as she entered headquarters. When she entered the main block of offices and was informed that "the boss wants to see you," she was more sure of it.

It got worse when she entered the office and saw Jack Summers sitting there like he was the school principal and she'd been called to the office. What a regulation shithead Summers was. What had she ever seen in him?

To Springer, Vegas was always an unnatural place. It was like they had a time-lock on the whole city; fifties ambience wrapped in the poor taste of the nineties. Cheap hustlers and hucksters and lounge lizards in alligator shoes cluttering up the flashy fraudulent ambience. And now, the flashy getting a make-over with a Disneyland facelift. Bring the kids. Never liked the place. Slot machines whistling and ringing in the airport as he walked through carrying his bag while Max, who already had three of those airline cocktail bottles of Scotch in him, was looking for the airport bar.

Flying over the Rockies and the Western plains, Max had actually acted semi-human. While Suzi was in the bathroom, he asked Springer what it was that had Suzi pissed off at him.

"I'm not sure I'm a source of wisdom in that area," Springer said, looking down at his Coke-and-ice.

"You get along with Suzi," Max said.

"Suzi's easy to get along with."

Max pursed his lips and looked out the window. "Usually she is. But, lately it's not going so good."

"That's your fault."

Max looked back at him. "Just what I wanted to hear."

Springer closed his eyes and leaned back in his seat. "You asked."

"So," said Max, his expensive aftershave strong as he leaned toward Springer. "What do mean, exactly?"

Springer opened his eyes. "You treat her like an after-thought," Springer said. "Like when we got on the plane you didn't ask where she wanted to sit, you just grabbed a seat and sat down."

"What?" said Max, spreading his arms, palms up. "She can't figure out where to sit?"

"And then when I told you it was better if you didn't stay at her place, you didn't ask where she wanted to stay, you just said you wanted to stay at the MGM Grand."

"I like the Grand."

"Maybe she does too. You said she used to work there and maybe she's tired of it. You should've asked her if that was all right with her, is all I'm saying."

"I thought women wanted to be our equals now and all that other stuff was condescending."

"It's more complicated than that." Springer sipped his Coke. "They want to be our equals, but still want to be treated like women. They want you to talk to them, but they don't want a man they can dominate, even though some settle for that. Which insures mutual misery. And they don't want to be dominated but they want us to still act like men."

Max sat back in his seat and looked at the ceiling. "Sounds like a balancing act."

"Mostly, I think they want us to be ourselves. Anyway, that's all I know about it. With you and Suzi, I don't think you see that she's just worried about you and you take it like she's telling you what to do. Probably has to do with having too much money most of your life and other people willing to take your crap in order to get close to some of it. Suzi's not here for the money."

"I'm damned near sixty. How'm I supposed to change?"

"You don't have to. Just give more thought to what she says and what you say to her. Sometimes you have to gauge the content of what she's saying against her mood and disposition."

Max screwed up his eyes and said, "That sounds complicated. Even beyond understanding."

"We *were* talking about women, right?"

So Max had been a little more thoughtful—in other words a little less like Max—regarding Suzi for the remainder of the flight. Asking if she was hungry, where she wanted to eat, if she wanted to go out somewhere when they landed. But as soon as they were on the ground Max was back in me-first mode, wanting to find a bar when Suzi just wanted to get out of the airport and check on her apartment. She wanted to get some things before they checked into the Grand.

Springer wanted out of the airport for other reasons. For one, he needed to look up a guy he knew to make connections on a gun as he'd had to leave his behind. The chance that he'd need a piece was slim as he didn't think that Ray Dean and Auteen had a clue that Max had left Aspen. But they worked for people who weren't stupid, and sooner or later they would check out Las Vegas as that was Suzi's home address. Springer was just trying to buy some time while he figured a way out of this mess. But they would have to go back to Aspen eventually as he was out on bond and wasn't supposed to leave the state of Colorado.

They'd have to go back. And he'd have to do something about the bad guys tracking Max. And, more important to himself, he needed to do something about the Whiskey Basin before he lost everything. He was near broke with the cash flow from the place dammed up as tight as a Corp of Engineers project. He needed to get a cash flow going, soon. The three grand a week Max was paying him would help for a while, but it would do him no good if he had to keep following Max around. A nightclub was the kind of business where the owner had to be on-site. He couldn't just turn it over to someone else for an extended length of time. He didn't want to lose the Whiskey either. It was about time he succeeded at something where he didn't carry a gun. He'd given up on the military. He'd given up on the Service. He'd given up on the place in Colorado Springs. Quitting things was a bad habit. It was getting easier, since Kristen died, to give up on things. Fewer reasons to care. Less motivation to improve. Some days it was even hard to think about shaving. Kristen had been so much of who he thought he was. Who he was going to be. She kept him on task, pointed in the right direction. His tendency was to let things go and change the tempo to suit his mood. He needed to make *something* work.

But first, he needed a gun.

Gerry Nugent, not *Knucks*, he told himself, trying out his new identity to see how it fit, stood around the circular belt and watched the parade of luggage, baggage, and boxes with the other passengers. Passengers who looked like tourists and salesmen and businessmen and business women. Wonder what they would think if they knew what it was that *he* did to turn a buck.

There it was again. He never used to think like this. Never gave any thought to what other people thought about him, or who he was, or what he did. He just did it and took the money. What was going on with him, anyway? Was it the fact that he was middle-aged? Or did it have to do with the fact that he didn't have a steady girl, just an endless line of power-fucking barmaids and chorus girls

that wanted to be near a tough guy with money? What if he didn't
have the money? What if he was just Gerry Nugent, insurance
salesman?

But, that was asshole thinking. What had Max said? "Knucks
is an asshole name." Yeah, that's what he said. And he was right.
He had an asshole name and now he was starting to think like an
asshole. He needed to keep his mind on what he was doing. He
only had a few hours to take care of the business he had in Vegas
and then he had to catch the charter to Aspen and do the job with
Max. And that was another thing—he wasn't looking forward to
icing Max. Hell, he liked Max. He was a funny guy. And he always
had a cigar for him. A good one. But that was the job.

He rented an airport locker and was walking to the Avis counter
when he saw them. Max and his girlfriend and some guy in the
airport lounge. Right here in the Vegas airport he had lucked onto
them. What were the odds? If he was getting this lucky then he
needed to hit the tables right away, maybe buy a lottery ticket. Max
Shapiro within a hundred feet of him and Gerry without a hammer.
What were the odds of that? First running into the guy and then
not having a piece to do the job?

The guy with them was good-sized. Rangy. Big shoulders.
About two hundred pounds. Guy was taking in everything with his
eyes without making it look like he was doing it. Casual. Moved
easy. A pro. Was this the guy that braced Ray Dean and Auteen?
Probably. Where'd Max come on this guy?

How to handle this? Tail them and find out where they're staying
and then wait? Or just walk up to them, let 'em know he was there?
Watch their eyes. Might work. See what the big guy's reaction would
be. He wanted to meet this guy, size him up. Scare Max a little. See
Max, there's not anyplace you can go that I can't find you.

But he didn't have a gun. Maybe the big guy did. But so what?
Guy wasn't going to cap him in a public airport, was he?

"What did you say Gerry Knucks looked like?" Springer asked Max,
as the bartender handed Max his drink. "About five-eleven, one
hundred ninety pounds, sandy hair?"

"Yeah," said Max, drinking his Scotch.

Springer nodded in the direction of the entrance. "Well, I think he's coming toward us right now."

Tobi Ryder got back in the Explorer after leaving the office. Still pissed. It hadn't gone as badly as she thought it might. Her supervisor, though sometimes a little uptight, was fair and he backed her up to Summers. Jack, for his part, tried to play it like he was an innocent. "I'm not saying she's done anything wrong. I'm just relating how the surveillance has been going. Detective Ryder and I are good friends." Then smiling at her while she was thinking about how he'd look upside down in a roadhouse toilet, dirty water swirling around his ears.

Some of this was Springer's fault. His free-wheeling style was like a broom handle stuck in the spokes of a bicycle. What was it about the men in her life? David, her ex, was a narcissistic DEA cop who listened to Madonna CDs and couldn't pass by a mirror without touching up his mustache. Fancied himself the hero-type cop who couldn't deny himself to the women he met. "What am I going to do?" he'd say, counting on his charm and good looks to sway her. "They throw themselves at me. No man can resist that forever. I try, hon. I really do."

She gave him a couple of chances before she found a pair of mauve hose and a pack of condoms left behind in his car. She hated mauve and she was on the pill. So, one night while he was snoring heavily, dreaming about one of his concubines, she wired him directly to an alarm clock, sending 110 volts through his worthless hide when the alarm went off at five A.M. Threw him right out of bed onto the floor. She left a note that said,

Good morning. This is the first day of the rest of your life without me. My lawyer will contact you. Don't call. Don't come by the office. If I see you, I will hit you upside the head with a nightstick.

Love and hisses,
TOBI

P.S. I think something terrible happened to your Madonna CDs.

Then, there was the unfortunate relationship with Jack the jerk. She'd been on the rebound, she told herself. She'd known him from before the divorce, running into him on a couple of investigations. He'd seemed okay. But after a couple of dates she got tired of him. He was a neat freak who rearranged things after *she* used them— pillows, writing pens, even her clothing. At first it was kind of cute, but then it got on her nerves. Picking lint off her jackets. Brushing the shoulders of her blouses like she had dandruff or something. She hated that. Once he straightened a scarf she was wearing. She just looked at him while he did it like she couldn't believe it was happening. When he wasn't looking, she put it back where it had been and *he straightened it again*. What did he think they were, mating baboons? Who needed that?

And he talked all the time. No let-up. You couldn't even get a word in. He talked about himself. *His* plans. *His* philosophy of life. Talked about his political beliefs and how he wanted to own his own bar. Nice place. Went on and on about different types of wine and beer and how he would make it work. Long boring mono- logues that were a form of verbal masturbation. His favorite topic? Jack Summers.

Boring.

And now, this guy. This Springer guy. In his own way he was more irritating than both David and Jack. But, it was in a way that was up-front, even honest. It wasn't an idiosyncrasy or a habit or a personal hang-up he was unaware of. He was irritating her *on purpose*. And he didn't think of his skills as a law enforcement of- ficer as something to be proud of, it was more like he just accepted it, like having brown eyes. In fact, he didn't even like doing it. He really seemed like he would be content to play his piano and just go through life without any outside excitement. The enigma was that she didn't think he could handle life without some sort of drama. Something to keep him interested.

A really different kind of guy.

But that didn't keep her from being ticked off at him. She still had questions to ask him. She drove out to his club to see if she could find him. She parked in the lot and walked inside the lounge but no one was inside except the guy she'd seen the first night she'd been in the Whiskey Basin with Summers. He was spraying

Endust on tables and wiping them down with a rag. He told her his name was Bruce.

"I'm sorry, Miss," said Bruce. "We're closed."

She looked around. "Is Springer around?"

"No."

"Do you know where he is?"

"You that lady cop?"

She nodded. "Do you know where Mr. Springer is?"

"I don't know where you'd find him," he said. But his eyes were evasive. This kid wasn't a liar and it showed. He was hiding something from her. Something to do with Springer.

"How about a beer?"

Bruce shrugged. "Sure. Why not?" He opened a bottle of Moosehead for her.

"You got a second?" she asked him.

"I'm not on the clock anyway."

"So, why's the place closed?"

"I thought you knew. The bank closed us down because of the incident with the football player." He looked at her.

"That doesn't make sense.

"Cole's a little behind on the rent."

"Oh," she said. "So, why are you here?"

"Cole paid us all a week's pay." He shrugged. "Feel like I should earn it."

She sipped her beer and touched the tiny ring-scar on her chin. "You must really like him."

"He's a good guy," said Bruce. "He's a great guy, in fact. Sometimes I feel sorry for him, though."

"Because of his financial situation?"

He gave her a funny look. "No, I don't think he cares about stuff like that. I mean, of course he gives it some thought, but I don't think he cares about being rich."

"But you feel sorry for him?" she said, leading him into it.

"You don't notice it?" he asked her.

"Notice what?"

He shook his head. "I shouldn't talk about it."

"Wait a minute. What are you getting at?"

Bruce looked down at the bar. He buffed a spot on the finish with his rag. "Cole's a hell of a guy. But he's the saddest person I've ever known. You can feel it in the vibes he puts off." He stopped buffing and looked up at her. "Hell, you can see it."

She looked at Bruce for a moment. "I don't see that when I look at him."

"Next time," said Bruce. "Look closer."

CHAPTER

Thirteen

MAX DAMN NEAR CHOKED ON HIS SCOTCH WHEN HE looked up and saw Gerry walking into the bar. Could you believe it? The kind of luck he was having he'd better stay away from the strip or he'd be bumming change to call someone to come get him. What the hell was Gerry Knucks doing here in Vegas? Walking right into the very town where Max thought he'd be safe.

But Gerry wasn't going to do him here. Not here, for Pete's sake. Surely not here. *Nobody* got hit in Vegas. It was a safe town. At least it used to be, back in the old days when the Big Bosses ran the town. The syndicate didn't allow killing in the city limits. It'd scare off the tourists. But who knew how things went anymore. Used to be a bottom-feeder like Nicky T didn't have any juice and now he had the best button man on the coast working for him. The world was upside down. Maybe you could have a shooter pop you in the Circus-Circus as part of the evening show for all he knew.

As Gerry got closer, Max noticed that Springer had moved closer, positioning himself between Max and Gerry. Guy knew what he was doing for all his other faults.

Gerry watched the big guy position himself. Smart. Nothing going on here, but the guy was making sure if something did go down.

"Hello, Max," said Gerry. "You on vacation?"

"Yeah," said Max.

"Don't believe I know your friends," said Gerry.

"This is Suzi," said Max.

Gerry looked at Springer. "And you'd be who?"

"Cole."

"Cole what?"

"Don't believe I caught your name," said Springer.

"Gerry."

"Gerry what?"

Gerry thought about it. "Nugent," he said, looking at Max. "Gerry Nugent." He put out his hand for Springer. If Gerry wasn't careful, this guy, Cole what's-his-name, could put you off-guard. The way he moved quietly into position was slick. Knew what he was doing. Gerry had the feeling he would've made him for what he was without Max's help.

Springer accepted the hand. "Springer," he said. "Cole Springer."

Tobi Ryder snaked up Red Mountain and then pulled the Explorer in front of Springer's house. The tires skated slightly on the snow as she stopped. She sat in the truck momentarily before getting out. She didn't see Springer's car. Maybe he wasn't here. Maybe she didn't care if he was here.

Maybe she did. She didn't know for sure.

She rang the doorbell. No answer. Knocked and got the same response. None. She looked around the grounds. The house off the road was boundaried on the west side by a grove of trees and on the east side by a hill which sloped back down Red Mountain to Aspen. The closest house was an unusual-looking one down the slope with no view of this one. She looked at the lock. It was a piece of cake.

She had B & E'd a couple of places before. Not to gather evidence and not to plant any. Both times it was to convince herself that she was after the right person and not wasting her time. Once she had proven herself right and the other time it had caused her to look somewhere else. She didn't like breaking the law or bending the rules and she didn't even know what she was looking for, but she rationalized that she wasn't trying to pin anything on him. What was she trying to do? Was it because he made her think about things he said and did? He was an intriguing guy and she wanted to know more about him. So, she picked the lock and eased into the house, closing the door quietly behind her as she entered.

As always, she felt the emptiness of the unoccupied house; the absence of vibration. No human voices. No appliances whirring or humming. No television, no radio. Silence had taken up residence and it always gave her a weird sensation. Like walking on another planet.

She remembered he'd said he lived upstairs. The downstairs was open and appointed with expensive furniture and paintings. She walked up the staircase and came to a landing that led to the apartment where she had seen him through her field glasses that first time.

The door to the apartment was unlocked. She opened it and saw the talcum powder on the floor. Nice trick. You walk across it, it leaves footprints. You clean them up, the powder leaves marks when you walk around. She removed her shoes and jumped over the powder, nearly falling when she slid on the carpet. She steadied herself and looked around the apartment.

She wasn't entirely ready for what she found.

Springer noted that Gerry Nugent was well-dressed. He wasn't carrying a weapon, either. If he was, it was well hidden. Springer also noted that Nugent wasn't what he expected, even though Max had described him in detail. Unlike Ray Dean and Auteen, Nugent wasn't obtrusive. The clothes were expensive, yet understated. The face impassive and non-threatening. And the man had a self-effacing way of carrying himself that was practiced—Gerry Nugent had apparently learned to submerge his toughness so he could get close. Yet when Nugent got close he let the tough guy peek through. It wasn't so much in the way the guy looked or what he said. It was just there and Springer could feel it. And he knew that Nugent knew that Springer felt it in the same way that a predator feels the presence of an adversary.

"So, what are you doing in town, Mr. . . . a . . . Nugent?" said Springer. "You did say Nugent, didn't you?"

"Yeah," said Gerry, looking into Springer's eyes, testing him.

"The problem with Mr. Shapiro is a misunderstanding."

"That right?" said Gerry.

Springer nodded. "No reason to continue with this."

But, as usual, Max missed another excellent opportunity to shut up. "You're talking about me like I'm—"

Suzi tugged on the sleeve of his coat and gave him a hard look. Max shut up but he didn't like it.

Gerry looked at Max. "Not my decision."

"You really ought to give it some consideration though," said Springer. "No reason to ruin the weekend with it. We'll be in town a couple of days. Give you some time to think about it."

"What's your part in this?" Gerry asked.

"I'm involved."

"Yeah? How so?"

"I'll feel inclined to take steps, before or after the fact, to either prevent or rectify the situation."

"Why would you want to do that?" Flat. Not really a challenge.

"Don't have much else going right now," said Springer. "Something to do."

"It could go bad."

"Always a possibility."

"Better to let it go."

Springer shrugged. "Already agreed to do it."

"With Max?"

"With myself."

"Works like that, huh?"

Springer nodded. "Has to. Otherwise, you're just hired help. How do you decide?"

Gerry massaged the corners of his mouth with a hand. "Hadn't thought about it much."

"What's it cost you to think about it?" said Springer, seeing something unexpected in the button man's face. He wasn't afraid of Springer. It was something else. It was a look that suggested a settled disposition of lassitude, as if he'd gone through this many times before. It was more felt than seen. Guy was thinking about it.

Nugent smiled. "I don't know. I've always done what I set out to do."

"Columbus was looking for something else when he found America."

"Another dumb wop," said Max, just when you thought it was safe to talk in front of him.

Well, ain't that the way it goes, thought Nicky Tortino. Kim Li had his underwear up his crack about a couple of his guys that disappeared.

So, Nicky asks him, "What's that to me? You think you got 'Missing Persons' here?"

Which pisses Kim off because he thinks Nicky has something to do with it.

"Why you think I got something to do with it?" Nicky asked. Fucking chink calling him in the middle of a movie his girlfriend had rented him. Her halfway out of her blouse.

Then, Kim elusive before he finally admitted that he sent them out to shadow Gerry.

"Gerry don't like being followed," said Nicky. "What's with you Chinese guys? Can't get any imported rice and the domestic stuff makes you crazy? Gerry never said nothing about a tail or doing any of your guys or . . . why'n the fuck am I talking to you about this, anyway? You lose two guys, neither of which has nothing to do with me, so you call up and start blaming me. Maybe they quit. Ever think of that? Maybe they don't like working for you? You ain't an easy guy to talk to, ya know? Either way, there's no reason for us to get in a squabble. Know what I mean? We can respect each other's territory. I'll ask around, maybe see if I can find out what happened. I'll tell you this though, if Gerry did take them down, they made a run at him first. And you need to hear this for future reference, you just don't come after Gerry, because there ain't no future in it."

Kim started blabbing off a bunch of chink chatter that Nicky couldn't understand and didn't have time for. The upshoot was that Kim would back off for now but they agreed they both needed

to stay out of each other's face for a while. Cool things off between them.

Which was okay with Nicky because he didn't like Chinatown
anyway.

Then he thought, would Gerry take out a couple of chinks and
not tell him?

Something to think about.

CHAPTER

Fourteen

RICKY JADE PEELED OFF THE BURGUNDY CALFSKIN DRIV-
ing gloves that matched the interior of the 300ZX, clicked off
his cell phone and put it back into the holder on the dash. Kim
Li, boss of the Chinatown rackets, had called and offered him
work. A hit.

"Who?" Ricky had asked Kim, not believing it.

"Gerry Knucks," said Kim.

"You know what you're asking?"

"You want the job or not?"

"That's high dollar trade."

"I'll pay."

Ricky told him how much and it was agreed upon. Ricky didn't
really like Li because Li and the other Chinese thought Ricky was
a mongrel—half-Japanese and half-Chinese. Ricky was born in
America and couldn't speak any Chinese and had only been to
Japan once. Ricky didn't give a damn one way or another about the
Tongs or about the Italians or even about Gerry Knucks. The money
was good.

Hell, Gerry Knucks? That was a tall order. Ricky knew about
Knucks. Everybody in town knew about the guy, but nobody had
ever seen him at work, and *nobody* went after him. At least nobody
had ever talked to anyone who had. There was no wondering why
that was the case. You only heard things. Probably exaggerations,
but Ricky had heard that Knucks had popped two Colombians that
came after him because he had iced one of their shooters. They
found the Colombian's bodies in the back of their boss's car.

Just the bodies. The heads were gone.

Before Ricky went after Gerry Knucks he needed to do some background work. Research was essential to performing his trade. Ricky Jade was a thorough man with a degree in statistics from San Francisco State University. He had initially set out to go into investment banking but gave up on it back in the late seventies when the stock market had fallen and the interest rates had risen. He had been a collegiate gymnast and his athletic ability, coupled with his active cognitive skills, made him perfect for the work he was now doing.

He'd gotten restless after college and toyed with the idea of joining the CIA but didn't get anywhere. He tried the FBI, same thing. So he joined the navy, got into the Seals program but washed out when he injured his back jumping out of a helicopter on an air-to-water drill, landing on a rock. All those years jumping off parallel bars and dismounting off the rings without serious injury and then he lands on a rock hidden in the murky waters of a lake. But he had completed most of the training before his discharge and his back didn't bother him all that much anymore. So when the investment business went to hell he got involved in some scams that put him in touch with some of the ruling crime families in Chinatown.

He was hanging out with a couple of young guys, Tongs, who he'd known from the clubs. They were drinking one afternoon and Ricky shared that he'd been in the Seals program. They asked, "They trained you to kill people? To sneak up on them and do it with your bare hands?" He had shrugged, his mind thick with gin, and nodded. "You think you could kill someone if you had to? Really pull the trigger, man?"

"Sure," he said, "Why not?"

"Could you do it for money?"

"Especially for money."

He found out that Knucks had a military background. U.S. Marines. Vietnam. Khe Sahn survivor. Made corporal. Worked for the New York people for several years. Came to the coast seven years ago to work for Nicholas Tortino. No arrests. Had been called in for questioning but had never spent a moment in jail. An amazing record. No wonder Kim Li thought that Gerry had assassinated his two soldiers. Two very strong and tough men. It wasn't his place to question such things, but Ricky wondered what Kim Li had thought when he'd sent the soldiers after Knucks? What did he think would happen?

Ricky asked around until he found out that Gerry Knucks was on his way to Aspen. Why Aspen? What business did Nicky T have in Colorado? And Aspen, of all places. Nothing there but snow and ski snobs. He called Kim Li back and told him he needed flight tickets to Aspen along with a car and a clean piece when he arrived. Li said it was done and that his people would contact him within an hour to give him details.

Taking down Gerry Knucks would make his rep. If he lived to tell it.

Tobi Ryder took inventory of Cole Springer's room. It was comfortable, the furniture more serviceable than decorative as if every piece had to be functional including a recording system which was patched to a computer. Guy probably programmed his music for his nightclub.

There were four rooms. The living room was large and open with the kitchen and dining area included. The centerpiece of the main room was a black baby grand piano. The piano was key-worn, the finish dull with age yet still a lovely piece. She had to admire how much trouble he must've gone to to get the piano upstairs. On the piano was a picture of a young woman. She was pretty; reddish-blond hair, green eyes, and a smile that gleamed like a toothpaste commercial. Probably the late wife.

There was another picture on the bay window settee. Her again. This time she was standing in front of Springer, his arms around her waist. They were younger, his hair a little longer. It was an outdoor picture, the camera capturing the wind lifting her beautiful hair away from her face. Springer's smile was confident, happy, contented. She'd seen him smile several times in the short time she'd known him, but it was a smile that suggested muted emotions. His smile was smug or sometimes wry. Even an amused smile, but nothing like what she saw in the photo. At present the confident smile had been replaced with smugness; the happy smile replaced with amusement, the contented smile supplanted with a wry acceptance of his circumstances.

Stop it, Tobi. You're reading too much into this. You're letting the employee's words in the deserted nightclub plant a subconscious message. He was just some guy who played the piano. That's all. And, he arm wrestled college boys to champion war vets, and advanced money to employees when he couldn't pay his own bail. And, he was protecting a money-launderer and showed up with a weapon and a wisecrack as she was cuffing a career criminal.

That's all. Plenty of guys like that.

She looked at his bookcase. Hunter S. Thompson, Hemmingway, John D. McDonald, Mark Twain, Joyce Carol Oates, Jack Kerouac, and Thomas Wolfe's newest—bookmarked with a small American flag. She looked through his music selection which was varied and eclectic, everything from Beethoven and Van Cliburn through the Beatles, Randy Newman, and John Fogerty. Even some Johnny Cash.

In a roll-top desk she found another picture of his wife and something else. An airline flyer. Had he left the state? He wasn't supposed to with the assault charge hanging over him. They wouldn't extradite for that and surely he wouldn't relocate just to avoid prosecution. But where was he? She kept digging through the drawers. Underneath some papers in the bottom left hand drawer she found a .357 Colt Python with a four-inch barrel. Loaded.

She put the gun back into the drawer, careful to place it as she found it and walked into the bedroom. The bed was made and the room was military-neat. There was another picture—framed and matted of his wife—on the bureau with a small lock of reddish-blond hair in a tiny plastic bag inside the frame at the bottom. Tobi was afraid to touch the picture. She almost left at that point. It was as if she had defiled a temple.

But her curiosity held her. She'd come this far, too far to turn back. She looked through the drawers. Socks and underclothing arranged neatly. Underneath the bed she found something you wouldn't find in the average bachelor's apartment—inside a slender briefcase she found an AR-15 in .223 caliber, broken down, and heavily oiled. There was a nightscope along with it. Just what every bachelor needed for that moment when you absolutely had to shoot someone in the dark.

What to do with the discovery, though? She couldn't ask for a search warrant to look for illegal weapons. Maybe the weapon was semi-auto and therefore legal. No crime to own a nightscope. How would she explain what her probable cause was?

Then she found something else you didn't find in a man's apartment. Particularly in a man of Cole Springer's peculiar talents. It was a diary, a journal actually. Inside she read his observations of his daily life since he'd come to Aspen. The purchase of the Whiskey Basin, people he'd met, even his arrest.

She looked through the pages at random and there it was. Something she shouldn't have read. It was a message to his late wife.

Kristen,

I'm hanging in, kid. Haven't stuck my gun in my mouth yet. Sometimes I think about it though. I'm not proud of it. I tell myself it's a coward's way out, the ultimate selfish act. And I tell myself that you wouldn't like it. It helps.

Not doing so well with the club. And yes, I stay away from the melancholy pieces. When I can.

I know you told me that after you were gone that I should find someone. I've tried. Well, that's a lie because I haven't tried at all. There's been a couple of women but they were more like incidents or traffic accidents than a relationship. Shaking hands would have been more intimate. Probably my fault. It's hard to give myself as it seems there's so little left to give. Now I'm getting maudlin. Sorry, but you were supposed to hang around longer.

I did meet a woman. An interesting woman. Attractive. But, I think I rub her the wrong way. And that's the way it goes, I guess . . .

There was more but Tobi closed the book. She felt like a voyeur and a ghoul. She put the book back and walked back into the living room. She felt a sensation of tightness inside her. She sat down and noticed her hands trembling, ever so slightly. What was wrong with her? She knew. She had looked inside a man who didn't want to be seen—a private man with a hidden grief. A grief that, while not torturing him, was tearing him down.

She was less proud of herself than she had been in a long time.

She left the apartment and walked back down the stairs, the silence following her, filling in the wake of her passing. She went outside and opened the door of the Explorer, the sound of the door hinges reminding her of routine and the reality of her existence. She started the vehicle and sat looking at the house. She had gotten rid of husband David and never gave it another thought. Jack Summers had been just an interim boyfriend, more like a trial or a sample of what single life was going to be like after being married for five years—pretending to care when all he wanted was a steady hump. And now this guy. Was she starting to think about him like he was a possibility? He was funny and intelligent and now she knew he was vulnerable which made him more intriguing yet less accessible.

But there were the similarities that disturbed her. Like David and Jack, Springer had cop in his blood. And though he was ambiguous about his law enforcement background, Springer had that air about him that David had; that bravado that caused him to do things as if he were the hero in some movie. Like turning his back on her when she had a loaded gun pointed at him—or was that the death wish of a suicidal personality? A man who had lost his love and had nothing to live for. Like Summers, he was a neatnik. Not obsessively like Summers perhaps, but from his apartment she could tell he liked things in order. His wife's death had upset his neat and orderly existence. He even referred to it in his journal, ". . . you were supposed to hang around longer." And now, Tobi had disturbed some kind of psychic rhythm by her intrusion into his tidy method of dealing with his pain. Would he feel the interruption in the vibrations of his sorrow? Slow down, Tobi, you're starting to over-analyze. Let's inject a little objective reasoning into this situation.

Springer was just a guy who'd lost his wife. He missed her. Many men had suffered similar bereavement. But now he was involved with criminals. They had fired him from the Secret Service because he wasn't a team player. He was a rogue. A malcontent. A maverick operator who couldn't, wouldn't, submerge his personality. He was assisting the object of an FBI investigation, a man who laundered drug money. He had a loaded weapon in his desk drawer. There was a shadow over this guy. She shouldn't ascribe romantic characteristics to a man who kept a night-scoped assault rifle under his bed. She needed to think of him as just another subject in the report she would be writing when this was all over. That's better. Don't get involved with this guy. He was just an extension of the bad choices she had made with men.

Then she thought about the lock of hair and the pictures. The piano keys worn by his touch. The way he could make the piano articulate those things he thought but wouldn't say. The funny wry smile he had when he thought he'd said something amusing. She hurt for him. Hurt for his loss and his spare lonely existence. Hurt for his smile that was a mask, hiding the bruises and the cuts underneath.

Damn him. Damn you, Cole Springer, for making me care. She put the Explorer in gear and pulled away from the curb.

There was something in her eye. Both of them, in fact.

"Max," said Suzi, unpacking her suitcase. "How can you say things like that?"

"Like what?" said Max. Lately Suzi was starting to get on his nerves. Like she was his mother or something.

"Calling Columbus another dumb wop in front of that Gerry Knucks guy. What is wrong with you?"

Geez, for a smart woman sometimes she wasn't very observant. "Gerry ain't no guinea. He's Polish or something. He didn't take offense."

She shook her head and made a dismissive noise with her mouth like steam escaping an overloaded radiator. They weren't getting along real well.

"Hey, you think there's some sort of etiquette about talking to a guy who shoots people for a living?" he said to her back. "Geez, Suze, this isn't some investment banker we're talking about here."

"Next time just let Cole do the talking."

"Springer? Why should I let him talk?"

"Because, unlike some people I know, he appears to know what he's doing. Like sending us on and keeping an eye on this Nugent guy so he can't follow us to the hotel. Would you have thought of that?"

"You'll note he worked it so we now have two rental cars. One for us and one for him."

"That's so he could protect you better. It was sharp on his part."

"Every time he has a great idea I've got to get out my wallet. Besides, I've been dealing with guys like Gerry for twenty years."

"Not when they've got the gun pointed at you. Cole is used to having the gun pointed at him. Let him handle this. Besides, Gerry doesn't seem that bad."

He raised his eyebrows. "He's a cold-hearted killer. He's not going to appear on *Oprah* anytime soon because his girlfriend left him and he's broken-hearted. I'll bet he's killed four guys. At least."

But she was ignoring him. He watched her as she hung up a couple of suits in the closet. "I believe you," she said. She turned around and smoothed the line of her blouse. "But there's something else going on inside the man."

"Yeah, he's pondering bullet placement."

"He had some hesitation in his face when Cole asked him what decided it for him. Like Cole had gotten inside his head."

"Yeah? So, now you can see inside people, right?"

She wanted to take a coat hanger and throw it at him. She started to say "women's intuition" but knew it sounded trite and that he would jump all over that.

She said, "I could just tell when I looked at his eyes."

"Well, come downstairs with me and look into the eyes of the blackjack dealer and tell me what he's thinking."

"Do you work at being a prick?"

"Really not that hard," said Max, glad to get the last word in for once.

Springer sent Max and Suzi on to the hotel while he tailed Nugent. Turn the tables on the guy. He wouldn't expect to be followed. And, keeping an eye on the shooter was better than wondering where he was. He'd rented a plain-Jane Ford Taurus to follow Nugent around. Oddly, Nugent was also driving a Taurus. A white one. They thought alike. He wasn't sure if that was good or bad.

Springer followed Nugent to Caesar's Palace. Watched him go inside. Springer waited. Moments later a bellboy came out to pick up his luggage and a valet started the rental car and parked it. One picked up the bag and one drove the car away. The image of the bellboy and the valet triggered something in his head. Springer waited a few minutes to see if Gerry came back out. He didn't. Springer had spotted a Mr. Bill's Pipe and Tobacco shop close by. There seemed to be about a million of them in Vegas.

He purchased a bent pipe and some tobacco and went back out to his rental. The desert air was hot. Quite a contrast from Aspen. He sat in the car for a moment and thought. He was a pretty good judge of character and body language and verbal clues. He had noticed the momentary lapse into introspection when Springer was talking to him. It was unmistakable. Was there a way of dealing with this guy that wouldn't require shooting him?

Maybe.

Didn't see how it could hurt to ask though. Guy could say no. He could get pissed. If he was intending to kill Max it certainly wouldn't accelerate that outcome. Max laundered money for Nicky T. Max had been good at it. Wonder how much they missed him?

He drove back to Caesar's and a plan began to form in his mind. It could work. It could just work.

If it did, it sure would solve a lot of problems.

Tobi Ryder called in to the office to give her location. When she did, the dispatcher said that Officer Tompkins, an Aspen cop, wanted to talk to her. She called in to Aspen P.D. and asked for Tompkins.

"Thanks for calling in," said Tompkins.

"What's up?"

"We found a Ruger .22 semi-auto pistol at the hotel where you put that perp on the floor."

"Where'd you find it?"

"Housekeeping found it. He threw it down the chute."

She thanked him and signed off.

And she smiled to herself.

CHAPTER

Fifteen

SPRINGER WALKED TO THE REGISTRATION DESK AND asked to be connected with Gerry Knucks.

"Who sir?"

"Mr. Nugent," said Springer. "He just checked in."

"May I ask who's calling for him?"

"Tell him it's the guy he met at the airport," said Springer. The desk clerk looked at him, Springer smiled.

"I'm sorry, sir. I'll need a name."

"Fortune. Tell him Fortune's calling."

The desk clerk forced a colorless smile and picked up the desk phone and dialed. When the connection was made he turned his body away from Springer. A few words were exchanged then the clerk said, "Yes sir, I'll tell him." He turned back to Springer and said, "Mr. Nugent will meet you in the bar in ten minutes, sir."

"What's his room number? I'll just go up, save him the trouble."

The clerk gave him a look.

Springer shrugged, pointed a thumb toward the lounge. "The bar, huh?"

The clerk nodded.

"Damn cigarettes are getting more expensive than cocaine," said Ray Dean, cracking the seal on a pack of Winstons. "Where is he? Guy couldn't just fucking disappear."

"Least ways not from some crackerjack manhunter like your-self," said Auteen. He had a quart bottle of Budweiser, his third, between his massive thighs. "Wouldn't be seemly."

Usually Ray Dean didn't mind Auteen's company, but after several days and nights of his mouth and his smell and his habits, Ray was getting nigger-fatigue. All the guy did was eat, drink beer, and give him shit. May have to do something about it, eventually. Even though the guy was a regulation bucket of shit, Ray still needed him for a while. Besides, he had to be careful about Nicky T not liking it if Auteen suddenly wasn't around anymore. "Yeah, well you ain't exactly been struck with any intelligence attacks lately. And, it's colder than a well-digger's ass. I'm gonna start the car."

Auteen, ignoring him, said, "Man ain't gonna like it he get here and you tell him you don't know where the Jew is."

"Who gives a shit what Knucks likes?"

"You do."

"Yeah. Well, you're in this too."

"I knows how you likes to be in charge."

"We'll find him."

"While we looking, see if you can find a Mac-Donald's."

Ray Dean gave him a look. "That all you ever think of? Eating?"

"Sometimes, I think about pussy," said Auteen. "Sometimes I think about kicking your cowboy-boot-wearin', Gomer Pyle ass. But at the present moment I be thinking about Big Macs."

Ray Dean put the car in gear. What could you do with this guy?

Auteen said, "We could go back, look at the man's house some more, see if we find anything." He looked at Ray Dean and gave him a toothy grin. "Maybe find something to eat."

Ray Dean nodded. "Might as well. At least we could maybe tell if he was coming back anytime."

"Just hope he's coming back before Knucks get here. I don't even want to hear what he got to say about this."

"Fuck Knucks."

"Yeah, that's easier to say than it is to do. He be fucking us we not careful."

Springer sat in a booth, sipping a Scotch-and-soda and waiting for Gerry Knucks. While he waited he examined his purchases. The pipe was a free-hand bent shape. A Brebbia. Hadn't smoked a pipe in years. Didn't know what possessed him to buy one now. While he looked at the pipe he turned things over in his mind. If he was wrong about Knucks he'd have to try something else.

He had a plan. A plan that could solve all the problems at once.

Though it seemed convoluted, it was really quite simple when you considered what everyone wanted. Max needed to walk away clean. Nicky T needed to save face. Nugent would have to satisfy his boss. And Springer needed cash. Lots of it. Nicky had lots of it. He wouldn't miss some of it if he thought somebody else had it, would he? And, if it all went as planned, Springer could get Max off the hook, which was primary. Get Max clear first and then think about the money. It all hinged on how badly Tortino's operation missed Max and whether or not Gerry of the multiple last names would buy into it.

The variables? Max's predilection to difficult behavior, the unbalanced nature of guys like Tortino, a top drawer hit man that could turn the whole thing upside down, and not least, a certain female cop.

The hazards were many, but the payoff could be great. The whole idea had come to him in one long fine flash as he was sitting there. His biggest asset would be that everyone involved had incentive to stay away from each other and therefore the likelihood of exposure was lessened.

Springer, you cad, you.

Gerry Knucks came up behind Springer and as if reading his thoughts, said, "Not good to expose yourself like that."

Springer turned halfway in his seat. "Didn't think you'd come in and shoot me in a public place."

Gerry sat down across from him. Fixed his eyes on him. "Don't count on anything. That's the first rule. Maybe I get you placed where I can see you then go visit Max."

"You don't know where he is."

"You don't know that."

Springer looked at him. "Sure I do."

Gerry smiled. "Followed me here." Not a question.

Springer nodded.

"Made you about the time we turned off on Flamingo," said Gerry.

The waitress came by and Gerry ordered cognac. Springer gave him an amused look.

"What're you looking at?" said Gerry.

"Cognac?" said Springer. "A man in your line of work?"

"What do you think my line of work is? Maybe I'm a wine merchant. Why'd you come by here?"

Springer opened the bag of tobacco and begin to fill the pipe. "To make you a proposition."

Gerry watched Springer fill his pipe. "You're doing it wrong," Gerry said.

"You haven't heard my proposal yet."

"No, I mean the pipe."

"Never did know how," admitted Springer. "Maybe that's why I could never keep the thing lit."

"Here," said Gerry, his hand out. "Let me show you." Springer handed him the pipe and the tobacco pouch. "See?" said Gerry, taking the pipe and placing it inside the pouch. "First, you fill the pipe half-full and then you tamp it until it's firm. Not tight or smashed in there. Firm. You got a pipe tool? You don't?" He pulled a Swiss Army pocket knife out of his pocket and tamped the to-bacco in the pipe. Springer noticed that Nugent had perfectly man-icured fingernails and a nasty three-inch scar across the back of his left hand. A defensive scar. "Then," said Gerry, "you fill it three-fourths and do it again." He dipped the pipe in the bag again, Springer watching. "Then, you overfill the pipe and tamp it again." He handed the filled pipe back to Springer. "Nice pipe. You just buy it?"

"Yeah."

"Really should just fill it half-full the first couple times you smoke it. That way you get a nice cake going and it won't go out on you as easily later."

"Thanks." Springer put the pipe down on the table.

"You're the guy braced Ray Dean and Auteen," said Gerry.

"Who?"

Gerry smiled. "Big fat black guy and dumb little white guy who dresses shitty. Little guy does most of the talking. Black guy does most of the eating."

Springer shrugged.

"Yeah, it's you. They're a pair of regulation morons, but they're not that easy to take. You shoot Ray Dean in the foot?"

"The little toe."

"What were you aiming for?"

"The toe next to the little toe."

"That's pretty good shooting."

Springer shrugged.

"You carrying?" Gerry asked.

"Always."

Gerry looked at him. "You're not very good at lying."

"Everybody has a weakness."

The waitress brought the cognac and set it down in front of Gerry and left. Gerry never took his eyes off Springer.

Gerry said, "I don't."

"Couldn't bring a gun through the airport. You couldn't either."

"Had one waiting in my room when I got here."

"Must still be in your room then," said Springer.

"You think I couldn't hide it from you, huh?"

"Nope."

"What'd you do before?"

"Before what?"

"What'd you do, before all this?"

"I play the piano."

"Yeah, I heard that. That's not what I'm talking about. How do you know how to do the things you do? You can talk the talk. You can shoot. You know your way around the life, like you had experience. How's it happen a piano player knows that stuff?"

Springer ignored the question. "Max says he always liked you. I get the impression you like him."

"Max's okay, but it's not relevant."

"What if there were a way out of having to carry out your a . . . obligation?"

"What obligation?"

"Max."

"Who you think you got here, Monty Hall?"

"You want to do that sort of thing forever?" said Springer.

"Do what?"

"Kill people."

Gerry was quiet for a long moment. Springer thought the guy might get up and leave. Gerry sipped his drink, looked at Springer some more. It was a dead-eyed shark look. A look that probably unnerved most people, but Springer was used to standing, impassively, for hours on end, listening to boring speeches with a communicator in his ear. People staring at him. He'd seen tough guys before.

Gerry said, "Just like that, huh? You think you can just come straight at me with it and knock me off my feet, right? You ought to give more thought before you open your mouth. Your style could get you in trouble."

Springer shrugged. "You don't want to do it forever. I know that much."

Gerry leaned back. "Why you say that?"

"I'm highly intuitive."

"You're also a smart-ass. You know what happens to smart-asses?"

"They end up getting the late slot on *The Tonight Show*?"

Gerry looked around the lounge, then looked back at Springer. The corners of his mouth turned up a sixteenth of an inch—a microscopic smile.

"Knew a guy once," Gerry said. He paused to sip his drink. He looked over the edge of it at Springer. "Thought he was pretty sharp. Going to break the bank at Vegas. Take it down. Thought he had this unbeatable system. Not a system at gambling. A system for robbing from the casinos without them knowing about it. Computer guy. Got away with it for a while, but then he got greedy. Bosses found out."

"What happened to him?"

"They sent for somebody. Found the computer guy out in a drainage pipe in the desert. Wouldn't have known about it but he clogged it up."

"Gee, that's a chilling tale. We going to talk about my proposition or are you going to tell me scary stories some more?"

The microscopic smile grew in intensity. Now it was up to an eighth of an inch.

Springer said, "What's it hurt to think about it?"

"I could shoot you."

"I might shoot back."

"Maybe I'll shoot before you know it."

"Don't miss because I won't."

Gerry looked at him some more. Springer smiled. Gerry looked off across the lounge, shaking his head. "You're a sketch, that's for sure. I'll bet you drive Max crazy. He likes numbers and clean sheets and everything in order. You'd fall in the category of something out of order. So, what if I decide to go along, then what?"

"A way out of the life. Some cash to go with it. You got any put away?"

"What's the catch?"

"Max walks away clean."

Gerry scratched the three-inch scar with the other hand. "How would Max walk away clean? Even if I left him alone, Nicky ain't gonna give up on it."

"I've got that figured."

"How?"

"You in?" Springer said, "Or not? No free samples."

Gerry nodded his head slowly. "Not today. I'll think on it but I wouldn't count on nothing." He started to reach in his pocket for his wallet but Springer stopped him.

"I got this," said Springer, reaching for the check.

Gerry said, "Thanks."

Springer said, "I'll call you later this afternoon and see if you changed your mind. What's your room number?"

Gerry shook his head. "No, I'm not going for that. Back here at eight o'clock tonight. I'll buy you dinner. Get that look out of your eyes. Nothing happens with Max until after we talk again. My word. No matter what you think about us wine merchants, I do what I say. The other thing is just a job." Springer nodded. Gerry started to walk away, stopped, and turned back around. "You know," he said. "Even if this doesn't work out I'm just here for Max. This doesn't have to involve you."

"Appreciate the gesture," said Springer. "But I'm in for the duration."

Gerry nodded. "What I figured."

Ricky Jade parked the 300ZX in the airport parking lot and picked up the Chevrolet Cavalier that Kim Li's people had waiting for him at the Hertz desk. The car was registered to a guy that was behind on the vig to Li. If the cops got onto the car, then Jade, or one of Li's soldiers would have another job to do. The guy that owed the money knew that, too. But the poor guy would have no choice. Rent the car or come up with the money he owed immediately.

Li's people had found out that Gerry Knucks was in Las Vegas. They didn't know why but he was there. Vegas was not a large town for all its notoriety. Knucks would be easy to find here. Wiseguys and hoods stuck to the strip and the nightspots. Knucks lived well. His one weakness or at least the one thing you could predict about the guy.

Jade tooled the Chevy out of the lot and onto Las Vegas Boulevard. He found a radio station that played alternative and turned the sound up. As he pulled onto the strip a white Taurus pulled up beside him. Ordinarily he wouldn't have paid much mind, but the sun caught the Taurus mirror and flashed across the interior of the Cavalier. Jade looked over and couldn't believe his luck. Gerry Knucks. Bigger than life, driving the Taurus.

Jade slowed down some and the Taurus moved ahead.

The Taurus turned left.

Jade slid in behind the Taurus two cars back.

"Ricky, you're living right," he said to himself. He turned the radio up some.

Gerry drove down the LV Boulevard south to Tropicana and then turned around and headed back north. That fucking Springer, he thought. Following him again. Keeping him in sight. Guess he figured if he always knew where he was then Max was safe. Maybe he'd play with him a little. Now, where was that turn-off that led to Shapiro's girl's dress shop? There it was, up ahead. Maybe he'd go in and buy his mother something for her birthday, so she'd get off his back about never coming to see her. Always talking about his brother, the insurance salesman, like that wasn't stealing. Making people bet they wouldn't die. No chance for that. Led nowhere.

He pulled in front of the store. Parked and got out.

But he didn't pay any attention to the Cavalier that pulled to the side and parked. Didn't see Ricky Jade sitting in the driver's seat.

Didn't even think about it.

CHAPTER

Sixteen

SUZI SET A CAN OF DIET DR PEPPER ON HER DESK AND went through her receipts and bills. She preferred regular Dr Pepper but thought it was bad for business to be drinking the stuff in front of customers who never touched the real thing. It would be like flaunting it.

She had had to get away from Max before she did Gerry Knucks's job for him. Max was driving her crazy. Whining and complaining and smoking cigars like they were Lucky Strikes. As she went through the books she once again realized how fortunate she was to have Margie working for her. She was a good employee. Efficient. Honest. Everything was in order. It was like Suzi had never left. Good to know you could trust her to take care of things.

It was good to be back at the shop. She enjoyed the work. Enjoyed the satisfaction of running a successful business, talking to customers. Larger-sized women were nicer than the starved, spoiled clientele that she ran into when she shopped for her own stuff. Her customers often asked her what a lady with a body like hers was doing running a queen-sized shop. She told them that she was really "a queen-size trapped in a size eight body." They liked that. A couple of them had become good friends of hers. They would have coffee at mid-morning or drinks at the Mirage after work.

She was checking on some new merchandise, no customers in the place, when Gerry Nugent walked into her shop.

"Hello," he said.

"What do you want?" she said, ice in her voice. She reached under the counter where she kept the Colt Detective's Special .38 Max bought for her after a couple of kids had robbed her.

"I'm looking for a nice dress for my mom," he said, looking around. "She's pretty big, you know."

"You don't have a mom."

"Everybody's got a mom."

"Except shit. Shit doesn't have a mom."

He leaned his head back slightly. "Why're you coming off like that?"

"I'm sick of you guys with guns coming around and bothering Max." She tried to keep from trembling. Both from anger as well as fear. "Why don't you just leave him alone? Why the hell are you here?"

"I told you. It's my mom's birthday. I want to get her something nice."

"Get out."

He looked at her. "I'm not here to cause trouble."

"You are trouble." She pulled out the Colt and pointed it at him. "See this?"

"Yeah, I see it. You think I never seen one before?"

"I know how to use it, too."

"Okay."

His calm in the face of the gun had been unnerving to her at first, but now it was relaxing her. He looked her right in the eyes.

She said, "Maybe I should shoot you and then Max would have nothing to worry about."

"At least he wouldn't have anything to worry about from me. Why don't you put that away, huh?"

"Why should I?" she said.

"Because I'm not going to hurt you. Just going to buy a dress. And I don't think you're going to shoot me."

"Could say you were trying to rob me," she said, slowly circling the gun around in the direction of his torso, enjoying herself now.

"Sure," Gerry said. "That'd work. A guy wearing a four hundred dollar jacket and a Rolex watch comes in and rips off a muumuu and a couple hundred bucks because it's a slow afternoon."

"I could say you tried to rape me."

"Much better. They'd understand that, looking at you."

She smiled, in spite of herself. "How do I get you to leave Max alone?"

"You could sell me a dress and maybe we could talk about it over coffee."

"Like I'd have coffee with a thug."

"I figure a woman who's got a Colt thirty-eight can do about what she wants."

Springer watched Nugent's Taurus pull up in front of Suzi's dress shop. Now what? Would he try to take her hostage and trade her for Max? No, that was Amateur Night crap. What was Nugent's angle here? Springer drove on by, did an illegal U-turn and pulled into a parking slot opposite the direction he'd come in. He sat and thought about things for a minute.

After leaving Nugent's hotel, Springer had met his gun connection and picked up a .380 Colt semi-auto pistol. One of the lightweight ones. He didn't like the featherweight guns but it was 89 degrees out, cool for Vegas but not for a guy who lived in Aspen, and he needed something that wouldn't require him to wear a jacket to conceal the gun. He just dropped the Colt in the front pocket of his khakis and pulled the shirttail out on his short-sleeved shirt, a silk T-shirt underneath that. The weapon didn't weigh much more than a wallet. Only four hollow-point rounds in the clip instead of six to make it even lighter.

He wondered if Nugent had made him. That could be it. Playing with him. Or, maybe the guy thought he could force Suzi to tell him where Max was. Or maybe wait until she left and follow her. But Nugent had gone inside, which would tip Suzi off and Suzi was a smart lady. She would know better than to head back to the hotel until she was sure it was safe.

Something else was bothering him. He was almost positive that they'd picked up a new player. A guy in a Chevy Cavalier had turned off behind Nugent. Might mean nothing but it was the kind of thing you watched for. His suspicions were further affirmed when the Cav turned onto the same street as Nugent.

Springer was wondering whether to get out and go into the

shop when the Cavalier door opened and an Oriental-looking guy got out. Late thirtyish. Stylish clothes. Expensive sunglasses. Nice summer-weight jacket like Californians wear. Not the kind of guy looked like a Cavalier driver. Guy looked more like a gymnast or a karate instructor. Tan driving gloves.

Tan driving gloves to drive a Chevy Cavalier on a hot day in Vegas?

He watched the guy go into Suzi's shop.

Springer got out of his car.

Ricky Jade checked the sidewalks out of the corner of his sunglasses before entering the boutique. He left his sunglasses on as he walked into the shop, easing the door open and slipping through the opening. What kind of place was this? Some kind of women's clothing store with clothes that looked like they fit professional wrestlers. Thick-bodied mannequins draped with expensive cloth. He heard Knucks talking, then the voice of a woman. He slipped the Walther PPK out of his shoulder holster, placing the gun hand at his back where it was covered by his jacket and moved quietly toward the sound.

The place smelled of strawberries and jasmine. As Ricky got closer he could hear what they were saying. The woman's voice was angry, but Knucks seemed calm. Then Ricky saw the gun. She had a gun pointed at Knucks. What was going on here?

"Like I'd have coffee with a thug," the woman was saying.

"I figure a woman who's got a Colt thirty-eight can do about what she wants."

"Just like that?" she said.

"I'll even pay," said Knucks. "Just put the gun away. What do you think's gonna happen here? You think I shoot women for recreation? Come on, put the gun away, nothing's going to happen."

Yeah, lady, thought Jade. Put the gun away. Please. If she didn't then he'd have to put them both down and that was messy. He could do that easy enough, but that would be a double homicide instead of just some San Francisco shooter getting iced. Besides, she might get lucky and put one in him. So, he had to decide. Did he take them both out or did he slip back outside and leave? Wait for another opportunity?

"Well," she said, shrugging her shoulders. "What the hell? Don't think I wouldn't shoot you for real."

"I believe you." Jade heard a drawer open. The gun disappeared and he heard the drawer shut.

Jade brought the PPK out from under his coat and stepped out from behind the clothes rack and—

Wham! Jade felt a deep pain behind his right ear, then a pressure on his carotid artery. Felt his legs give out from under him as something dug at the back of his knees. Next thing he knew he was face down on the floor, something heavy and sharp digging into his kidneys.

"Don't move," said Springer, putting the Colt pistol at the back of the Oriental man's neck. "Unlace the fingers on the weapon. Do it."

Jade complied. Springer took the Walther from the prone man and placed it in his left hand.

"What the fuck?" said Gerry Nugent at the sound of the commotion.

"Oh my God," said Suzi.

"You know this guy?" Springer asked.

Nugent moved closer. He knelt beside the guy and looked at him, nodding his head. Looked up at Springer and nodded again. "Yeah, I know him." Then to the man on the floor, he said, "Ricky Jade. What are you doing in Vegas? Feeling lucky?"

Jade said nothing.

"Who sent you?" Gerry asked Jade.

Nothing.

"He's not going to talk," said Springer.

"He's part Japanese. Pretty inscrutable."

"I thought it was the Chinese who were inscrutable."

"Yeah, I think that's right."

"What is it with you two?" said Suzi, brushing hair away from her face. "A man with a gun walks in and you're talking about his cultural heritage. I'm calling the police."

"Wait a sec," said Gerry. "I got some things I wanta ask this guy."

"Yeah, hold off, Suze," said Springer.

"Where'd you get the gun?" Gerry asked Springer.

"Guy I know here in town."

"Yeah? He a piano player too?"

"Strong union."

"You can put it away now." He looked at Springer.

"Not yet."

"Ricky ain't going nowhere."

"Maybe it's not for Ricky."

"Thought that was a possibility. You already got a scenario fig-ured, don't you?"

Springer nodded. "Yep."

"You shoot me with Ricky's gun, then you do Ricky. You and Max's girl," he nodded in Suzi's direction, "tell the cops that Ricky shot me and you took Ricky. Like that?"

"Pretty close."

Gerry smiled and shook his head slightly. "You're a quick study. I'll give you that."

"You're not going to kill them are you, Cole?" asked Suzi, panic edging into her voice. "Not in my shop."

"Not in her shop, she says," said Gerry. "Women."

"I'm not going to shoot him," said Springer. "That's not the way to start a partnership."

"What does that mean?" asked Suzi.

Gerry looked at Springer. "You're setting me up, aren't you?"

"I wouldn't do that."

"Maybe I won't be forced."

"Up to you."

"What about him?" said Gerry, indicating Jade.

"I find him useful."

"I'll bet you do. What if he sneaks back and pops me? He'll do you too because he doesn't want any witnesses. You could make him to the cops."

"It's a problem all right. We could take him out back and beat the shit out of him. Get some exercise out of it and then we kill him."

Gerry nodded. "Yeah. We could do it like that. Pretty hot out-side, though."

"Or," said Springer. "Ricky here . . . your name's Ricky, right? Ricky Jade? Wow, that's so exotic."

"Fuck you," said Jade.

Then, to Gerry, Springer said, "Or, Mr. Fuck You here, could tell us who sent him and maybe we let him walk. What do you think?"

Gerry acted disappointed. "Be more fun to shoot him."

"Well you can't have everything."

"Listen Ricky," said Gerry, standing up. Jade was prone, his arms outstretched. "I'm just going to ask you one time. Who sent you?"

"Fuck y—"

Gerry stomped Jade's right hand, breaking it. Jade flinched with the impact, but didn't make a sound.

"Oh shit," said Suzi, putting her hand over her mouth and closing her eyes.

"Not even a whimper," said Springer.

"Ricky's tough," said Gerry. "But, sooner or later they all have to give it up. Hate to see it happen to Ricky. Good-looking guy. Likes the ladies. Likes to hit the discos, you know. He's a dancer. But, it's tough to dance after somebody clips your Achilles tendons with a razor."

"Stop it! Stop it right now," said Suzi. "I won't have this."

"What's it gonna be, Ricky?" Gerry said. "You're a pro. You know what you're looking at. Make it easy for yourself. I don't have to hurt you."

"Please," said Suzi.

"Take a walk, Suze," said Springer. "Put out the CLOSED sign and go somewhere."

She looked at him, surprised by the coldness in his voice. But he winked at her, letting her know it was all right. She gathered her things and left.

"Okay, Ricky," said Gerry, after she left. "I'm going to go easy on you. You don't have to say anything. Just nod your head. Hold out his left hand, there, would you Springer?"

"Sorry," said Springer. "I'm real busy here. Both hands are full." He hefted the pistols for effect. "What do you want to do?"

Gerry took a deep breath, looked around, then back at Springer. Deciding something. "That's the way it's going to be, huh? You want something. Okay, what've you got? I'm listening."

"Not now," said Springer. "First, we have to do something with 'Have Gun Will Travel' here."

"I got some ideas on that."

"Figured you might. Like what?"

"I'll have a couple guys I know here in town come by and bundle Ricky up and tell me what I want to know."

"What about our deal?" asked Springer.

Gerry looked down at Jade, then back at Springer. "I'll be in touch."

Jack Summers looked around before he pulled out the burglar kit and slipped a pick into the lock. After a couple of tries he felt the tumblers click and the knob turn in his hand. He'd checked and found out that the owner of the house was in Bermuda, probably smoking Montecristos and drinking Jamaican rum right now. Once the door opened, Summers made a show of waving as if someone were inside and letting him in.

Inside, Summers made his way up the staircase, a little spooked by the silence of the large house. He'd creeped a few places in his time, but this time he felt like a criminal. But he'd convinced himself that this Springer guy was dirty and he needed to get him out of the way so he could concentrate on Shapiro and Tortino. Springer was a wild card and Summers was just re-shuffling the deck. He couldn't trust Ryder to do her job right with this guy around. She had that look in her eye whenever he mentioned Springer's name which she tried to disguise as anger but Summers knew reflected deeper emotions. Summers had been watching people's nonverbal signals for nearly two decades now and his instincts were always right. She had something for this guy—this paradoxical piano player with the dark background. He could get something on Springer then he could plant doubt in her mind. Besides, he just didn't like this guy. Springer had to go.

Once in the apartment, Summers pulled the baggie out of his coat pocket and hefted it. The white powder inside shifted and settled like sand.

Then he looked down at the floor. This fucking guy had put

talcum powder on the floor like he was James Bond or something. What kind of paranoid crap was that? He slipped off his shoes and looked around the place for a vacuum cleaner. He found one and plugged it in, and cleaned where he had left prints. When he was done he wound the cord back around the vacuum cleaner and placed it back in the closet. That done, he looked in the guy's bedroom and bathroom until he found the powder and re-salted the carpet. But now how was he going to get out without disturbing it again? Finally, he settled on putting an amount in one of his shoes so he could dust the carpet after he was in the hall.

He looked around for a place to hide the cocaine. He decided the roll top desk was best. He removed some old letters out of a cubbyhole and placed the baggie at the back of the empty cubicle then placed the letters back, hiding the cocaine.

Then he took one step in the powder, then one in the hall with his clean foot, put the shoe on the foot with powder on it and sprinkled powder from the other shoe on the footprint. Not perfect, but it'd have to do. Might be a good idea not to underestimate this guy.

Special agent Jack Summers walked down the stairs and left the house, the door shutting with the finality of a jail cell.

Then he drove to a bar and had a drink to celebrate.

Good-bye Springer.

CHAPTER

Seventeen

TOBI RYDER PUT THE PHONE DOWN. NO ANSWER. SHE called the Whiskey Basin. No answer there either. No sign of him. Nothing. Nowhere. Nada. She checked around and found that Max Shapiro had booked a charter to Las Vegas. Three passengers. One of them had to be Springer. Springer, the wise-ass ex-Secret Service agent, who wasn't supposed to leave the state without permission of the court.

One of these days he was going to learn the hard way that he wasn't as clever as he imagined. But she had to give him style points. She was angry, frustrated, and yet felt an ambiguous sense of regret, as if she had something to say to him but didn't know what it was. It had to do with creeping his apartment. No, that wasn't *all* of it. That was only a symptom of what was troubling her.

She looked at the picture of her dad on her desk. He was dressed in his police uniform. "What do I do with this guy, Dad?" she said aloud. She touched the edges of the frame and smiled. She knew what her dad would do. He would do his job. Her mother would tell her that Springer was not worth the trouble. That he had betrayed his trust with his superiors at the White House. That would be Mother's take—that Springer didn't know how to properly serve his masters.

But she had plenty to do without worrying about Springer. First, there were no prints on the .22 Ruger pistol they'd found at the hotel so she couldn't link it to Ray Dean Carr. None on the clip or ammunition either. Wiped. Knew it had to belong to him but there was little she could do about that. Right now the immediate problem was they'd found a local guy, a jet-set drug merchant, dead in his house up on Red Mountain. Shot twice in the face at close range with a large caliber weapon. It was an ugly crime for Aspen. His live-in girlfriend found the body after returning from skiing. The local law enforcement had asked her to look around.

The dead dealer was known around Aspen as the source for the celebrity crowd—movie stars, rockers, and the moneyed classes who frequented Aspen on an infrequent basis. The dealer was known to his clientele only as "Charlemagne," aka "Charles Wheelwright," aka "Charley Wheels." A street punk and failed actor from L.A. who had taken two falls for "possession with intent to traffic" in his younger days before he hit the motherlode and moved his cheap act to Aspen and insinuated himself into the circle of beautiful people. Charlemagne was loosely associated with the Denver Castellano family. Aspen was laid back about drug traffic when it flowed into the hands of the rich. Don't hassle the tourists, especially those who made Aspen the snow capital of the American West. Was it a mob hit? Why? The mob wasn't this sloppy. Maybe a client that was pissed off? Who knew?

The list of suspects was extensive. People willing to talk to her about Charlemagne would be less extensive. Movie stars and celebrities didn't like to talk to cops and they especially didn't like to talk to cops about murder and drugs. She'd had to threaten a *National Enquirer* reporter who arrived on the scene within minutes of her arrival. How did those rodents find out about this so quickly?

The reporter, a ponytailed guy she'd seen around before with a camera hanging around his neck and a pair of amber Remington shooting glasses on his face, hadn't taken the hint when she'd told him that he wasn't getting anything until she'd had a chance to look at the scene, and maybe not even then.

"You think it was a drug deal gone bad?" he'd asked.

"I don't think anything yet because I haven't been inside. And you can quote me."

When she turned to walk toward the chalet he started to follow her.

"You need to step back, sir," she said, firm but cordial.

"I'll just hang around," he said, a wide grin on his face.

Detective Ryder turned to a uniform and said, "If this guy is still here when I come back out I'm going to be severely distressed. At you. Do you understand? I want him behind the tape. Way behind."

"Hey, I got a right to be here," said the reporter.

She took a step in the reporter's direction, leaned close to him and said, "If you don't back off I'm going to pick you up by the scrotum and swing you over my head." She leaned back away, smiling, and said, "Does that compute for you, sir?"

The guy moved back and she went in to view the crime scene.

To add to her stress, David, her ex-husband, showed up at her house later.

He was just sitting there—as if it were the most natural thing in the world instead of incredibly irritating—in her apartment when she returned home after filing her report. She was tired and stressed and the last thing she wanted to see was her asshole ex-husband sitting on her couch, smoking a cigarette, and drinking her Absolut. He had his jacket off so she could see his shoulder holster as if that would prompt her to tear her clothes off and jump on his lap. David always had this idea that his tough-guy cop routine was sexy. Probably was at one time. But now the whole thing was *so* played.

"Hello, beautiful," he said, as if he'd never left. "How was your day?"

"You told me that you'd given me the apartment key when I threw you out. Give me the one you have now."

"I picked it."

"Maybe I should shoot you then. We have tough vermin control laws here. Or maybe it would be breaking-and-entering with intent to annoy."

"Why the attitude, Tobe? Aren't you glad to see me?"

"David, I'm tired and you're smoking cigarettes in my living room." Her cat came out of hiding and rubbed against Tobi's legs. Tobi reached down and pet her. "What did you do to my cat?"

He shrugged. "She don't like me. I just tried to pet her and she hissed at me."

"That's because cats can't talk. If she could talk she'd call you dirty names. And put the cigarette out."

"All right, all right." He looked around for an ashtray. Toby fished an empty Heineken bottle out of the trash and handed it to him. Like a mischievous child he took one more drag, looking up at her as he filled his cheeks with smoke, before dropping the cigarette in the bottle and handing it back. She took the bottle into the kitchen and came back.

"Okay, David," she said. "What do you want?"

"Just came by for a visit."

Tobi sat down in her favorite chair. She reached out and picked up the Absolut bottle, removed the cap, and drank from the neck. She felt the heat of the vodka, warm against her gums then in her throat.

"We're not going to have sex, David," she said. "So get it out of your head."

"Come on, Tobe, that's not what I'm here for," he said, but his look said she nailed him.

She laughed. He could be cute sometimes. He was a good-looking guy. Curly-blond hair, blue eyes, wide shoulders, narrow hips. Unfortunately, too many women had thought he was good looking. And David had no resistance. "That's what you're always here for. You're always on the make. You've never resolved your sense of post-adolescent ennui. But I'm all grown up now and it makes me tired when I see you. Why don't you go down and hang around the high school? You could sling your jacket over your shoulder and show them your holster. I'm sure that'll impress the cheerleader types you're used to."

"Don't be so hard-ass. You know you still care about me."

She shrugged. "Okay. I still care. But that's miles away from wanting to have you around. And I'd rather have my kneecaps removed than jump into bed with you."

"It wasn't that bad."

"Whatever you want to believe."

"You seem . . ." pausing, then giving her the smile he thought was charming, he said, "Sexually repressed?"

She stared at him, momentarily. This is what had ended it for her. David's presumption that he could fix any bad behavior, any stupid act, with a boyish grin.

"And," she said, "you're the antidote. Right?"

"Why not?"

She took another sip of the vodka. A smaller one this time. "Turn it off, David. I'm so immune."

"Still seeing that Summers guy?"

"That'd fall under the heading of none of your business. But, no, I'm not."

He smiled. "Oh. So what happened? Give me the details."

She took another pull on the bottle. She should really get a glass. Starting to look like a lush drinking right out of the bottle. This is what David did to her. He made her unbalanced. Kept her emotions out there on the edge of the precipice where it dropped straight down to bitterness.

"There are no details. He's an asshole. A self-assured asshole." She thought about Cole Springer. "I seem to be attracted to smug assholes."

"Meaning me?" he said, a smile on his face.

"No," she said. "You're a prick. An immature prick. See the difference?"

"So," he said, dismissing the insult. "You want to get something to eat?"

She shook her head, slowly. "No. I'm going to pour some of this in a glass with ice and take a long, hot bubble bath and listen to Mozart."

"Maybe you need someone to scrub your back," he said, standing.

"You're not on the program," she said. "Nice to see you, David, but I really want you to go." She stood to help him get the message.

He stuck his hands in the pockets of his black Levi's and said, "How about I order us up some Chinese, maybe a bottle of wine and then . . ." He paused again, which was really played now, Tobi just wishing he'd go before she socked him in the nose, ". . . well, you know." He smiled, moving closer to her, showing teeth. Capped teeth, which she had to pay half of, back when they were married.

She shook her head.

"I'll just wait until you're done then."

"No, David," she said. "You're going to leave. Please."

She grabbed him by the elbow to steer him toward the door. He reached down and took her hand in his. She jerked away but he was quicker, snatching her by the wrist. She tried to pull away but he tightened his grip.

"Let go, David."

"In a minute."

"Now." She was getting pissed.

"I got something to say."

She pulled back and he twisted her wrist. He was hurting her. She forgot how strong he was. She kicked at his knee but he must have anticipated that because he dodged the kick and caught her behind the foot and dumped her on the floor, hard.

"You ought to save that policewoman bullshit for strung-out jack boys," he said. "Doesn't work on me."

She brushed the hair away from her face. "Just get out."

"How about dinner sometime?" he said, not getting the message.

"Man, you gotta do something 'bout your temper," said Auteen, between bites. He had a box of French doughnuts they'd bought at this fancy pastry shop in his lap. Cost ten bucks a dozen. "Ten bucks?" he'd said to the bakery guy. "Will there be little gold nuggets inside or something?" He was on his fifth one. No nuggets yet.

"Little prick had it coming," said Ray Dean. He was sitting on the motel bed flipping through the channels with the television remote. Still keyed up from shooting the creep. "Fucking smart-ass sitting there drinking cognac and dragging on that pipe like he was fucking Hugh Hefner instead of some L.A. piece-a-shit with a face lift."

Auteen licked his fingers. "Man, you can't cap everybody pisses you off."

"Yeah? First you think I won't do it and now you're bitching when I do it. Besides, you heard what Nicky said."

"He didn't say shoot nobody in his face."

"We made the offer and the guy starts with that bullshit about all the important people he knows and how we were bringing "grief into our lives" because we "don't know who we're dealing with." Guy wearing fucking spandex leotards talking shit out the side of his mouth like he was a bad-ass instead of a faggot. I don't have to take that. Fuck him."

"But the man want to use him. Told you he want the guy to work for us. He'd already set it up with Denver. Save having to set up brand new. Guy had the contacts already."

The way it went down was like this. Nicky T had been eyeing Charlemagne's drug business for a little while. He'd known Charley Wheels from his L.A. days. Wheels had made the mistake of getting too big too fast with no real sponsor. Really raking in the bucks. Guy was loosely connected to the Castellanos in Denver. Nicky T wanted a slice of the take. So, he worked a deal with Denver. Wheels could keep a fourth, Nicky wasn't greedy. Nicky would send a piece to Denver and a percentage to Guardino in Frisco. In return, nobody would muscle Charlie. But now that he was Charlemagne, the guy had got it in his head that he was "somebody" and that he "knew people." As if guys that pretended to be hard cases in movies were swinging dicks in real life. He liked Bob De Niro on the screen but would ice him in a New York minute if the guy ever talked shit to him.

They'd driven up Red Mountain in the Chevy Blazer that Auteen had boosted from a resort parking lot, driving right up to the door, trampling the guy's bushes and shit. Guy came to the door when they knocked, wouldn't let them in at first. But Ray Dean explained the situation to him. Said it was a "business" proposition. He mentioned Nicky Tortino and a guy in Frisco that Charlemagne knew.

"It can go easy or it can get uncivil," said Ray Dean, looking past the guy's shoulder as if unconcerned, then straight at him. "Whatever you want. We have to come back, it's going to be the second one. What do you think that means for you?"

So the guy let them in. Okay so far. But then after they'd talked a while and discussed terms the guy started getting obstinate and panicky.

"You fuckers don't get it, do you?" Charlemagne said, getting little sparkly drops of spittle at the corners of his mouth, like to make Ray Dean sick. Guy was wired up on something. Fucking dealers. All the same. They were all users. "This ain't Frisco. This is fucking Aspen. You see the difference, don't you? No? This is where guys like the president and Axl-fucking-Rose and Richard Gere, for crissakes, come and get high and ski down the slopes. You get that? Hard-ons don't make it here. Especially hard-ons with pompadours and cowboy boots. Where the fuck do you shop? You don't fit here."

Guy started to laugh nervously. His eyes didn't look too good, like they were shimmering with some kind of weird inner light. "You start walking around here and they'll have the fucking FBI and the CBI and every other alphabet crew crawling up your ass with a magnifying glass and a razor. Can't you see what a shit-storm you'd stir up for me? For yourself? And I know people that know people and they'll come down here and go through your life with a pair of tweezers, man. Are you listening to—"

"Look, asshole," Ray Dean said, a hand up, interrupting the guy. "You just need to relax. I don't give a shit about Axl Rose or Axl Petunia or whatever the fuck his name is. You're over the line here and you need to back up because I'm not going to fuck around with you all day. Now, you need to focus on the reality of the situation. Our people are making you a legitimate offer. One that protects you from other people like us. One that allows you to keep living in this place and wearing dance clothes like some kinda wimpy fucking ski-jump asshole instead of a piece of dog shit which is what you are."

"You can't talk to me like that," said Charlemagne, screaming now.

"Are you on something?" Looking at the guy funny now. Geez, what was with this guy? "What's wrong with you?"

"You fuckhead. I'll have your ass."

Ray Dean looked away, making a face, then back at the guy. "Quit screaming at me. I don't like it."

"Chill, motherfucker," said Auteen. "We just talking at you."

"Fuck you! Get out."

Starting to really piss Ray Dean off now. "I'm telling you, don't do that."

"GET THE FUCK—"

Ray Dean interrupted him again. But this time he did it by shooting the guy in the face. Twice. Once, after the guy was laying on the floor. Then Auteen started acting all neurotic.

"Damn. Why you shoot the guy? That is some fucked-up shit. Man, the more I hang with you the more I think you belong in the fucking zoo, people throwing peanuts at your sick ass. Shit. That's some crazy-assed way of acting, man. Ain't no doubt about that. You are one confused white boy. Why you do that shit?"

"How long you think I'm gonna listen to that shit? How long? Huh?"

"You coulda winged him or something. You ever think about anything like that? Coulda punched him. You coulda had me punch him. We coulda held him by the ankles off his balcony. No. Not you. Not Billy-the-fucking-kid. You just start blasting people's faces. You shoot fucking Tinkerbell she was here."

"Quit whining," Ray Dean said. "I gotta think. We gotta get outta here."

"No shit? You think we should? I thought we'd hang around, drink the guy's brandy and watch TV. You one cagey motherfucker. You on top of everything. 'We gotta gotta outta here.' Why didn't I think of it first? It's a motherfucking miracle you not the head of a big corporation you such a big thinker."

"Just shut the fuck up, huh?" Auteen starting to piss him off now but enjoying the guy's jumpiness. The gun going off had scared the big man. Ray Dean liked that.

"And, I can't hear shit, either. My ears are ringing. You and your fucking guns. Damn. Nicky ain't going to like this. Gerry neither."

"Yeah, well fuck Gerry." Ray Dean could feel something swelling inside him. Some sense of inner peace. Sort of like after sex. Something inside had broke loose and floated downstream.

Auteen said, "You keep saying that and the spooky muthafucker's gonna hear it and he's gonna start shooting *your* narrow ass."

"He ain't Superman, ya know."

"Ain't Tinkerbell neither."

Max was getting tired of being left alone. He might as well let Gerry Knucks shoot him as stay in his hotel suite, channel-surfing and going off his nut. He'd called room service to bring him up a Reuben sandwich, some peanuts, and another bottle of Scotch. Springer had told him not to call down to the desk because he didn't want anybody in town to see him.

"Nicky's probably got connections all over town," Springer had told Max. "So you can't even let the help see you. Nugent's already seen you and he'll put out feelers, probably some sort of bounty on you. Some room service waiter who'd like to make a week's pay would turn you without batting an eye. In this town everybody's a greed-head and you're just another mark so don't do anything impetuous."

That's the way the guy talked to him. Like he was some putz. Paying the guy three G's a week and he talked to him like *Max* was the employee. But even that wasn't as bad as sitting around this room. Here he was in Las Vegas, for crissakes, and he couldn't go out and hit the tables, see the shows, or visit some of his buddies. Suzi and hotshot, for crissakes, got to leave, while he sat there and waited. Waited for what? For somebody to put a bullet in his brain? Could do it himself, save them the trouble. Even that would be better than this. It was getting so bad that he was thinking about shooting the television again. Maybe shoot the mini-fridge for a change of pace.

So, after he ate the sandwich and drank some Scotch he wanted something else. What did he want? He wanted something that would jump-start his circulation. Something that would create a little excitement and knock the edge off this three-hundred-pound hairball of tension at the back of his neck. Suzi had been distant lately. And with Suzi, distance equaled frigidity. She was cold as ice in bed right now.

A little trim would relax him. Hell, he was in Nevada. Legal prostitution. He knew a couple of places. Looked them up in the

Las Vegas phonebook he found under the Gideon's bible in the nightstand. He rang up "Caroline's Cowgirls" and the girl that answered told them they had a special on the "Lash Larue" treatment. He told her he wasn't interested.

"I don't want anything aberrant or unearthly," he said. "None of that handcuffs or leather underwear shit. I just want somebody to come up here and put my day right. The prettiest girl you got. The best."

"You want the 'Hopalong Cassidy.' "

"Whatever you call it." Geez, it was like ordering at McDonalds. "Just get somebody over here. Soon, cause I'm flipping out."

She told him they charged more to come to his hotel and he said he didn't care.

"The hotel you're staying at frowns on our girls showing up unescorted."

"So dress her up nice and send her. I don't care what they like. I'll call down and tell them my niece, Jennifer, is coming. They know me here." But they didn't know he was here, he thought. He couldn't tell them. It was Springer and Suzi who had checked him in. "Tell them to ask for her Uncle Cole, Cole Springer, if anybody stops her." He smiled, thinking about giving the desk Springer's name, then gave her the room number.

She agreed to that and told him that "Jennifer" would be there in forty-five minutes.

He hung up and took a shower.

He sang "My Way" while the water beat down on him.

CHAPTER

Eighteen

CHERRY BLOSSOM COULDN'T BELIEVE HER LUCK.
She had just had implant surgery and it had cost a fortune. Well, not a Las Vegas-sized fortune but a fortune for a girl from Rogers, Arkansas. Next, she needed to get the tooth fixed, the one that had got chipped when that prick insurance adjuster hit her in the mouth. He wanted S&M he shoulda asked for another girl. Guy got away before Brownie Biceps, a former circus strongman and the house bouncer, could catch him. With the implant and the tooth fixed she could get a dance job on the strip and then maybe head out to L.A. and see if she could make it as an actress. She didn't spend her money on drugs like some of the girls. She had plans. Goals. She wasn't a call girl, she was a dancer and an actress. This was just a temporary situation.

Her real name was Nicole Maxwell. She went by Cherry Blossom because Caroline's made them come up with a work name so the sick fucks couldn't track them down and mess with them. When she went to Hollywood she was going to change it to Chantel Maven. She was good looking, with nice legs and eyes, and made good money working for Caroline and she got the best gigs. Straight missionary most of the time. Some hand-action once in a while, but no anal stuff and a limited amount of Monica Lewinsky crap. Sometimes she had to dress up in weird outfits but she wasn't like the rest of the girls. She was going places.

Right now she needed money, so when she heard the guy's East Coast accent and saw the cigars and the Scotch she thought she had her guy. He was Jewish too, just like Carmine, who worked at the Nugget, told her. A Jewish guy, who smoked cigars and drank Scotch, from Back East. Fiftyish. Not bad looking. If he was the guy it was worth five C's.

When she asked to be paid up front the Jewish John said something like, "What're you? Some kind of romantic?" Then he opened his wallet. When he pulled out the two C-notes she saw his driver's license.

Max Shapiro, it said.

Bells ringing, all cherries. Chantel Maven here I come.

Suzi couldn't believe she'd just had coffee with a hit man. What was wrong with her anymore? With *the* hit man that was sent to kill Max. It was like something out of a romantic comedy. But he didn't seem like such a bad guy. The only reason she went was that she wanted to take a shot at trying to talk him out of shooting Max. Her Max. For all his faults she didn't want anything to happen to Max. He'd been good to her and even though the relationship was headed south she still cared about what happened to him.

But Gerry Knucks didn't even seem interested in Max. He kept asking questions about Cole.

"You trust this guy?" he asked, stirring his coffee even though he'd ordered it black.

"That's a strange question, coming from a man who works for criminals. Why should I tell you anything?"

He shrugged. "That's fair. But do you think this Springer guy is stand-up?"

"You mean, does he deal honestly with people?"

"Yeah, like that."

"Haven't known him very long." She put her cup down and placed a mauve-colored fingernail along her jawline. He wanted to know what *she* thought. But why? Why did he want to know about Cole? She *was* pretty good at sizing-up people, like deciding what clothes looked best on them or if they were the type of person that would do what they said or just talking to hear themselves speak. Ever since she was a little girl she had this sort of insight into the way people would be after only talking to them for a few minutes.

Her mother said it was God's gift to her and she should use it right. Like this guy, Gerry Nugent. He was a tough guy, sure. Even a bad guy. But, there was something else about him. Something that caused her to trust him. Besides, knowing whether you could trust Cole Springer wasn't exactly a state secret. So, she said, "But yeah, I think so. He's very direct. Something about him makes you feel, you know, safe. Like he's got things under control. Take when he saw you in the airport. I liked to wet my pants, but he just took it in stride and controlled the situation. Didn't panic. Didn't act like it bothered him at all."

"So, you think he tells you something you can count on it, right?" asked Gerry.

She pursed her lips, causing her chin to dimple and nodded her head. "Yeah. So far that's the way it's been."

"He's kind of a smart-ass though. Always talking like what he says means something else that he thinks is funny. Only nobody else gets it but him."

"Oh yeah. Definitely. But, I don't think he means anything by it. It's more like he's entertaining himself, you know? It's like he's inside his head and enjoying what he's seeing. It's the way his mind works. Must have something to do with his former job."

"So what did he used to do?" asked Gerry.

"I don't know if I should tell you or not," she said, moving her coffee cup closer to her.

"Not important," he said.

"But getting back to his sense of humor, he thinks something's amusing, he says it. Lot of people don't get to do that. It's not nasty or mean, it's just, well, kind of dry and offhand, like he doesn't care if you heard it or not. He drives Max crazy sometimes because Max is used to getting the last word. He's been in charge for too long to change."

"But, you trust Springer, right?"

"Yes," she said. "Yes I do."

He nodded his head as if deciding something.

She uncrossed her legs and watched his eyes trace the outline of her calves. "Why are you asking these questions? I want you not to shoot Max."

"Maybe I won't," he said. "Haven't decided."

She re-crossed her legs. Slowly. Leaned back and considered him. "What do you mean 'haven't decided'?"

He shrugged. "Sometimes things can go another way. Depends on the way things fall."

"How are things falling?"

He smiled a very brief and very small smile. "Picking up."

She cocked her head at him. "Can I ask you a personal question?"

"Depends on what it is?"

"Do you like your line of work?"

"I'm good at it."

"That's not what I asked, 'are you good at it?' " Not believing she was asking this stuff. But it was exciting. She leaned forward slightly and rested her chin on the back of her wrist. "Do you like it?"

"It's work. I'm good at it. Pays good. I wear good clothes. What else is there?"

"But you're tired of it. Right?"

He rubbed a scar on the back of his hand. "Maybe. Sure, why not? Everybody gets tired of their job, don't they? Sooner or later. Don't know what it has to do with anything."

I knew it, she thought. Wait until she told Max. See if he made fun of her, what did he call it? *Omniscient insight*, that's what he called it and then gave her that patronizing look, like all knowledge was going to die with him.

"You want something to go with your coffee?" Gerry asked her. "You know, cookies or something? They got some of those fancy cookies here." He looked around the place, nice little place made up like a Swiss chalet and then looked down at his coffee.

"No. Thank you. You seem a little uncomfortable."

"I'm not uncomfortable. I just don't get to sit down and talk with nice people all that often."

She felt her face burning. "Thank you. That's very sweet of you."

He shrugged. "So, if things work out you mind if I call you sometime?"

"Oh . . . I don't know if . . . that is—"

He waved a hand. "Forget it. It was a dumb question."

"No it wasn't. If you don't, you know . . . I don't know how to say this I guess. But, if you don't do what you've been hired to do, with Max, that is, then things might be different."

He looked at her. Nodded his head a couple of times. He had nice eyes, she thought. "Okay," he said. "I'll give that some thought."

She smiled. He smiled back.

"Secret Service," she said.

"What?"

"Cole was a Secret Service agent at one time."

He nodded his head slowly. "That makes sense."

When Springer returned to his room he called Bruce back in Aspen.

"Hey, Springs," Bruce said. "Glad you called. That lady cop was here looking for you. Called too. She mentioned interstate flight and other cop shit. You'd better get back here. Said your ass was in a sling if you left the state."

"Did she seem at all concerned? Or, maybe like she was harboring a secret longing for my return?"

"It's more like she wants to put you inside and laugh while the cons are raping you."

Springer laughed to himself. "She's messing with you, Bruce. The assault beef isn't a big enough deal to attract a high-speed badge like Ryder." What was her interest, then? Still interested in Max? Something else?

"I don't know, man. I like her but she's got this, I don't know, this aura about her, you know? Puts out these vibrations."

"She's a cop, Bruce. Cops make people nervous. They do it on purpose. You've got to get over that New Age crap. She hasn't got any aura, she's just a cop."

"I don't know. She's spooky. She comes on nice but she's got this tone, subtle, that lets you know not to cross her."

"Don't ascribe too much mystery to her. I'll be back there within forty-eight hours."

It was *time* to come back. For one thing, he wanted to see Tobi

Ryder again. There it was. First time he had admitted it to himself. Also, he had just gotten everything straight with Gerry Nugent. But, as usual, Max was screwing things up with his stubbornness and his unwillingness to take directions—directions made for Max's own good. Protecting politicians was easier. At least they understood what they were up against.

"I know where Max is now," said Nugent, earlier in the evening when Springer had sat down at the table in the bar. "A working girl gave me his location. Called one up to his room and used your name. Cost me five C's but it's worth it to see the look on your face right now." Nugent looked pleased, though he didn't smile. "So you got new problems."

"What'd you do with Ricky Jade?" asked Springer.

"You sure you want to know?"

"Probably not."

"I didn't do him."

"That's decent of you."

"He's your problem, now."

Springer looked at the defensive scar on Nugent's hand and said, "Why's that?"

"I subcontracted the work on Max." Nugent sat back and smiled his one-sixteenth of an inch smile. "I don't like what you tell me or you try to dance me around or fuck me over, and Ricky finishes Max. Maybe you, too."

"What about Jade's contract on you?"

"Got that figured."

"What if you like what I say?"

"Then I pull Ricky off until the deal's done."

"When the deal's done what about Ricky?"

"I pay 'im and he goes away."

"What if he gets greedy?"

"Then he disappears off the earth."

Springer nodded at the waitress and ordered Jack Daniels and water. He could hear the lounge singer butchering "Games People Play." Could hear the noise of the pits and the slots pinging and scrolling. Losers hoping to be winners. He waited until the waitress returned with the drink before speaking.

Springer said, "You know, my alternative might be to take you out and then Ricky. Maybe not in that order."

"Most guys don't say shit like that to me. I don't think you can do that, but watching you, I know you could come closer than most so it's something I need to keep in mind. But, it'll go better you don't mention it again."

"You sure Ricky'll stay hitched if things go bad? He heard me say that we were partners."

Nugent nodded. "Yeah, you thought that was clever on your part thinking he'll go back and put the word on the street that I'm with you." He shrugged. "Guys that fuck up confuse clever with smart. But you're no dummy. That's why I'm going to listen to what you say. Not because you boxed me in and not because you're holding shit over me, but because I think you're quick and smart and you got nerve. I don't think you scare and I don't think you go at things without thinking them out. You try to come on as spontaneous with the comedian act but I'm thinking you do that to throw people off. You calculate things. I don't think you make a move you haven't already considered the possibilities. You read people pretty good."

"So, what are you saying?" asked Springer.

"I'm throwing in with you. That's what I'm saying. For all of it. Ricky's just insurance. I figure a Secret Service operative knows how to plan things."

Springer looked at him.

"Don't worry about it. I don't care if you were in the fucking CIA. And, you're right about one thing." He sat back and looked at his watch. "I want out of the life."

Springer nodded. Smiled. He picked up his drink and gestured at Nugent. "Here's to changing the routine."

They ordered more drinks. Nugent lit a cigarette. A woman from another table gave him a look of disapproval but he stared at her until she looked away.

"You ever kill anybody?" Nugent asked.

"I'm not sure."

"What kinda answer's that?"

"Got in a firefight once in Iraq. Ran into a squad of Iraqi regulars. We exchanged fire. It happened quick." He took a drink, looked at his hands. "They ran off and left two bodies behind."

"And you think you may've killed them?"

Springer shrugged. "I was the best shot."

"Doesn't always matter."

"I was alone, too. So that could be a factor."

Gerry Nugent, hit man, leaned away and considered him. "You are a fucking question mark, aren't you? You ever give out information that isn't . . ." He waved his arms in the air as if trying to conjure something up. "What's the word? Ambiguous?"

"The guys you killed. How'd you feel about that?"

"What do you mean, how'd I feel?"

"Feel guilty?"

"The guys I whacked were dirtbags and low-lifes. I never killed no citizen."

"Law enforcement people?"

Shook his head. "No cops either."

"How would you feel if you did?"

Nugent took a drag off his cigarette. He looked at the woman who disapproved. He smiled, exhaled the smoke in a direction away from her and ground out the butt. "Different," he said. "I'd feel different."

"What about Max?"

"He's part of why I want out I guess. Rather not shoot him. Hadn't thought about it until now. You charge for these therapy sessions?"

"It's a package deal."

It was time to tell him, Springer told himself. What he had in mind. How he planned to get Max off the hook. How to get Nugent out of the life. And, how to get both of them a pile of cash.

"How good is Max at laundering cash?" Springer asked.

"He's the best."

"How badly did it hurt Nicky T when Max wanted out?"

Nugent shrugged. "Wasn't traumatic or anything. Nicky can line up somebody else. But Max kept the cops out of the picture. Knew how to litter the paper trail. He was subtle, knew what the red flags were and avoided them. Made it tough for the cops and the IRS to track it down. Impossible even. Little more dangerous if

Nicky used somebody new. I mean he can get somebody else, but it won't be somebody as smart as Max. Guys like Nicky don't like things coming at them out of the dark. He can handle the pimps and the badasses, but IRS accountants at his door give him the runs. That's why he has Max. Max is smart and tough but he knows smart ain't enough and that thinking you're smart can get you in trouble."

"He doesn't act very smart sometimes."

"Maybe about some things. But not about money."

"What if you tell him that Max has reconsidered and wants to do business again? You think you can talk Tortino into using Max?"

Nugent thought about it. Fished a cigarette out of a pack of Marlboros, tapped the filter on the table top to settle the tobacco. "Maybe." He lit the cigarette. "But Nicky wants to be a made guy. He can taste it. He's connected and a good earner but he ain't been straightened out yet, you know?"

"What's that got to do with Max?"

"If the bosses think Nicky can be shit on by a Jew banker-type then Nicky'll think that'll keep him from getting recommended." He moved in his seat. "But what if I *can* get Nicky to go along? How do you and I come out if Max goes back into business with Nicky?" He took a sip of cognac.

"You and me steal the money."

Nugent coughed like the cognac or the smoke went down the wrong pipe.

"The fuck is wrong with you? You want to scam Nicky out of some money? What did I just say to you? Steal it? From a connected guy? Then what? We kill everybody on the West Coast? That it? Because we'll have to."

"No. We just kill Max." He took a sip of his drink, smiled and nodded at Nugent. "And you."

Nugent scratched the scar on the back of his hand. Looked around the bar. "You're not on something are you?"

"I'm fine."

"So if Max and I are dead how do I come out on this? You don't mind my asking, do you, because it seems like it might be tougher to for me to spend the money if I'm dead."

"We just make it look like you're dead. If Nicky thinks you

and Max are dead, then he'll have no reason to come after either of you."

"Nicky'd have to see that. You can't call the guy up and say nobody can find me. He'll have to be there or see the corpse. Especially if he ends up with money missing."

Springer nodded.

Nugent sat back and looked sideways at Springer. "You can do that?"

Springer finished off his drink. "Already figured out how. I just need you to arrange a meeting for me with Nicky Tortino."

"That's all, huh? You want a sit down with Nicky?"

"That's it."

"Yeah, sure, why not? I mean what the fuck? You didn't ask me to whack the Easter Bunny. You didn't ask for a personal meeting with Jesus Christ, just a meeting with Nicky T, who'll fucking shit when I ask."

"Tell him I can deliver Max and get some of Max's money, a lot of Max's money, and give it to him."

"He'll ask why you'll do this. What's in it for you?"

"Sixty-forty split."

"Sixty for who?"

"Me."

"Pretty stiff cut. Nicky likes things in his favor."

"Gives me a strong opening bid and I can negotiate down to an even cut, make him think I'm a tough bargainer and that he bargained me down. Give in too easy he'll think it's a setup." Springer paused to sip his drink. "I'm a former fed, remember?"

"I see where you're going. It could work, we both don't get killed. We scamming Max?"

"No. Just Nicky."

"So, how do we get Max to give us his money?"

"We ask him."

"That'll be something."

"He wants to live, he'll have to bait the trap."

"Max likes his money. More'n he likes himself."

"I don't think so. He wants to stay around to spend it, he needs to get some insight into why this will work."

Now all he had to do was convince Max, thought Springer, which might not be easy.

"Tell me you did not ice Charley Wheels," said Nicky Tortino, yelling into the phone. "Please tell me you didn't do that."

Ray Dean squirmed on the motel bed, and said, "Hey, Nicky, I'm not sure this phone is okay. Maybe—"

"Shut the fuck up and answer me. And, if you think the phone's not right then don't use names, you dumb shit. What did you do with Charley Wheels?"

"Things got kinda out of hand, boss," said Ray Dean. "You see, first Auteen ran over the guy's bushes and shit and then—"

"You did shoot 'im, didn't you, you stupid fuck? What is it with you? How is it you keep finding the worst way to go about things? It's like a special ability with you guys. I went to a lot of trouble to get permission to make this move and now, thanks to you two bozos, I gotta start all over."

"Wait a minute boss, let me explain." Ray Dean had thought over his cover story before calling Nicky. He hated to lie to Nicky, not because he minded lying but because if Nicky knew he was being lied to then you might as well book a seat on the next moonshot. "The guy threw down on us. He was all wired up on some shit, he's a fucking hype or something, and was talking crazy and then he gets this moose rifle or something and starts threatening us with it. So I had to do 'im. Auteen'll tell you."

Ray Dean looked at Auteen, who made a face and rolled his eyes. Look at 'im sitting there, eating Cheetos outta one of those four-dollar bags, his fingers all yellow with that shit. Yellow smears on his pants where he'd been wiping them off. Fucking Auteen.

"So, how're you doing on the Jew?" asked Nicky.

"Can't find him. He's not at his house and he's not at any of the hotels in town. I think he left town."

"What do you mean he left town?"

"He's coming back. His stuff's still at his place."

"Is Gerry there yet?"

Ray Dean felt his ass tighten up. "Gerry Knucks?" Auteen threw up his arms, acting pissed off. Ray Dean gave him the finger.

"No, Jerry fucking Lewis, moron. I'm sending him out there because I think you're so fucking simple we need to have a telethon for your dumb ass. Yeah, I sent him out there. Should be there by now."

"Ain't seen him." Why did he send Knucks? Said he was going to wait two days. Lying sack of shit. The last thing he wanted was Gerry Knucks hanging around. For all he knew Nicky sent Knucks to whack him and Auteen. This wasn't good. Auteen was shaking his head.

"Well that's weird," said Nicky. "Something ain't right. I don't know why I'm talking to you about it. Nothing you could do about it even if you knew how. Which you don't. Have him call me the minute he gets there. You got it?"

"Yeah, I got it." Good, he wanted him to let Nicky know when Knucks got there. A good sign. Maybe he wasn't taking a run at them.

"And listen. Don't do nothing stupid until he gets there. What am I saying? You do anything, it'll be stupid. Don't do nothing. Go tie yourself up or give yourself an Excedrin P.M. and lie down or something. And don't shoot nobody either or I'll personally come out there and rip your nuts off. Y'understand?"

Ray Dean started to say he understood, but he heard the phone click in his ear.

He turned to Auteen and said, "Nicky's pissed."

"You think? And all the time I be thinking maybe the man call us saying how happy he be to have us work for him. What with you killing everybody in sight when you not getting your toe shot off and all. What did he say about Gerry Knucks?"

"Said he was on his way here."

"Aw shit, man." Auteen made a face and his voice was high-pitched. "See? I fucking told you this would happen. Now you got me in on the lie to the man. Fucking Nicky's crazy, too. All you fucking white people are crazy. Auteen crazy to listen to you."

"Man, go wash your hands. I'm about to fucking puke looking at that yellow shit on your hands."

"Man, who died and left your skinny ass in charge? We *gonna* die though, we fuck up enough with Gerry Knucks. Be your fault too."

"You know," said Ray Dean, thinking about it, "we're going about this all wrong."

"Naw." Auteen shook his big hand at him. "Don't be thinking about nothing now. So far you thinking has been way messed up."

Ray Dean had been thinking a lot about shooting Charlemagne. Kept playing the whole thing over in his mind. Pow, and the guy shuts up. Acting like Ray Dean wasn't nobody and suddenly it was a different story. Bust a cap and this guy isn't talking no more. He remembered shooting the homo. It was too quick and he had to run away. The guy back home, in Texas, that one went bad. All he had was a cheap .25 pistol that only put a little hole in the guy's shoulder, then misfired before he could line up a good second shot. Guy was screaming and running out into the street bleeding. Did it in front of *witnesses* if you could believe it. But this last one was nice. He could see himself doing Gerry Knucks. Gerry giving him that fish-eye look like Ray Dean was something stuck to the bottom of his shoe or something. Fucking Gerry. If Gerry wasn't around anymore then Nicky'd give Ray Dean the good work. No more collecting change out of vending machines or rousting gamblers who owed nickels and dimes. He'd be the man. Yeah, he could see himself doing Gerry Knucks.

"Maybe Gerry Knucks's coming is a good thing."

"Yeah," said Auteen. "Like getting cancer is a good thing 'cause you won't die in a plane crash."

He could see himself doing Auteen, too, the guy didn't shut up.

"I don't believe this," said Max, his arms out, when Springer and Gerry Nugent entered the hotel room. The fucking guy who was hired to *kill* him, for crissakes. "What the fuck is wrong with you?" He slapped his forehead with his palm. "Are you a hopeless mental case? This guy wants to shoot me. He gets *paid* to shoot me." Max started laughing. Crazy laughter. "I mean you tell me to hide out in the hotel room, 'Don't go out, Max, don't call room service, Max, don't stand near the window, Max.' That's what you tell me and now you bring the guy right in here." He unbuttoned his shirt and pointed at his chest, gray hairs peeking out over his silk undershirt. "Here you go, just let me have it. Right here. Let's get it over with."

"He seems upset," said Gerry to Springer.

Springer exhaled. "Max, cut out the theatrics. There's no—"

"No wait!" said Max, interrupting. "Why don't *you* shoot me? Yeah, that's it. That way you could charge me for the bullets again. Shit. You bring the guy right *here*." Max's voice was getting high-pitched. Max looked at the guy who was supposed to protect him from the guy standing there not ten feet away like they were college roommates or something.

Springer scratched his temple and said, "He already knew where you were, Max."

"What?"

"Cherry Blossom ring a bell for you?"

"How do you know about . . . hey, you're not going to tell Suzi, are you?"

"No, Max," said Springer. "I figure soon enough, you'll be able to screw that up all by yourself."

"Did you pat him down?" asked Max. "How do you know he's not carrying?"

"He's not carrying."

"Oh? You got X ray vision like Superman, now?"

"I'm not going to kill you, Max," said Nugent.

Max looked at him. He turned his head sideways. "You're not?"

"No."

"Why not?"

"Why not?" said Gerry, as if the question mystified him. He looked at Springer. "He wants to know 'why not?' Not, 'good, you're not going to shoot me.' Not, 'that's good to hear.' No. He asks 'why not?' Nobody else like you, Max."

Max looked at Springer. "You fucking bring Gerry Knucks into my fucking room?"

"Nugent," said Nugent.

"What?" said Max, making a face.

"Call me Gerry Nugent. That's what I want to be called from now on."

Max shook his head and stared off, looking at nothing. "What's going on?"

"Sit down, Max," said Springer, "and I'll explain it to you."

There was a noise outside the hotel room door and then the doorknob turned. Springer reached inside his jacket. The door opened and Suzi was standing there with a couple of plastic grocery sacks in her hand.

"What's he doing here?" she asked.

"Springer's bringing his work home," said Max. He looked at Springer. "He figures it saves time to bring the killers here, then they don't have to go looking around all over Vegas. You have to look at it from a time-efficiency viewpoint, that's all."

She smiled. "Well, it's good to have company. I brought some champagne and some cheese. How are you doing, Gerry?"

"I'm fine."

Max stared at her, as if his autonomic nervous system had just shut down. Then, recovering, he sat down, heavily, and said, "I'm not believing any of this. This is *Alice in Wonderland* shit. Freaking goys're all crazy. My mom told me, I wouldn't listen. No, I gotta be the punch card for the entire Rocky Mountain shiksa society. Five thousand years of suffering ain't enough for you people?"

"You think it's bad now," said Nugent. "Wait until he explains what he's got in mind."

CHAPTER

Nineteen

"DAVID'S IN TOWN," TOBI SAID, SIPPING FROM HER REGU-
lar Colombian coffee, sitting in the specialty coffee shop. She didn't
tell Summers about the altercation she had with David. Afterwards,
David tried to play it off by asking her to dinner, but turned sheep-
ish when she said to him, "You're such a tough guy. Instead of
dinner maybe you can slap me around, make yourself feel better."
Then he'd left. When she got up the next morning she noticed the
bruise on her wrist, that she now had covered with a long-sleeved
shirt with lacy cuffs.

The waitress asked Tobi if she wanted some pastry and she
shook her head.

Special Agent Summers was deciding whether to have a French
vanilla cappuccino or a caffé latte, making the waitress stand there
waiting for him to decide. Might be too much sugar after he just
had a chocolate eclair, she thought. Summers always worrying
about what he looked like. Like David. Why did she always end up
with these juvenile cretins? "What's Dave up to?" he asked her.

"What he's always up to," she said. "Annoying me and trying
to insinuate himself into my life."

"There's worse things."

"For who?"

"Have you heard from your boyfriend, lately?"

She gave him a look. Knowing what he was going to say.

Jack said, "You know. Springer. I heard he skipped bail."

"Here's a news flash, Jack. He's not my boyfriend, he hasn't
skipped, and you've graduated to full prickdom. Congratulations."

The waitress said, "I can come back if you need some time." Looking uncomfortable.

"That'll be fine," Tobi said, then after the waitress left, she turned to Summers and said, "And, skipping bail on a minor assault charge isn't a news maker. Springer will be back."

"You know something? Have you had contact with him?"

She stared at him. "Get the decaf, Jack. You've had too much caffeine."

"Why're you so touchy this morning?" He signaled the waitress and ordered the house blend. Asks her to go through the whole list and then orders the house blend.

"I'm going to squeeze Springer," said Summers. He pushed the sweetener bowl and the creamer bottle together with his hands. "I'm gonna squeeze him hard until he spills."

Here's a guy really needs to stop watching *NYPD Blue*. "How about just saying we're going to try to get Springer to talk to us and provide information? Simple, direct, doesn't sound stupid."

He took his hands off the condiments, sat back in his chair, and laughed. "Funny, hearing a state cop who works a yuppie theme park say something like that. You could learn a lot from me." He paused and raised his eyebrows. "A lot."

Listen to this guy, like he was in a movie or something.

"Get over yourself, Jack," she said.

"You're touchy because I'm bearing down on your boyfriend."

Her turn to laugh. "Please."

"That's it, isn't it? You're wondering what it would be like to be with him."

"The fact he doesn't talk in television dialogue would be a nice change."

He scratched the side of his neck. "I've got something on him. Something that puts him in my hands. He cooperates or takes a fall."

She felt a pin-prick of apprehension along her shoulders. "We could use a little clarity here. What are you saying?"

Now he was smiling. What an arrogant bastard. "You don't like that, do you?" he said.

She didn't, but she wasn't telling him. "I'm not listening to you about this."

"He's a user," he said. "Coke. I got a tip that he's got some stashed and I'm going to use it to leverage him."

"He's not a user."

He put his hands out to his side, palms up, and shrugged. Winked.

"You shithead," she said. "You planted something, didn't you?"

"Good cops don't have to do that."

"But mediocre ones with prick diplomas do."

"I need the information he's got."

"Maybe he doesn't have any."

"A Secret Service agent who's protecting a dirty millionaire from a mob hit?"

"It's not the mafia. It's a slimy San Francisco wannabe."

"Tortino is connected," said Summers. "My information says Tortino is working to be a made man."

"So how does Springer figure in? So far you've got a bunch of vague information and loose connections."

"You think the guy doesn't know anything. But he knew enough to blow town."

"He'll be back."

"And how do you know that? I find that intriguing."

"That's because you're easily intrigued."

"What do you know that you're not telling me?"

"You're obsessing. You're so jealous of this guy—which, just for the record, I'm not dating . . . you either for that matter—that you can't think straight. You're reading him the wrong way. You don't have any feel for people. He's not a drug dealer and he's not a user. I find out you planted anything and I'll personally arrest you. That Gestapo crap you think is cute is just symptomatic of the meltdown that characterizes your narcissism."

He smiled. "And you make fun of the way I talk."

She said, "When are you going to realize that we enforce the laws, we don't make them?"

"Would you relax?" he said. "I'm not going to put the guy inside."

"Inside what? An envelope? Inside a box? Once, just once, Jack, say 'put him in jail' or 'arrest him.' "

"All right," he said. "I'm not going to arrest him. But he's in with Shapiro and we could use him to close Max out and maybe force Nicky Tortino out into the open."

Which was a possibility, she thought. Once in a while Summers had an actual thought. And he really was a good cop when he wasn't on stage. "What if he won't cooperate? He strikes me as the type who rarely does what other people design for him and nearly always does what you don't expect."

He raised his eyebrows and smiled. "You go for the mysterious types?"

She closed her eyes and turned away.

Could you believe this guy?

Nicky Tortino clipped the end of the Cuban cigar. A Hoyo de Monterrey double corona. Hard to get. He had a guy, a pornographer down in the district, that he had a piece of, that brought the Cubans in for him. Made the guy run customs for him. Guy was happy to do it like Nicky was fucking royalty or something.

Nicky was checking on his new boat, *The Bella Donna*, a big cruiser, with two big diesels, two screws, cabin, galley, sundeck. Cost Nicky about fifty G's. Woulda cost more but the guy owed him. Joey "the Neck" Guardino got hold of him on the ship's phone. Joey was the top captain of the San Francisco crew. It was a good call.

"You been making good money for us," said Guardino. "You been keeping a low profile. You handled the chinks. People are impressed downtown. Your name comes up. I'm thinking maybe I can recommend you for that thing we talked about before. Maybe get you straightened out once and for all. What do you think about that?"

Nicky knew what he meant. Guardino was telling him that he was going to be a made wiseguy. What he'd always dreamed about. It would change the way he operated. More freedom. He would probably make less money, initially, but he could do what he wanted, go where he wanted without having to ask permission.

"You know that's what I want."

"I need somebody I can trust to do my business. You're like my brother. Nobody can tell you to do something they don't ask me."

"I don't know nothing you don't tell me."

Guardino said, "I've got a big deal coming down. Can you lay off some cash for me?"

"Anything, you know that."

"How's it you know you can do this, I don't tell you how much?"

"Because you tell me you want it done and that's good enough," said Nicky. "You say you want it done and I do it or you wouldn't ask."

"Good. That's good. But what's this bullshit with this Charlemagne character? What's with your people? That's kinda unnerving. I thought we had an understanding on that."

"Guy got heavy with my people. No choice in the matter."

Guardino went silent on the other end. He did shit like that from time to time. It made Nicky's sphincter tighten up when he did that. Guy did it on purpose. Kept you guessing. Kept you on edge.

Then, Guardino said, "It happens. We can get that straightened out with the people out there though, right?"

"I'm sending somebody already. He should be there." He needed to get hold of Gerry, have him straighten this out. Where was that sonuvabitch anyway? Gerry was acting weird lately. Did he ice the chinks and not tell him? He'd suspected that Gerry had done stuff like that before. He asked him about it once and Gerry said, "I don't tell you and they call you to the witness stand, you don't know nothing. Can't perjure yourself. You even pass the lie detector." Which made sense, except with Nicky this close to being a made wiseguy he couldn't have Gerry whacking people without going through the proper channels. And he was out of touch. Usually Gerry called every day and now it had been forty-eight hours without a call. "He'll talk to people, get it straightened out."

"You still working with the Jew?"

Here it comes, thought Nicky. Fucking Max was making his life difficult. Guardino had mentioned it before, even suggesting that Nicky take care of it personally or have Knucks take care of it. But it was hot here in town now, what with the problem with the chinks and all and Nicky's guy inside SFPD told him the feds were sniffing around his operation and watching Max so Nicky had to keep Knucks around until some of that got fixed. Nicky couldn't move on some things with the heat watching him.

"I can."

"You can?" said Guardino. "What's that? I heard he left the fucking reservation. You better secure him."

"That's what my guys're working on."

"May want to slow down some. I need this problem I'm talking about cleaned up. It's large. And, it's sizzling. You tell nobody we talked about this, y'understand?"

How much was Guardino talking about and what did he mean asking about Max? Did he want Nicky to use him again? Or was he testing him? He said secure him. Whack him? Or, bring him back into the operation? You never knew with these guys. Always talking in code in case the phone was tapped.

"We need the Jew? That's what you're telling me?"

"One more time, maybe," said Guardino. "Or, find out how to do this thing and then let him go. It's a tough thing, but he's making you look bad."

Let him go. Kill him. But he wanted to use Max or just have Max tell him how it works.

Then Guardino said, "You can do it either way you want, as long as you cool down this fever we got going right here. This is large. Big enough that maybe you need to take a personal hand and go see the guy. The people I'm talking to want to know everything's all right."

So Nicky could use Max then take him out. Nicky was still pissed at Max. Max had got to acting like Nicky had bad breath or something even before the cancer thing. Which was a hell of a thing. Guy thinks he's got cancer so he grows a pair, gets ballsy with them and then runs out and hires a gun when he finds out it ain't true.

What kind of appreciation was that?

But if Nicky could launder Guardino's money and then ice Max it would show he could get things done. The money would be taken care of, then the loose ends would be tied off. Nothing to worry about. The guys Guardino talked to would like that.

He needed to talk to Gerry, see what he thinks.

Where the fuck was Gerry anyway?

CHAPTER

Twenty

MAX WHINED ALL THE WAY BACK TO ASPEN. HE WHINED about having to get up five A.M., whined about riding in a Chevy and the crummy seats he said were hard on his back.

Max wanted a Lincoln or a Mercedes, Springer told him they didn't need to call attention to themselves by driving an expensive vehicle. Springer had decided against flying back, which Max wanted to do, as the car would be harder to track than a charter jet that would leave a trail of flight plans, departure times, and a passenger list. Springer thought about the female cop tracing him to Vegas, about running into Nugent in the airport. A car gave him some mobility. Some room to move. Also, he didn't have to ditch his gun this time.

This thing doesn't even have a CD player, said Max. Springer said, yeah, but it had air conditioning. Max arguing it was only fifty degrees before seeing that Springer was playing with him, again. Max not liking the restaurants they saw and having to stop at five or six places until he found one that would let him smoke cigars as Suzi wouldn't let him smoke in the car. Then both of them fighting about that.

Oh yeah, it was an enjoyable ten hours.

Springer envied Nugent who had flown ahead to Aspen. Nugent went ahead so he could find Ray Dean and Auteen and keep them off Max until they could contact Tortino and pull him into their scam. Which is what it was, a scam, no way around it. But it made Springer smile to think about turning it around on a regulation thug like Nicky T.

Scamming the mob. Could be a book title.

It made Max anxious, Springer could tell, thinking about Springer's plan, which made Max drink and they had to stop and get a bottle of Maalox which Max drank along with a six-pack of Beck's. The Beck's, of course, came in bottles, so they had to make another stop to get an opener. Max asking questions about the scam then swilling Maalox and chasing it down with Beck's, making Springer wince whenever he watched Max do that. But Springer understood why the guy was nervous. He was being asked to deal with a known gangster, then trust a piano-playing ex-Secret Service agent and a hit man who, only a few hours before, had come to kill him.

That was a lot for anyone.

"So, you're saying I contact Nicky T and tell him I want to come back," asked Max. "That it?"

"No, Gerry does that," said Springer. "You just be ready to negotiate when Nicky calls."

"Negotiate what?"

"I'm going to be your go-between. I'll talk to Nicky, tell him you want to come back but you're reluctant to trust him after he sent Auteen and Ray Dean to kill you. Then when they contact you, through me and Gerry, that's when you negotiate for the opportunity to show Nicky you're a stand-up guy and can be trusted. But you have to do it in a way that makes the guy think you're scared."

"*Think* I'm scared? I *am* scared."

"You'll be more convincing."

"This ain't gonna work," Max said, then tipped the Maalox bottle. Making a face which Springer could see in the rearview mirror. Max sat in the back, not understanding why he couldn't sit in front. Springer tried to explain that if something happened he wouldn't have to climb over Max and Suzi to get into position and that Max could get on the floor of the car if something went down. Max was saying, that ain't gonna happen. Springer telling him that he had to deal with possibilities instead of what might not happen. Suzi telling Max to shut up and do what he was told. Max throwing his hands in the air.

And now Max said, "This ain't gonna work."

"Yes it is," said Springer. "Because we're going to entice Nicky."

"Entice him?" Then, turning to Suzi, Max said, "And you think this guy is smart? What's with this enticement thing? Like we were on *Fantastic Island* with that Fernando Lamas guy and the midget and we got a couple of wishes or something."

"Fantasy Island," said Suzi, correcting Max. "Not 'Fantastic Island.' "

"And it was Ricardo Montalban, not Lamas," said Springer.

"What? You write for the *TV Guide* or something? And, entice Nicky with what?"

"Your money."

"My money?"

Springer nodded, looking in the rearview.

"My fucking money."

"I think you're starting to get it."

"Why we gotta give him my money?"

"You prefer dead?"

"I prefer to know what the hell is going on."

"Look, guys like Tortino aren't motivated by trust or friendship," said Springer. "They're motivated by greed and paranoia. He thinks he might get something out of the deal, it'll appeal to him more. If he thinks it's too easy then he might shy away, so I tell him I'm taking a cut of the money."

"A cut of the money. My money?"

"To con a guy like Tortino I have to convince him I'm on the dodge and trying to take advantage of you. I give in right away he'll think something's up. So, I've got to dangle the money, your money, in front of him so he'll go along. Keeping his mind off me and you and keep it on this sweet deal where he comes out large and still has to pay me. But, in his mind he still comes out ahead."

Max moved around in the back and the seat made a "squirching" sound. "So, what happens if Nicky decides to let me clean up his money, takes my money, then decides to whack me anyway?"

"That's what I'm hoping he'll try to do."

Max shaking his head now, looking up with his palms raised.

Saying some words in Hebrew. Then saying, "So, you're hoping Nicky'll take a run at me so you can what? Pick 'im off from behind a rock? Take a video of him killing me so you can get a conviction?"

Springer said, "See, I knew you'd like it."

Springer took Suzi and Max to the Aspen Ritz-Carlton which finally made Max happy. Then, Springer was going to Pitkin-Sardi airport to pick up Max's Jag and turn in the rental. Before he headed for the airport he stopped by his place to check his mail. He leafed through the mail as he got out his house key. A couple of bills, a flyer from a sweepstakes house telling him he may have won three million dollars, which he was sure he could blow paying bills, and building a new place. An Eddie Bauer catalog. More bills. Then, a letter from his landlord telling him he was selling the house. Springer had a month to find something else. Let's see, no cash flow from his business, no place to live, and the most expensive place to live in the whole country. What could be better?

Unless, of course, you factor in thugs and an assault charge—then it was near perfect. Springer, you have mastered living richly.

He entered the house, smelling its neutral smell, and feeling its familiar vibrations. Not much longer, though. But climbing the stairs, something didn't feel right. He didn't buy into karma or intuition but something felt out of sync, feeling it the way a deer feels a disturbance in his woods.

Was somebody inside? He had his gun with him and he pulled it out now, chambering a round.

He looked at his door. No scratch marks, but then, he hadn't locked it up when he left. Not many burglars in Aspen made less than he did. Hadn't thought to check the front door. He eased the apartment door open, the gun sweeping in front of him and looked down at the carpet. He kneeled down to get a better look. Was he imagining it or did some of the powder look fresh?

A quick check satisfied him that he was alone. Nobody waiting to spring out and blast him. He was almost disappointed.

He put his mail on the rolltop and got the vacuum cleaner

out to clean up the powder. As he unwound the cord, which wrapped vertically up the arm of the apparatus he noted that it had been wound *clockwise*. Springer always wound things, cords, garden hoses, anything like that, counterclockwise. Somebody had been here.

He checked his room, looking under the bed. He pulled out the case underneath. The nightscope and rifle were still there. There was no money in the apartment. What were they looking for?

He made a systematic search. Bedroom, bathroom, living room. Swept it a section at a time. After an hour he decided nothing had been removed. Maybe they weren't looking for something in the apartment. Maybe they, whoever it was, left something. He checked the phone, taking it apart, looking for a bug. Looked inside the lamps, under the furniture. Inside the piano. Nothing.

Why were they here?

He sat down at the desk and gave it some thought. Here's what he thought. He thought he needed a beer. The rental could go back tomorrow. He picked up and headed for the Caprice.

Gerry Nugent arrived at Glenwood Springs Memorial Airport at 10:55 A.M. Rocky Mountain Time. He got off the jet, rented a white Pontiac (they didn't have any Tauruses), and found a pay phone to call Nicky. He hadn't talked to Nicky for a couple of days so he expected the guy to be all churned-up and having to do his pissed-off boss act. He wasn't disappointed.

"Where the fuck you been?" Nicky said. "You can't believe what's going on here. There's going to be a change in management at the top. Mostelli's gone. I got people calling me, asking about you, it's fucking nerve-wracking here, and I got to act like a jilted bitch, not knowing what the fuck you're doing."

"Your friend in Chinatown sent someone."

"What do you mean sent someone? Wait, call me at this number in five minutes." Nicky gave him the number which Gerry figured was a pay phone. Nicky was as bad as the wiseguys now. Can't talk on the phone, always wanted to meet in the street. Asking about anybody new who showed up in his orbit, afraid they might be FBI plants. But if Carmine Mostelli, the big boss, was dead he had reason to worry. Gerry waited four minutes and forty-seven seconds and dialed the number, Nicky picking up.

"Who'd he send?" said Nicky, first thing out of his mouth. Not hello or nothing.

"Ricky Jade."

"Where's Jade now?"

"Iced." Which was like a joke, really. The two imbeciles he had used to work on Jade had gone too far and Jade had checked out. He knew this when he'd talked to Springer, not wanting to tell him, make him think Jade was insurance in case Springer was playing him. But Gerry no longer thought that. The two guys asked Gerry what to do with him, did he want them to take him out to the desert and bury him? Gerry thought about it for a while before he came up with the answer.

"Wrap him up and take him down to the locker plant, rent a big box, and put him in it."

The guy said, "What? Are you fucking crazy?"

"Do what I say, huh?" Gerry had it in mind to send Kim Li a present.

He wanted word on the street that Jade was gone, but not just yet. And while he didn't like it that these two muscle-bound bozos had bitched the job, Gerry wasn't broken-hearted. Jade couldn't go back and tell Kim Li he couldn't get the job done, so he would have had to hang around until he popped Gerry and maybe even the girl, Suzi. Funny, it was thinking about the danger to the girl that made it all right for him. Besides, maybe he had some use for Jade yet.

So, that's why he made the joke about "iced" so Nicky would think Gerry had wasted him. "So, Jade is gone. Like the two chinks, right?"

Nugent ignored that. "I found Max in Vegas."

"Vegas? What the . . . You put 'im down?"

"Jade bitched things by showing up at the wrong time."

"So, where's Max now?"

Gerry thought about it. Considered lying to him about it. Should he tell him Max was back in Aspen? If he did, would Nicky put Ray Dean and Auteen on Max? While he was deciding, Nicky said, "Don't do Max. Not yet. Things have changed."

Gerry waited. Nicky was used to telling Gerry to go and do things and Gerry doing them, so questioning him might confuse the guy.

Gerry said, "So, what do you want me to do?"

"Find Max and tell him the heat's off. He comes back we forgive him."

Which meant Nicky needed something from Max. Probably a money deal. Which is exactly what Springer wanted. This was strange. Gerry had been deciding how to lead Nicky on, playing it over in his head and now the guy just volunteers to do what they wanted. But Gerry had to play it straight. React like he would if he wasn't in on the deal with Springer.

"Max ain't gonna believe that. He's gonna think we're setting him up."

"Convince him."

Gerry had to play this just right, as Nicky was a paranoid. Anything that didn't sound just right would send the guy right up the wall. Nicky wasn't the smartest guy in the world but he was a wary bastard. Guy had a sixth sense about things, like he *knew* ahead of time that something was going to happen. Gerry needed to be careful with him.

"I'm okay with letting Max off the hook, Nicky," Gerry said. "But, I'm not sure I can get close enough to him to tell him that. He's got the bodyguard and he's scared."

"What are you saying?"

"May take some time."

"Shit. Well . . . do what you gotta do and get back to me. And, don't fucking wait three days to call again. That makes shit crawl up my back and stuff. You know what it's like here without you around? Huh? Fucking Li's pissed and Joey the Neck wants things done. You know him. He wants it done right now. He wants it done fucking yesterday. And this shit he wants done is priority. Understand?"

"It'll get done," said Gerry.

"That's good to hear."

Gerry hung up. He needed to call the dynamic duo and tell them to chill. He called the motel number. Auteen answered. Gerry identified himself, told them to lay off Max.

"Why's that?" said Auteen.

"Because I told you to."

"Man, I don't mean nothin', askin'."

"Where is Max anyway?" Playing with the guy now.

"Haven't seen 'im."

At least he didn't lie. Ray Dean would have lied, pretended to know where Max was. "That's because he's been in Las Vegas."

"Yeah? Be wondering where the man went."

Gerry told Auteen to stay put with Ray Dean, not to leave the room until he got there, which could be a while. That would keep them out of his way and out of sight where they wouldn't be screwing everything up. Gerry had some things to do. Like go see Suzi. He hung up and walked away from the phone.

A woman, dressed in some weird shit he'd never seen before, hair too long for someone her age, and a ring on every finger of her left hand, came up and asked him if he was Gene Hackman. He looked at her for a minute.

"I look like I'm losing my hair to you?"

Ray Dean's toe, or where his damned toe used to be, was throbbing like a blue-ball hard-on. He had used up the prescription sample the doctor had given him. He had taken his last two Advils and was drinking Jim Beam straight from the bottle. He couldn't even get the new pair of boots on he bought to replace the damaged one, the thing hurt so bad. Worse than yesterday. Was it getting infected? It had been hurting worse since that bitch cop sat on him, making it bleed all over again. Was okay until then. Fucking cunt. Between her and the smart-ass guy that shot him, Ray Dean didn't know which he hated the worst. Before he left town he was going to pay one or both of them a visit and square things. Maybe shoot one of their toes off.

Ray Dean said, "Whyn't get off your ass and see if you can score me some Percs or some morphine. I'm dying here."

"Go get it your own self," said Auteen, munching carmel popcorn and drinking from a quart bottle of Colt 45. "Auteen be watch-ing TV now." Guy was watching some kind of Kung Fu movie on television. Ray Dean hated that shit, about worse than anything. Bunch of fucking short slant-eyed pussies who weighed about 120 pounds jumping around beating the shit out of an army of guys. It was bullshit. But not as bad as some three-hundred-pound asshole calling himself by his own first name and eating carmel popcorn.

"Fucking hurts, man. I can't even put on my boots it hurts so bad."

"It ain't nowhere near your heart, babe. You gone live. 'Sides, the way you popping Motrin and drinking whiskey I give you any-thing else you gonna fly off sideways into the i-onosphere."

This fucking guy, look at him, sitting there eating shit twenty-four hours a day. No wonder the sonuvabitch weighed three hundred pounds. "See, you don't know shit. I'm taking Advil, not Motrin."

"Advil is Motrin."

"The fuck you know about it?"

"More'n you. You don't even know Motrin is ibuprofen which is the same ingredient in Advil and Nuprin. It's like Tylenol is ace-tominophen."

"Yeah, so what's aspirin?"

"Aspirin's aspirin. Anything else I can help you with?"

"Yeah," said Ray Dean, taking another pill. His stomach was hurting from taking the Advil. "You can go out and get me some-thing for this fucking toe. Some Tums, too."

"Gerry Knucks said stay 'til he got here."

"That was ten hours ago."

"The man said stay, we stay."

"So, who the fuck is he?"

"He Gerry Knucks, the bad motherfucker. And he our boss."

"Nicky's our boss."

Auteen held up his hand. "Man, I ain't talking to you 'bout this no more. Now shut up, I'm trying to watch the flick. Whoa, bro, look at that." Excited now. Like a high school kid. "That little guy just did a three-sixty and kicked two guys in the face." He stood up and got in a stance. "You imagine what a muscular Afro-American male like me could do I could move like that?" He threw a side kick and swung his arms around like he was Chuck Norris instead of some fucking street punk who ate too much. "Shit. I'm tellin' you."

Ray Dean, pissed now, said, "You're scared of Gerry, that what you're saying?"

That got his attention. "Say what? Me scared? No. No way. But we got a job to do and we gotta do it."

"We don't need Gerry."

"We don't need 'im," said Auteen swinging his arms like those dipshits in those gangsta rap videos did, "but we got 'im."

"What if he wasn't around no more? Huh? Think about that. Then you'n me'd be Nicky's guns. More pay. More respect. A piece of the action maybe."

Auteen turned his head and shook a hand sideways, like motioning at someone to stay away. "Man, get your mind off that shit. We got enough to think about what with that bodyguard shootin' at us. Man, I like to shit when he stuck that gun to my ear and said, 'Try the pastrami.' Man's one cold dude."

"He said, 'try the corned beef.' "

Auteen cocked his head and put his hands down to his side. "Now you were there, right?"

"You told me he said, 'try the corned beef.' "

"The fuck difference do it make?"

Ray Dean shook his head like he had something in his ears. "Man, please go get me something for this toe."

"Okay. Make you a deal. I go get it but you gotta say 'try the pastrami.' "

"What? Are you fucking mental? That's it, you're fuckin' looney tunes."

Auteen put a hand to his ear. "I didn't hear it. 'Try the pastrami.' C'mon, just say three words, bro, and Auteen take care of you."

"That's fucking—"

"C'mon, my little bitch. Say it."

See? This is what Ray Dean had to put up with. Toe throbbing and a three-hundred-pound coon wanting him to say "try the pastrami."

Auteen sat down. "I be right here, you need anything."

So, what could you do? Ray Dean said it.

"Thank y'all," said Auteen, standing up, big smile on his face. Ray Dean wondered if he pulled out his gun would the guy keep smiling. "Daddy be right back, honey."

Auteen left and Ray Dean put him on the list with the cunt and the smart ass. Maybe at the top, even.

What Auteen had in mind on his way to the convenience store was to buy some Tylenol, maybe the generic stuff, and tell the hick it was Demoral. Wouldn't know the difference. Man didn't even know Advil and Motrin was the same shit. What Ray Dean didn't know is that Auteen was planning on going out anyway, because he was out of malt liquor. Man couldn't watch no Kung Fu movie without a quart in his lap to suck on. It was fun to play with Ray Dean. Easy too. Because he was a dumb cracker.

He looked through the pharmaceutical rack at the convenience store. Had corn pads, Tums, and stuff for toothaches, that gel stuff that numbed your gums and your tongue too when it touched the stuff. He looked through the pain-killers. There was aspirin made by Bayer, Bufferin, which was twice as fast as aspirin, Excedrin, Tylenol in caplets form and there was some kind of off-brand generic acetaminophen. Cheap too.

He was reaching for the generic when a voice behind him, said:

"Ibuprofen's what you want. What I'd use I was missing a toe or something."

CHAPTER

Twenty-One

GERRY NUGENT TRIED TO CALL MAX BUT HE WASN'T registered at the motel Springer said he'd be at. Which wasn't dumb on Springer's part and didn't piss Gerry off. Guy was taking care of Max. Springer was cautious, that's all. Making sure. However, Gerry *had* told Springer where he would be staying, which made him smile a little when he thought about it. This guy had a way of making you trust him but was still a wary bastard.

Gerry spent the afternoon getting used to the layout of Aspen. It was like a postcard, this place. It had a small-town feel which he hadn't expected, like a Disney movie with the old timey houses and the street lamps. The mountains looked like cake and ice cream, all dark and sprinkled with white. The air was clear and cold, but he didn't feel cold because the sun was warm when it burned through the thin mountain air. Gerry was used to San Francisco where even when it was warm it was cold. Now, here was a place where even when it was cold, it was warm. The people seemed relaxed and complacent. And rich.

He gassed the rental at a convenience store on Main Street and a Rolls Royce Corniche pulled in just as a Range Rover pulled away. This guy gets out of the Rolls and Gerry recognized him but couldn't bring up his name—Gerry was better with faces, which he never forgot, than he was with names, which weren't required in his line of work. Guy was dressed like Donald Trump but was a middle-aged character actor that managed to appear in about three movies a year. Guy always played a senator, or a cop, or a high-ranking military officer. Not a great looking guy, but a four-star female, all legs and flowing golden hair got out on the passenger side. Wasn't his daughter.

Wonder which attracted her the most to the actor—was it the money or the fame?

During the day, Gerry also saw a former governor of California, one of the members of Fleetwood Mac, and a Hall of Fame football player. All dressed in Abercrombie and Fitch or Donna Karan or ski clothes and driving cars that cost more than a three-bedroom house.

What was a guy like this Springer doing here? He didn't fit.

But then, neither did Gerry.

Gerry drove the streets in the rented Pontiac seeing where the streets went. Which ones dead-ended and which ones led back to Main. Force of habit, checking escape routes. Snow everywhere. He hadn't seen much snow since he left back East. Nice to see it again. He used to like the snow when he was a kid. Snowball fights down on the street with some of the Italian kids in his neighborhood who used to put rocks in the snowballs so it'd mark you when it hit. Gerry getting cut up and crying the first time, then his mom telling him to be a man. "Don't take none of that, Gerald," she'd say in her thick Eastern European accent. "You come back at them. Then they stop. Your momma clean you up when you're done." So, Gerry learned not to cry and would make his own snowballs packed with rocks, wetting them a little with water from the house. He marked himself some Italian kids and then things got better.

Long way from here.

This place smelled of money. Money in the hands of people it would be easy to take it away from. No wonder Nicky had wanted a piece of Charlemagne. Bet he was pissed at Ray Dean for screwing that up.

Just a matter of time before Nicky would send him to see Ray Dean and take care of that problem. Ray Dean too stupid to see it coming.

Gerry ate lunch at a sidewalk cafe which had a glassed-in porch, and pastry in a glass case, which is where he saw the member of Fleetwood Mac. The setting of the cafe made him think of himself as if he were in the European Alps, what with the mountains and all, even though he'd never been to the European Alps. Go to the Alps. That might be something to do when this was all done and he was clear of Nicky T. Change his life around when this was done. If he wasn't dead. He wondered if Springer gave any thought to the prospect of violence. Sometimes, the guy gave the appearance of not really worrying about anything and yet there was something there, something underneath the surface that was chewing on the guy. You couldn't really see it but it was there. Gerry had spent too much time studying people's attitudes and dispositions not to notice it. But if you *weren't looking* for it, you could miss it, you really could.

He ate dinner at Boogie's before going back to his room at the old Jerome Hotel, this place that had been there a hundred years and had this great dining room on the main floor, to call Springer and ask where the hell Max was. Really wanting to know where Suzi was, though, but hiding it. Screw Max. Screw Nicky too.

The message light was on when he got back to his room and the printed phone instructions said for him to hit pound seven which he did and a recording said he had two messages. The first one was from the wise guy, Springer.

"Nugent. This is Springer. By now you may realize I didn't tell you a couple of things. But I'll come by and take you there. I trust you but Max is about ready to jump out of his skin and if you go there without me I'm afraid he'll die of a heart attack or shoot an appliance."

Called him "Nugent." First time he'd heard that in a long time.

The second message was the good one. "Gerry, this is Suzi. Max's friend. Wanted to see if you made it all right. I'll call again later. Can't give you the number because Cole said no one could know the number or the place we're staying until he says so. Enjoyed coffee the other day. Maybe we can do it again. Bye for now."

She had a nice voice. *"Maybe we could do it again."* A little promise in the nice voice. *"Bye for now."* Gave him a funny feeling. Something he wasn't used to feeling. Maybe not the time for such feelings. When then? He was sure if Springer knew the way Gerry felt about the girl, Springer would smile that *Cool Hand Luke* smile of his and without saying anything say a lot.

Springer pulling his strings. He had a way about him, Gerry

had to admit it. Guy was sure of himself but Suzi told him the guy's business sense was terrible and he was in money trouble. Funny how some attributes didn't transfer to other things. That's why Gerry had gravitated to his line of work. He was good at shooting people and keeping his mouth shut so he did that. He intimidated people into doing things his way by not saying much and looking people straight in the eyes. Most people couldn't take that. When he tried it with Springer it seemed to amuse the guy. Springer got people to go his way in a manner that seemed almost like it was the *natural* thing to do and there wasn't another way. You just found yourself going *along* with the guy without thinking too much about it.

Gerry liked the guy. Been a while since he'd met anyone he liked. Counting Suzi, that was two now.

Well, Max, he guessed. But less. Still, it felt good to decide not to shoot somebody for a change. Might as well be Max he didn't shoot.

Driving back up the hill to the motel, Auteen thought about his second encounter with the spooky white guy. It was a small town but this motherfucker just *appears* out of nowhere. Second time. Right behind him, saying, "Ibuprofen's what you want." Then mentioning Ray Dean cracker-ass's toe like he had a camera or something in their room.

So Auteen stood up to his full height, letting the man see what he was up against, looking at the guy, saying, "The fuck you want here? They ain't no bitches here to come to the rescue of."

"That's pretty good," the man said, nodding his head. "The standing up, taking advantage of your size. Probably effective most of the time." Like Auteen was a science experiment.

"But, not with you, right?"

The guy shrugged at Auteen.

Auteen saying, "Man, maybe I bust your ass."

Then, the guy looking at Auteen like he said something funny, before pushing his jacket to one side showing him the gun. The same one he shot Ray Dean in the foot with.

Auteen saying, "Maybe I be packing too."

Smart-ass said, "Yeah, where is it? In the back of your pants? Down in your crotch in your stylish form-fitting pants you guys from the hood like to wear, never thinking about accessibility? Mine's right here. Close. Easy to get to. Probably go through the whole clip while you're playing with your zipper."

"You wanta go somewhere see what it's like, boy?"

Then the asshole smiled his asshole smile and said, "Like in the Old West? You and me in the alley, guns blazing? Sounds good to me. I got nothing else on right now." Real confident mother-fucker, like it wasn't gonna be nothing to blow holes in Auteen. "You're a big target. Might be fun. Really rather shoot your boss."

"My boss?"

"The big-haired guy with the cowboy boots and the bad toe."

"Ray Dean? Man, he ain't the boss of nothin'."

"So why are you here, you got a headache?" Then, the moth-erfucker just looked at him and smiled like he knew something, pissing Auteen off. Meaning to do it, too. Smiling at Auteen because he was thinking Ray Dean told him what to do, where to go.

"Ray Dean ain't my boss, motherfucker."

Now the man really smiling.

Auteen mean-mugged him, saying, "You don't have the piece, I kick your punk ass."

Guy didn't even blink, just looked Auteen up and down, and said, "Well, you're big enough. But what if you can't do it? Ever think of that? Then what?" Looking at Auteen, calmly, but getting ready, moving his legs a little, bending them. Guy had big shoul-ders. He ready to go. Right here. Man was crazy, stupid, or bad. Auteen didn't know which.

"Some other time, bitch."

"Some other place," the guy said, winking at Auteen, then started looking at a bottle of merlot like Auteen had disappeared.

Auteen drove back to the motel, parking the rental two streets over and having to walk because some dipshit in a Porsche had taken his place. Slipped on a patch of ice and busted his ass on the asphalt. Made him think about keying the guy's ride, but knowing that might bring the cops as rich people were touchy about their shit and maybe they put their whole force on car vandalism since they not used to real crime. Except now that Ray Dean was in town and grabbing women and shooting people, that could all change. That boy was going to get them both thrown inside which Auteen didn't want.

And Ray Dean liking to give orders, making fun of Auteen while he was eating. Thinking *he was* the boss. Auteen didn't like that, either.

May have to talk to the boy. Show him the way.

Auteen was looking at the Porsche, thinking about keying it, when the familiar voice said:

"Where the fuck you been?" said Gerry Knucks, scaring shit out of him.

Twice in one night. Fucking white people. Who needed this shit?

Tobi Ryder was strolling through the walking mall when Springer just walked up to her and said, "So, where have you been?" as if he hadn't disappeared for several days in violation of his bond and was now looking for a reaction from her like a kid that had sneaked out of his room when no one was watching. She had just gone off duty and was looking to have a drink or coffee after returning from the Charlemagne crime scene. She'd wanted to look at it again. It wasn't like cop shows where you found some minute evidence or someone broke down and confessed just before the last commercial. With her it was more hoping that being there and studying the scene and reflecting on it would jar something loose in her own experience as a police investigator. Or maybe she could envision how it went down.

So, she was thinking about that when he walked up. That lingering half-smile on his face like he was considering some inner thought. She said, "I've been at the courthouse getting a warrant for a smart-ass bail jumper thinks he's cute."

He stuck his hands in his jeans pockets, looked around the walking mall, and nodded his head. "Must be a headache."

"Believe me, it is."

"I've been looking for you."

"And now you've found me." Then she had another thought. How *did* he find her just now? There were no coincidences with this guy. He showed up when he wanted and disappeared when he wanted.

"I think someone was in my place while I was gone."

She felt her eyes begin to widen but checked herself by running a hand through her hair. Was he testing her? Did he know it was her? She studied his face. No, he didn't appear to be looking to knock her off stride. How did he know anyone was in his apartment? So she asked him how he knew.

He shrugged. That's all. A shrug. You ask him a question and you get a shrug or a smile, or a question or a half-answer. He never gave out information unless *he* thought it was important for you to know. She was getting real tired of that. But he knew someone had creeped his apartment.

"They didn't take anything and didn't bug the place," he said, now. "Don't know what they were looking for. I'm not missing anything important."

"Did you call it in?" she asked.

"What would I tell them? That it *felt* like someone had been in my place but they didn't take anything? Cops are real cynical about that kind of thing. But I'm telling you and you already know about cops."

She looked at him. There was a pause between them. A long pause, with her looking into his eyes, which lasted maybe two seconds too long before he said, "Buy you a cup of coffee?"

She nodded. "Okay," she said.

They found a place and after they got their coffee, he said, "I followed you from the courthouse."

She gave him a look.

"You were wondering how I got here," he said, reading her mind, which spooked her a little. She wasn't used to that. Made her uncomfortable that he could do that. "Whether it was a coincidence or not. But you don't believe in coincidences. And you especially don't believe in coincidences where it concerns me because you think I'm facile."

This time she was unable to hide her surprise.

"So," he said, "I was right."

"Why are you following me around?" she asked, trying to be the cop again.

"I thought maybe you'd like to come look at my apartment."

She felt heat at the throat of her blouse. "Why would I do that?"

"Because you're a cop and I'm a citizen and I just told you that someone was in my apartment while I was out of . . . away from it." Playing with her again. "You could come by, if you're not doing anything, look at the place." But, that wasn't what he meant, to check out his apartment for a break-in. What did he mean? She remembered the journal entry to his late wife. About meeting someone new.

"Call it in. They'll send someone out."

"I don't want someone else to come." Now he was looking right at her. Straight into her eyes. He had soft, dark eyes. Looking right through her. Unsettling, but pleasant. Probably could see her throat coloring like it always did when she felt emotion. It was a damn giveaway and he wasn't the type to miss something like that.

"I don't work break-ins."

He shrugged. "Who said anything about a break-in? I said someone was in my apartment. Didn't say they broke in. Didn't say I wanted an officer to come and take a report. I asked if you wanted to see my place," He said. "From the inside."

"Now?"

"You got something better on?" he said.

Springer put on Chopin when they got to his apartment. Tobi felt uneasy in his place with him. Not because of the erotic tension between them, and there was a lot of that—she could feel it when they were driving up the mountain, nothing much being said, the interior of the vehicle feeling too small to contain what she was feeling. She felt strange having broken into his apartment like a thief and now she was there as a . . . as what?

"This is a lovely place," she said.

"It'll do," he said, before sliding his arms under hers and kissing her on the mouth. Hard. And urgent, rocking her back on her heels. At first, she was surprised, then she thought, "what the hell," before surrendering to it. It was a macho move on his part. Something men didn't do anymore. Something she wasn't ready for. Something new. Different.

He backed her up until they were next to the couch and then, gently, as if she was a cloud and he was the wind, he had her seated next to him, continuing the embrace. The Chopin tune was building and driving and throbbing in her head.

She leaned away from him, not really wanting to, saying, "This probably isn't the right thing to do."

Searching her eyes then, with his. The smart-assed look gone from his face.

"I don't give a damn about what the right thing to do is," he said.

She looked at him for a moment, brushed the hair at his temples, then said, "Neither do I."

And they fell into each other with an urgency she hadn't felt since she was in college.

Afterwards, lying in bed, her leg across his stomach, running her fingernails through the brown hair on his chest, spent and warm and reflective, she thought about the number of times she had been spontaneous in her life. Counting this time? Once. The only time.

Springer's body was firm like David's but somehow more comfortable, like she fit him. Summers was two or three inches taller, with a roll around his middle and arms like noodles but thought because he had a belt in Karate that would ward off all harm. Springer's shoulders were muscular. He didn't look that muscular with clothes on.

Boy, would Summers freak out if he could see her now.

She asked, "You do this a lot?"

"Constantly. Sometimes it's all I get done."

"You think that's the best answer to give a girl you just took advantage of?"

"I didn't take advantage of you."

"Maybe I took advantage of you."

"Hard to do."

She smiled and pulled herself closer to him, his body hard and warm against her. "Are you okay with this?"

His turn to be surprised, now. Did she see him swallow hard? Looking at her with a question mark in his eyes, then the question mark turning to an acceptance of something as if he had settled something in his mind. "Yeah, I think so. Why ask?"

Her turn to be oblique. "Because I don't think you're facile."

"Good to know."

They made love again and then he got up and discreetly put on his jeans. It carried a modesty inconsistent with his normal demeanor. But, very cute, she thought. When he left the room she stretched and yawned. Then she heard the water running in the bathtub. She wrapped the bed sheet, which had been torn from its moorings, around her and asked what he was doing.

"You've been working hard," he said. "Thought you might like a hot bath while I make you something to eat."

"Is this the same wise-ass that skipped bail?" she asked.

He stuck his head into the room and said, "Why officer, that would be illegal."

"So?" she said. "Did you?"

"Do you like hamburger? It's all I got." Not going to answer. Playing her off.

"I'm not sure that's true." Being coy and girlish now and liking the feeling. "But, a hamburger sounds fine."

He left and she heard him open the refrigerator. She went into the bathroom and lay in the tub and let the heated water swirl and envelop her. The tub had jacuzzi jets which he had turned on for her. She lay back against the headrest and closed her eyes, thinking, well, this isn't what you set out to do today.

After her bath she put her clothes on and ate a hamburger. He ate two. He'd made her a salad and some thick-sliced steak fries and opened a bottle of merlot he'd had with him when he got out of his car. She drank it with her food which tasted delightful.

When she reached for her wine glass, the sleeve of her blouse rolled up to reveal the discolored marks on her wrist. She saw him looking at the marks and she pulled her arm back quickly.

He said, "How'd that happen?"

She hesitated a beat too long. "Car door shut on it," she said.

He wasn't buying it though. He said, "Noticed it before. That's a defensive bruise. The kind you get when you pull away from somebody." Looking at her, trying to see inside. She could *feel* his look. Here's someone she had way underestimated. "Anybody I know?"

She shook her head. "It's not a big deal."

"Somebody you arrested?"

"Yeah."

"No, it isn't," he said, doing it again. Looking into her head and plucking out things to examine. Which is probably how he knew she wanted him to take her. "Summers do that?"

"Jack? No. My ex-husband, David. He's in town and . . . well, we weren't arguing. Not a domestic squabble or anything. Nothing like that. He just grabbed my wrist and wouldn't let go and I didn't like it."

"Sometimes it happens."

"Didn't you ever grab your wife by the wrist or the sleeve and try to restrain her?"

He was starting to sip wine when she said it. He stopped the glass, the dark brown eyes clouding up like a storm, the disarming smile gone and said, "Never."

A dumb thing to say to a guy who was still broken up about his dead wife. How could you be so stupid, Ryder. Suddenly, she said, "It was Summers who was in your apartment."

"Yeah," he said. "What I figure too. Before or after you?"

CHAPTER

Twenty-Two

SPECIAL AGENT JACK SUMMERS TOOK THE CALL ON HIS mobile phone. It had been patched over to Aspen from San Francisco via the D.C. office. The caller, one of the young guys just out of the academy, told Summers that the bureau had information that Gerald A. Nugent, aka "Gerry Knucks," "Knucks," and "Gerry the Hammer," had disembarked from Las Vegas, Nevada, at 9:47 A.M. and arrived at Glenwood Springs Memorial Airport at 10:55 A.M. Rocky Mountain Time, on this date. All the recent graduates talked like Efrem Zimbalist, Jr. or Jack Webb. It was like a disease they gave them before they issued the badge.

"We'll fax you a description and an artist's rendering of the subject," said the rookie. "You can pick it up at the Aspen office."

"Artist's rendering?"

"There are no available photos of the subject."

"You're kidding."

"He has no recent criminal record. He has been a rumored participant in four homicides but there has never been any *prima facie* evidence establishing him as a legitimate suspect. He's never been brought in for questioning. Our intelligence also relates that he possibly disposed of three other members of rival crews but the bodies have never been found. We do know that he was a decorated marine in Vietnam—purple heart, bronze star—IQ of one hundred and thirty-five. Very dangerous."

"A hero torpedo with intellect?"

"There's more."

"So, is it caught in your throat? Let me have it."

"There has been a disturbance in the power structure in the Bay area mob. Carmine Mostelli died."

"Killed?"

"Natural causes. It looks like Joey 'the Neck' Guardino is making a run at the big boss's seat. Our information also tells us that Guardino is bringing along Nicky Tortino, aka 'Nicky T,' 'Nicky the Knife'—"

Summers interrupted him. "Yeah, yeah, I know who he is. Is Tortino made?"

"It looks like it's in the works and when he is he'll be made with a bullet. Guardino will shoot the guy right up the ladder. Tortino's dying for it. Also, there is a rather large amount of money which has disappeared from Mostelli's war chest."

"How much is a large amount?"

"Three million."

Summers whistled. "More than I made last year."

"Guardino is blaming Sonny 'Blue Bart' Bartoloni, his chief rival for Mostelli's chair, for its disappearance. Bartoloni is furious and keeping his crew members close."

"Hell, this could get nasty." Let the fucking goombahs blow each other away. Less paperwork.

"Looks like it. The chief thinks Max Shapiro could be a key to blowing the lid off this thing."

Summers gave the scenario some thought. If Gerry Knucks was in Aspen to do Max then Sonny Blue had the money. If Knucks was in town to secure Shapiro, after they had originally had a contract out on Max, then it meant that Guardino had the three mil and Nicky T wanted Max to launder it. In either scenario Shapiro was probably a dead man since they couldn't afford to keep Max around after laundering stolen mob money and keeping it. Which was fine with Summers.

Maybe that would give him a chance at the girlfriend. Comfort her and work on her a little.

Summers said, "Okay, send me the stuff. Something else. I'm having a little trouble getting a warrant issued by a local judge. Says I don't have the evidence to justify the warrant. Need someone high up to jack this judge up, let him know our intentions are serious."

"I'll talk to McMillan as soon as I sign off. Who's the warrant for?"

"Guy named Springer. Cole Springer. Aspen, Colorado. Possession with intent."

Gerry clicked off the television and took the whiskey bottle away from Ray Dean, not asking or nothing, then said, "Tell me again why you had to pop Charley Wheels?"

"I just told you," said Ray Dean. Guy staring at him with those hard eyes, hard to be comfortable when he was doing that, but pissing Ray Dean off anyway. He didn't like being treated like he was something washed out of the gutter.

"Tell me again." Gerry poured the whiskey out in the lavatory sink, looking at Ray Dean while he did it, daring him to say something. "And, I'll listen real close because Nicky's put out about this. This is not a good time for you to cowboy the operation."

"I told you, the guy was hopped up. Ain't that right, Auteen? All nervous and jumpy. Then he got out a gun—"

"What kind of gun?"

"I don't know. A rifle."

"What kind of rifle?"

"Whadda you mean, what kind of rifle? You mean like was it a Remington? I didn't have time to check the fucking trademark while he's pointing it at me."

Knucks narrowing his eyes slightly, letting Ray Dean know to watch his tone of voice. Then, Knucks says, "Was it a lever action? A bolt action? Semi-auto?"

"Lemme think." He looked at Auteen for help but the fucking moron was looking away, not wanting anything to do with this. "I think it was a lever action. Yeah, that's it. One of those deer rifles like in the old western movies. That's right, ain't it, Auteen?" Auteen, soon to be writhing in pain from a gutshot wound, shrugged and said, "Can't 'member." That's right, the motherfucker shrugged. Could you believe that? Ray Dean swimming in the deep end of shit lake and this guy don't help him.

"Whadda ya mean, you can't remember?"

"Don't know nothin' 'bout long guns. Man whip out a Sig or a Colt Python, Auteen identify that shit. Like the gun the bodyguard got? One he uses to shoot toes off and shit?" Look at 'im, smiling now. "Thass a Beretta. But a rifle? Auteen don't deer hunt. He coulda had a pump action elephant Ba-zooka I wouldn't know it."

"I told you guys to stay in the room but you sent Auteen out to get medicine."

"He never *sent* me," said Auteen, looking offended. "He don't send me places. He wasn't feeling good and I got him something for it."

"Now you're a nurse."

"Then I run into the man again, the bodyguard."

"Yeah, what did he want?"

"Man just show up. Don't know where he come from. Made a crack about Ray Dean's toe and showed me his gun."

Ray Dean was watching Knucks's face. It was different somehow. "Showed you his gun?" Did Knucks think that was funny?

"Yeah, he a crazy white boy. Show me his gun, I tell him maybe I show him something and then him saying something about guns blazing like in the Old West, acting unconcerned 'bout the whole thing. Even smiled."

"He smiled?"

"Motherfucker always smiling like he know something you don't."

Did Knucks smile just then? Ray Dean asked himself. Couldn't remember Knucks thinking anything was funny.

"How do you know he didn't follow you back?" Knucks asked.

Auteen's face went blank. "He didn't follow me back."

"Followed you to the store, you didn't know it."

"That was a accident." But he could see Auteen thinking about that.

"You don't know if he followed you back or not, do you?" said Knucks, looking disgusted now. Ray Dean was glad he was on Auteen's case and off him for a while. Knucks always made your insides knot up like you couldn't take a deep breath when he was around and this time was worse because Ray Dean was already having stomach trouble.

"Man, he didn't follow me back."

"He could be waiting right outside, right now, waiting to blow your shit away when you walk outside."

"He's not a shooter," said Ray Dean, thinking, what the fuck did you pipe up for? Knucks isn't bothering you right now. Knucks swiveled, fixed his eyes on Ray Dean.

"You shoot yourself in the foot, then?"

"I mean he *can* shoot but he ain't gonna whack nobody in cold blood. He ain't got the balls for that."

"And you gained omniscient insight while I was away, right?"

"What?"

"It means . . . never mind." Knucks shook his head. Knucks sat down, opened his coat and Ray Dean could see his shoulder holster. Guy still wore a shoulder holster like it was the eighties or something. Man, *everybody* wore their gun on the hip or in back nowadays. And, the guy carried that big blue-steel Colt cannon like it was World War II when everybody was carrying poly-framed nines. Sonuvabitch was dated.

"You guys know where this guy lives?"

Ray Dean and Auteen looked at each other. They *didn't* know. Auteen voiced it.

Knucks said, "Guy finds you whenever he wants and you have no idea where he is. You don't know nothing about him." Knucks shaking his head now. Letting them know how dumb he thought they were. "Look at you two fucking guys. One of you limping around and the other getting ambushed every ten minutes by some off-the-street wise-ass. You guys fucked up going into Max's place and messing with his girl. What if she'd called the cops? How fucking stupid is that?"

"We'd been all right," said Ray Dean, his arms flying about, "if fucking Superfly over there didn't have to raid the fridge every fifteen minutes like he was on life support."

"Man, fuck you," said Auteen. "You weren't up there slapping the girl maybe you'd know the man was in the house."

Knucks's eyes narrowed and he turned those gun metal eyes on Ray Dean, full force. "You hit the woman? Max's girl?"

"Yeah," said Ray Dean, his arms out, palms up, like he was holding off the look. "The cunt was mouthing me."

"There's another thing," said Knucks, standing up now, his eyes hot. "Don't ever call her that again. In fact, you even talk to her again, I'll rip your fuckin' throat out. Understand?"

"Sure, Knucks. Okay, man."

Now what the hell was that about? thought Ray Dean.

Springer could see that he had surprised Tobi Ryder, bringing up about her being in his apartment, her denying it but him seeing through it. She was too genuine to be comfortable with a lie and it showed in her eyes. Still, he couldn't be sure she was in his apartment, or why, so he let it go for now and thought about the FBI agent, the Summers guy, being in his apartment. So, he asked her.

"What was he doing here?" he asked.

"I don't know," she said. "Trying to get something on you, I guess. May I have some more wine?" Springer got the feeling she really didn't want the wine, just wanted to avoid the question.

He got it for her. Poured it. Sat down again. She moved away slightly when he sat down next to her. Now what? What is it about women that makes them so mysterious? What motivates them to put the veil up? One minute they were hugging themselves to you, grasping and holding on like everything depended upon it, giving themselves to you fully and then you could say one thing—a word, a phrase, or even make the tiniest drift in your demeanor—and suddenly they wanted to put a little more distance between themselves and you. He didn't think it had anything to do with him personally. Though it had to be somewhat about him; he got the feeling that it had something to do with the cop in her, making her wary. She probably wasn't even aware of it, Springer only alerted to it from years of watching the slightest change in someone's disposition.

Like with Gerry Nugent. Although Nugent's new drift in his life stream was glacial, its impact on Springer's awareness was as plain as if he wrote it down and had it broadcast on CNN. Guys were easier to read, even guarded guys like Nugent.

Women though . . .

She said, "I'm working a murder up close to Aspen Meadows. A local dealer, a creep called himself Charlemagne."

"Charley Wheels?"

Surprising her. "Yeah, you know him?"

Boy, if she only knew.

"Heard of him. He's been in my place a few times. He sells to a couple of my regulars, semi-celebrities that want a toot now and then and say they know him. Thinks it makes them appear to be hip Aspenites."

He didn't tell her that eighteen months ago, when he was short on cash, he had gone in heavy, giving Charley Wheels the DEA scam, pretending to be an agent and shaking the guy down. The way he did it was to glass the place for a couple of days, wait until he was sure Wheels had received a shipment, and kicked the door in wearing a DEA jacket he'd more or less stolen from a DEA agent at a party after a seminar on surveillance devices back when he was still with the service. DEA guy was a jerk. Married guy who was talking bullshit and hitting on one of the female agents at the party. Saying what his wife didn't know couldn't hurt her. Big handsome guy with curly hair, the type that wore expensive leather jackets and was always on the make. Guy was drunk, being obnoxious, so Springer lifted his DEA jacket for a joke and left with it while the guy was nuzzling the female agent.

Something fun to do.

That was back when Springer was working for the government, already deciding he wanted out of that life. The jacket had come in handy a couple of times since.

Anyway, he busted into Wheel's place, a bandanna over his face, big nickel-plate Colt Python in his hand, hollering like on the cop shows, "Get the fuck down! GET THE FUCK DOWN ON THE FLOOR, DIRTBAG!" Using the wheel gun because they were scarier than auto pistols, ratcheting back the hammer and letting the guy see the big hollow points rotating in the cylinder. Scaring the guy before he could think, cuffing him then searching the place, finding the stash, holding it in Wheel's face, telling him that he was going to take a big fall, get passed around and rear-ended in the shower by weight lifters with swastikas cut into their forearms. Stuff like that, letting it work on him.

Then, after planting seeds in the guy's imagination, a guy used to living large with rock stars and the L.A. crowd, he'd made a phony call to his own phone, acted like he was calling in to head-quarters and told them he was *outside* Charlemagne's place and *about* to go in. Then, after he hung up, he'd turned to Charley Wheels and said, "What'll it be, puke? Did I find anything here or can we make some other arrangement?"

Charley Wheels coughed up five grand and couldn't give it to him fast enough.

It was really kind of fun. It wasn't like stealing, he told himself. Not like he walked into a bank with a gun. Wheels was raw sewage anyway.

"Anyway," Tobi said. "It looks like a hit. Like someone was mad at him."

"Job hazard. Should've gone into real estate he didn't want people shooting him."

"Who do you know that would do something like that?"

"How about the guy you tackled in the motel?"

"Ray Dean Carr?"

"That's him."

"I thought about him as a possibility. How do you know that creep?"

"I'm supposed to protect Max, remember?"

"You've never said."

"But, now I'm feeling charitable toward you. I think sex does that. But, I'm not always sure." Smiling inside as he watched her face when he said it.

She said, "They found a .22 pistol in the hotel laundry. Wish I could have stuck it in his face. He did some hollering about 'false arrest' and saying he was going to sue."

"Guys like Ray Dean don't sue and they don't go through the court system on purpose. Bet the gun was wiped clean, bullets too."

She nodded.

He said, "Those guys are socially retarded but they know their business."

"Whatever was wrong with his foot was nasty. He bled all over the place after I took him down."

"Like he'd had his toe shot off?"

She stopped and cocked her head to one side. "Yeah, as a matter of fact, that's what happened. What do you know about it?"

"I shot him there."

"Boy, suddenly you're forthcoming. Quite a change. You realize you're reporting this to a police officer?"

He shrugged, a good one. "I'll deny it. Tell them how you and the FBI creeped my apartment. B and E doesn't look good when it's the cops doing it."

"You don't know that."

"You know about my wife."

She looked uncomfortable now, wetting her lips. "I don't know what you mean. What has that got to do with anything? I don't know anything about your wife."

"Earlier you mentioned something about how pretty she was."

"I said I'll bet she was lovely."

"It was more like an assertion backed by knowledge rather than a guess. Besides, what you said was, 'I *know* she was lovely,' when I mentioned her."

"That's just an expression," she said. "Like I meant she'd have to be lovely for you to love her so much."

He shrugged. "If that's the way you want to go with it, it's okay with me. But, I think you've seen her picture."

"I've seen it, it's right over there on the bay window."

"You're right. It is. But, since you've been here you haven't been pointed in that direction."

"It's in your bedroom too. I've been in there. Alone. I saw it then."

"But you knew about the picture in the bay window. You want a key I'll get you one. Save you some trouble."

That stopped her.

She said, "I shouldn't have told you about Summers."

"But you did."

"And you shouldn't have told me about shooting Ray Dean."

"Maybe. But I didn't castrate him and the shot wasn't post-mortem."

She gave him a look. A good one. "You make love to me then you take me over the hurdles? You think that's a way to romance me?"

"Actually, I thought about playing the piano for you. Something romantic and dreamy. That's the way I thought I'd do it. I'm just passing on possibilities and information right now. Nothing like threatening a guy with arrest on hearsay evidence, for shooting a recidivist thug like Ray Dean Carr, when that's not what you want to do."

"What is it I want to do?"

"You want me to help you make the bust of your career."

"And you think you can do that?" She shook her head. "Men, all men, amaze me with their high regard for their power to change the world around them."

He shrugged. "So, what are the alternatives?"

"Are you blackmailing me?"

"No, just giving you something to think about. But you don't have to worry about what I'll do. I'd never give you up."

She started to say something but stopped, giving him the look again. "What . . . how do I know what you'll do?"

"Because I think I'm in love with you."

Her lips parted slightly and Springer felt something stir inside him.

"Play something for me," she said.

Later, after making love to Tobi Ryder again and she had left the apartment, deprived of her sound and movement but the residue of her perfume on him, Springer put on the Temptations' "I Wish It Would Rain." It was Kristen's favorite. It played through once and he hit the repeat button on the remote and played it again. And again. Sang along with it like a sappy junior high kid.

He blinked his eyes halfway through the second repeat, voice catching and let out a deep breath. He felt a tightness in his chest and thought about her. Feeling almost unfaithful for the first time since she'd left. He couldn't think of her as dead. He'd had a couple of one-night stands. The women had been attractive and knew all the right moves, the right things to say, straight out of a romance novel. But this time something had happened inside his head. Should've made him happy. Instead, something was working out on him.

Tobi Ryder. A cop. A smart cop who also happened to be more woman than anyone he'd met since Kristen . . . died, there, he could say it. Thinking about her, now.

That's when he knew he was going to read her letters again. The ones he kept in the cubbyhole in the rolltop desk.

CHAPTER

Twenty-Three

MAX HAD TO ADMIT IT, SPRINGER WAS TAKING PRETTY good care of him. Max was alive and staying in a nice place, the guy sent to kill him was on his side, and now Nicky T had called off the dogs and wanted to negotiate. Max could sit on the sundeck of the Ritz courtyard, look at the mountains, all purple and stately, smoke a cigar and actually think about the future for the first time in a couple of weeks.

Only now, Suzi was treating Max like he was caries active, acting distant when she wasn't being outright hostile. What had he done to deserve it? Hadn't he treated her like an equal like Springer said? Hadn't he shown her that he cared about her? He thought so. But when he asked her to make him another drink, she'd snapped at him like a rat terrier to get his own and she wasn't his maid.

Women. Who could figure them?

Still, he wasn't out of the woods yet with Nicky T or he'd cut Springer loose which he couldn't wait to do, guy was always making oblique statements whenever Max said something or smiling that irritating smile he had like he didn't want to use too many mouth muscles to get it done. Or like there was a comedy playing in his head and Max was the star.

But, overall, hiring Springer had been positive. Guy knew what he was doing. Still, the plan he had to get Nicky off his back was a little scary. Lot of things could go wrong. Here's the part he liked the least—putting up some of his own cash as bait. And, if he didn't know better he'd think Springer and Gerry were looking to rip off Nicky. But that was crazy. They wouldn't do that. *Nobody* would do that to a legitimate psychopath like Nicky Tortino. Would they? It made Max ill to think about. He knew for a fact that Nicky had once sewed a guy's lips shut then stuck cocaine up the guy's nose until he suffocated. Yeah, that's the kind of crap that sick bastard was capable of. But there had to be some reason Gerry Knucks, now Nugent, had switched teams. There had to be a pay-off somewhere.

Springer said he knew a guy who would fake a death certificate, look like the real thing. But who was going to die? Where was the body? "Don't worry about that," said Springer. "I've got that worked out." Always saying things like that. Not making Max feel a whole lot better. For some reason, though, when Springer said things Max was beginning to just accept that it would get done. He was that kind of guy.

Even with the crazy plan and the danger, Max was miles better off than he had been a week ago when he was waiting to see which he died of first—cancer or a bullet.

He was thinking about that and where to go when this was all over—sitting on the deck in his ski sweater, smoking an aged Macanudo, which cost thirty-five bucks a stick, but not much better than their regular cigar that cost about six bucks—when this guy he'd never seen before came up and sat down beside him. Put his feet on Max's chair like they were old buddies. Guy smelled like a fed. Reeked of it. Who else would wear a London Fog overcoat and Florsheims in Aspen, for crissakes? Guy wasn't undercover anyway. Good-sized guy. Rangy like a basketball player. Late thirties. Red-and-blue striped tie. Said his name was Special Agent Summers, letting it hang.

"That supposed to mean something?" Max asked him.

"It will. I'm going to become an important part of your life."

Then, Max gesturing the guy's legs with his cigar. "Your feet are on my chair."

The G-man moved his feet, adjusted himself to a fully erect position. Guy had good posture, you had to give him that. "You're a known associate of Nicky Tortino."

"A *known* associate? How do you achieve that status? Is there some kind of chart down at your office gauges shit like that? Known associate. How about this? I heard of the sonuvabitch and I stay away from him because people he knows and don't like don't have life spans of any consequence."

"I heard he had a contract out on you."

Max looked around like he was wondering what he was hearing. "Are you sure you're a fed? If Nicky Tortino had a contract out on me would I be sitting here smoking a cigar and watching the sunset?"

"I can help you."

"Maybe if you were an osteopathic surgeon. My back's killing me. You want to know about pain? Can't sleep sometimes it's so bad. And waking up and stretching? Takes twenty minutes just to put my feet on the floor. So, unless you're some kind of doctor, I can't think of anything you could do, unless you brought a box of Monte Cristos. The real ones. From Cuba."

Summers never changed the FBI-issue expression on his face. Summers said, "Heard you were tough to crack. That you keep your guard up. But the heat's not on you here. At least, not as long as you help me. I know I can help you."

Max looked up at the mountains. Laughed. "You fucking guys. How many times you think I heard that one? How you're going to help me. Nice of the Bureau to send someone around periodically to help me. What would I do without you? You guys take a class on that at the academy? Come on, you look pretty sharp, try something original."

"You want Nicky Tortino off your back?"

"Don't know him. Know of him, that's all."

"Did you know that Carmine Mostelli's dead?"

"My condolences. Don't know him, either."

"How about Joseph Guardino? Sonny Blue?"

"Drawing a blank here."

"Gerry Knucks is in town."

"Him I'm supposed to know, right?"

Mostelli's dead, thought Max. Oy. That was going to create some shit. Maybe Nicky wouldn't have time to do anything with

Max. Sonny Black and Joey the Neck would be fighting it out for the boss's chair. Dangerous shit. Glad he wasn't on the coast right now. But those guys had long arms. This could change every damned thing.

"How about this?" Summers said. "You let me take down Nicky T and Gerry Knucks and I let you go free, clean up your file."

"How about losing my file entirely?"

G-man shrugged. "Could happen, the right things occur."

Max looked at the end of his cigar. "If I had any interest in this, and I'm not saying I do, that sounds pretty thin to me. I mean, so what, I'm free right now."

"What if you come out ahead?"

"How far ahead?"

"Way out in front. Bucks ahead?"

"Could you turn the volume up on that a little, I can almost hear you."

"How about all the above, change of identity through witness protection and I let you keep any money that's floating around."

Max finally looked at the agent. "You smoke cigars?"

Nicky T decided he wanted to drive out to Colorado. See the country. He had this brand new Firemist Mercedes E55 he wanted to try out. Listed at sixty-nine grand. Sonuvabitch was a land rocket besides being like driving your living room around at one hundred and ten miles an hour. One hundred and ten feeling like fifty, the thing was so smooth. The Mercedes dealer owed him a favor because Nicky was his alibi after the guy fell in love with one of Joey the Neck's hookers, a high-dollar girl from Brazil who was half Italian. A real looker, almond-shaped eyes, dark skin, and the best legs Nicky'd ever seen. The Mercedes dealer wasn't a great looking guy but the working girl liked the toys he bought her. Guy needed someone to cover him with the wife and Nicky wanted a deal on the E55. Got it for the cost of a Ford. Nicky pointed out what a divorce would cost him in real dollars as opposed to losing a few grand on a new car.

Made Nicky feel like a matchmaker. Nice to do nice things for people.

Nicky took Donny Black with him to Aspen. They were going to stop over in Las Vegas where Nicky was going to put the money in a safe deposit box at the Bank of America. Keep it there until time to do the business on it. Donny Black was a 240-pounder played football at San Francisco State University back in the eighties. Former Oakland cop. Got in trouble for taking freebies from hookers. Donny wasn't much of a shooter but he was tough and strong. And he hit like a truck. What with Nicky hauling nearly $3 million around he thought he could use Donny. Donny didn't know about the money. Which is another reason Nicky didn't fly out. He didn't want the airline to lose his luggage and the three mil. And, this money was hot. Thermonuclear it was so hot. Fuck this up and Nicky and the E55 would end up in the bay with the stereo on.

With a lot of other people.

David Ryder nosed the Jeep Cherokee into the motel parking lot space, the one the owner kept for him whenever he was in town. A good guy, didn't mind giving a break on the rent for a drug enforcement agent. He'd tell the manager some true crime stories about taking names and dodging bullets and the guy ate it up like popcorn. Guy's favorite program was *NYPD Blue*.

He had a date in a couple of hours with this amazing redhead from honest-to-God, Akron, Ohio. He'd bought her a couple of stingers last night and told her his life story, embellishing here and there and watching her green eyes widen with appreciation. She brushed against his arm with her fingers and moved close so he could smell her perfume. Nice. She was the type looked like she was trying to squirm out of her clothes when she walked to the ladies room. There was no doubt about what they both wanted. It was naked and out front. The way it should be. None of this I-have-to-appreciate-you-on-an-intellectual-level bullshit like he used to get from his ex-wife. She didn't say it that way but you *knew* that's what she meant when she started giving him her look and making smart-ass statements she thought were cute.

Reflecting on Tobi, he decided that while she was a hell of a woman she was high maintenance. Might have to give up trying to get over on her. She was too headstrong. Always had to be her way. But what a great ass. And eyes you could swim in. But, she possessed some irritating personality traits—hardheaded like her mom with her dad's acerbic sense of humor. Dad never liked David, anyway, especially after the first couple of affairs. Mom did, though. Mom was still a babe and her in her late fifties. More ambitious than Dad who was more interested in sitting around and telling jokes, exchanging cop stories with Tobi, the two of them tuned in on a level David never understood. David could always charm Mom but Dad would just look at him like he was waiting for David to say something that he could appreciate.

Tobi was gorgeous and smart and articulate but only so-so in the sack. Why were smart women always disappointing in bed? Give him one of those ex-sorority chicks every time. Somebody named Buffy or Dana whose worldview rotated the spectrum from new clothes at Saks Fifth Avenue to which restaurant to eat in.

Tobi and him never had that much in common anyway. Still, he'd like to bed her down one more time. If nothing else just for the satisfaction of making that smirk disappear off her face. Still, he felt bad about grabbing her. He'd never done that before. She just had a way of irritating him that no one else had. He was thinking about buying her something as a peace offering but could see her looking at him and saying something wise like, "And, this squares things, right?" Her hand on her hip, rolling her eyes. That kind of shit she did.

He was thinking about that when he saw the guy, leaning against a Jag, like he was taking in the sights at the motel. Except the guy was eyeing David. Not really *eyeballing* David, but considering him, like he was looking at a painting that David was a part of. And, the guy didn't move, like those Palace guards in England, but with a more relaxed posture, arms folded on his chest, ankles crossed, leaning against the car. Not dressed for Aspen but dressed more like a guy from North California or Oregon that only went to town for supplies.

The guy looked familiar. Someone he'd arrested? Maybe. But,

he had more of a cop smell to him. And yet, not exactly like a cop. What then?

David got out of the Jeep and reached down and touched the Glock nine clipped on his belt. As he walked to his room the guy's head moved with him. What the fuck was this about?

"David Ryder?" said the guy, smiling at him.

"Yeah, who wants to know?"

The guy scratched his nose, gave a small shrug, said, "Nobody else here. So, I guess me."

Guy was an inch or two shorter than David. Pretty good build. Had this complacent look going, like the guy was detached from this place. Friendly looking guy but something else underneath it.

"What do you want?"

Guy looked around a little bit, not getting to it. One of those guys. Thought he was smart.

"Talk, that's all," said the asshole, standing there still.

"What do you want to talk about? I got things to do."

"Well, maybe—"

David interrupted him, holding up a hand, giving him the cop voice. "I don't know you. And, I don't like talking to people I don't know. I'm a DEA agent. That connect for you?"

Now the guy was smiling. Big smile. It was a smile of recognition. Did he know this guy?

Guy said, "You think I have drugs on me? That it?"

"No. I think you're a wise-ass that'd better come across with what he wants before I bounce him around the parking lot."

"Well, now I don't know if I can talk. What with my voice quivering with fear."

"It could happen."

The asshole's eyes turned hard. "Tobi gets any more marks on her, you'll get your chance."

"Tobi? My wife?"

"Your ex-wife. I think that's how she describes it."

"She send you?"

"Doesn't know I'm here."

"Then there's no reason for you to be here, is there, asshole?"

"May need to be more careful when you grab women. Never know who their friends are."

That's it. David had enough of this shit. "You better blow before bad shit starts happening to you."

Guy was smiling again. " 'Better blow'? Damn, you're a colorful talker. Must be the DEA training."

"Look, motherfucker, you want a piece of me? Get this straightened out?"

"You gonna hold me by the wrists?"

"What? How . . . look, that's between me and her. None of your fucking business."

"Well, you could be right. I don't know. You don't look like the type who'd beat up a woman. Probably didn't mean to do it."

David stepped up and swung at the guy, but the asshole was quick. He stepped outside the punch and before David could react, the guy had David's arm pinned behind him and leaning over the Jag, kissing the hood, which was warm. David tried to reach for the guy's face but the guy pinched him along the base of his neck. Electric waves of pain rippled through David's neck and shoulder. Paralyzing his left side, his right arm pinned behind him. He was reaching the sick realization that he may have underestimated this guy.

The guy said, "Let you go, you act nice. Didn't know you were going to act like a cheap punk and take a swing at me. Is it my manner? You think that's the way a federal officer acts?"

A skinny guy, early thirties, came out of one of the rooms with a plastic ice bucket in his hands. Eyes wide. Asshole said, "How are you, sir? Nothing to worry about here. We're old friends. Playing around. I'm just demonstrating a new hold to my old buddy here. What do you think, Dave? Really works, doesn't it?"

"Yeah, it's a . . . it's something."

The skinny guy left. Asshole let Ryder go, his neck still burning. Sonuvabitch was stronger than he looked. A lot stronger. Now they were facing each other, David fighting the impulse to reach up and rub his neck but in no hurry to take another swing at him. Who was this guy?

"Let's just talk. Sorry about the neck. You still think a workout will make you feel better we can go somewhere. Not what I want, but not here in a parking lot with people driving by."

"Yeah, fuck you."

The guy shrugged. "That's it? 'Fuck you'?" Guy looking around now, like he was bored. "Come on, you can do better."

"Wait a minute," said Ryder, recognizing the guy now. "I know you."

"Yeah," asshole said. "I think you do."

"You stole my fucking jacket."

"Borrowed," the guy said. "Borrowed it. You want it back I'll get it to you."

"Why did you take it?"

"A joke. Kind of like looking at it. Pretending to be a G-man. Always wanted to be one."

"Really?" David said, cynical.

"No," said the guy, shaking his head. "Not at all."

Springer dropped by the club before going to see Max and call Gerry Nugent. Bruce was inside the place when he got there. Bruce, a weird twenty-something who believed in UFOs and had nineteen-inch biceps, but a good worker. A loyal guy that had stayed hitched when things had gone bad. Something to remember.

"What are you doing, kid?" Springer asked, as a way of greeting. Bruce was wiping glasses with a hand towel.

"Hey, boss," said Bruce. "Just cleaning up. So, we can open up when you're ready."

"Might be a while, yet."

"Maybe sooner than you think," said Bruce. He brought out an official-looking document in an opened envelope. "This came while you were gone. I opened it. Hope you don't mind."

Springer said he didn't and pulled out the court document. Smiled. "The football player dropped the charges."

"Yeah," said Bruce. "Heard one of the assistant coaches at the university like to shit when he heard the guy was trying to take you to court. Said the head coach would eat him alive, take his aid, if he found out he was involved in a bar fight. Got some alumni to pick up the tab on the ER and sent this, too." Bruce handed him a check.

"Fifteen hundred bucks? For what?"

"Guy came by, looked like a lawyer or an accountant. Linebacker was All-Big 12 last year. Said the guy sent it for your inconvenience and so you don't say nothing about it to anybody."

Springer thought that was funny.

Who would he tell?

CHAPTER

Twenty-Four

MAX WAS ACTING WEIRDER THAN USUAL, SUZI THOUGHT. He was in way too good a mood for the Max Shapiro she knew. He was acting like he'd just won the lottery instead of whining around and asking her to do stuff for him. Walking around the motel room singing, which he never did, and with good reason if you'd ever heard him sing. When she asked what he was so happy about, he'd just smile and say, "Hard to explain."

Part of it, she knew, was that he could move around again without worrying about getting shot full of holes. But there was something else there, too.

Oh well, she might as well enjoy it. It was better than the whining.

She was thinking about Gerry Nugent, too. Seeing him scratch the scar on his hand, telling her he didn't get to talk to nice people very often. The hardened look dropping off his face as if taking off a mask.

Springer seeing the difference in her. Asking her if it was okay if he called Nugent to come over, smiling when he said it like he knew something.

"What're you smiling about?" she asked, smiling herself.

"I'm smiling?" Springer said, giving her that look he had, innocent.

"You think I'm crazy, don't you?"

He shrugged. "We're all crazy here. What was that old song back in the sixties? 'We're all bozos on this bus.' "

"You wondering why I just don't ditch Max. Right?"

"I figure you have your own reasons. But, I'll guess you don't like to leave a guy when he's up against something. Would make you feel like a coward."

She smiled at him. "That's pretty good."

"You're not a coward, Suzi. You're a good woman. Lot of guys could use a good woman. Max can. Even Gerry. What's wrong with Gerry having something nice happen to him?"

"You don't think it's weird to have feelings for a man who does what he does for a living?"

He pursed his lips and gave his head a little twist to one side. "That part would be tough. Don't know what to tell you about that. He's out of that life now. Or will be soon. Not much we can do about our feelings. The ways of love are mysterious and given to those willing to risk the ache of loss."

"Who said that? Browning?"

He shook his head. "Cole R. Springer. The 'R' stands for Romantic."

"So are you going to call Gerry?"

"Already did. He's on his way."

"You think you're pretty clever, don't you?"

"Aw shucks, ma'am," he said. "It's nothing."

David Ryder had a headache and the inside of his mouth felt like Styrofoam. The redhead from Akron, Ohio was asleep, passed out anyway, next to him, in the king-sized bed. All that red hair spilling over the pillow and sheets. Girl should have been a gymnast the way she was all over the place last night. What'd she say her name was? Was it Anna or Annette? Anita?

The message light was flashing on his phone as he had told the desk no phone calls. He called the front desk and asked what the message was and the clerk said, "A Special Agent Sommers called." The guy meant Summers but David didn't correct him. The clerk said that Summers wanted to meet him at the Ritz-Carlton hotel bar for a drink and some "interesting" conversation at 2:00 P.M. It was 11:30 A.M. now.

Summers and David used to be pretty thick. Used to chase the bush around, Jack serving as his alibi a couple of times while he was still with Tobi. Then, when things went bad in the marriage, Jack started hitting on Tobi. But that didn't last. David knew it wouldn't. He knew Summers would start trying to run her life. Tobi's personality didn't have a co-pilot setting.

What the hell did Jack want now?

After he hung up the phone, he got out of bed, ate a couple of aspirin and called Tobi to tell her about his visitor yesterday.

"Some guy came by my apartment," he told her. "Made some threats. Said he was a friend of yours."

"What guy?"

"Some guy who told me I shouldn't grab you by the wrists."

"Well, he was right about that," she said, and hung up before he could say anything else. He tried to call again but she had the recorder on.

Oh well, what could you do?

There was a drink waiting for David Ryder when he arrived at the Ritz-Carlton lounge. Jack Summers was sitting there, the only guy in town in a Brooks Brothers suit. Shoes shined. His tie perfect.

"You want Cole Springer by the balls?" Summers said to David first thing after he sat down.

"Good to see you, too, Jack. Who's Cole Springer?"

"The guy that has the hots for your ex."

"I thought that was you."

Summers made a face. "Yesterday's headline, David. You want to go through all that again? You were out of the picture, she's an extremely attractive woman so I dated her. So, shoot me for having good taste." David looked at him like he'd had worse ideas. "Now she's carrying a torch for this ex-Secret Service agent that plays piano down at the Whiskey Basin Tavern."

Carrying a torch? Summers always did talk weird.

"The Whiskey?" said David. "I knew I'd seen the guy before." Other than at the party where the guy boosted his jacket. Why did he do that, anyway? Weird guy. "I've been in there a couple of times. Is this guy about six foot one, around two hundred, big shoulders, kind of a smart ass?"

"Thinks he's a comedian."

"He came by yesterday. Give me some shit about my—" He started to say wife, then changed to—"about Tobi."

Summers leaned forward. "Is that right? What did he have to say?"

David didn't want to say anything about grabbing her by the wrists or that the guy took him down, so he said, "I guess he thinks Tobi's still got a thing for me and he's jealous. We had words."

"You think he's jealous?" said Summers, cocking one eyebrow like he didn't believe that, which ticked David off some. "Of you?"

"What's your interest in this, Jack? You think I got time to come down here and talk about my love life with you? What do you want?"

Summers smiled. "I want Nicky Tortino."

"A minute ago you wanted Springer. Now it's Tortino. What's one got to do with the other?"

"Springer's been hired to protect Max Shapiro, a Frisco real estate broker and accountant that does some work for the Joey Guardino crew and especially for Nicky Tortino. Tortino is a regulation bucket of dog shit who is rising in the ranks on the coast. There's a large amount of money floating around and I think Nicky T will want Shapiro to clean it up. But as long as Springer's around, Shapiro will feel safe—from Tortino and from us. I've talked to Shapiro. Springer annoys him—"

"I can see where the guy'd annoy almost everybody."

Summers nodded. "Anyway, Shapiro would like it if he didn't have to rely on Springer. But, he's not ready to totally trust us. That's where you come in."

"Where do I come in?" said David.

"The DEA's still interested in busting coke dealers or is everybody down there on the take? You know what we call the DEA? 'Don't Ever Apprehend.' That's pretty good, isn't it?"

David narrowed his eyes. He'd forgot how Jack could piss you off with his patronizing tone of voice. Acting like the FBI was on one level while the DEA and the ATF were just a cut above the Keystone Kops.

David said, "You wanta get to it, Jack?"

"Sure, buddy. You're going to like this."

Cole Springer called Gerry Nugent at his hotel and told him what was going on. "We're at the Ritz-Carlton."

"Am I going to drive over there and find another clue, like a scavenger hunt?" asked Gerry.

"What? You don't think this is fun?" said Springer.

Springer and Gerry and Max met in Max's room at the Ritz-Carlton. Springer was drinking the room service coffee which was excellent and eating the sandwiches Suzi had ordered up for them. Suzi glanced occasionally at Gerry and Springer saw it, making her give him a look. Gerry was all business but was polite with her.

Springer left with Gerry Nugent after meeting with Max. Max had been all over the place while Springer was trying to map out the scenario concerning Nicky T. Max was laughing and making jokes at inappropriate times. Interjecting questions about why they needed his money when they had Nicky's.

"Because we have to bait the trap. I've already explained this, Max," said Springer.

"But, if Nicky isn't mad anymore I don't see the reason for it."

Gerry said, "If you think Nicky's over you walking out on him then you're not as smart as I think you are."

Max said something weird at the end like maybe he'd be where Nicky couldn't find him anyway. But he still wanted Springer to go through it.

So Springer went through the whole thing again with Max rolling his eyes and throwing his hands in the air. Suzi said to ignore him, he just liked to gripe.

Then a funny thing happened.

As they were getting ready to leave, Gerry said something about wanting a drink. It was about 2:15. A little early for him but Springer said okay. Going into the lounge Springer saw two familiar figures. Jack Summers and David Ryder. Now, wasn't that something?

"See those two guys over there?" Springer asked Gerry.

"You mean the two feds?"

Springer must've looked surprised.

"What?" asked Gerry. "You think I can't tell a fed when I see one? One of them looks like FBI. The suit. The other guy has to be ATF or DEA. Most likely DEA. Leather jacket. Fancy boots. Jeans. The joke around the guys is that DEA agents on the take all have leather jackets they buy with money we give 'em." He looked at Springer. "That what you were going to tell me?"

"Close."

"So, do we need to get out of here?"

"No, just the opposite. Let's join them."

Gerry looked at him. "You all right? I mean, it seems like we should avoid people like that. I don't know. My experience is that you avoid the G. Never know what you might catch. Sometimes I'm wondering if you got wires and shit stuck in your brain."

"You in or not?"

Gerry shrugged. "What the fuck, huh?"

They walked over to the table where the two G-men were sitting and Springer said, "What's up, guys? Why we would be glad to join you, of course." Then, spinning a chair around and sitting down before he got an answer, he leaned his arms on the chair back. Giving them the folksy act. Ryder and Summers looked at each other. Gerry sat down slowly, looking with gunslinger eyes at the FBI man.

David Ryder glared at Springer. "What the fuck do you want now?" Ryder turned to Summers, jerked a thumb in Springer's direction and said, "This is the asshole I was telling you about."

"Yes, I know," said Summers. "Cole Springer. I'm Special Agent Jack Summers and this is David Ryder."

"Of the Drug Encouragement Agency?" said Springer.

Summers smiled and looking at Gerry said, "And you're Gerry Knucks."

"Nugent," said Gerry, correcting him but not saying anything else. Eyes flat.

"What do you do for a living, Mr. Nugent?"

Gerry looked at Springer. "I design Brooks Brothers suits."

Ryder laughed. Summers's face flushed and he nodded, a terse smile on his face. "That's pretty good. What do you call this particular suit I'm wearing?"

Nugent looked him in the eyes and said, "It's from our uptight asshole line."

"You think this is a funny situation, Mr. Nugent?"

Gerry looked at him. Said nothing.

"We have quite a file on you, Knucks," said Summers, emphasizing the nickname. Gerry didn't change expression. "On you too, Springer."

"Did you read the part where I single-handedly saved Kuwait from the Persian menace?"

"I read the part where you threatened a superior officer."

The superior officer was a British officer, not an American. Guy told Springer to get his "Yank carcass off his chair." Springer told the guy to move his Yank carcass off the chair himself, that he wanted to see that. Then the Brit took a tone with him and Springer told him he'd be glad to get up, if only to knock the guy on his English ass.

"Just tried to help the guy regain some perspective. Let him know we were all in this together in the spirit of cooperation."

"There are other incidents."

"What's a life without other incidents?"

"What did you hope to accomplish here?" said Summers.

Springer looked at him and said, "I see you, you see me, we see each other. You've been following me around for days so I just thought I'd swing by and say hello. Friendly."

"We're not following you."

"See? Now you're going to ruin things by being disingenuous."

Gerry got up and walked to the bar and stood with his back to the table. "Well, fellas," said Springer, getting up. "Looks like my friend is ready to leave."

"Smart-assed bastard," said Ryder.

"No," said Springer. "Don't ask us to stay. We have to go. Good talking to you guys."

As Springer walked by, Gerry joined him. As they walked out of the bar, Gerry said, "What the fuck are you doing?"

"Getting their attention."

Gerry shook his head. "You don't brush back the feds unless you're fucking mental. Now they're going to be all over us."

"That's what I want," said Springer. "We need them."

"Well, I guess you know what you're doing."
"Don't know what I could've said that'd make you think that."

Tobi Ryder drove out to Springer's place, drumming her fingers on the steering wheel, chewing vigorously on her lower lip. He wasn't home. She got back in the Explorer, slammed the door shut and looked out the window. Picked up the radio mike and called in. Asked the dispatcher if a Max Shapiro was registered in any of the hotels in Aspen, taking a chance.

"That may take a while," the dispatcher said.

"Check the more expensive ones first."

"I don't know. You know how these places are about the privacy of their patrons. I could work on this for two days and not get anywhere."

Tobi signed off. Turned on the car stereo. Stevie Nicks's voice came on. Then she got a break. If you could call it that.

Springer pulled up in front of the house.

Tobi got out of the Explorer and walked toward Springer, who was getting out of his car, looking like he was glad to see her.

"Where the hell have you been?" she asked.

"Gee whiz, Mom," said Springer, giving her a Beaver Cleaver voice. "All the other guys get to go out and do things."

"Who put you in charge of protecting me?"

That stopped him. For the first time since she'd known him, he didn't have a smart remark or a smile. Good.

He started to say something, stopped. Then he coughed.

She said, "You think I can't take care of myself?"

"That isn't why."

"Well, you want to tell me why? What did you do?"

"Ask him."

"I'm asking you."

"Just wanted him to give some consideration to how he should treat a . . . how he should treat you."

"How he should treat a woman? That right?"

Springer shrugged. "Yeah."

"Did you hit him?"

"He say I did?"

"Don't answer questions with a question."

"Do I do that?" Smiling now. Back in smart-ass mode.

"Did you hit him?"

"No."

"What'd you do? Be specific."

"Just told him I didn't like him grabbing you."

"And?"

"Pissed him off. So he took a swing at me and I sorta had to subdue him a little."

"Subdue him a little, huh?"

He nodded.

"And you probably thought I'd never know about it?"

"Didn't know he was going to tell on me." Giving her the look now. Thinking he was cute and getting to her.

"Well, I don't need you to do that for me."

"Okay."

"That all you have to say?"

"You want to go inside? Have a drink?"

She shook her head and walked back to her vehicle. Left him standing there. Let him think about that for a while.

CHAPTER

Twenty-Five

RAY DEAN WAS DRUMMING HIS FINGERS ON THE HOOD OF the Mercedes E55. He was cold. Gerry Knucks was standing there with his hands in his coat pockets, saying nothing, looking at nothing, standing there like he was on a street corner in L.A. instead of freezing to death in an Aspen parking lot. They were standing outside Nicky's new car in this big grocery store parking lot. Auteen was leaning against the front fender. They were waiting for the guy.

Going to see the smart-assed guy again for the first time since he shot his toe. Toe was doing better today. He'd gone back to the doctor and they'd given him some stuff. Rewrapped it and told him to stay off it for a couple of days. Gave him a cane which caused Auteen to go into convulsions because he was dumber than shit. Couldn't believe Nicky drove in all the way from the coast for a meeting with this guy. Which meant they were going to do business. Which meant Ray Dean couldn't pop a cap in the guy's ass.

The driver's side window rolled down.

"Cut that shit out," said Nicky, from inside the car.

"What?" said Ray Dean.

"Drumming your fingers on my ride. Why you think I want fingerprints all over my car? Who you think you are. Gene Krupa?"

"Who's Gene Krupa?"

"That's right," said Nicky. "They probably don't teach that on *Sesame Street*."

Ray Dean looked at Gerry Knucks and shrugged, his palms up. Knucks just looked at him with those killer shark eyes. Knucks.

Fuck him and Nicky, too. What a couple of shitbags. Why'd he have to put up with all this? And now he'd have to put up with the wise-ass guy that shot him. What a fucked-up life.

"Tell the fat guy to get off my fender, too," said Nicky.

Auteen stood up. Ray Dean wanted to laugh when he saw Auteen's jaw tighten up, knowing the large homeboy was pissed off.

"We got a job to do and we gonna do it," Ray Dean said, imitating Auteen.

"Man, you fuck yo'self."

Ray Dean pursed his lips in a mock kiss.

Nicky said, "And shut the fuck up out there, huh? I'm trying to think and I don't want to hear your voices. Gerry, where's this guy?"

"He'll be here," said Gerry, not changing expression.

"How you like this car?"

"It's nice."

"Fucking thing's like driving a cloud. Ain't it like riding in a cloud, Donny?"

"Yeah," said Donny Black. "Just like riding in a cloud."

Good gosh, thought Gerry. How long before this shit was over?

"Here he comes," said Gerry.

It was twilight when Springer pulled into the parking lot, the fading sunlight breaking up into unusual colors over the mountains. He could hear the river rapids bubbling to the north, late afternoon bikers coming up off the bike trail which ran along the river. He looked at the two cars parked near the back of the large lot. A blue rental job and a factory fresh Mercedes Benz. Three men standing outside. One of them would be Gerry Nugent.

Gerry had told him that things were upside down back in Frisco. The Big Boss, Mostelli, had died and now Nicky's boss, Joey Guardino and Sonny Blue were vying for control of Bay area rackets. There was three million missing and Guardino was making noise about Sonny Blue ripping it off.

And Gerry warned him about Tortino.

"Nicky'll want me to frisk you because he's paranoid and he'll wanna be the show, you know what I mean? Let him be the man

but hold your own. Talking to Nicky T is a high wire act. He'll be
trying to intimidate you, scare you, but you've got to come up with
a way of making him see you're a serious player, y'understand? Just
don't pimp him in front of the help 'cause then he'll go into his
Capo act and it's just getting old to hear it.

"And, another thing," Gerry said. "Don't get in the guy's face
with your attitude."

"I have an attitude?" said Springer.

"Boy, do you have an attitude."

As Springer pulled closer, he could see Auteen and Ray Dean
moving around the car. Gerry didn't move. Smarter than the other
two. Already standing where the car blocked him from the street,
behind the back door where he could get it open in a hurry for
cover, knowing from which direction trouble would most likely
come.

Springer parked his car in front of the Mercedes, forming a "T."
He had the Colt Python in a shoulder holster under his coat and
the Beretta Tomcat in the back pocket of his jeans.

What he hadn't told Gerry was that he'd already figured something out on his own. And it had to do with Nicky Tortino driving
himself to Aspen instead of flying. Guy had a reason for driving.

Springer got out of the car.

Gerry watched Springer's car coming toward them. Springer pulled
the car in front of the Mercedes, the passenger door toward them.
Smart. Blocking them from going forward and allowing Springer to
get out of his car on the side away from them. If shit started he
had a car to stand behind and they'd have to back out to leave.
From what Gerry had seen so far, Springer would go down hard if
they tried to take him, if they could take him, which he doubted
they could do without Gerry's help.

Gerry touched the jagged scar by his eye and looked at the
others.

Ray Dean and Auteen moved around to Gerry's side, Ray Dean
trying to look tough, letting a cigarette dangle from his mouth and
slouching like he was some juvenile delinquent with a Brylcream

D.A. and a switchblade in his pocket. Auteen was standing up, bulling his chest, his arms hanging at an angle from his sides because of his size. Both were frowning like they'd just escaped from a Robert De Niro festival. Mad at Springer. A couple of carnival freaks, though Auteen was a handful and Ray Dean was a dirty little bastard that'd break his own mother's fingers if she were behind on the vig. Gerry didn't underestimate anyone.

Springer got out of the car, wearing a dark leather bomber jacket, black jeans, and hiking boots and walked slowly around to the rear of his car. Stood there, his legs slightly apart, framed by the mountains in the distance. Guy knew how to use his rangy frame and shoulders to make an impact. It was a no-bullshit stance. Doing it on purpose.

"Where is he?" asked Springer, demanded it actually. "He in there?" Indicating the car with a nod of his head.

Gerry nodded, almost smiling. Springer coming on hardcore, letting Nicky know he wasn't afraid.

"What the fuck did that sonuvabitch say?" Nicky asked, from inside the car.

"Wanted to know where you were, boss," said Ray Dean.

"I'm right here. Is he fucking blind?"

"He sees you," said Gerry, not looking at Nicky.

Donny Black got out of the car on the driver's side. All 240 pounds of ex-cop. He opened the door so Nicky could get out. Nicky got out, buttoning up his topcoat, a silk scarf tucked into the collar. Black kid leather gloves. Springer looked at the five of them and smiled.

"Well, you guys must've heard what a bad man I am. Five guys." He let out a low whistle. "I'm flattered."

"Don't let it go to your head," said Nicky. "You wanta talk? We're here to talk."

"Not in front of the kids," said Springer, nodding at Ray Dean and Auteen.

"Say what?" said Auteen.

"Shut up, Auteen," said Nicky, not taking his eyes off Springer. "You think you can come here and decide who goes where? That it?"

"I came to talk to the man who can say yes to this deal."

"That'd be me."

Springer nodded.

"You a tough guy?" Nicky asked.

"I get by."

Then Nicky said, "Yeah? Look at this guy." Meaning Gerry. "He's the best there is. I tell him to take you down and you disappear. Got that?"

"So," said Springer, expression unchanged, "do I avoid pissing him off? Or you?"

Gerry's eyes widened in disbelief. What is it with this Springer guy?

"You think you can come here and talk shit out the side of your mouth? To me? You whitebread cornball-looking motherfucker? What're you smiling at anyway? You think shit can't happen to you?"

"This schoolyard stuff wastes time. You have to act tough and I'm sure you are, even though I'm not the one who brought four guys with me and then I have to say something shows you I'm not scared and it just, you know, wears on me. You want to hear what I have to say or not?"

"I'm listening."

"Before I say anything you need to cut back on the muscle," said Springer. He motioned at Gerry with his hand. "He can stay. The others need to back off."

"Frisk him, Donny," said Nicky. The ex-cop took a step toward Springer.

Springer said, "No need. I'll show you what I got." He unzipped his jacket and showed them the Colt Python. "And, I got a .32 auto in my pocket. I'm not going to use them. You think I came here to shoot all five of you in a parking lot? Then, go inside and buy a loaf of bread and some milk?"

"Still got to check you," said Donny Black. "See if you're wired."

Springer shrugged and raised his arms while Donny Black checked him.

"Whoa, that tickles," said Springer, doubling up. Gerry watching. Did Springer make some kind of funny move? His hands had gone to Donny's side. What was he doing? Gerry couldn't tell. Donny stood up quick and told him to knock it off, then resumed his frisk. Satisfied, Donny stepped back. To Nicky, Donny said, "He's clean."

"You guys take a walk," said Nicky to Ray Dean, Auteen, and Donny. Ray Dean glared at Springer before he walked away. Springer winked at him.

Nicky moved closer to Springer and said, "You're the guy wants to talk to me? What've you gotta say that could interest me? A guy drives a piece of shit like that?" Pointing at Springer's car. "Take a look at that beauty behind me. That's an E-Fifty-five Mercedes Benz. Seventy grand, list. Got a Bose stereo and eight speakers. Fucking stereo cost more than your whole ride."

Springer smiling. "So what now? You want to unzip our pants and compare length?"

Gerry wondering what made Springer say shit like that to a demented bastard like Nicky T. The guy was as fucking crazy as Nicky in his own way.

Nicky turned to Gerry and said, "Tell me again why I'm talking to this motherfucker."

"He's got a deal for you."

Nicky folded his gloved hands over his chest, and said to Springer. "So, what is it?"

"I know where Max is and he wants to make friends."

"What if I don't want to make friends with him?"

"That'll be your choice," said Springer. "You can keep trying to kill him and maybe you get him. Maybe you get me. Maybe I get one of your guys. Maybe I even get you."

"You think you could do that?"

"I'm pretty good at it."

"That would be the biggest mistake you'll ever make."

"Made 'em before," said Springer. "You have to ask yourself if I'm worth the trouble. I've got a federal background and it might shake people up who work for the government. Who killed this guy that used to guard the president? Why was Nicky Tortino in Aspen? Did it have anything to do with Carmine Mostelli's death? You think that won't occur to them? I don't think you want that. The alternative is you put Max back to work and you both benefit. Guy thought he was dying or he wouldn't have acted so crazy."

"What's in it for you?"

"Piece of the action. Max puts up good-faith money of his own and I take a cut."

"Why would Max do that? Doesn't make sense."

"Consider it a payoff. Max puts money down and he lets you know that he wants to be friends. He wants to live. Like Henry Kissinger says, 'Everyone is rational about their own survival.'"

"Who?"

"Henry Kissinger. He used to play linebacker for the Bears."

"Yeah," said Nicky, nodding as if it just came to him. "I remember him now."

Gerry not believing any of this.

"So, why don't I just take all the money?" Nicky said. "Clean it myself?"

"Because the money you want cleaned up is hot. Scorching. You don't dare get caught with it. I get caught with it or Max gets caught with it, then you're clean. And Max is the best at it. He'll hide it and no one, not the feds, not the wiseguys, nobody, will connect it to you. You can go ahead and get someone else to do it, you want to, but Max still wants to walk away from this with your blessings."

"What do I need you for?"

"Max is too scared to give it to you directly. I'm the bag man. If you've got money you want to lay off I give it to him."

"You think I'm going to give you money to clean? My money? You think that? You're a fucking piece of work. I don't work with independents. I work with my people."

This was the part that Gerry had told him was dicey. Nicky wouldn't want to let Springer touch his money.

Springer said, "So, your man there," meaning Gerry, "goes with me. Wherever the money goes."

"Why don't I just send him and you stay out of it?"

"Because Max is afraid you'll send him to hit him. He'll want me there."

"What if I send one of the others?"

"Max trusts Knucks, not the others. Besides, from what I've seen, you're not going to give real money to the gimp or the big kid."

"How much is Max willing to put up?"

"A hundred grand."

Gerry could see Nicky thinking on it. The possibility of getting several thousand dollars when he was going to use Max anyway was working on the guy. "What's the cut?"

"Sixty-forty. Plus Max gets his usual piece of any money he cleans up."

"Meaning sixty for you?"

"Sure, why not? I'm setting up the deal."

"Max know you're cutting yourself in?"

"Hasn't a clue," said Springer. Springer sinking the hook in Nicky's jaw now. Knowing Nicky would be okay with a deal where somebody was conning somebody else. Classic wiseguy thinking. If Springer was screwing Max it must be a good deal.

Nicky looked at Gerry, thumbed in the direction of Springer, and said, "You believe the balls on this guy?"

Gerry said nothing.

"Okay, tough guy," said Nicky. He looked off at the mountains like he hadn't noticed them before, then back at Springer. "We do this and I get fifty-five percent."

"No."

"No? What have you got I don't go along?"

"The satisfaction of knowing I'm doing the right thing."

"What would the right thing be?"

"Taking care of Max Shapiro who hired me to watch out for him."

"Could get you dead."

"Always a possibility."

"But, that don't bother you, right?"

"Something you factor in when you take the money. It's like skiing or sky-diving. You know something bad could happen. Something dangerous. But you do it anyway. And you don't think about it. Keeps it interesting."

"You want to work for me?"

"No thanks."

"Fifty-fifty cut. Take it or I walk."

Springer pretending to think about it now. Appearing hesitant before agreeing to it. Guy was pretty good at this.

"All right," said Springer. "Fifty-fifty cut, but we do it my way and Max is square with you."

Nicky nodded. "When's this gonna take place? And where?"

"Two days. My club."

"You own a club?"

"The Whiskey Basin Tavern."

Tortino laughed. "Catchy name." Making fun of it.

"I like it and 'Pastafazoola' was already taken."

That stopped Nicky, who was getting little white balls of saliva at the corners of his mouth like he did before he blew his stack. What the hell was Springer thinking about? Guy couldn't let anything go. No wonder he didn't stay in government work. Son of a bitch took no shit at all.

Nicky's head was bobbing up and down like a wind-up toy. "Yeah? You're a fucking clown, you know that? Keep fuckin' around and see what happens."

Springer shrugged. "Just making conversation."

Nicky jabbed a finger in Springer's chest. "This better work like you say."

Springer looked down at the point where Nicky had poked him and for a moment Gerry was afraid the guy was going to pop Nicky. It was the first time Gerry had ever seen the guy mad. Showed in his eyes. Nicky was too fucking dumb to know he was crossing the line. Gerry was just realizing Springer could be a scary bastard.

Finally, Springer raised his eyes and between teeth set in a straight line, said, "It will."

Springer got in his car and left. Before he got in his car, Springer pointed a finger at Ray Dean and with his thumb mocking a gun hammer acted like he was shooting Ray Dean. When Springer finally left Gerry exhaled, not realizing he'd been holding his breath.

"That motherfucker," said Ray Dean.

"Man said 'bang' to you, boy," said Auteen.

Ray Dean grabbed his crotch and said, "Whyn't you come over and bite this."

Nicky turned to Gerry. "What about this guy?"

"He'll do what he says," said Gerry.

"He'd better."

Gerry looked at Springer driving away. Hoped Springer was aware of the danger in this situation. But, you didn't know with this guy.

"When this is over I want that motherfucker dead," said Nicky, jabbing a finger in the direction of Springer's departing car.

"That might not be the best way to go," said Gerry. "Like he said, he might attract attention, being an ex-Secret Service man."

"I'll fuckin' do it," said Ray Dean.

"Yeah?" said Gerry. "You've done real well with him so far."

Springer drove back to the club and waited for Gerry, listening to Mozart on the classical station. Helped him think. It had gone like they'd wanted but the encounter was a little surreal. Springer had seen mob guys before. Had turned some of them away from official White House gatherings, even when they had invitations. They blustered and bitched but left anyway. But he'd never really had an encounter with them like this one. And Gerry said Tortino wasn't even made yet. Springer almost pushed it too far, but couldn't stop himself. This creep in his expensive clothes and car, didn't know who Henry Kissinger was, but pretending he did anyway. There was something about Tortino that suggested just a touch of madness. Like he was capable of having Gerry and the other goons waste him on the spot just because Springer pissed him off.

The amount of gorilla power Tortino could bring to bear on the situation was something to think about. A little scary, in fact. He needed to cut down the odds. Which, if everything went right, he may already have done.

But now he was committed and there would be no turning back. All or nothing. Live or die. What the hell, though? Nobody lives forever.

Springer saw the plain-Jane Taurus rental pull into the lot and watched Gerry Nugent's big shoulders emerge from the driver's side. The enforcer looked around the lot before walking to Springer's car and getting in on the passenger side.

First thing he said to Springer was, "What the fuck are you thinking about? I told you not to yank Nicky's chain, but no, you gotta do it anyway."

"Yes, you're right. It is a beautiful evening."

"What do you think that smart shit's gonna get you? Huh? First, you do it to the feds and now you do it to Nicky. And let me tell you something, the guy is a functioning psychopath who'd give no more thought to blowing your ass away than to what color socks he's gonna wear."

"I want him to be thinking about me. Not about Max. Not about the money. I want him to dislike me."

"Well, you accomplished that. He wants you dead when this is over."

"Did he seem to express any sense of remorse about that?"

"Yeah, make jokes," said Gerry. "This shit ain't funny. Guy nods his head in Frisco and people die and you think it's a source of humor. He wanted me to do it, but Ray Dean liked to shit himself volunteering to ice you."

"Ray Dean?" Springer said, brightening now. "How's he going to do that? Limp over to my place and shoot me with a cane gun?"

Springer was smiling now, enjoying himself. Gerry looked at him, and started smiling with him. Really smiling. Gerry said, "You're a crazy bastard, that's for sure."

"More fun that way."

"You get us killed I'm gonna kick your ass."

"Might be hard to do. Besides, it'd piss Suzi off. She likes me, you know."

Gerry was quiet. He looked at Springer. Not a hard look. More like he was thinking about what he was going to say but not sure he wanted to say it.

Springer helped him out. "She talks about you."

"Who?" said Gerry.

"Don't hand me that 'what are you talking about' crap. Suzi, that's who."

"Yeah?" Gerry looked out the passenger window. "What does she say?"

"She likes you."

"She's nice."

"She likes you a lot."

"She's Max's girl."

"Was."

"She's still with him. What about that?"

"She's not the type to run out when things are tough."

Gerry said nothing for a few moments. Then started slowly shaking his head. "No. There's no way she could have anything for me. Wouldn't work."

"Why don't you let her decide that?"

Gerry shrugged. It was quiet again for a while.

"You listen to that classical shit?" said Gerry, finally.

"Mozart. One of his more famous pieces. The name of it is—"

"Yeah, I know," said Gerry. "It's *Eine Kleine Nachtmusik.* I heard it before."

Springer looked at him funny. "Well, check out the enigmatic Gerry Knucks, mob enforcer."

"Aw, fuck you. You think all I do is go around and shoot people?"

CHAPTER

Twenty-Six

TOBI RYDER HAD FOOLED HIM THIS TIME. SHE WAS DRIVING an impounded Thunderbird she'd checked out from Aspen P.D. Tied her hair up and stuck the whole thing under a Colorado Rockies baseball cap. She kind of liked the look. She followed Springer to the supermarket parking lot where he turned in. She drove on and parked across the street at the little strip mall where she could see what he was up to.

She watched him through Bushnell binoculars. There were five other men there besides Springer. All of them looked like thugs. One of them was Nicky Tortino whom she recognized from the FBI files Summers had shown her. What was Tortino doing in Aspen? She watched a heavy-set guy pat Springer down then step back. What was going on? Why was Springer meeting with Nicky Tortino? Springer was keeping a lot of balls in the air and her cop intuition was going off like a fire alarm.

And now she'd followed him back to the Whiskey Basin where he sat like he was waiting for someone. A woman? Why did that thought come into her mind?

Five minutes passed and a white Taurus pulled up. One of the men she'd seen at the supermarket, the oldest of the crew, who looked like a cross between a younger Gene Hackman and Nick Nolte got out of the Taurus and into the car with Springer.

What the hell was going on?

Springer meets with five thugs and then goes somewhere else and one of the hoods meets him again. Why? What was Springer doing? Was it a deal to get Max off the hook with Nicky T? Or something else? Would Springer do something illegal?

He was broke and his club was in trouble. How desperate for cash was he? She'd heard that the assault charge against him had been dropped. Would that be something that Nicky T could arrange? In Aspen? Doubtful. She couldn't bring herself to think that Springer could do something illegal. Wasn't the type. But how many times had she heard a family member or a wife say that "he couldn't possibly do that. He's not like that." She was a cop and could not rule out that possibility.

There was a lot to Cole Springer that remained unanswered in her mind. She thought he just liked to play at being cryptic but maybe he had another reason for being mysterious. Underneath it all—the half-smile, the glib banter—was another dimension to the man. She'd seen it, felt it when he held her. Read it in his eyes.

And still she hadn't told him that she thought Summers had planted drugs in his apartment. Why hadn't she told him that? Maybe she was hoping Summers couldn't be that much of a jerk. If Summers could do that, who was the bad guy here? Where were the lines? Her dad had always told her, "Lacey," he'd say, he called her Lacey when Mother wasn't around. "The difference between us and the bad guys is we play by the rules. Don't plant evidence, don't take short cuts, or take a bribe because that's the first step to abuse of the badge. If everyone breaks the rules, how do you know who the good guys are?"

And, for whatever reason, Springer reminded her of her father. Couldn't put her finger on it. Maybe it was because they both seemed to function separately from the pack mentality. Lived by their own code. She could see her dad telling the president's chief of staff the same thing Springer did. And walking out with a smile on his face. That must be it. Their reaction to situations was dictated by their sense of individuality and not by other people's priorities.

They were different. Unique. Dinosaurs. Both of them. And she loved them both for it. There it was. She loved this man. This outlaw piano player. It just came to her.

So, why did she have him under surveillance?

He was going to drive her crazy if she let him.

Right then she decided she was going to tell him that Summers may have planted something in his apartment. But, she'd have to wait until the heavyset man left.

Several minutes passed before the heavyset man got out of Springer's car, started the white Taurus, and left the lot. Now the Taurus was coming this way. She leaned down like she was getting something out of the glove box, taking her time. Did the Taurus slow down as it approached the Thunderbird? Finally, she sat up and saw it in her rearview mirror getting smaller.

She looked up just as Springer left the parking lot of the Whiskey Basin. Headed in the opposite direction. Damn. Now where was he going?

She was following him again, now. Staying back but not worrying too much as she didn't think he'd recognize this car. She had stayed a good distance behind earlier so she didn't think he had noticed the T-bird before.

After a few minutes she realized he was headed for his apartment. She dropped back and took her time, turning off about a mile from his place. She drove up the off-road, did a three-point turn and headed back for the road to Springer's.

It was then she saw them.

David Ryder and Jack Summers. They were in David's federal car on the road to Springer's place. And they were in a hurry.

She was going to be too late.

Springer was getting out of his car when he saw them pull up, skidding to a stop like it was crimebusters incorporated. The DEA agent and the FBI man. Both with reason to enjoy rousting him. They were accompanied by another man in a DEA jacket.

The trio of federal agents got out of the car, a Dodge Intrepid, and came toward him. Ryder slipped, then regained his balance, as he got out of the car.

"Cole Springer?" said Ryder.

"Haven't seen him."

"Mr. Springer," said Summers, official now. "Special Agent Summers, FBI. Agents Ryder and Maxwell of the DEA. We have a search warrant, signed by a federal judge, to search your premises."

"I threw out all my *Playboys* so it's a waste of time."

"We have information from a reliable source that you are trafficking in a controlled substance. Specifically cocaine."

Springer stopped, narrowed his eyes at them. "Reliable source, huh? Who would that be?"

"Of course we can't reveal that," said Summers.

"Of course," said Springer. "Just trying to trip you up."

"You're going to be a smart-ass right up to the end, aren't you?" said Ryder.

"Well, come on in," said Springer. "*Drew Carey*'s coming on pretty soon and I don't want to miss it."

Springer looked up as a Green Thunderbird pulled up behind the Intrepid. The three men stopped and watched as Tobi Ryder got out of the car, a baseball cap on her head. Looking girlish and good with her slender neck exposed.

"Another cop?" said Springer. "I maybe need to swing by the post office and see if my picture's down there." He waved at Tobi, and said, "You're just in time. Toody and Muldoon here have a warrant to search my apartment. Guess you didn't want to miss this."

"It's not like—" She stopped herself. "I'm not with these guys."

"Might as well come along, anyway. Participate in the arrest of the biggest crime lord in the Rocky Mountains. Maybe you can help them beat a confession out of me."

"Yes, Tobi," said Summers. "Come along. I think this will interest you."

"Nothing you do interests me," she said, bristling. Springer impressed by the force she could put into an expression. Maybe she *didn't* know what was going on here.

"I think this will be different," Summers said.

Springer unlocked the door, stepped back and swept his arm for them to enter ahead of him.

"Quit clowning around," said David Ryder. "Lead the way."

"Don't know why," said Springer. "Your buddy knows where everything is."

Ryder gave him a funny look. "What's that mean?"

"Nothing. Just being oblique. I'm often oblique."

Ryder said "fucking smart-ass," under his breath while Summers gave Springer a look. Tobi looked concerned.

Springer led them up the stairs to his second-floor apartment. The door was unlocked. Once inside he said, "You care if I play some music?"

"Do what you want," said David Ryder.

"Any requests? How about 'You Ain't Got Nothin' Yet'?"

"If you tell us where the stuff is," said Summers, "We won't have to tear things up."

"No," said Springer. "Go ahead. Enjoy yourself. But, if you're really serious, why don't you just start with the desk first?"

That stopped everything.

"What the hell does that mean?" said David Ryder. "You being oblique again?"

"I notice you wear your watch on your right wrist," said Springer to Jack Summers.

"Yeah. I'm left-handed. So what?"

"Well," said Springer, looking at Tobi. "It was a left-handed guy that went through my apartment when I wasn't here."

David Ryder looked at Summers. Summers looked at Ryder, then at Tobi and finally back at Springer. "If you think this will keep us from going through this apartment then you're fooling yourself. We've got a legitimate search warrant here and—"

"You know what pisses me off the most? What really cooks my balls? You touched her letters. You touched them. You shouldn't have done that. That'll cost you."

"That sounds like a threat."

"You never get it, do you? You just keep peddling that tired G-man act. Why don't you come right at me? It's all about her, anyway." He indicated Tobi with a nod in her direction. "That's what it is with both of you." The two men were staring hard at him now. Tobi's mouth was open, her eyes wide. Agent Maxwell looked confused.

"This is ridiculous," said Summers, avoiding Tobi's look. "I'll check the bedroom, Maxwell, you take this room and David—"

"I'll sit here and watch," said Ryder, folding his arms across his chest.

Summers said, "Suit yourself."

"He knew we were coming," said Ryder. "Someone tipped him off." He looked at his ex-wife now. "You?"

"Oh, screw you, David," Tobi said. "You chose to throw in with Efrem Zimbalist, Jr. So, this is what you get. You trusted a guy who hits on your wife before you're divorced."

"You didn't have to go out with him."

"You two ever going to get over that?" said Summers, heading for the bedroom.

"I'm way over it," said Tobi, glaring at David.

She turned to Springer. "I didn't have anything to do with this," she said.

"But, you knew about it, right?"

She had a look on her face that was halfway between hurt and angry so Springer didn't push it. Like he didn't push the left-handed thing with Summers which had nothing to do with which way he wound the cord on the vacuum cleaner, but Summers didn't know that.

Springer knew that Summers would have to go through with the search, even though he wasn't going to find anything. He had to carry out the search warrant or give away the fact that he had planted the cocaine.

After an hour of going through Springer's apartment Summers gave up the charade. By that time, Springer was playing the piano. Some Scott Joplin, some classic Chopin, and for the benefit of his guests he played the Pink Panther theme but nobody laughed, although David Ryder's jaw tensed.

"This is bullshit," said David Ryder. "I'll wait outside. I need a cigarette anyway. You coming Maxwell?" Maxwell nodded. The DEA men left, Ryder giving Summers one last look of disgust before he walked out.

Springer was looking at Summers. Summers said, "What's your problem?"

"I'm waiting for you to say, 'curses, foiled again.' "

Summers raised his chin and considered Springer momentarily. "Look, a . . . Springer, I guess I made a mistake."

"No mistake. You tried to burn me."

"My information said that you were trafficking—"

Springer started laughing. "Aw, please. You planted the stuff and thought you'd come up here and catch me with the goods.

Instead, you look stupid. The thing I don't get is why? What did you hope to accomplish? Make me look bad to her?"

"Tell him, Jack," said Tobi. "Tell him or I will."

Summers pursed his mouth. Sat down on a overstuffed chair. "All right," Summers said. "I want your help in taking down Nicky Tortino and Max Shapiro."

"Why didn't you say so?"

Summers leaned forward. "You'll help us?"

"With Tortino. Max isn't on the menu. He walks."

"I don't know," said Summers.

"Knock it off, Jack," said Tobi. "You don't want Shapiro and you can't get Tortino without his help. He can get you for breaking and entering, for planting evidence. And I'll testify against you."

"Hearsay evidence."

"Hearsay evidence taken in direct testimony by an officer of the State of Colorado to a grand jury? How do you think that will sound? Anyway you cut it you won't look good. You'll end up indicted for sure and you'll lose your job. You're bluffing with Shapiro. You don't have anything to bargain with here. You overplayed your hand with this sham search. Get Tortino and be done with it. You said yourself that you've been trying to make a case against Tortino for years and now you have your chance. This would be a big arrest for you."

"Maybe I don't need Springer."

"What does that mean?" Tobi asked.

"He thinks he's got Shapiro in his pocket," said Springer.

Summers's mouth almost fell open but he caught himself. He looked at Springer.

Springer said, "What do you think, Jack? You think I trust Max? A guy whose every first thought is what Max wants? What's good for Max? A guy who would deal with a piece of raw sewage like Tortino? I'm the guy checked him into the Ritz. I'm the guy knows the head of security there. Guy I go elk hunting with every fall. They kept an eye on Max for me. Told me what he did, who he talked to. Told me when you got there and when you left. Max kept your visit a secret from me. Don't know what else you two could've been talking about."

Summers shoulders slumped an eighth-of-an-inch. "Will you help us?"

"Hell, why not? But Max is clean when this is over and you don't tell him that you and I have a deal. I want him to think that you and he are on the same page. It'll make him feel like he's screwing me and that'll make him happy."

"I can do that."

"And, I have another request."

"Yeah, what's that?"

"The guy with me in the bar? Gerry Nugent? He walks away clean, too."

"What? Gerry Knucks? Are you crazy? The man is a killer."

"But he dresses well."

"No way."

"I can give you Tortino and by implication, a line on Joey "the Neck" Guardino. That change your mind?"

"Maybe."

Springer looked at Tobi. "Man's the king of the non-comment." He turned back to Summers. "Choose. Right now."

Summers was struggling with it. He had looked bad in front of the ex-girlfriend and fellow cop. He had looked bad in front of the DEA. He was having to deal with a guy he didn't like. But he was a cop and he didn't want to go away empty-handed.

"All right," said Summers, finally. "It's a deal. I can swing it for Shapiro and Nugent. But Nugent has to testify."

"No. He won't do that anyway. He'd rather die. It's all or nothing."

Summers nodded his head. "Okay. Nugent walks. Anything else?"

"Yeah, you pay to have my place cleaned up."

"When will I know what's going down?"

"I'll tell you where to be and when to be there just before it happens. You come alone and it's your bust."

"So, I'm just supposed to wait around until you tell me something?"

Springer nodded. "It'll be worth it to you. Promise."

"Why should I believe you?"

"I have no idea."

"What in the hell did you do with the cocaine?"

"I think it may be in the coat pocket of an ex-cop named Donny Black. You put those DEA guys on it and I think you can redeem yourself with them."

Tobi Ryder sat on the sofa and sipped the Dr Pepper Springer had poured over ice for her. Summers had left.

"Why did you meet with Nicky Tortino?" she asked Springer as he sat down facing her.

"You saw that?"

She nodded.

"Followed me. That's pretty good. Forgot what I was doing for a moment," he said. "Or . . ."

"Or what?"

"Or, I let you follow me."

"If that's what you want to believe," she said.

"You were going to let them bust me with planted evidence," he said.

She felt her face flush. "I was coming to tell you."

"Quite a delay between knowledge and revelation. Must've been pretty conflicted."

"You came out all right."

"What if I hadn't?"

She looked into his eyes. "I'm sorry, Cole. I should've said something. I wouldn't have let them make the case."

He relaxed his shoulders and leaned back in the overstuffed chair. "You're a cop. You couldn't rat out a fellow officer. I understand that."

"What's going on with Tortino?"

"I should tell you, huh?" he said.

"If you want to."

He looked at her. She looked back. Finally, he exhaled and put his hands behind his neck. "Okay, this is what I think is going down. You know who Carmine Mostelli is?"

She nodded. "I know he died."

"Mostelli was the Big Boss in the Bay area rackets. There's three million dollars missing, too. Mostelli's getaway money. If the feds put the heat on, he was going to use it to go someplace and wait it out. Anyway, Tortino originally wanted Max Shapiro dead. That's what Ray Dean Carr was doing the day you tackled him. He was sent to kill Max. You stopped it.

"Then, Mostelli dies and out of the clear blue, Nicky decides to forgive Max. Why? Nicky works for Joey Guardino, one of two San Francisco underbosses who want Mostelli's seat at the big table. The other guy is called Sonny Blue. Guardino is making trouble for Sonny Blue, telling the other wiseguys that Sonny took the three million. Everybody bracing for war. Meanwhile, Nicky Tortino personally *drives* out to Aspen to meet with me and he wants Max to do some work for him. Guys like Nicky T don't drive to see somebody like me unless someone tells them to. They fly or they send someone. He got sent. Why come to see me? Why did he drive?"

Tobi thought about it. "Because he doesn't want the airlines to handle bags filled with cash."

"Exactly. The money is too hot for him to trust someone else with it. And the deal is too big for him to send a subordinate. You might want to check local banks to see if Nicky or Gerry Nugent checked out a safe deposit box. So, I make a deal with him to get Max to launder some money, which Nicky never says how much, in exchange for Max's life. Now, you need to understand that Tortino is a legitimate psychopath who will never allow me or Max to live. I know this because first, he doesn't like me, second, he's mad at Max for walking out on him, and third, he doesn't like witnesses. Not because he's afraid of the cops, though. It's because he's afraid of the very people he works for. Anyone finds out he laundered stolen mob money, then Nicky T is a dead man. Guardino too. They eat their own."

"How does this connect with Charlemagne's murder?"

"I don't know yet," said Springer. "But, from what I've seen of Ray Dean Carr, I think maybe he just lost his temper and killed the guy. For his own reasons. But that's just a guess. Maybe there was a contract on Charlemagne. Nothing makes sense when you're dealing with recidivist imbeciles like Ray Dean Carr."

"Who was the guy you met with in the Whiskey Basin parking lot?"

He looked at her. "You're pretty smart. For a girl." Giving her the smile now. "His name is Gerry Nugent. His name on the street is Gerry Knucks. The best enforcer on the West Coast. He is what makes Nicky T a force."

"The guy you want Summers to let off the hook. So why is he meeting with you?"

He shrugged. "We need some mystery between us."

She bristled a little. Didn't like it that he was smiling at her reaction. "Don't play games with me. I care about you."

"And I care about you," he said, his face softening, and Tobi could tell what he looked like when he was a boy.

"I care about you," she said, "but if you're running a crooked game, I'll close you out."

"A tough broad."

"I'm not kidding."

"Okay."

They looked at each other for a moment. These moments were becoming provocative and intense, but she didn't know what to do about that. He made her feel things she didn't normally feel.

He said, "You ever see *The Thomas Crown Affair?* Not the new one. The sixties one with Steve McQueen and Faye Dunaway?"

"A long time ago," she said. "He was a millionaire and she was some kind of insurance investigator. I remember there was a lot of steamy looks between them."

"McQueen plays this millionaire industrialist who's so bored with making money that he plots and carries out perfect crimes for entertainment. Dunaway, the investigator, sets out to seduce him so she can get him to make a mistake and trip him up. Along the way, she actually falls in love with him."

"Which she hadn't expected to do," said Tobi.

Springer looked at her and nodded. "Right. So then she has this dilemma. She loves this guy and doesn't want to bust him but she has to bust him because that's her job. She's all torn up inside going into the final scene because McQueen's told her to meet him at the payoff of his latest job. She's waiting with a contingent of cops to take him down and the whole time she's tortured with the thought of betraying him."

Tobi shifted in her seat. "I forget what happened then."

"McQueen knew."

"He knew what?"

"He knew she would bust him anyway. So he worked it where she couldn't. The last scene shows him looking out the window of a jet, a satisfied and enigmatic smile on his face."

"Satisfied because he'd tricked her?"

"Not exactly. He was smiling because he had pulled it off. Smiling because he had avoided the trap and saw it coming."

"What about her?"

"She's frustrated. She doesn't get to arrest him. And she loses the great love of her life."

"But, she didn't want to arrest him anyway."

"No, she didn't," he said. Then, he cocked his head and smiled at her. A satisfied smile. "But it's just a movie."

"So," Tobi said, "how're you figuring to come out of this?"

"I'm still working on it."

CHAPTER

Twenty-Seven

"THANKS FOR INVITING ME TO THE CLUSTER FUCK," DAVID Ryder said to Jack Summers as they drove back to town. "It was a high point in my law enforcement career. Guy made jackasses out of us. That may be a regular occurrence for you but I don't personally care for it."

"Everything isn't always like it appears," said Summers.

Ryder rolled his eyes and made a dismissive noise with his mouth. "Don't go philosophical on me. It's a waste of time. You tried to buzz one under his chin and he knocked it the hell out of the park. No use trying to spin it some other way."

"But I may get Nicky Tortino out of this."

"That wouldn't be too bad. Like to see that."

"Might have something for Springer, too. When this is all done."

Now Ryder was shaking his head. "Give up on this guy, Jack. Give up on her, too. She don't want you and she don't want me."

"What makes you think it's about her?"

"What makes you think it's not?"

"I don't know why we gotta deal with that prick," said Ray Dean Carr, meaning Springer. Ray Dean had his semi-auto pistol broken down and was cleaning it. *I Love Lucy* was playing soundlessly on the television. "You wanta take a stab at explaining that to me?"

"Because Nicky says," said Donny Black, sprawled across a motel chair, sipping on a brown bottle of Budweiser, an El Producto cigar smoldering in his hand.

"Why did Nicky drive himself out here?"

"I don't know. Nicky didn't say. Maybe he wanted to drive his new car."

"You didn't ask?"

"Nicky says 'Let's go to Aspen.' I say, 'Okay.' We drive here. The less you know, the better off you are."

"Yeah? Well you can bet Gerry Knucks knows exactly what's going on."

"I'd say you're right," said Donny Black, flicking ash on the floor. "Here's a conversation tip. Have a fucking point."

"Why the fuck does he get to know and the rest of us are left in the dark? Tell me that."

"I was you, I wouldn't think on this too much."

"Yeah," said Auteen coming into the room. All he had on was a pair of boxer shorts. Three hundred pounds of Afro-American dumb-ass. Disgusting. "Thinking ain't 'zactly your best use."

Ray Dean put up a hand and averted his face. "Go put some clothes on, willya? Whatta you think this is? A homo bathhouse? Huh? Who wants to look at that?"

"I look good," said Auteen. "Have a beautiful chocolate-brown body."

"You have a disgusting fat body that I don't wanna have to look at."

"Why? You getting a hard-on? You want me, honey?"

"We were talking here, okay?" said Ray Dean. "Before you come parading through in those ugly shorts. Where you get shorts that big? At army surplus? Go look in the mirror and see what we have to put up with."

Donny Black shook his head and took another pull on his beer. Donny was kind of a weird guy. Got busted out of the cops for beating up perps and tasting nookie off the Oakland whores he didn't arrest. But he was ten times better company than the human garbage disposal in the boxer shorts.

"Donny," said Auteen. "Tell the boy that he shouldn't talk about Gerry Knucks."

Donny nodded and looked at Ray Dean. "It doesn't pay to talk about the ice man. Just leave him alone. I was a cop for ten years and never run across anyone else like him. Sonuvabitch is scary dangerous."

"Anybody can bust a cap."

Donny raised an eyebrow. "That's what you think makes Knucks?" Shaking his head. "Shit. No use talking to you about it, that's what you think."

"Well, then you tell me."

Donny sipped his drink, took a pull on the cigar and sat up in the chair. "Okay, it's like this. It's all attitude. Gerry's got it. Everything about him says he don't care about what you're gonna do or what anyone's gonna do because he knows what he's gonna do and there's nothing you can do about it. Savvy? He's got his own agenda going. It's like with Nicky. He lets Nicky think he's the boss but Gerry's still doing what he wants."

"Bullshit."

Donny shrugged. "You were a cop, you'd see it."

"How's he let Nicky think he's the boss?"

"He's smarter than Nicky. Son of a bitch is smarter than about anyone I've met in the life."

"He could get whacked like anyone else."

"Yeah? Wouldn't want to be the guy who tried it."

Which was what Ray Dean had been thinking about for a while. Earlier, Knucks had been on his case, telling him to quit giving tough looks to the Springer guy and talking about how he was going to fuck 'im up.

"Talking about it isn't the same as doing it," Knucks told him. "Something you don't fucking get. You talk too much and you telegraph everything." Then Knucks paused like he'd said something important, Ray Dean glaring at him, before Knucks added, "Everything."

After Auteen got dressed the three of them went out. Nicky giving them some time off while Nicky visited this woman he knew. She drove in from Denver to see him. The three of them stopped at a bar where everyone had on those ski clothes and was sipping wine and other pussy-looking drinks. Ray Dean tried to talk to one woman, a good-looking blonde who was drinking some kind of weird foreign beer, all dark brown and frothy.

"So what do you do for fun around here?" Ray Dean asked the blonde.

"Pardon me?" she said, like she couldn't hear him, her face all screwed up like she'd swallowed something.

"What? You can't hear?" he said, arms out, head bobbing. "What're you doing, tonight? Huh?"

She turned away from him, ignoring him, so he grabbed her by the elbow. "Hey, I'm talking to you here, y'know." She'd pulled away from him and then some preppie-looking asshole tells him that, "The lady doesn't want to talk to you."

"Oh yeah?" said Ray Dean, bulled-up now. "And I don't want to talk to you either, you fucking jerk."

The guy rolled his eyes and turned away from him.

"Hey, motherfucker. Don't roll your eyes at me. You got that?" Then he grabbed the guy by the shoulder and turned him around, the guy trying to look tough when he turned around.

"I don't want any trouble," said the preppie.

"What if I sliced one of your ears off? Huh? Would that be trouble? Because it'll be no trouble for me." The guy's eyes getting big now. His yuppie friends staring.

"What the fuck is this?" said Donny Black, moving closer. Then, to the prep, Donny said, "My friend just had a downturn in the market and he's not feeling real well." He patted Ray Dean on the shoulder.

"This asshole is fucking with me," said Ray Dean. "Sticking his nose in my business."

"Hey, a . . . what's your name?" Donny asked the preppie.

"Carlisle."

"Carlisle?" said Ray Dean. "What kind of fucking asshole name is Carlisle?"

Donny moved between them.

"Listen, Carlisle," said Donny. "Can I call you Carl? Carl, I was you, I'd move to another part of the place and have a Becks while I settle my friend down."

Carlisle took the advice and moved on but a couple of burly-looking twenty-somethings were moving their way now. "Time to go, Ray," said Donny.

The two weight lifters moved closer. The taller one said, "Are we having a problem here, gentlemen?"

"The fuck these guys want?" asked Auteen, standing away from the bar now.

"They're the bouncers," said Donny Black.

"Sorta dainty, ain't they?" said Auteen, looking down at the two.

The tall bouncer said, "You guys have worn out your welcome. Hit the door."

"Say what?" said Auteen. "What happens, we don't?"

"Whoa, whoa, whoa," said Donny. He scratched alongside his nose. "Nothing's gonna happen here. We were just leaving, right guys?"

"Fuck that," said Auteen.

Fucking Auteen, thought Ray Dean, smiling now.

"Aw come on, man, we don't need this shit," said Donny.

"They gotta ask nice," said Auteen, mean-mugging the two bouncers. "Then Auteen leaves."

Donny looked at Ray Dean. Ray Dean shook his head, saying, "He's not kidding. They'll have to say it."

Donny leaned into Ray Dean's face. "You listen to me, you ignorant fuck. We have got to get the hell out of this place. We can't get arrested, do you understand that? You want Nicky to go fucking nuts?"

Ray Dean shrugged.

Donny moved away from Ray Dean. The two bouncers didn't look so resolute with Auteen looking down at them, like a giant redwood towering over two saplings. "Look, Auteen," said Donny. "Let this go."

More staring. Like they were all in the fucking yard at Soledad or something.

"Come on guys," said Donny, to the bouncers. "Help me out here. Just ask him to leave."

The tall bouncer, who only came up to Auteen's chin, said, "Sir, I'm requesting that you leave. If you would do that I would appreciate it."

"Yeah, okay," said Auteen, nodding his head, happy now. "Check out the bitches in some other cheap-ass place."

Ray Dean smiled and waved at everyone as they left.

Outside at the car, Donny said, "You fucking guys. What the hell are you thinking about? We can't afford no trouble with the cops. Nicky'll have Gerry cut our balls off with a paper-cutter we bring any shit down."

"Guy got in my face," said Ray Dean.

"And weight-room boy givin' Auteen shit," said Auteen.

Donny looked at them. "Gerry was right. You guys don't have no fucking sense."

"What're you saying, Donny?" said Auteen, moving closer.

"Back off, A. I'll blow your fucking nads off. You got that?" Donny giving Auteen the tough cop look. A pretty good one, too.

"Okay, okay," said Ray Dean. "Relax, Auteen. Listen, Donny. We're sick as shit of hearing about Gerry Knucks and what he's going to like and not going to like, y'know? I mean, how much of that shit we gotta put up with?"

"You gotta put up with all of it until we're through here in Aspen and head back to California. That's what Nicky wants."

"So, what's Nicky doing here?"

"I'm telling you I don't know, but for some reason you can't seem to keep that in the front of your fucking head."

At that moment a Dodge Intrepid pulled into the lot and a tall, curly-hair guy in a leather jacket, looked like a movie star, got out and walked toward them. Another guy was with him. Now what? thought Ray Dean.

"Donny Black?" said the guy. Had to be a cop. They all sounded alike.

"Don't know 'im," said Donny.

"You're him," said the curly-hair guy. "I'm Agent Ryder of the DEA and I have a warrant and an extradition order here for you from the State of California."

"A warrant?" said Donny. "A warrant for what?"

"Failure to appear in federal court."

"I thought my lawyer straightened that all out. This is just a misunderstanding. Man, I used to be a cop. Seriously."

"Sir, would you please place both hands against your car?"

"Why?"

"Because I'm going to have to search you."

"Search me? Aw, shit. Don't do that. I'll go with you. Won't give you no problems."

"Please place your hands against the car, sir," said Agent Ryder. "You other two gentlemen, just move away from the car."

"Glad to, Officer," said Ray Dean. "Always glad to help out the cops."

Donny shot him a look.

"Look, a . . . Agent Ryder," said Donny. "I've got a .38 Chief's Special in a clip-on at the back of my pants. I'll get it for you."

Ryder pulled out a semi-auto pistol. Looked like one of the new Walther nines. "Get against the car, now! Maxwell, keep an eye on the other two." The other cop got out his gun and more or less pointed it at Ray Dean and Auteen.

"Hey, hey, hey," said Ray Dean. "Everything's cool."

Donny put up his hands, closed his eyes, and exhaled loudly. He turned and placed his hands against the rental car.

"Spread your feet."

"Yeah, yeah, I know the drill. Put all the weight on my hands. Done it a million times. Told you where the damn gun was, didn't I?"

The cop found the .38 and handed it to Maxwell. Then he patted down Donny, turning his pockets inside out. He reached down into the left pocket of Donny's top coat and pulled something out.

"What's this, Black?" said Ryder. "You got a sweet tooth?"

Donny looked back over his shoulder. Ryder was holding up a baggie of white powder. "Where the fuck did that come from? Hey, that ain't mine."

"Yeah, you're the first to ever tell me that."

"Naw. No shit. Somebody must've put it there. You guys planted it on me. This is a chickenshit bust. I don't do that stuff."

They put Donny Black in the back of the Intrepid after they'd cuffed him, placing a hand on top of his head as they put him inside.

"Bail me out," Donny said to Ray Dean as they were putting him in the car. Ray Dean just smiled at him.

They drove off, leaving Ray Dean and Auteen alone in the parking lot.

"And he was worried about you and me getting busted," said Ray Dean.

"And him carrying nose candy all the while," said Auteen.

"Nicky ain't gonna like this."

"No, he ain't."

"That leaves you and me."

"And Gerry Knucks."

"Yeah," said Ray Dean, watching the taillights of the Dodge. "And Gerry Knucks."

CHAPTER

Twenty-Eight

BRUCE POURED THE CONTENTS OF THE BLENDER INTO A rocks glass and handed it to Springer. "Here, try this," he said.

Springer looked at the glass with one eye closed. "What's in this?"

"Rye whiskey, B and B, Courvoisier, and black tea."

"Black tea? God, no wonder it's that color."

"Try it."

"There's no fish by-products in it, is there? Powdered elk antler?"

Bruce gave him a hurt look. "You going to drink it or not?"

Springer looked at the dark liquid, gave Bruce a smile that was almost a grimace, and took a sip. It tasted like cold burnt coffee, only worse. And the alcohol content was off the scale.

Bruce said, "So, what do you think?"

"It's . . . a . . . very different. Refreshingly so." He meant it was different than anything potable. "What do you call it?"

"The busted wheel."

"The busted wheel, huh?" Springer thought the busted toilet a more appropriate name. "Listen Bruce, we're going to open the club back up on Monday. I paid my creditors."

"Great."

"I got more good news for you. I'm going to make you a partner. Also starting Monday."

Bruce looked stunned, then looked like he was going to tear up and cry. The guy had biceps like Arnold Schwarzenegger and was as emotional as Sandra Bullock. "Why? I mean, thanks. But I don't understand. How much is this going to cost me?"

"Nothing. No, wait. You have to promise not to concoct new potions for our customers." He held up the dark liquid. "This stuff is swill, you know."

"I can't accept this for free."

"You got no choice. I've already taken care of it. Anything happens to me you get the whole thing. My insurance policy will take care of any outstanding debts. All you'd have to pay was the taxes."

"What do you mean, 'if anything happens to you'?"

"I don't mean anything by it. Starting Monday you're a partner in the Whiskey Basin. If I ski off the side of a mountain then you get the whole thing."

"You always use the beginner's slope."

"That's because I don't like to show off. Another thing, I need you to take off until Monday. I've got some recording to do for the nightly shows and I've got people coming in over the weekend for another business deal and we can't be interrupted."

"So, what are you telling me?"

"Get lost until Monday, Bruce."

Every town has its own network of people connected with law enforcement—bail bondsmen, retired cops, private investigators, and hotel security operatives. Aspen was no exception. It's how Springer was able to tell Agent Summers that he knew he'd visited Max at the Ritz. It's how Springer was able to keep tabs on Ray Dean and Auteen. The contact's name was Bailey Collins, a retired Denver cop and former Green Beret who gave ski lessons up on Ajax Mountain.

Collins had been following Mutt and Jeff for days. He'd also tapped their motel phone and had a listening device installed in the room smoke detector. In addition to being a high-speed, go-fast, legitimate marine war hero, Collins was something of an electronics expert. Also a demolitions guy.

Max had been paying the tab and hadn't griped once about it. "It's good to know where those morons are," he'd said.

But now Springer needed something different from Bailey Collins.

Which is how Springer came to be standing on the intermediate slope, waiting for Collins to finish with his class. Collins was in his fifties but still looked forty. Slim waist, big shoulders. A Vietnam veteran. Two tours, two bronze stars, and a purple heart. Collins was a regular at the Whiskey Basin and they had talked about their different experiences in combat on several occasions. Collins had been in the shit in 'Nam and had walked the walk.

The air was clean and clear and thin as Springer watched Collins work with the skiers. The sun was bright against the white sheen of snow. Collins dismissed the class, removed his skis, and waved at Springer. Walked in Springer's direction with a slight purple-heart limp.

"Well, hell, if it ain't the Secret Service," said Collins.

"And if it isn't Aspen's favorite jarhead snake-eater. What's up, Bailey?"

"How about some coffee?"

They walked to the ski office which was a converted storage shack. There was an old overstuffed couch and a faded oak desk with a Sony boom box sitting on top of it playing New Orleans jazz. The lodge had a nice ski office with a computer terminal and contemporary furniture but Collins only used it with new clients and preferred his makeshift office. Collins poured coffee out of an old thermos bottle with a wine cork he'd stuck in it because he'd lost the cap. The coffee steamed as he poured it. Collins liked his coffee thick and black and strong.

"I need some C-4," said Springer.

Collins cocked his head. "Why don't you quit beating around the bush with all the small talk and get to it?"

"Also some mercury switches."

"Mick Jagger would say you can't always get what you want."

"But, sometimes you get what you need."

Collins smiled.

"Can you get it?" asked Springer.

"What the hell are you going to blow up?"

"This lodge." He pointed up the moutain. "That ski lift. Maybe your car."

"Yeah, I can get them," said Collins. "But they're exotic and will cost."

"Money is no object."

"That's an interesting take for a guy who got his place closed down by creditors. You come into some money?"

"Not yet. By next week you'll either get a big bonus or never see me again."

Collins arched an eyebrow. "You're not going to hit another crack house, are you?"

"Not this time."

"It's kinda fun," said Collins, suggesting he wouldn't mind. "Always wanted to be a DEA agent."

"Not this time."

"You going to need some help?"

"I'll let you know."

"How soon you need this stuff?"

"Soon. Yesterday will be okay."

"You haven't told me what you're going to use it for yet."

"You're right," said Springer, lifting the mug, steam drifting around his face. "I haven't."

Collins looked at him. Rubbed his chin with a thick hand.

Springer said, "Need two remote switches. One should be a dummy and one real one. And enough C-4 and fertilizer to blow up a car. Really blow up a car."

"You're not going to kill anyone, are you?"

"Nobody that doesn't have it coming." Then he shook his head. "Shouldn't have to."

"Good to know."

"Where's Ray Dean and Auteen this fine morning?"

"Same place. I figured they might move after you set up their buddy," said Collins, rising from his fabric-worn executive chair. "You think that was nice to plant coke on the guy?"

"I thought it was necessary. Anything new on the Bobsey twins?"

"Yeah. Interesting, too. Sounds like the guy with all the hair, Ray Dean, doesn't like Gerry Knucks. Auteen doesn't like the way Gerry treats them but he's kind of in awe of the guy."

"I can understand that."

"I think Ray Dean wishes that something would happen to Gerry."

"Like what?"

"Like maybe Gerry would catch a bullet. And that Ray Dean would be the guy to pull the trigger."

Information he could use, thought Springer. "Well, get the stuff for me and I'll get you a nice Christmas card. I'll let you know if I need anything else. Okay?"

Collins nodded his head, slowly. He smiled, then said, "Semper Fi."

"Do or die."

"Hoo-rah."

Ray Dean woke up at 10:30 A.M. because of Auteen's snoring. If the guy wasn't eating or running his mouth, the guy was farting and burping and snoring. Guy was a freaking symphony of obnoxious sounds and bad smells. Ray Dean padded into the bathroom and relieved the pressure of too many beers the night before. He had to walk around on his heel because he couldn't find his cane. The motel room was a mess. An obstacle course of fast food sacks and containers and beer cans and empty quart bottles of Colt 45. Guy ate every two hours like he had a six-foot tapeworm or something.

Ray Dean wasn't no housekeeper himself but Auteen was an environmental disaster. Look at this shit, he thought, stepping over a plastic plate full of gnawed rib bones and stepping into something. Something wet.

He quickly lifted his foot, causing him to put his weight on the bad foot too quickly and he fell to the floor crushing a beer can and a bag of potato chips.

Shit.

Did the guy piss on the floor or what? He felt the heat rising to his neck and face. He was furious—sick of this stupid motherfucker and his shitty habits. He almost screamed out but instead he grabbed his gun and wracked a shell into the pipe.

He walked over to Auteen's bed and placed the muzzle close

to the sleeping man's ear. "You motherfucker," hissed Ray Dean, his chest heaving. He could see himself blowing the side of Auteen's head off, leaving a mess of gray slime and red froth and splintered bone all over the bed sheets. Which made him think of the drug guy, Charlemagne.

Yeah, he'd liked that. One minute the punk talking shit and in the next second the gun bucking in his hand and the guy's face exploding. No more talk. No more bullshit. Felt good. Ray Dean had been thinking about that for days. He never realized he liked it so much. The other time when the fag tried to cop his joint he was too mad to enjoy it. And the guy with the knife? He only wounded him but he liked the way the guy screamed in pain, Ray Dean standing over him and starting to bust another cap when he heard the siren and had to run. He'd had time to look at Charlemagne.

Still, when he put all of them together it made a nice tight little ball of delight in his head and he knew what he wanted to do. He could be like Gerry Knucks. Better than Knucks. For one thing all he knew about Knucks was rumor and booze talk with the guys down at the pool hall. Knucks never talked about it. It could all be bullshit.

He put the gun even closer to Auteen's ear. Could see himself screwing the muzzle end into the big man's ear then squeezing the trigger as Auteen woke up. No, that wasn't the way to do it. He wanted him awake, looking at him. Ray Dean talking to him before he did it.

Saying, "You know how you like to eat stuff? Well, here's some lead." Naw, that wasn't it. How about, "Well, Auteen, guess who's not eating any Cheetos today?"

Not bad.

Ray Dean put on his clothes and walked back over to Auteen's bed, and using the gun he knocked on the headboard which was screwed into the wall.

Auteen rolled over and one eye opened up. He smacked his lips and squeezed his eyelids then opened them. Mumbled something. Mouth working, eyes closing again.

"Hey, sleeping beauty," said Ray Dean.

"The . . . fuck you doing, man?" Eyes open now. "What you got a gun for?"

"I thought about blowing your brains out your ears but changed my mind. I'm in a good mood." He liked that, acting like he was kidding around but really meaning it. "I'm going out."

"So go."

"Want me to bring you back something? You know, like twenty-five Egg McMuffins and two gallons of milk and a Shetland pony to eat? You could leave the skeleton on the floor here for us to look at and step over."

"Egg McMuffin sound good." Rolling away from Ray Dean now. "Couple big O.J.s. What was that other thing you said?"

See? What a dumb shit.

Ray Dean started up the rental and drove to McDonald's, then changed his mind and drove past it. Fuck Auteen and his Egg McMuffins. He'd have to eat something else. He drove to the bakery place on main he'd heard everyone talking about.

He went inside and picked up a dozen doughnuts, some bear claws, and a large coffee for himself and walked back outside. That's when he saw the guy sitting in his car. *Ray Dean's* car. Ray Dean looked around the lot to make sure he was looking at the right car. He walked to the car and saw who it was.

It was the wise-assed guy. Springer.

Wise-ass rolled down the window and said, "I've already eaten, thanks."

"Get the fuck outta my car. Whatta you think this is? You think we're best friends or something?"

"Just want to talk to you. Nice morning, isn't it?"

"No. It's too fucking cold like it always is in this air-conditioned deep freeze. I hate it here."

"Better keep that down or the Chamber of Commerce will hear it and deport you. They're sensitive about that kind of talk here."

"Yeah, like I give a shit." Ray Dean didn't know what to do. His hands were full since he had to buy a ton of shit for Auteen. Couldn't get to his gun and couldn't hit the guy, though from looking at him that wouldn't be the smartest thing to do. Guy was too big for anything physical, what with the bad foot and all.

"Just get in and we'll talk," said the guy.

Ray Dean gave up and got into the car. What could you do?

When Ray Dean had settled into the driver's seat the guy said, "Looks like you have a hearty appetite."

"You wanna get to it? Stuff gets cold fast around here."

"Got a business proposition for you."

Ray Dean looked at him. What was this about? He looked for something behind the statement. Guy wasn't smirking now. He looked for real, like he really had something.

"Yeah? What is it?"

Guy looked out the side window, then back at Ray Dean. "You want to make some money? Big money?"

Ray Dean chewed on the inside of his lower lip and looked at the guy. Still couldn't read nothing in the guy's face. Guy had a funny way about him. Ray Dean didn't like him but something about the guy made him want to trust him.

"Sure," said Ray Dean. "I can always use some more money."

"There's even more to this deal than that."

"Like what?"

"Like maybe you can move up in life. Become Nicky T's main man."

Then the guy just sat there and looked at Ray Dean. Not a hard look and not a wise-ass look. It was different this time, like they were sharing something. Guy's clothes weren't what Ray Dean liked but they were nice, guy-next-door clothes. Like he was your neighbor and could help you get your cat out of a tree. The kind of guy who raked leaves and washed his car on weekends. You could trust this guy.

"How would I do that?" asked Ray Dean, interested now.

"You need to keep this to yourself. Because if you don't then you'll screw it up for yourself and I'll go ahead with the deal like it is and hope for the best."

Ray Dean turned in his seat so he could see the guy better. "What're we talking about here?"

"You want to be Nicky's go-to guy? You like the way Gerry Knucks treats you? I heard him the other day in the parking lot. Notice he got to stick around and you had to back off."

"That's because you said it."

Guy was shaking his head. "That's what Knucks told me to say. Think about it. You're a sharp guy. Who set this deal up at your end?"

Ray Dean did think about it. "It was Knucks."

"Right. And who talked to me before they talked to Nicky?"

"Knucks again."

Guy nodded his head. Smiled. Didn't say anything, like he was waiting for Ray Dean to say something else.

"So, what does it mean?"

"There's a lot of money involved here. A lot. More than you can ever imagine spending. More than you can ever visualize having for your own."

"Yeah?" It had been bugging him that they didn't know what was going on. Only Nicky and Gerry Knucks knew.

"Knucks has already cut down the number of people who might share the cut."

"What's that mean?"

"Where's Donny Black?"

Ray Dean thought about that. Made sense. Donny busted for a baggy of cocaine. Ray Dean never knew the guy to use drugs. Donny looked surprised when the cop pulled it out of his coat. Saying it was planted on him. Donny coming all the way from Frisco with Nicky and now he was in the can, Nicky refusing to bail him out. Nicky hated drug use. Everybody in the crew knew that. Gerry Knucks knew that. Knucks planting drugs? Why? Maybe it was like this guy was saying. Knucks had something going and didn't want to share.

"So, what's it mean?"

The guy leaned forward slightly and said, "I think maybe Knucks is going to try to burn Nicky and take the money."

Ray Dean leaned back. "What? No. Gerry rip off Nicky T? That's crazy."

Guy shrugged and sat back. Ray Dean waited for him to say something. Something that would convince him that Knucks was up to something. But the guy just sat there.

"So, Knuck's gonna . . . I mean, you think Knucks wants to make a big score and take off with it?"

"Could be."

"Why tell me?"

"You think Nicky T would believe me if I told him his number one man was going to rip him off?"

"No way. Nicky thinks the guy walks on water or something." Guy nodded at him.

"So, you want me to tell Nicky about this?"

Guy smiled. "You think he'll believe you any more than he'd believe me?"

Ray Dean looked out the windshield, nodding his head in agreement. "No. He won't."

"There it is," said the guy.

"So, what do I do with it?"

"You wait. But, you're prepared for the possibility if it goes down. You become the hero. If everything goes right and Knucks doesn't pull anything you haven't said anything. But, if something does go down then you've got the preventative."

"What preventative?"

The guy reached into his pocket and pulled out this little box with a toggle switch on it. "With this."

"What is it?"

"It's a triggering device."

"For a bomb?"

"C-4 plastique. Knucks is buying a car this morning. Bet you didn't know that, did you?"

"Why would he do that?"

Guy shrugged at him. "Not sure. But, I'll bet it has something to do with taking the money. He can't run away in a rental and he can't take Nicky's car. Besides, when he shows up in a new car you'll know I'm telling you the straight skinny. Right?"

Ray Dean nodded to himself. "So, why I got this triggering thing?"

"If Knucks tries to get away with the money then you're the guy that can stop him."

"Yeah?"

Guy nodded. "The range is about five miles. He takes off, you blow him up. Save the day."

"Won't that blow up the money too?"

"No. It's a small charge and I'll plant it under the driver's seat. May not even kill him but it'll sure stop him. The only thing I ask is that you don't blow him up near my place. Bad for business."

"How I know I can trust you?"

"You don't." The guy waited a couple minutes before he said, "But, what've you got to lose? If I'm not right and you don't say anything then you have the same status with Nicky that you do now. I'll wait and give you the trigger the morning of the switch. If I'm right and you save the money? Well . . . you think about that one yourself."

Then the guy got out of the car, got in his own ride and left.

And Ray Dean did think about it. A lot.

CHAPTER

Twenty-Nine

"HE WANTS TO PUT THE MONEY IN BEER COOLERS? WHY'S that?" Nicky asked Gerry. "Three million dollars in Coleman coolers? What's that about?"

"Says nobody'll take any notice since it's a bar. Says people come in with coolers all the time. Won't draw attention that way."

"I don't fucking like this guy."

"I don't either," said Ray Dean.

"Who the fuck asked you? When's he want to do this?"

"Four-thirty in the morning. At his place."

3:15 A.M.

Max handed Springer a carrybag. Inside was one hundred thousand dollars.

"So, now I'm out over a hundred G's and this may or may not work?" Max said. "I can't believe this is happening."

"Would you rather be dead?"

"I'm going to die of a heart attack waiting for this to happen anyway. And why does Gerry need a new car anyway?"

"He needs it. Didn't cost that much anyway."

"Ten grand ain't much, right? In addition to the hundred grand. You know how much work it is to get your hands on that much cash in this short a period of time? And then just hand it over to some crazy shiksa so they can give it away like we were on *Let's Make a Deal*? No, of course you don't. All you do is come up with bizarre schemes that always end up costing me money."

And on and on.

"Go outside and wait like we agreed on," said Springer.

"Yeah, yeah, you and your fucking ideas."

"Just go, Max. I've got stuff to do."

"I'm going. I'm going. Shit."

After Max left, Springer set the timers and auto start features on the machines. Coffee machine upstairs set for 4:00 A.M. Video-tape set to go on at 4:30. He could activate the audio recording manually.

He checked the clip on the .380 Colt. Full. One in the pipe. He dropped the weapon in the flapped pocket of his tweed jacket and loaded the Beretta hideout gun with silver-tip hollow points and wrapped it in a bar towel and placed it on the bar. Good thing about hollow points is that they usually stopped in whatever they hit. No use shooting up the place.

If it came to that.

Springer sipped some coffee and was feeling pretty good. This was at least exciting. It wasn't a meeting with creditors, coolly considering him and dividing up his life wondering where the interest was. Might be better if all his business was conducted before dawn with a loaded gun under his jacket. This was more what he liked.

Let's see, Tobi Ryder upstairs. The FBI man, Summers, in the sound room. Max outside waiting. Suzi a mile away, sitting in Max's Jag. Bailey parked next to her in his four-wheel drive. Gerry driving a used car mined with C-4. Ray Dean unknowingly set up to be Springer's inside man. What could be better than cops and robbers?

He had two coolers behind the bar in a large cabinet. Two Coleman coolers with the identical markings that Tortino had made Gerry put on the other two coolers. Knowing Nicky wouldn't trust him, but Gerry would take care of that. Springer's coolers had several thousand dollars in hundred's, fifties, and a few thousand ones to approximate the weight of the cash in Tortino's cooler. He had a dummy remote switch in his pocket to give to Ray Dean.

It would be up to Gerry to delay Tortino from coming inside the place until they could switch the coolers. Tortino *would* come in. "Telling him he can't will make him want to," said Gerry. It was in Tortino's nature. But they would need a couple of minutes to make the switch before Tortino and Max came into the place.

Beats standing around looking steadfast.

Detective Tobi Ryder tapped her fingers absently on the computer keyboard in the office of the Whiskey Basin Tavern. Nice place. It was like a hiding place. Woods and soft browns. A bay window with native wood fretting that looked out on the parking lot. A man's office. Definitely fit Cole Springer.

She looked at her watch, 4:00 A.M. She'd had to get there by 3:30 to get in ahead of Jack Summers who would throw a fit if he knew Springer was letting her in on this. Springer even had a video camera set up so she could watch the money exchange. Summers had wanted a video camera but Springer told him it would scare off Tortino. Springer told her later that he had a hidden one, placed in the lounge by some ski instructor friend of his who used to be a Green Beret. That's the kind of guy he was—the kind that knew Special Forces crazies who set up surveillance systems. There was nothing on the screen now except the empty lounge with Springer walking through occasionally. Unconcerned. Unflappable. As if he were having a bunch of old friends over rather than a gang of killers.

"You realize Springer is scamming us," said Summers after Springer had laid the scenario out for them.

"How is he going to do that?" she asked, exasperated. "You'll be right there in the back room and able to hear everything."

Still, she was a little concerned. First, there was that enigmatic look Springer had on his face when he talked about the scenario. And she could still remember the reference to Steve McQueen and the way he'd pulled off his scam with Faye Dunaway watching. You could tell he really liked that. Now, *she*, Tobi Ryder, would be watching. If there was money involved and Summers was going to arrest Tortino then maybe the money would be available.

But why ask her to come? Why have Summers waiting in the back room? There was no way for Springer to pull anything with that much going on. Was there? Why did he make her so nervous? Why did she love him?

If he was pulling something she *was* going to bust him. She'd already decided on it. That was the job. Her job. He'd better play this one straight.

From 4:25 to 4:30 A.M. she was supposed to look out the window and stay there until Tortino and his hoods got out of the car and came inside. He'd given her a pair of night goggles to use. They were hard to look through. Took some getting used to. Where did he get night goggles anyway?

"I need for you to watch them in case we end up downtown explaining this," Springer had said. "You're my alibi if anything bad goes down. I can't predict these people and I could use someone to watch my back. See if anyone tries to sneak into the place from another way. Maybe you can make an arrest out of this thing. Advance your career and piss off Summers in the bargain." Giving her that grin when he said it, never knowing what the grin really meant.

He'd made coffee for her. She poured some out of the Mr. Coffee machine into a cup and sipped it. 4:15 now. Pretty soon she'd have to go to the window. She wouldn't be able to see the live cam on the monitor while she was at the window looking through the night goggles. Which was no big deal. Nothing going on in the lounge until they were inside anyway.

At 4:24 she got up and walked over to the bay window. Waited.

Special Agent Jack Summers checked his watch. 4:25 A.M. Springer had called him at 3:35 A.M. so all he'd had time to do was pull on his pants and a jacket, grab his weapon, and hurry down to the Whiskey. Springer didn't give him much lead time. He complained but Springer said that Nicky T didn't give him much lead time either. Summers had arrived at 4:05 and had been sitting in the storage/sound board room of the Whiskey Basin Tavern since he'd arrived. He had a headphone set on which was wired into the main room of the place so he could listen in on the money exchange. There was a tape recorder at his fingertips. Springer told him that he'd try to get Tortino to say something provocative. Make a threat. Make a confession. Anything.

Summers said, "Guys like Tortino don't tell guys like you anything."

Springer told him, "Nicky seems a suspicious sort of man. He probably has some deep inner resentment." Even now the guy was a smart-ass. "But I'm pretty charming. So, you never know."

Springer was a pain in the ass but bringing down Nicky T would be huge for Summers. He could already visualize the headlines in tomorrow's paper. "FBI Busts Mob Underboss!" and getting a commendation for the bust.

He could almost taste it.

Max fidgeted in the car seat. It was dark, he wanted a cup of coffee, and he needed to pee. Damned prostate acting up. Drank too much last night, nervous about the next morning. He hated getting up early. Hated it when he was in the army. All that rolling out and marching around in circles. Real he-man stuff. Jerk-off sergeant acting like marching and humping up hills with a full pack would win the next war.

And now Springer had his ass up at this god-awful hour and giving him orders.

"Max," Springer had told him. "Do not leave your vehicle before 4:35 A.M. Not for anything. Don't come inside and don't open the door or the light will come on inside and you'll scare them off."

"Scare them off?" Max said. "Who you think is gonna be scared here? I'm about to shit thinking about it."

Max didn't know why Springer and Gerry just couldn't shoot Nicky when he showed up. Springer shook his head and made a noise with his mouth.

Gerry had just looked at Max like he was stupid, then said, "Because, Max. If we shoot Nicky then Joey the Neck will send someone to shoot us. You just do what Springer tells you, huh?" Giving Max a little pat on the cheek like Max was seven years old.

And now it was dawning on Max that he had given Springer one hundred thousand dollars in unmarked bills and Max was supposed to sit in the car until 4:35. And the guy already had money troubles. Why not just take the hundred G's and split, leaving Max to deal with Nicky T and his goons? But what choice did he have at this point?

Sit and wait. Sit and wait.

Nine more minutes to go.

Man, did he ever have to go.

It was funny, thought Springer, pouring himself more coffee. He was enjoying himself. It had been a long time since he'd felt like he was having a good time. Was it because of the situation, danger turning him on? Or was it the way he felt about Tobi? Hard to tell. But, he hadn't felt this way since before Kristen died. In fact, this was the best he'd felt since before the doctor told him Kristen wasn't going to make it.

"She hasn't much time left, Mr. Springer," the doctor had said. "She wanted me to tell you because she doesn't want to talk about it. She said she wants to make the most of the time she has left."

And she'd had less time than the doctor told him. She gets less time and Max gets misdiagnosed and gets to live. It wasn't right.

For a time he'd drank too much. Johnny Walker Red and Jack Daniels had been his companions. But, they had quickly worn out their welcome. Never was much of a drinker but he didn't like crying all that much so he did it. The counselor said the drinking kept him from getting over her death. "You can't grieve if you numb your feelings," she'd told him. But he couldn't stop—drinking or grieving. Finally the drinking stopped but the grief went on and on . . .

The Whiskey Basin was a different place this early in the morning. Quiet. He liked the place but he was bored with it now. Bored with his life. He'd even become kind of bored with himself. Living in someone else's house. Living someone else's life.

This scenario was stimulating. Back in the jungle, poking sticks at the wild beasts. Messing with Ray Dean and Auteen and he especially liked watching Nicky T's eyes narrow and burn, knowing that no one talked to the guy like that. Life nearest the bone was sweetest. He liked the edge. Liked looking over it. Why was he like that?

Maybe that was why he had an FBI agent in the back and a state cop upstairs. Doesn't do any good to pull a rabbit out of your hat if no one is there to see it.

FBI man in the back room. CBI cop with nice legs upstairs in his office. Max outside in a car probably squirming around and cussing him, imagining Springer ripping him off somehow.

At least Springer thought she had nice legs. Still hadn't seen her in a dress.

Something to think about.

4:26 A.M.

Gerry Knucks was getting to be a weird bastard, thought Nicky Tortino. Ray Dean, too, for that matter. But Ray Dean already had a start on that. Ray Dean kept saying, "Everything is going to be all right, boss." Said it twice already like he was reassuring him. Like Ray Dean was his guardian angel or something.

And that bonehead Donny Black getting himself tossed in the slam for drugs. Why'd Nicky have to do everything himself?

Nicky was sitting in the backseat of the Mercedes. Ray Dean was driving. Auteen was sitting in the front passenger seat. Money in the trunk. The worst part was getting the money out of the safe deposit box and worrying about it all night.

Now Gerry had decided he wanted to drive his own car to the meeting. A cheap piece of shit he'd bought only yesterday. What was that about? Nicky couldn't remember the last time Gerry hadn't been an arm's length away during an important meeting. There were other things. Gerry had suddenly come up with two ways of talking. The street way he'd always had of talking and then another way like the guy was a fucking accountant instead of the best button man on the coast. It was almost like Knucks was turning into someone else.

But the guy had a point.

Gerry'd said, "With that much money in the trunk, it's best I follow behind. No telling who this wise-ass Springer guy's told about the money exchange."

Nicky agreed with that. "But he don't know how much," said Nicky.

"He knows it ain't no small amount. Otherwise you don't need Max. Don't underestimate the piano player, Nicky."

They hit a pothole in the road and Nicky spilled coffee on his topcoat which had cost him five C's, *wholesale*, for crissakes. Sonuvabitch would have to be dry-cleaned now.

"The fuck you doing there, ya dumb shit? Keep the goddamned car out of the ditches, couldya? That be too much to ask? Look at my coat. Shit."

"Sorry, Nicky," said Ray Dean. "It's darker'n shit out here. Can't see anything. Everything's gonna work out fine. Why we gotta do this before God even wakes up, anyway?"

Geez, this guy was thick.

"Because, you moron," said Nicky, dabbing at his coat with a handkerchief. "Nobody's awake yet. That way nobody sees us and nobody knows what we're doing."

Auteen chuckled to himself in the front seat. "Boss said you a moron, boy."

"Fuck you, Auteen."

What a pair of halfwits he was riding with.

And three million dollars in the trunk.

"This is it," he said to the halfwit driving the car. "This is the place. Pull in, here."

The other halfwit grunted.

Man, he'd be glad when this shit was over. He had to piss. And he needed to do it soon.

CHAPTER

Thirty

GERRY WATCHED THE TAILLIGHTS OF THE MERCEDES BUCK and trail red streamers in the darkness when the car hit a bad spot in the road. If he knew Nicky, Ray Dean was catching it right now.

Nicky was already pissed off about Donny Black getting tossed in the can. Another Springer stunt. Knew he was pulling something in the parking lot when he acted like Donny was tickling him. But, it worked out well—one less guy to worry about. And, like Springer said, Donny was the biggest worry being an ex-cop. Nicky didn't buy it when Donny told him that somebody must've planted the dope on him. Nicky didn't like his guys using drugs. Mr. Consistency. Sold them but went crazy if any of his crew was using them. Wouldn't even bail Donny out. Told him to call his mom.

For the first time since Vietnam, Gerry was nervous. Not that he wasn't scared sometimes. But scared didn't help when he had to put somebody down so he just ignored it. Besides, *he* was in control of those situations and didn't have to rely on anyone else. This time was different. This time he was counting on Cole Springer, a guy he'd only just met, to pull this off. No strong-arm stuff. All of this was way out of Gerry's experience. This was a Newman-Redford money scam. Guy even played the piano. In fact, the guy started playing that Scott Joplin stuff on the piano when Gerry asked him if he was sure this was going to work. Just looked at Gerry and then sat down at the piano and started playing that shit.

This is what Gerry'd got himself into—scamming a psychotic

wiseguy wannabe with a scheme worked out by a half-crazy, piano-playing ex–Secret Service agent.

It was like the car thing. He had Max give Gerry ten grand to buy a used car. Max, of course, went nuts. At first Gerry didn't get the car deal but after Springer explained what he had in mind it made sense. Guy had thought this out. Hell, this might just work.

And the other thing that made him nervous?

Suzi.

She would be waiting for him when this thing was over. She had sneaked away from Max last evening and they'd had a drink together and then they'd spent some other kind of time together. He had feelings for her. Feelings he'd never had before and couldn't understand. Was he ready for this? Any of this?

Suzi had told him a couple of stories about Springer she'd heard from Max. Guy apparently had done something really terrible to the president's top guy. Made fun of him or made some crack and gotten himself fired. When Gerry asked about it the guy just shrugged and said, "Can't remember, but it must've been significant."

But, looking at the guy you knew he remembered. In fact, the memory seemed to give him some sort of weird satisfaction. Guy was broke, a widower, his business going in the tank, and about to scam the mob which could get them both killed, or worse if you were familiar with the way the mob handled these things, and it all just seemed like some sort of vague joke to the guy. Like he couldn't die. Or maybe he just didn't care.

Or, like he was having the time of his life.

Springer was offbeat, that's for sure. The kind did things to amuse himself.

Suzi said the only thing that Springer was sober about was the dead wife.

"He gets this kind of faraway look in his eyes when he mentions her like he's looking inside something in his head," Suzi said. "It makes him look different. Like the man we're seeing isn't the real Cole Springer. Almost as if he's hiding behind this new guy. This wiseguy adventurer that isn't afraid. But, when the wife look gets in his eyes you can see that he's . . . well, sad. And lonely. But, he's got something going with the female cop, that Ryder lady. They strike sparks when they're together. I don't know, maybe I'm just being silly. Max says I imagine that I have this insight when I don't."

"Max doesn't know shit," Gerry said.

She'd looked at him and smiled. Nice.

Knowing that Springer and the lady cop had something going was a little unsettling for Gerry. Maybe the guy was planning to throw them over for her. Let her make a designer bust—get Nicky T and most of his crew in one sweep. But, Gerry knew the lady cop was upstairs and the FBI man was in the back room. Springer wanted them there so he could make the switch with the cops right there. Then there'd be no question. He had to trust somebody sometime. Might as well be Springer. Guy trusted Gerry and he wasn't sure why. He understood now why the guy could feel something for the Ryder woman. When this was over Gerry was taking Suzi with him. He'd just come right out and asked her like Springer told him to. He couldn't believe she agreed to it.

"What about Max?" he'd asked her, after she said okay.

"What about him?" she said, giving him a look, with a fist on her hip that said there was no use talking about Max anymore.

For the first time in a long time, Gerry felt . . . what? Satisfaction? Yeah, that was it and not all of it. He actually felt happy.

And he could see why Springer could hurt inside when he lost someone.

Gerry got out of his car, the used Mercury Sable he'd bought only yesterday. The starter on the damned thing was starting to go out. Only noticed it this morning when he started it up and it sort of caught and spun. Then it coughed and chugged before catching, finally starting.

That didn't make him feel better. Not to mention the explosives right under the driver's seat. And a thawing corpse in the trunk.

"We triumph without glory when we conquer without danger," Springer had told him when Gerry balked at the C-4. The guy turning philosophical but it wasn't *his* ass sitting on top of enough plastique to spread pieces of him all over the Rockies.

Springer assured him it wouldn't go off without being triggered.

Gerry'd seen the stuff used in the war. Saw what it could do. Wasn't pretty. Some guys put some in a Saigon whorehouse to get even with the proprietor who they thought had ripped them off. It took a whole wall out of the place. The slope they were after looked like bad hamburger after the explosion. They blew it during Tet if you could believe that. All that shit going down and these guys ice a cathouse owner. Lot of that kind of shit going on over there.

So, the stuff made him nervous. But he had over a million reasons why he'd chance it.

The Mercedes Benz pulled into the dark parking lot and cut its lights like Springer told them to. Car doors opened and Auteen and Ray Dean got out of the car. They walked around scoping the lot before Ray Dean opened the back door and Nicky got out of the car, buttoning up his topcoat and looking around like he was John Gotti or something.

Ray Dean pointed his hand at the car, an electronic beep sounded, and the trunk lid opened.

Auteen reached into the trunk and pulled out the coolers. He handed one to Gerry.

"I can carry one," said Ray Dean.

"Auteen'll carry one," said Gerry. "I'll carry the other."

"I don't like it that I'm not going inside with you," said Nicky.

"You don't know he ain't setting you up," said Gerry. "I'm going to recon the place, scope it for cops. Besides, the guy's nervous. He's going to pat me down, make sure I'm not carrying before he lets us see Max."

"You ain't gonna have a piece?" said Ray Dean.

"Don't need one." Of course he had a gun, you moron. "I'm not gonna shoot nobody. There's no danger here."

"Yeah?" said Ray Dean. "That's good to know." Gerry didn't miss the bastard's smile, not even in the dark. Little bastard was up to something. Come on, Ray Dean, take a chance. Roll the dice. See what you get.

"I gotta piss," said Nicky.

Gerry looked around. "Pick a spot."

"I'm gonna take a leak here in a parking lot like I'm some kinda wino? Besides, it's freezing out here. It could go brittle and break off or something."

Fucking Nicky. This is just the kind of shit Gerry'd warned Springer about. You couldn't predict Nicky Tortino because he was looney-tunes. Timetables and appointments didn't mean shit to the guy unless Joey the Neck set them. It had been like a circus trying to get this freak show to the parking lot on time. Honest-to-God it was all he could do not to park a bullet in Ray Dean's mouth this morning.

Gerry controlled his feelings. Kept his face deadpanned. "He sees you before he sees the money and we don't see Max."

"Then I'll go in first, then come out."

Unbelievable.

"I'll talk to him," said Gerry, not liking any of this.

"Well, hurry up," said Nicky. "I don't go soon my eyes'll turn yellow."

Ray Dean was laughing. "Good one, boss."

"Shut up," said Nicky. "Can't you see we got us a situation here?"

Auteen chuckled.

Well, here we go, Gerry thought. All they needed was some Scott Joplin now.

Max's bladder felt like it was going to burst. 4:29.

He turned on the radio and tried not to think about it. Bounced his leg to the music. Rocked back and forth in the seat.

Couldn't wait any longer. It was either go or wet himself.

He threw the door open and jumped outside as quick as he could.

The interior light didn't come on. Springer must've disconnected it. That son of a bitch knew Max would get out of the car. Of course, he also knew that Max was getting out at 4:35 so he'd removed the light and then told Max not to get out because the light would come on. Bet he thought that was some funny shit.

Like he'd said all along, this Springer guy could piss you off without even trying.

———

They were in the parking lot now. Springer checked his watch. 4:29. Good. Gerry was doing his part. He stepped behind the bar and looked at the VCR. Come on, come on. 4:30. The VCR panel lit up like the scoreboard at a Rockies game. Now, if Tobi was looking out at the parking lot she wouldn't notice the blip on her monitor when it switched from closed circuit to "play."

He took another sip of his coffee, patted the Beretta.

"Showtime," he said, smiling. Feeling good.

Why did Tobi Ryder think something was wrong? Something *felt* wrong. She saw three guys walk to the front door, lost them when they stepped under the porch roof. She walked over to the monitor. She saw Springer and the Nugent guy talking. She went back to the window. Looked through the night goggles which were giving her a headache. It was Ray Dean Carr, standing by the Mercedes, twirling his pistol like he was practicing for a western.

Maybe the other two were waiting on the porch where she couldn't see. She should've told Summers she was going to be there. But it had just been too delicious a thought—watching the whole thing without Summers knowing she was there. Knowing it would drive him crazy later. Sometimes she was *too* much like her dad.

Now she saw the big black man, Phelps, walking back to the car. Where was Tortino? She went back to the monitor. Still just Phelps and Carr. Wait a minute, where was Tortino now? He hollered something to the two men by the car. She couldn't hear exactly what he said. Something about "getting their asses back in the car."

She went back to the monitor now. Springer and Nugent were placing two coolers on the floor of the bar. Everything looked okay. Maybe she had just been imagining things.

Why was she so suspicious?

Something wasn't right.

———

Springer watched through the front window. Saw three men walking to the front porch. Three? Now what? It was just supposed to be Gerry. If Tobi was looking at the monitor she would be seeing a videotape of just Gerry and Springer that they'd taped the morning before. What if she saw Auteen go back to the car alone? Where would she think Nicky went?

He heard the coded knock on the door. Three knocks if everything was okay. Two knocks, a pause, and another two more knocks if something was wrong. He got the second knock. Springer took the Beretta out of his pocket and clicked off the safety.

He opened the door.

Gerry stepped in and said, "Nicky's gotta take a leak if you can believe that. Like I'm taking a kid to the zoo and he's gotta stop at a gas station."

"Tell him to use the lot."

"I did. You can't tell Nicky anything."

Springer rubbed his neck. "Well, what the hell, let him in and tell Auteen to stay on the porch until Nicky comes out. Then get them both the hell back to the car until we do what we have to do."

Gerry nodded and stepped back out.

Nicky stepped in. "Where's the bathroom in this dump?"

Springer pointed. "It's that door over there, the one that says 'Men' on it. We code them like that to confuse our customers. It's a lot of fun."

Nicky gave him a look. "Keep shoveling the funny shit. I really like it."

Springer didn't say anything. Nicky went to the bathroom.

Then, he heard a noise. It was the back door opening. Now what?

Max.

He hurried across the lounge to the rear of the building. Max was just coming in looking around like a lost pup.

"Max," hissed Springer. "I told you to wait in the car until 4:35."

"I gotta pee."

What was it with these city guys that they couldn't take a leak outdoors?

Springer said, "Use the women's bathroom, it's right over there."

"Using the ladies' like I'm a bitch now, right?"

"Look, Nicky T's in the men's room." Max's eyes widened. "Just do what I say and you make it through this alive. You go in the ladies' and you stay there. Don't you come out for anything until I come get you." Springer's teeth were clenched together now. "And, Max, if you come out before I tell you, I'm going to break your damned neck. Promise. And I'll like doing it."

Max started to say something but Springer grabbed him by the coat lapels and dragged him to the women's bathroom. He opened the door and pushed Max inside just as he heard the urinal flush in the men's room.

Tortino came out and said, "Why'nt clean that place up, huh? It's like an outhouse in there."

"You didn't rifle the condom machine while you were in there, did you?" said Springer.

"Don't run your mouth at me, asshole. It ain't healthy."

"I'll try to remember that. And, don't come back in. Got it? Just stay in the car until I tell you to come in. You come in ahead of my signal and you don't get to see Max."

Tortino took a step forward and glared at Springer. Springer met his gaze and looked back, giving the guy his indifferent look.

"Don't tell me what to do, again. You got it?"

"You forgot to say 'or else.' The heavy always says 'or else.' Where've you been? Don't you ever go to the movies?"

Tortino pointed a finger at him. "I'm gonna enlighten you about something. You keep running that mouth and I'm gonna have someone sew your lips together. See?"

Springer hoped Summers was getting all this. But, it wasn't enough.

"You mean you have people that would do something like that? What else do they do?"

"You need to be careful." Tortino said, giving him a vampire smile. "That's all I'm telling you. Never can tell what'll happen to a guy. It's a dangerous world."

"When you're through scaring me to death we got business to attend to."

Tortino looked at him, started to say something, but instead

shook his head and went back outside. It was getting more satis-
fying by the minute to burn this guy.

After Tortino left, Springer punched on the cassette player he
had piped into Summers's headset. Hoping Summers wouldn't give
any thought to the sound of the tape clicking on. And wouldn't
notice when the tape ran out and it switched back to live audio.

Gerry and Auteen came in. They set the coolers down and
Auteen left. But first he mean-mugged Springer. He was making
new friends at an alarming rate.

"What'd you say to Nicky?" asked Gerry, after Auteen left.

Springer told him. Gerry smiled. "No wonder he's pissed off.
Wants me to cut your balls off."

"That'd hurt, wouldn't it?"

"Some."

"Max the dumb-shit is in the ladies' room. He had to go to the
bathroom too."

"It's like an epidemic or something."

"Let's get this done."

They each picked up a cooler and carried them into the bar.
Springer opened the large cabinet under the bar, which he had
cleared out the night before, and they placed the coolers inside.
Then they dragged the other coolers out into the open.

Springer walked to the women's bathroom and told Max to
come out. It was 4:36. A little off-schedule but not bad. He walked
Max back into the bar.

Max saw the two coolers, said, "That the money?"

Gerry nodded.

"Open it up, let me see it."

Gerry shook his head. "Nicky had me seal them. Can't be
opened without breaking the seal. That way he knows no one's
lifted anything out of there."

Max looked at Springer. "So, what I do with it I can't open it?
You think I can run it through the Cayman's and set up dummy
corporations like that? Tell 'em, 'Trust me, the money's in there'?"

"Max," said Gerry. "You sure you and Nicky aren't related? You
can open the coolers after Nicky's satisfied."

Max looked up from the coolers. "What do you mean, satisfied?"

This was the part they hadn't told Max about.

Gerry said, "Nicky has to see you. Wants to know Springer really has you and ain't trying to rip him off."

Max put his hands on top of his head and walked around in a circle. More theatrics. "That's 'cause he wants to whack me. You don't know that? For all we know there is no money in there. He sealed them up. We don't know what's in there. There could be dynamite in there."

"I saw the money," said Gerry.

"Great. I feel better."

"You gotta trust me, Max."

"Trust you? There's three million dollars involved here. I don't *trust* nobody right now." He turned to Springer. "You hear what I'm saying? You trust this guy?"

Springer looked at Gerry, momentarily. Their eyes met. Max had a point. Springer didn't know they were going to place a seal on the coolers. Gerry hadn't told him that and Springer hadn't thought to look in the coolers when Gerry brought them in.

Still looking at Gerry, Springer said, "Yeah, I trust him."

"That's because you're a bozo," said Max. "You're dealing with fucking mobsters here. Wiseguy wannabes. You listening to me? You have no idea what you're up against. I've been trying to tell you, you won't listen. No, not you. You know every fucking thing."

"Then walk out of here, Max," said Springer. "I'm tired of hearing you whine. I'm committed to this. How long do you think it'll be before Nicky finds you? A week? A month? Tomorrow? Decide. You in or out? Tell me now because this could get ugly real fast."

Max looked around the room then back at Gerry and Springer. He shrugged. "Shit. No way out, is there?"

"None," said Gerry.

"Then let's roll the dice."

Springer walked over and turned off the audio tape.

CHAPTER

Thirty-One

"GET YOUR DUMB ASSES BACK IN THE CAR," SAID NICKY, when he got back. Ray Dean jumped, startled by the sudden yelling in the quiet that surrounded this place. It's what he didn't like about this Aspen that he couldn't put his finger on before. Too quiet all the time. No sirens, no street noises. "Cop drives by and sees two thugs like you hanging around a parking lot and he's gonna wanna know why."

"Cops here are real laid back, boss," said Ray Dean. "Like they don't see much crime."

"Gotta tell you everything twice. That the way it is?"

They got back in the car. Auteen and Ray Dean in the front. Nicky in the back.

Auteen reached over and turned the key and rap music came on.

"Turn that shit off," said Nicky. "You think I want to hear that jungle bullshit at four-thirty in the fuckin' morning? Turn the car on, Ray Dean. I'm freezing here."

Really wasn't that cold out, thought Ray Dean. But Nicky lived in California all his life and didn't like the cold. Didn't like the cold in Frisco either. Then Ray Dean had a thought. Show Nicky that he thought things out. "What if a cop comes by and sees the smoke from the tail pipe?"

"You know, that's not bad," said Nicky. "But turn it on for a while and then shut it off if you see headlights."

Ray Dean started the car and smiled to himself. Making progress now.

Nicky said, "Auteen, get out and give a look around, see if everything is okay."

The car shifted as Auteen got out and walked off into the night. Then, Nicky hit Ray Dean with a bombshell.

"When this shit's over," Nicky said, "I'm going to get finished off."

"Finished off?"

"I'm gonna be a made wiseguy."

"Hey, boss, that's great."

"Yeah, it is. But Joey the Neck says we can't have no niggers no more. Not after I'm made. The commission don't like it. So, Auteen has to go, you understand what I'm telling you here?"

"What about Gerry? I thought that was his stuff."

Nicky said, "Not this time. You do it. And I'll use Gerry you fuck it up."

Ray Dean knew what that meant. He did Auteen, which he would enjoy, or Knucks would do Auteen and Ray Dean. Guardino wanted Ray Dean tied to Nicky. Ray Dean iced somebody for Nicky and then he owed Nicky. That way Ray Dean could never flip Nicky to the feds because Nicky had him on a murder. Nicky would own him.

Which was okay. Because, if the piano player was right then Knucks was going down too.

What the piano player didn't know was that Ray Dean was going to put him down as a bonus. A reward to himself. Was looking forward to it. Had been deciding which way to do it—use the big .40-caliber Glock under his jacket or maybe use the little Taurus .38 he had strapped to his ankle which he'd been wanting to try out since he took it out of the drug dealer's house. Maybe use the big one for Knucks and Auteen and then let the wise-ass have it with the .38. Get rid of Knucks and Auteen and then the wise-ass.

Ten minutes went by before Auteen returned. He got back in the car and the whole thing dropped down with his weight.

"Everything be cool, Nicky," said Auteen.

"Thanks, Auteen. You do good for me," said Nicky.

Ray Dean smiling now where Auteen couldn't see it.

Things were looking up.

The headphones were starting to make his ears hurt so Special Agent Jack Summers lifted one side off his ear and listened to only one. He hadn't heard much. Bathroom flushing sounds, some talk. He'd heard Springer baiting Tortino, trying to get the guy to say something or at least just piss him off. He'd heard Nicky T obliquely threaten Springer but it wouldn't stand up. Springer didn't back off, though.

Guy had balls. He'd give him that.

Door opening, closing.

An electronic noise. A brief second where there wasn't any noise, then:

> NUGENT: "Nicky's ready to do this thing."

Why couldn't Tortino tell him that?

> SPRINGER: "All right. I'm ready."
> NUGENT: "Max here?"
> SPRINGER: "He'll be along in a minute."
> NUGENT: "Nicky wants to see Max."
> SPRINGER: "Why does he need to see Max? That wasn't in the bargain."
> NUGENT: "Nicky wants to make sure you're not fucking him. Wants to make sure you really have Max. Doesn't want to hand over one hundred G's to you if Max isn't here. No Max then the deal's off."
> SPRINGER: "How do we know that Max is safe? How do I know you guys won't kill him if I bring him in here?"
> NUGENT: "You have my word."
> SPRINGER: "That's not much to go on."
> NUGENT: "It's all you get."

Another electronic noise.

Then, a long silence.

Finally a door opened and he heard loud knocking. A door opening.

TORTINO: "I want to see Max and I want to see him now."

Okay, we're here, thought Summers. The final scene.

Springer heard the banging at the door. He looked at Gerry and smiled. He walked to the door and Nicky T was standing there. Ray Dean was at the bottom of the porch stairs.

Nicky said, "I want to see Max and I want to see him now."

"All right," said Springer. "But, I've gotta frisk you and he stays out here." He pointed at Ray Dean. "You come in where your help can't see me do it. That way you don't lose face."

"You're learning."

This guy, huh?

"I'll frisk your boy outside," Springer said.

Nicky stepped in and said, "I ain't carrying. I never do. Don't have to."

"It'll put my mind at ease. Raise your arms." Springer patted him down.

"You've done this before," said Nicky.

"Wait here while I check Ray Dean."

Springer stepped outside, feeling the cold, crisp Aspen air. He always liked that early morning feeling. The smells. The distant sounds.

"I gotta have your gun, Ray Dean."

"I don't give up my piece, man."

"Okay, but I got this for you," said Springer, reaching into his pocket and pulling out the dummy mercury switch. Ray Dean smiled.

Ray Dean said, "You think it's going to go that way?"

"Don't know yet." He gave Ray Dean a conspiratorial wink and walked back inside.

Ray Dean pointed at him like they were best buddies.

Springer's Gambit 283

This was too easy, thought Springer.
Which might not be a good thing.

Special Agent Jack Summers knew something was wrong. He knew it the way any cop knew it after two decades of smelling things out. Couldn't put his finger on it—didn't know whether it was the fact that he was in a soundproof room, why a soundproof room? he asked himself, or if it was because he couldn't see what was going on and had to rely on the headphones? He didn't know. But it didn't feel right.

He took off the headphones. Then he reached down and removed his Beretta from the clip-on holster on his belt. He jacked the slide on the weapon to chamber a round. Set the safety. Here we go.

CHAPTER

Thirty-Two

WHEN IT HAPPENED IT WENT DOWN FAST.

When Nicky T saw Max, he smiled, affecting a mock hurt posture, his hands turned inward toward himself the way the wiseguys did. Talking with that mob-street voice. "Max, how could you treat me this way? What have I done to deserve such disrespect from you, huh?"

Max, for his part, looked like he had a chili pepper caught in his throat. "I . . . look Nicky, nothing ever happens the way I want it to."

"You got the money?" Nicky asked.

"I've got it," said Springer. He reached under a table and brought out the satchel with the hundred grand in it. He placed it on the floor, gave it a little shove with his foot and stepped back. "Count it if you want."

Nicky jerked his head at Gerry without taking his eyes off Springer. "Knucks, take a look, huh?"

Gerry stepped forward. His footsteps against the wooden dance floor were the only noise in the room except for the low electric hum of the furnace. He kneeled down, unzipped the bag, lifted out a couple of packets, and thumbed through them, before placing them back inside the bag and re-zipping it. He stood up still holding the bag.

"Looks okay," Gerry said.

"That's good," said Nicky. "Max, in those coolers is two million, nine hundred fifty-seven thousand dollars. I want it cleaned up and back to me within six months." Then he turned to Springer. "And,

for you, wise-ass, I got something else. Gerry, shoot this motherfucker between the eyes."

Gerry removed the Colt .45 from his shoulder holster.

"Thought we had a deal," said Springer.

"What I need you for, now?" said Nicky, shrugging. "I got Max,
I got the hundred G's. So," he looked around with his shoulders
hunched up like he was playing to an audience, "fuck you."

"So, you're just going to let him shoot me and take off? You
don't think it'll attract attention? How do you explain something
like this?"

"It's fucking before dawn. Your piece of shit nightclub has been
shut down for days. Nobody's gonna know we were here. You're
just some Aspen asshole who was killed. The cops'll look into it
but they'll never figure it out. This shit happens sometimes. Business decision."

The last two sentences Nicky spoke echoed from upstairs. Very
loudly.

Tobi Ryder looked at the monitor. What just happened? The screen
blipped and then suddenly there were different people in the room.
Seconds before it had been Springer and the mob enforcer, Gerry
Knucks. Now Nicky Tortino and Max Shapiro were also in the
room. She knew Tortino and Shapiro would possibly be there but
why the sudden blip? Had the camera malfunctioned?

Or was it something else?

The cooler was there on the floor between the men. There
was no sound on the monitor because Springer said he didn't
want any noise coming from upstairs and said there was something wrong with the volume control anyway. Didn't want to
spook Tortino.

But what could it hurt to turn it up just a little?

She picked up the remote and hit the volume button. Nothing
happened. Now what was wrong? She pointed the remote at the
monitor and punched the control. Still nothing. Finally, she tapped
it rapidly several times.

And it worked.

And it was loud.

Really loud.

"What the fuck?" said Nicky, and his words reverberated like the voice of some offstage giant.

"I don't know what kinda shit you got going with your sound system, wise-ass," said Nicky and the echo faded suddenly. "But we're going. Grab a cooler, Max. I'll take the bag. Gerry, put this guy down then bring the other cooler."

Gerry Nugent, the black Colt down at his side, shook his head, and said, "Change of plans, Nicky." Then he raised the gun and pointed it at his boss.

Tobi had to unplug the monitor to shut it off. It'd only been on a few seconds but it was still on too long. She watched the enforcer remove a gun from his coat.

They had to hear that downstairs.

She removed her weapon, hands shaking, and headed for the door.

Now what? Had she blown the whole thing? What did she have?

She started to ease the door and found out it was locked.

Springer.

That sonuvabitch.

"What the fuck is this?" said Nicky, looking at Gerry like he'd suddenly grown a third ear. "Put that fucking thing down. Shit, Gerry."

Gerry shook his head slowly. He hefted the bag slightly. "This is my retirement, Nicky."

"I fucking knew it," said Nicky, spittle forming at his mouth. A little dab spewed out as he spoke. "You're throwing in with that fucking Li. You ungrateful piece a shit. You know what's going to happen to you when the guys in Frisco find out? They'll fucking rip your balls off with pliers."

"You gonna tell 'em?" asked Gerry. "Who knows about this except you and Joey G?" His face was placid, serious. "You can't say a thing. You can only hope they never find out you had this money. You can't say anything and you can't make a move on me. Who you gonna send? Ray Dean? How do you explain it to the commission? You think about that? No, Nicky, you don't think about shit. You're a dumb motherfucker. I see anyone come near me I call people I know in New York and they'll call Sonny Blue. In fact, I may give part of it to Sonny Blue and tell him it's all I could get away from you and he'll send somebody out to rip *your* nuts off with pliers. Oh yeah, another thing, Ontario is in fucking Canada, you moron."

Then, just like on television, Springer not believing it could happen like this . . .

"FBI!" yelled Special Agent Jack Summers, bursting into the room. "Place your weapons on the floor and—"

That's when Nugent's Colt bellowed and he shot Summers through the right shoulder. Summer's weapon clattered on the bare floor as he sunk to his knees. Gerry grabbed Max by the back of his coat and pulled him close.

There was a noise from the second floor and Tobi Ryder came down the stairs, gun pointed at Gerry, saying, "Police! Put the gun on the floor. Now!"

Gerry shrugged, shook his head no.

Nicky T said, "What is it, a fucking cop convention?"

"Don't do it, Tobi," said Springer. "Let him go. Nobody's hurt yet."

"What about Summers?" she said, eyes bright, intent upon Gerry Nugent.

Springer looked at him, then back at her. "Except him, of course."

That was when Ray Dean Carr burst through the door, a short-barreled revolver in his hand.

Springer slid his hand into his pocket and slipped the .380 Colt out.

"What the fuck's going on?" asked Ray Dean, not knowing who to point his gun at. "I heard shooting—"

"Fucking Knucks lost his mind," said Nicky. "Shoot the motherfucker. Even if you have to shoot Max first."

Max let out a strange whimper.

Springer raised the Colt and pointed it at Ray Dean. "Nobody shoots Max. No matter what else happens, Max walks out of here on two feet or everybody else dies. Especially you, Nicky, because I don't like you. I can do it and there's not a damn thing anyone can do about it. Nothing you can do about it either, Gerry."

"Something to find out maybe," said Gerry, his eyes flat and hard as gun metal.

Tobi Ryder was yelling for Springer to put his gun down. Ray Dean was hollering, asking Nicky what to do. Nicky was saying something Springer didn't catch. Springer didn't even look in Tobi's direction. "No. You'll just have to shoot, honey. Can you do that? I'm betting you can't. Let this thing happen."

He looked at Ray Dean. "Ray Dean, you put that gun away or I'm going to shoot you through the eye. You know I can do it. You can't watch me and Gerry both. One of us'll get you."

"Shoot somebody!" said Nicky to Ray Dean.

Ray Dean looked indecisive. Springer winked at him and Ray Dean made his decision. He leaned down and placed the revolver on the floor and stepped back.

"What the fuck are you doin'?" screamed Nicky.

"It'll be all right, Nicky," said Ray Dean. "You'll see."

Nicky made a pained face, his eyes closed.

"Put your weapons on the floor and move away from them," said Tobi. "Now."

Springer put his weapon on the floor and kicked it toward the stairs with his foot. "Okay," he said. "Mine's gone."

"Think I'll keep mine," said Gerry. "Ray Dean, you grab a cooler and you," motioning at Springer, "You get the other one. Max goes with me. Anybody moves wrong I shoot that person. Even if it's you, Nicky. Hell, especially if it's you."

Nicky looked like he'd just come down with the stomach flu. Springer almost felt sorry for the guy. Almost.

Too much was going on now. It was getting beyond his control. Things were unfolding fast and too much of it was unexpected. Summers getting shot was a bad variable. Springer didn't like that. Starting to worry about Gerry now.

"I need to check on him," Springer said, motioning at Summers. Gerry nodded and Springer grabbed the towel off the bar, palmed the .32 Beretta he'd placed in the towel earlier, and walked to Summers. As he bent down he slipped the Beretta into his pocket. He bound Summers's wound as best he could. It was a good shot by Gerry—it had torn a hunk out of the point of Summers's shoulder—it would heal up but leave a nasty scar. Summers closed his eyes and nodded in thanks.

Gerry had Springer pick up the guns and place them in the cooler. Tobi had moved down the stairs now and once again told Gerry to surrender his weapon.

Gerry said, "I had enough of this shit." He pointed the gun at Springer. "You toss your gun down here or I shoot Springer."

"Don't give up your piece, Ryder," said Summers.

"I don't bluff," said Gerry.

She looked at Springer, he met her eyes and she took a step onto the floor, put the gun down and kicked it toward Gerry. Gerry motioned for Springer to pick it up. Gerry had Springer lock the two cops up in the bathroom before the rest headed outside. It was tough getting Summers there as he was in a lot of pain.

Gerry pointed the gun at Nicky and said, "You lead. Hands on the back of your neck, fingers laced. Watch what you do or you'll get one through the hands into the back of the neck. Leave you with no fingers, no pulse."

They walked outside and Nicky told Auteen not to do anything. Auteen looked confused. Ray Dean and Springer placed the coolers in the backseat of Gerry's car and shut the door. He told Max to drive and got in on the passenger side.

Without a word they left.

"You sonuvabitch," said Nicky to Springer. "You fucked everything up."

"I don't think so. Who was going to have me killed?"

"No, he didn't fuck it up, Nicky," said Ray Dean. "I got this." He pulled out the remote switch and held it up.

"So, what's that?"

"Watch," said Ray Dean.

Springer pulled out the .32. Pointed it at Auteen who was reaching down into his pants. "No. Don't do it yet, Ray Dean. Take the weapon out and toss it, Auteen," said Springer. Auteen threw his gun into the night and it skidded and scraped across the asphalt. "Now get on the ground." Then to Ray Dean, he said, "Wait until I tell you. I want him out of town. The switch has a thirty-second delay on it and a five-mile range. I'll tell you when."

"What's going on?" asked Nicky.

"It's gonna be all right, boss," said Ray Dean.

"Would you quit saying that shit? How do you know it's going to be all right? What the fuck do you know about it?"

Springer waited several seconds, looking east in the direction of the continental divide, toward the pass. There it was. Two quick flashes.

He spoke quietly to Ray Dean so only he could hear it. "Now."

Ray Dean clicked the remote switch and was trying to pull up his pants leg to get at a gun before Springer shot him in the knee. Ray Dean screamed and a snub-nosed .38 clattered on the pavement. Springer kicked the wheel gun away from Ray Dean and pointed his Colt at Nicky T. "Auteen, you and this dickhead get in the car and get out of here."

Auteen didn't hesitate. He hustled his boss into the car. Ray Dean clutched his knee, a slick of blood forming on the pavement beside him.

"You fuckin' shot me again."

"You don't miss a thing, do you?"

Springer turned his back on Ray Dean. Walked away. Tobi Ryder was running out of the Whiskey Basin when the fireball erupted in the eastern sky, throwing a brief intense light just a heartbeat before the explosion boomed across the canyon, rattling windows and shaking the ground . . .

And then rolling and crackling and receding across the mountains, purpling with the first bright ribbons of sunlight.

It was morning in Aspen and the day had started with a bang.

Epilogue

SPRINGER TOOK THE COLLECT CALL FROM BILL MEDLEY, who sounded remarkably like Gerry Nugent. He swirled the Glen-fiddich, forty bucks a fifth, around in his glass. Nice to be drinking single malt again.

"Why Bill Medley?"

"Always liked the Righteous Brothers."

"How's Suzi?"

"What?"

"I said, how's Suzi?"

"She had it a little rough when she told Max they were done but she's doing fine now. My damned ears are still ringing from the blast. One of my ear plugs fell out when your buddy, the ski instructor, and I were loading Ricky Jade into the front seat. I thought Max was going to go into shock when the car blew."

"So where are you headed?"

"Rather not say," said Gerry. "It's not I don't trust you. This way you don't have to lie if they ever ask if you know what happened to me. They can be pretty persuasive."

"Well, if you're ever in the area, I'll buy you a beer."

"You never know."

Springer was leaving the Aspen locker plant when the Mercedes Benz pulled up beside him. Springer put locker-key number 117 in his pocket as the darkened driver side window whooshed electrically to reveal a large black face.

"Whatcha doin' man?" the driver said.

"Just taking care of some things. Nice ride."

"Yeah. How you like this? Don't figure Nicky be needin' it no more."

"Might as well somebody got some good out of it."

"Gonna drive it back to the hood let my homeys see it."

"Be careful you don't get it keyed. Or stripped."

Auteen shrugged. "Yeah, you could be right. Just wanted you to know I got no hard feelings."

Springer put his hands in his pockets and looked off at the mountains. "Me neither. You did know they were going to pop you when Nicky got made?"

"Yeah. I been thinking about that. Not too many brothers in La Cosa Nostra. I'm gonna miss Ray Dean, though."

"Why's that?"

" 'Cause he an odd little motherfucker I could laugh at."

"What little trace of a human being we could find in that blast turns out to be of possible Oriental origin," Tobi Ryder said to Springer, sitting in the Pitkin County Sheriff's office in the basement of the courthouse. It was two days after the explosion. They had taken Springer into custody the morning after the explosion ripped across the valley, then released him. Now, he was back for a follow-up interview. "Why is that?"

Springer shrugged. He wasn't going to help her.

She gave him the look, the one that said "I'm not buying the innocent act," and peeled back a page on her clipboard. "In your statement here you say that Nicky Tortino wanted Max Shapiro to launder a large amount of money in exchange for Shapiro's safety. So, you had no choice but to go along with it."

Springer nodded. She looked good in her jeans, her jacket off, a freshly laundered lavender blouse on, her shape pushing against the fabric at the right places. He looked at the coffee she had brought him. He was deciding whether she would be insulted if he didn't drink it. Probably not. He remembered the coffee from the holding cell and wondered if it came from the same place. It smelled like burnt toast. Maybe it would taste better without handcuffs.

"So, you're saying that Tortino would've killed Shapiro had he not agreed to launder the money?"

He nodded.

She said, "How much money was involved?"

"He didn't say." Shrugged. "Guess we'll never know."

"I guess not." Sarcastic now. "Pretty convenient, isn't it?"

"I guess." He didn't look away when she tried to bore in on him. It was a cop thing to do that. He knew the game. He looked right back at her. He had to hold up his end.

She said, "I mean, Nugent is dead, the money's blown up, Shapiro's off the hook and Nicky Tortino and his pet barracuda have been indicted for conspiracy. Only Auteen Phelps and you walked away from this. Very neat. Couldn't have wrapped it up any tighter if I planned it myself." She cocked her head and considered him. He tried not to smile. "It's one of the cleanest cases I've ever seen. Everything just sort of fell into place. Never experienced anything like it before in my twelve years as a police officer. These things are always a little messy but despite the complexities this was an easy one. Also clever to have two police officers there for an alibi, wasn't it?"

"It wasn't entirely neat," he said. "They must've used a ton of explosives to make a hole like that."

She placed her pen down on the desk. "Yeah, it's almost like they wanted a big explosion so we couldn't identify the body. We couldn't even find any teeth for a dental I.D." She looked at him, an irritated smile tugging at the corners of her mouth. "Even more interesting since it was a sophisticated device, mercury switches and C-4—a person who could rig something like that would certainly know it was overkill. Pieces of the car were all over the pass. The brass and the FBI are too busy congratulating themselves over netting Nicky T and putting the mob bosses in a turmoil to consider anything which takes the shine off the biggest bust in Aspen history." She took a sip of coffee and made a face.

"So, why look for problems?"

"Because you make way too many cute moves to be an innocent bystander."

He put his fingers around the Styrofoam cup. Patted the fingers of his other hand on the desk. Started to bring the cup to his lips, then changed his mind.

"You're certainly reticent today," she said. "How unusual."

"I've been working on my reticence. Thought it might come in handy someday."

"Especially now, huh?" She was leaning toward him now.

"How's Summers?"

"Wound was clean. He's had a religious conversion regarding you. If I didn't know better I'd think he was protecting you even though I think he believes you pulled something."

"I grow on people."

She almost smiled. Making progress.

"Nicky T made bail yesterday," she said. "Only a couple of hours after they found Joey Guardino shot through the head and his hands cut off."

He nodded. "Business decision. Reduction in force. Nicky'll never make trial."

"Why do you say that?"

"The money was mob war chest money that Joey the Neck had stolen from Carmine Mostelli. Those guys are losing influence but they still know how to deal with their own. Nicky's a dead man."

She leaned back in her chair. "You figured that from the start, didn't you? You had everything figured from the start, didn't you?"

He looked at her for a moment. Smiled.

"You ever wear a dress?" he asked her.

She looked at him for a moment. Suspicious. "Only for someone I care about."

"So what are the possibilities of that happening when I'm around?"

"Nonexistent if you're playing me for a mark."

He looked at his coffee cup for a moment and then pushed it away. He caught a trace of her perfume when he leaned forward. He reached into his pocket and produced a small key.

"If I were a crackerjack state cop looking to move up I'd look in meat locker number one-seventeen down at the Aspen locker plant," said Springer. He placed the key on the desk and gave it a small push in her direction. He sat back and put his hands behind his head. "This might help. You won't have to shoot the lock off this way."

She looked at the key, then up at him.

"How much is in that locker?"

"A bunch."

"Why are you doing this?"

"I think I may be in love."

"You realize I could put you away for this."

He shrugged. "It's about time to take a chance, I guess."

She pushed the key back toward him. Her eyes blinked and she reached up with one finger and touched the corner of an eye. It was very quiet in the room for a few minutes. Electronic white hiss of climate-controlled furnace pushing warm air. Noises down the hall. She looked at him. He looked back.

Finally, she said, "You know, the people above me are very pleased about the way this thing is tied up with a pretty bow. So, who am I to ruin it for them?"

"Who indeed?" he said, palming the key before she changed her mind.

"You think this is going to work out?"

"As much chance as anything, I guess. I'm kind of on a streak anyway."

"I might not be doing anything later tonight, you know," she said.

He shrugged. "That's funny. Me neither."

"But I'll probably want to go someplace pricey and waste money on ridiculous things. Did you know that despite the fact that I've lived in Aspen for ten years I've never drunk Dom Perignon?"

"How about Glenfiddich Scotch?"

"Never tasted caviar either. Think you can handle that?"

"I think so," he said, smiling. "You think you could wear a dress?"

She gave him a look. A good one.

"You never know," she said. "Anything could happen."